DAYS OF
WAR AND FAMINE

DAYS OF THE APOCALYPSE, #2

MARK E. FISHER

Extraordinary Tales

Publishing

DAYS OF WAR AND FAMINE (DAYS OF THE APOCALYPSE, #2), BY MARK E. FISHER

Extraordinary Tales Publishing
P.O. Box 6196
Rochester, MN 55903

First Extraordinary Tales edition October 2022

Print Book ISBN: 978-1-950235-13-1
eBook ISBN: 978-1-950235-14-8

Cover art purchased from 123rf.com
Cover design and interior formatting by Booknook.biz
Editing by Deirdre Lockhart of Brilliant Cut Editing

To learn where to buy this book or for more information about this and the author's other books visit: MarkFisherAuthor.com

Library of Congress Cataloging-in-Publication Data:
Fisher, Mark E.
Days of War and Famine (Days of the Apocalypse, #2) / Mark E. Fisher 1st ed.

Printed in the United States of America

CONTENTS

CAST OF CHARACTERS

THE PRINCIPALS

- Caleb Turner—Brother to Dylan and Chelsea and a Minneapolis native, he was a budding author and blogger before the vanishing. His brother, Dylan, recently arranged his escape from a Unitum Imperium prison.
- Chaim (Cam) Weinberg—A Jew from New York City, he also goes by the name of Camden or Cam. On the Raleigh-Burke class destroyer, the U.S.S. *Avenger*, he's a gunner's mate second class.
- Chelsea Turner—Sister to Dylan and Caleb, she's a fervent believer in climate change and liberal causes. Chelsea now works as a personnel researcher for her father, Adam Turner, the former head of security at Veritas Systems which, under the Unitum Imperium, became the Ministry of Truth.
- Dylan Turner—Brother to Chelsea and Caleb, Dylan helped arrange the release of his brother and other prisoners from one of Davato's underground prisons.
- Margot Durand—A Belgian woman whom God directed to paint visions of the future. After her father and brother were raptured, Dylan came to her.
- Tanya Baranov—A Chicago resident and granddaughter of the previously raptured Uri Baranov, the famous author. She and Caleb are good friends.

THE UNITUM IMPERIUM

- Aldo Conti—Head of the Department of Prosperity within the Ministry of Charity.
- Angelo Pisano—Truth Squad member.
- Adam Turner—Former CEO and founder of Turner Enterprises, he's father to Dylan, Caleb, and Chelsea. Recently, he was promoted to head the Ministry of Truth and its Central Security Agency, headquartered in Rome.

- Carlo Scutari—Davato's personal aide and bodyguard.
- Davato—The Antichrist and ruler of the Unitum Imperium, the man of lawlessness, also called the beast. He is Satan's evil representative in the end times.
- Dino Castiglione—Head of the Central Security Agency under Adam Turner.
- François Desroches—Vice president of the Unitum Imperium.
- General Eric Hofmann—Supreme commander of all Unitum Imperium forces.
- Sebastien Rey, the Prophet—Green-eyed false prophet sent to corrupt the message of God, part of the unholy trinity of Satan.

THE ISRAELIS

- Baruch Abramovich—Leader of the Great Assembly, a group of 144,000 men chosen by God to bring the message of Christ to all who would believe during the Tribulation. Dylan, Margot, and Chelsea recently released him from a Unitum Imperium prison.
- David Benjamin—Jewish friend of Baruch Abramovich.

THE AMERICANS

- Grady Wilson—Lieutenant in charge of Chaim Weinberg's unit on the U.S.S. *Avenger*.
- Kamryn Harper—President of the United States during the time of the vanishing.
- William Cole—President of the United States after Kamryn Harper.

THE NAZARENE FRIENDS

- Marcel and Gabrielle Blanchet—A farming couple who run the farm and manage the livestock.
- Pasqual Berger—The founder and leader of the Nazarene Friends.
- Danielle DuBois—Woman who was rescued from Marseilles.
- René LeClerc—A former spy and a friend of Sergei, the spy who helped Dylan and Margot escape from Chicago.
- Victor Marceau—The farm's tech wizard and guitar player.

THE IRANIANS

- Bayat Mahdi—Chief of the Islamic Revolutionary Guard Corps.
- Jaleel Hasani—Portly president of Iran.
- General Mir Ansari—Commander of the Islamic Republic of Iran Army.
- Muhammad Najafi—Iran's supreme leader, the Grand Ayatollah, and supreme commander of all Iranian forces.
- Perviz—The supreme leader's aide and household servant.

THE ISLAMIC COALITION

- Ahmed Umar—Chairman of the presidential council of Libya.
- Bayat Mahdi—Chief of the Islamic Revolutionary Guard Corps.
- General Hassan Al-Kalifa—President of Sudan.
- General Mir Ansari—Commander of the Islamic Republic of Iran Army.
- Omid Noor—Leader of the Sayf Alsharaf, the terrorist league of hill fighters from Afghanistan, Kazakhstan, Turkmenistan, Uzbekistan, and Kyrgyzstan.
- Suleyman Aydin—President of Turkey.

THE RUSSIANS

- Alexander Petrov—President of the Russian Federation.
- Colonel Vladislav—President Petrov's liaison at the front.

PREFACE

We have entered the time of the end. The signs are there for all to see: the regathering of the Jewish people in Israel; the formation of the European Union from the old Roman Empire; apostasy in the church of Christ; the beginning of a cashless society; and governments embracing globalism, ignoring their constitutions, and seizing more and more control over the people. Anarchy, chaos, and lawlessness are increasing everywhere. Brutal tyrants wage war against their neighbors. And many of us now struggle to remember that everything that happens is for the good of those who love God and who are called according to his purpose.

Some will ignore the signs, pretending they don't exist. Or they accept what is happening and, to their peril, mold their beliefs to the culture.

But the world has abandoned God for so long, it can no longer discern good from evil, right from wrong. The evil sweeping the country at breathtaking speed and spreading across the planet is only the latest in a long series of offenses from a people who have abandoned their Creator. And when, time and again, a people turns its back on God, a terrible thing happens—God abandons them and gives them over to their sins.

But this is not the path of one whose heart is sealed with Christ. Christians must turn their eyes from this world and look to the next.

This leads me to the goals propelling me to write this series:

First, I write for those who believe in and follow Jesus as the Son of God. Perhaps through telling the story of the end times, I can provide some meaning in these troubled times, thereby shining a ray of hope against the world's increasing darkness and despair. Knowing that what is happening is in God's plan and that Christians will be taken out of this world before the terrors to come should be of great comfort.

Second, for those who do not yet believe—and are not married to sinful lifestyles or ideologies—perhaps these novels will begin a search for truth. Then, not only might the reader escape a fiery eternal fate, he or she might also be blessed to enter the family of God under Christ.

The first book in this series tells the story of the Rapture, its aftermath, the breaking of the first Revelation seal, and the coming of the Antichrist.

This, the second book, tells the story of the next thirty-two months of the Tribulation when the second through fifth seals are broken. It relates how God's judgment directs men's actions against himself and how God gives people one last chance to turn to him before he begins the wrath decreed for all who would follow the beast.

Revelation 1:3 (HCSB) tells us this: "The one who reads this is blessed, and those who hear the words of this prophecy and keep what is written in it are blessed, because the time is near!" By inference, those who hear *the story* of Revelation—perhaps even through a series of novels?—and who believe the Revelation prophecies are also blessed.

Originally, I had planned this series to be a trilogy. But as I delved into the biblical storyline and plotted what's to come, I discovered that three books simply cannot encompass all that must occur. Days of the Apocalypse has now become a five-book series.

I have based the series on the prophetic passages from the books of Revelation, Joel, Ezekiel, Daniel, Matthew, and many others. I have relied heavily on the work of end-times scholars such as Mark Hitchcock, John MacArthur, and Ron Rhodes. I also thank Jan Markell and her Understanding the Times weekly radio and internet broadcasts. All this is to say that, for me, faithfully following the biblical storyline is paramount.

This is, however, a work of fiction, which requires the invention of fictional events and characters. Without that, there can be no story.

Many chapters begin with a Scripture quotation, a handful of which may be difficult to interpret. Please refer to the Scripture References section in the back of the book for detailed explanations of the more obscure passages. This will be especially helpful to decipher the ancient place names in Ezekiel 38 and 39.

Once again, this book contains a chapter describing one character's journey to Hell. It was based on one of three types of Near-Death Experiences reported by people who were declared dead, who went to Hell, and who returned to life. Hellish experiences are far rarer than those describing journeys to Heaven. One speculates this is because the journey to Hell is so horrific, the mind reels and suppresses it. Note that this is *not* the second death in the lake of eternal fire—the final destination of the unredeemed after the Great White Throne judgment.

The spiritual worlds are real. Heaven and Hell exist. And the God who created the beginning did so with a plan for the end. He created the world with a purpose—to make a people for himself under Christ, one whom he could love, who would love him, and with whom he would live forever. That is the great message of Christianity, a message of hope and love.

As the world spirals ever downward, knowing the future that awaits the Christian is something to live for, to hold on to, and a reason to hope.

Yet for all who reject him, who embrace the agendas, morals, and evil ideologies of the Adversary, a terrible judgment awaits.

So, take heart and hold on to hope. When the end comes, those whose hearts have turned to Christ will be released from the trials, suffering, and agony to come. Instead, they will experience an eternal future so blessed and filled with wonder and love that no words can possibly express it.

Mark E. Fisher
Rochester, Minnesota
May 2022

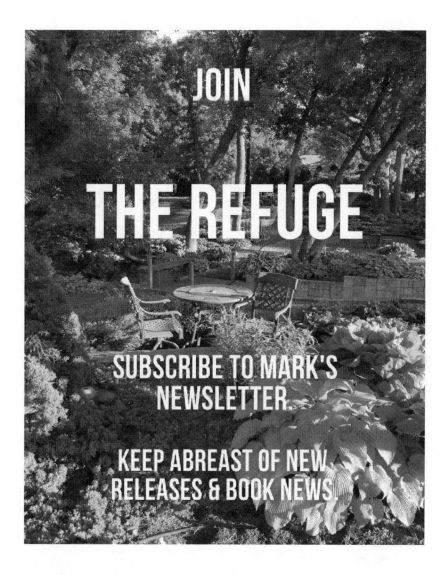

JOIN

THE REFUGE

SUBSCRIBE TO MARK'S
NEWSLETTER

KEEP ABREAST OF NEW
RELEASES & BOOK NEWS

The shadow of the Tribulation already darkens our world. Know what's to come, stay true to the faith, and seek refuge in Christ.

Subscribe to Mark's newsletter and receive two free gifts:

1. 10 Reasons Why the End Times Could Come Tomorrow
2. How the Green Agenda Prepares the Way for the Antichrist

Go to: www.MarkFisherAuthor.com/newsletter

PROLOGUE

Came a day at the end of the age when the Ancient of Days opened the great scroll and the planet shook. Written at the beginning of time, the scroll decreed the events at the end of time.

All whose names were written in the Book of Life were taken out of the world. Then chaos and anarchy swept the planet.

In the great throne room of the Lord of Hosts, angels gathered, and the first seal was broken. The man of lawlessness was revealed, and the Antichrist began his time on earth.

But the God who was, who is, and who is to come would not let evil reign unhindered. Here and there, he chose a few to stand against the Adversary, to take from him as many souls as would listen, and to remind him that, one day, good would forever triumph over evil.

This, then, is the story of some who were chosen and some who were not, of some who recognized their part in God's plan and worked to advance it and some who did not.

YEAR ONE

THE FIRST
AND
SECOND SEALS

Revelation 6:1–4 (HCSB): *Then I saw the Lamb open one of the seven seals, and I heard one of the four living creatures say with a voice like thunder, "Come!" I looked, and there was a white horse. The horseman on it had a bow; a crown was given to him, and he went out as a victor to conquer.*

When He opened the second seal, I heard the second living creature say, "Come!" Then another horse went out, a fiery red one, and its horseman was empowered to take peace from the earth, so that people would slaughter one another. And a large sword was given to him.

CHAPTER 1

A PRIVATE DINNER

2 Thessalonians 2:9–12 (NLT): This man will come to do the work of Satan with counterfeit power and signs and miracles. He will use every kind of evil deception to fool those on their way to destruction, because they refuse to love and accept the truth that would save them. So God will cause them to be greatly deceived, and they will believe these lies. Then they will be condemned for enjoying evil rather than believing the truth.

Rome, Italy – December, Year 1

It was December, four months after the vanishing, and Chelsea Turner lived in the ancient city where evil now made its home, not far from its headquarters. In her upscale, top-floor apartment, chosen and paid for by the Unitum Imperium, she was just beginning her day. But she was late for work.

As she headed for the door, the phone rang. She froze in midstride and lowered a hesitant gaze to her purse and its ringing contents. Had they finally found her?

All night, she'd tossed, waking at every noise from the hall, from the street, from the kitchen ice maker, wondering if the city's *polizia* had somehow traced the arson she'd committed yesterday back to her. At the crime scene, she'd heeded her brother Dylan's warning, hidden her license plates, and wiped her fingerprints from the gas cans. She'd smashed the throwaway phone she'd used to call the fire department and laid the pieces on the kindling. But after the timbers on the vacant lot erupted in flames and lit the night, people had run into the street behind her rental car. Would they remember the make and model? Would they recall a woman with reddish-blonde hair squealing away downhill? What madness had possessed her to strike against the government of the person her brother was calling the Antichrist?

Her fingers shaking, she fumbled, pulled out her phone, but didn't recognize the caller. "Y–yes?"

"Is this Chelsea Turner?" The voice sounded all too official.

Her heart skipped. They'd found her. They'd traced the crime back to her. It was all over, policemen with guns would soon burst through the door, and she was going to jail.

"Y–yes," she managed to say.

"This is the appointments secretary for the president of the Unitum Imperium."

Davato's office? Did they somehow know what she'd done? "What do you want?"

"Your presence is kindly requested this evening at nineteen thirty hours for a private dinner with the president at Worldnet headquarters. Are you able to attend?"

She sucked in air. A private dinner? With Davato himself? So it had nothing to do with her setting the fire?

But what could Davato possibly want with her? Then she pressed cold fingers to her forehead, remembering their dance at the reception, how lustful eyes had swept her up and down, and how earlier, as she'd hidden under the desk in her father's office while Davato talked with Father, Davato had called her a "charming creature".

"I–I guess."

"Is that an affirmative?"

To refuse the most powerful man in the world would be unwise. "Yes, I can come."

"Good. The president asks if you would wear the same dress you wore to the reception. A car will pick you up outside your apartment at nineteen hundred hours. Is that agreeable?"

"Yes, of course. All right." She breathed out. "I'll be there."

But after she hung up, she found a chair in the foyer, slumped into it, and wiped her brow. That dress was outrageous, showing too much skin, and now she regretted the purchase. Again, she wondered what Davato could want with her, of all people, and why he would want her to wear *that* dress? At the reception, she was sleuthing, trying to find out all she could about Veritas Systems, the company she worked for, now part of the Ministry of Truth.

She'd worn that dress to attract attention. It had worked all too well.

Then she remembered a rumor that Davato had slept with nearly every young woman—and young man?—on his staff. But was it true? A shiver raced down her back. How could she get out of this?

A glance at her watch revealed she needed to hurry. She stood, smoothed her slacks, again wiped her forehead, and hurried for the door. Too late to walk, downstairs, she hailed a taxi. As the car sped toward the Veritas building, she tried to slow her breathing.

At least tonight's affair wasn't about the arson.

*　*　*

AFTER WORK, THE TRAFFIC WHIZZED by as she strolled the avenue leading to her apartment. The December breeze, cool again after warmer weather, drove fallen leaves, tumbling and crinkling across her path. She pulled a heavy sweater over her head. Work had been the usual, digging deep into the backgrounds of applicants for positions in the security division of the Ministry of Truth.

The Ministry of Truth—hah! Could anyone spell 1984?

Her task was to ferret out applicants' social media faux pas. Find any pre-vanishing associations with conservative or religious groups. Look for recent emails critical of Davato or anything posted against the previous liberal governments, what the ministry now considered "subversive". She hated it all. But sometimes the higher-ups checked her work, and she had to follow their guidelines. She'd promised Dylan she'd stay on at her job as a spy. At least her efforts had freed Caleb.

Forty minutes before her pickup, she opened the closet door. But her hand fell, not on the outrageous dress that so turned heads at the reception, but on a more modest outfit she'd bought for dinners out—a silvery satin shirt with full-length sleeves and a high neckline. With accompanying tan slacks and leather belt, the ensemble was smart, yet conservative.

Her glance returned to what Davato requested. A sleeveless black thing with a ruffled *V* cut running between her breasts to her navel, it boasted a side slit starting above her right hip and dropping to her ankles.

Each step revealed leg and hip. The whole outfit showed almost too much skin.

But this was what the most powerful man in the world wanted. Taking a deep breath, she pulled it on.

The shiny black limousine picked her up. As it sped through traffic, she sank back against the black leather seat, ignoring the wet bar in the passenger compartment and the silent uniformed driver up front behind a plexiglass border.

At the Worldnet building, a smiling young blonde in her twenties met her at the door. "Welcome, Chelsea Turner. My, you do look smart. I'll take you up top."

The woman led her charge through a security checkpoint beyond which waited a private elevator. "I hope you enjoy your evening." The woman slid a card through the reader and punched a button for the penthouse. "It's not many who are invited to Davato's personal dining room."

Chelsea could only nod and watch the floor numbers mount. Halfway to the top, a shivering started in her shoulders and ran down her torso. She hugged her arms about her chest, trying to stop it. It was as if some unseen, powerful presence here, in the very building where she worked, was sending a hidden warning on some invisible wavelength deep into her soul.

"Are you okay, signorina?" asked the young blonde.

Chelsea shook herself and tried on a smile. What she felt was silly, wasn't it? There was no such thing as a sixth sense connecting her soul to someone—or something—else. "I'm fine. Really."

"We're almost there."

At the top, the woman guided her across a wide vestibule into a dining room whose walls were encircled by marble statues of ancient Greeks and Romans in various stages of undress. "Make yourself comfortable." She waved to a red velvet chair, one of only two before a glass-topped table supported by ornamental iron legs.

The woman departed, and Chelsea sat. She tried to still her racing heart, to lose herself in the soft background music and the aroma of roses from a bouquet in a standing vase.

Moments later, a far door opened, followed by the familiar voice of the man Dylan called the Antichrist. "I am so glad you could make it." His hand out, a smiling Davato strolled to her side, and again, his smooth words, so authoritative and kind, made her wonder if what Dylan said could possibly be true. With his silver hair swept over his forehead and his twinkling eyes, she couldn't help but smile back. How could she think ill of the man?

She rose to meet him. "Thank you, sir, for inviting me."

"I often make time for private dinners with some of our employees, especially when their father holds such an important position as yours."

She nodded, not knowing how to respond.

"But I'm hungry, and you must be too." He clapped his hands, and two young men in tuxedos entered. One bore a bottle of Chianti. After the first poured, the second served a salad course of caprese. Later came an antipasto dish.

After Davato had eaten the last bite and before the next course, he turned to her. "How do you like working for the Ministry of Truth, Chelsea?"

"It's interesting work. And I've always wanted to be in Rome."

"Yes, it's a fascinating city, the cradle of civilization, and once, the center of an empire. But the Unitum Imperium will surpass all that went before it. You should feel privileged you are here at the beginning."

Her fork stopped halfway to her mouth as, again, she struggled for a response. "I am. It is exciting. And things are certainly changing. All for the better, I'm sure."

"They are, and I'm glad you agree. But the changes started with the Great Catastrophe. Let's never forget that. Most people believe that UFOs were responsible, and I'll do nothing to dissuade that opinion. But there's another theory of which we do not speak, that the Enemy of all we are doing is complicit. And we cannot, must not, let him win."

Chelsea nodded, shoved the last of her antipasto into her mouth, and swallowed. Was he speaking of God? She shivered.

"But here's the pasta course, and next we'll have the meat course. I do so love our Italian customs. They are so . . . civilized." As he spoke, one waiter brought in plates of ham ravioli smothered in pesto sauce while the other refilled their glasses.

Davato's gaze occasionally swept her while they ate. And whenever she'd look up, he'd smile. Finally, he said, "You are a beautiful woman, Chelsea Turner, and I am so glad you are here tonight."

She should have been embarrassed. But somehow, his honeyed words slipped through her defenses, and she smiled back. "Thank you," was all she could think to say. It was difficult to dislike this man.

The main course was steak, rare of course and smothered in sautéed mushrooms. Every few minutes, the waiters topped their wine glasses. Her head was beginning to swim.

After more small talk and she'd eaten half her portion, she wondered if she should ask a question that had troubled her for some time. Bringing it up might be dangerous, and she hesitated. Perhaps it was the wine or his disarming presence, but throwing caution aside, she forged ahead. "I've been asked to do new, deeper background checks on several employees working for something called the Truth Squads." She swallowed. Was she feigning too much ignorance? "What is a Truth Squad?"

Davato set down his fork and placed both hands on the table. "Some of our methods may seem harsh, Chelsea, but believe me, they are necessary. The government I'm forming is looking to do something no government has ever done before. We are not only bringing peace, prosperity, and security to the world, we are also reshaping the minds and hearts of the people."

As he spoke, his voice changed, and she found herself listening with increasingly rapt attention to every syllable. Somehow, it all made sense. "Before me, anarchy, chaos, and war had free rein over the planet. But I propose to change all that. To that end, we must seek out and stop all who would sabotage what we are doing. Freedom is what I offer, Chelsea, freedom to pursue whatever a man or woman desires most. Unfettered pursuit of happiness and pleasure—that's what, deep in their hearts, people yearn for, long for. And what do you think stands against that most worthy of goals?"

"I don't know."

"First, the dogmas of the old, threadbare religions. Let me ask you a question, Chelsea. Do you believe in God?"

Startled by the question, she drew a quick breath before collecting herself. "Not really."

A slow smile spread across his lips. "Well and good. The second thing standing in the way of our goals is the old, tired structures of governance. Democracy was good in its day, but the people don't really know what's best for them, do they? What they need is a great leader with authority, someone with a grand plan, a superior intellect, someone who will purge the poison of old, tired dogmas and backward thinking. And that's what the Truth Squads and the Central Security Agency are all about. They will ferret out the antagonists, the naysayers, the rebels, those who would stop us before we've even begun. Your father heads the CSA, and I'm surprised you asked the question. But know this, Chelsea: The ends do justify the means."

When he'd finished his speech, she nodded again. With such a grand vision, such great goals for humanity, how could anyone disagree?

The waiters reentered bearing strawberry flan, followed by tiny glasses of limoncello. As she and Davato sipped the sweet liquor, they made small talk about the weather turning colder.

When the coffee was poured, a warm glow filled her, and she couldn't remember when she'd ever had a more pleasant evening.

She glanced at her watch. Two hours had passed since she'd left the apartment.

"But you have to return to work tomorrow, and I have to catch a plane to Brussels for a meeting." Davato pushed back from his chair. "Before you leave, would you dance with me once more? Just once. I promise."

Her heart beating faster, she nodded.

He went to a console on the wall, punched some icons, and the soft background music changed to a quiet Latin beat. He led her to an open spot on the tiled floor. Smiling, he raised his arms, inviting her to join him.

She stepped into his embrace, and they danced. He was charming, graceful, and seemingly the perfect gentleman. As they whirled about the room, she felt secure in his arms. All her earlier doubts and fears fell away. And as the dance ended, she wondered again if Dylan knew what he was talking about. Surely, he was wrong. How could this charming man be the Antichrist?

He led her to the door and clapped three times, and the young blonde who'd brought her up the elevator reappeared. "Please escort Chelsea to the limousine."

The woman nodded, and Chelsea followed her into the cabin.

"How was it?" asked the woman with eager, questioning eyes.

"I wasn't expecting it, but I had a wonderful time."

A knowing smile crossed the other's lips. "That's what they all say."

A warm glow followed Chelsea home to bed, and when she woke the next morning, the night before seemed like a dream. Only then did she realize that, since she'd entered the top-floor suite of the president of the Unitum Imperium, not once had she dwelt on the crime she'd committed two days ago.

But with that realization came another—the person whom Dylan had called the Antichrist had completely disarmed and entranced her.

And she didn't mind at all.

CHAPTER 2
RENÉ LECLERC

Paris, France – December, Year 1

Dylan Turner exited the TGF fast train at Paris's Gare de Lyon station, his heart pumping fast as he scanned the platform for their pursuers. And yes, there they were—the two men in black and gray business suits, who had followed them into their first-class car at Nice. They stood together, about twenty yards away, pretending to talk. And just as he had on the entire eight-hour journey, the taller bearded man sent a furtive glance in Dylan's direction.

On the trip, Dylan had sat with Margot. It had been a mistake to whisper to her about their two pursuers. Afterward, she had shifted in her chair, started to read a book, then stopped, then gazed out the window, then picked up the book again. "How can we ever lose them?" she asked several times an hour. He should never have told her.

As agreed, Caleb and Baruch traveled together, sitting a few rows away.

When Dylan and Margot visited the dining car, the tall man followed, leaving his partner behind. And later, when Caleb and Baruch rose from their seats to eat, the shorter, towheaded man was close on their heels.

Baruch and a smiling Caleb now approached Dylan on the platform. Caleb arched his back after the long trip. "What is this address we're supposed to find?"

Dylan nodded toward the men. "Don't look, but those two have been following us ever since we changed trains in Nice."

Surprise widened Caleb's eyes, and he began to turn around until Dylan shook his head.

"Everyone, just head for the exit. Pretend you don't see them. Somehow, we have to lose them."

Again, he glanced behind. The tall man was staring at him, standing motionless with his partner as the crowd passed on either side. Dylan averted his gaze and started walking.

The others followed, and he picked up the pace. At the platform's end, a mirror for cart vehicles told him the two men were, indeed, on their tail. How could he lose them?

Had the men been tracking the four ever since they boarded the train in Florence? If so, who sent them? Surely, they worked for the Unitum Imperium, possibly the Ministry of Truth. He shuddered. His own father now ran that ministry.

In the main hall, where arriving and departing crowds mingled, he headed for a sign announcing the metro entrance.

Just ahead, a portly man was frantically searching his pockets while, beside him, a frowning woman in a checkered dress planted hands on hips. "Are you sure you didn't put it in your bag?" she asked.

Dylan slowed, the better to hear their conversation.

"No. I've been robbed!" The man wiped his forehead, and his widened eyes swept the passengers around him. Both hands rose to the top of his head. "All my credit cards. All my cash. What are we to do?"

Dylan approached, keeping his voice low. "I couldn't help but overhear. Don't turn around, but those two men coming toward us—the short, blond one, and the taller bearded one—I saw them leave you then pick another man's pocket a moment ago." The lie was bitter on his tongue, but necessary.

The portly man's mouth opened. His wife glared with venom at the approaching strangers.

"After they left you, they stole that guy's wallet." Dylan pointed in the general direction of some men heading toward the departure platforms. "Now they're coming back this way, probably thinking no one noticed what they've been doing."

"Jean"—the woman pointed—"there are two gendarmes over there."

The man's eyes, now filled with venom, focused on the alleged criminals. Then he spun. As fast as his weight would allow, he hurried toward the policemen.

Whirling, Dylan joined his three companions and hustled them toward the metro entrance. They stopped at the kiosk to buy tickets, and he stole a glance behind. The gendarmes were arguing with Dylan's frustrated pursuers while the woman stood with hands on hips and the man's accusing finger wagged.

With tickets in hand, the four crossed through the turnstiles into the metro on the same level. Seconds later, a westbound train stopped, headed for La Défense-Grande Arche, bringing the smell of ozone, the screech of wheels. They boarded.

As the train whooshed out of the station, neither of the men appeared on the platform.

Dylan found an empty seat, plopped down beside Margot, and breathed out. "We lost them."

"What did you say to that couple back there?" asked Caleb from the seat ahead.

"I told them that our pursuers picked the man's pocket."

Caleb grinned.

"Who were those men?" Sitting beside Caleb, Baruch twisted in his seat, his smiling brown eyes narrowing.

"Government agents. It's troubling that they followed us all the way from Nice. I suppose they could have followed us from Florence."

Margot's dark brows drew together before she brushed aside her thick black bangs. "Why didn't they stop us sooner?"

"Who knows? Maybe they wanted our contact. But we've lost them." Dylan studied the metro map above the door. "We can change at Les Halles for Porte d'Orléans. That's where we need to get off."

They rode the rest of the way in silence.

* * *

THE ONLY INFORMATION THEY HAD about René LeClerc was a phone number and instructions to call him from a certain bench in a certain Paris park. That's all that Sergei, the former Russian FSB agent who'd helped them escape from Chicago, had given them. The four exited the metro at Porte d'Orléans and climbed the stairs to the street.

Dylan shivered as they donned the parkas, stocking caps, and gloves supplied by the bishop. Frost coated the grass, and an icy wind shifted piles of dead leaves. They walked the short distance to the park where streetlights shed yellow circles across the walkways and glinted off occasional puddles of ice.

It was dark when Dylan called the number.

"Âllo?" answered a ragged voice.

"Is this René LeClerc?" he asked in French.

A pause at the other end. "Who wants to know?"

"Friends of Sergei in Chicago. He gave us this number to call."

"If that's true, then where are you calling from?"

"From a bench overlooking a frozen pond in the Parc Montsouris."

"All right, monsieur, then what is the password?"

"Just a moment. It's dark." Following Sergei's instructions, he circled to the bench's rear. Switching on his phone's flashlight, he examined the graffiti. The three words painted in red, repeated on another corner, had to be the password.

"Étrangers au paradis." *Strangers in paradise.*

"Très bien. You are from Sergei. What is your name? And please describe yourself."

"My name is Dylan Turner. I've got blond hair, a medium build, and am wearing a blue ski parka." Then he mentioned he had three friends with him.

"Four of you! Stay where you are. I will be there in . . . thirty minutes. Oui?"

"Yes. We'll be here."

They spent the half hour watching the passersby. Two couples in winter coats strolling hand in hand after dinner. An elderly woman leading two teenage girls bundled in parkas. How strange it was that since V-Day, he hadn't seen a single child under the age of eleven.

Dylan stiffened as three young North Africans sauntered by. One carried a knife, and they eyed the four but passed without incident. France was one of the countries least affected by the Rapture. Even so, crime was now rampant and, like everywhere else, nearly out of control.

After the Christians were taken out of the earth, only those without the Holy Spirit and God's redeeming presence remained.

When a tall, slim man in a ski jacket with black slacks and a stocking cap passed them for the second time, Dylan nodded. The man circled back. He stopped, stubbed out the cigarette he was smoking on the cement, and his glance swept the four.

"You must be Dylan."

"I am."

René offered his hand, they shook, and he asked Dylan what he needed.

"A plane ticket to Chicago for my brother and one to Jerusalem for our friend. And new passports and identities for all of us. And credit cards. With new bank accounts. I have cash."

René rubbed his chin, and again a dark, intense gaze examined each of them. Dylan had never seen a man with such deep eye sockets. It was as if his eyes were eternally cast in deep shadow. "That's a lot to ask. Why do you need new identities?"

"Because men from the government are after us. We lost two of them at the Gare de Lyon."

René frowned. "What have you done to arouse the ire of the Unitum Imperium?"

Dylan narrowed his eyes. How much should he tell this man? What if he was in sympathy with what Davato was doing? "I'd rather not say." Dylan held his breath, fearful of the man's response.

"But you've done something that has gotten you into trouble? Oui?"

Hesitating for a moment, Dylan nodded.

"All right. I will do as you ask. But you must pay in advance. Seven hundred euros is my fee. I don't work for free, and soon, I'm getting out of this business altogether. I will need cash for the accounts up front."

Dylan swallowed. "I'll pay you half now and half when we receive the documents." His account, thanks to his father, had plenty of cash. Before leaving Florence, he'd withdrawn as much as they allowed and converted it to cash, now bulging in his backpack.

"*Bon.* Do you have a place to stay in Paris?"

"No."

René wrote an address on a piece of paper and handed it over. "Use this hotel. Text me your room numbers. I will be there tomorrow morning to take passport photos and get personal information for the accounts.

I can have your documents ready by the end of the day."

Dylan paid him, and they shook hands before they parted.

* * *

THEY SPENT THE NIGHT IN two rooms at the moderately priced Hôtel Mistral, eating a late breakfast of rolls with jam, butter, and coffee. At midmorning, Dylan admitted René, who took their photos, asked a number of personal questions for the accounts then left. He promised to return by nineteen hundred hours. The rest of the day, they napped, strolled the nearby streets and parks, lounged in corner cafés nursing coffee, and relaxed after the previous weeks of frantic activity.

But several times that day, gangs ambled down the street. Then the café patrons or sidewalk strollers would grab their coffee, food, wine, or themselves and flee to the interior of the nearest shop, everyone waiting until the youths had passed. One couple, too slow to depart, was robbed at knifepoint.

That evening, all four gathered in Dylan's room, waiting for the return of their French spy. Nineteen hundred hours came and went, but no René.

"Do you realize," said Caleb, "that back home, we just missed celebrating Thanksgiving."

Dylan cocked his head. "I doubt anyone will be celebrating anything this year."

Baruch asked, and they told him what the holiday stood for. "Then, my friends, we still have much to thank God for. I hope your countrymen—those who are now believers—celebrated."

Forty-five minutes passed. Caleb stood, paced to the window, and returned. "He's not coming back, is he? He took our money and fled."

"Give him time." Sitting on the couch beside Margot, Dylan again checked his watch. "Maybe he ran into a problem?"

"He's taken our money, and—"

A knock on the door interrupted. Baruch answered and admitted a sweaty-faced René wearing a backpack. But after a cursory greeting, their French companion went to the window, gazed down, then closed the blinds. He found a chair, sat, and dropped his pack on the floor. Fumbling in his pocket, he brought out a pack of cigarettes and lit one with a match. Blowing out smoke, he eyed them. "There are problems."

"What?" asked Margot.

"I was followed. I lost the tail, but there's worse. Through certain contacts, I discovered the Ministry of Truth has the descriptions of Dylan, Margot, and Caleb. It's been sent to their network of secret operatives. The network is new, but functional. It will be some time, if ever, before they implement their worldwide facial recognition web, but somehow, they traced you to me. My cover should have been solid. Also, I tried to reach Sergei this afternoon, and the reply I received was troubling."

"What kind of reply?"

"It was not according to our agreed-upon exchange." He took another long drag on his cigarette. "I fear he's been compromised."

"Oh no." Dylan swept a hand across his forehead.

"You say you lost your pursuers, and I'm trying to believe you. Sergei is the only other person who has my contact information. If they found his safe house with instructions to that park bench, they might have been waiting for us. Or . . . they sent you to entrap me. In any event, I was followed." René rose, paced the room, and returned.

Dylan exchanged a worried glance with Margot.

"I have what you asked for, but you have put me at great risk." René dropped his cigarette to the floor, crushed it with his foot, then reached into his pack. Instead of bringing out their documents, he produced a pistol.

He waved it at Baruch and Caleb. "You two—sit down!"

With stunned expressions, they lowered themselves to the bed.

René narrowed his eyes at Dylan. "Unless you tell me the truth, you'll get nothing. Either you will tell me all you know, or—God forgive me—I will be the only one to leave this room alive."

His heart beating wildly, Dylan stared at the weapon then raised his glance to the man with a face as cold as ice.

CHAPTER 3
A PROPOSAL

Joel 2:11–13,16,17 (NLT): *The day of the LORD is an awesome, terrible thing. Who can possibly survive? That is why the LORD says, "Turn to me now, while there is time. Give me your hearts. Come with fasting, weeping, and mourning."* . . . *Return to the LORD your God, for he is merciful and compassionate, slow to get angry and filled with unfailing love.* . . . *Gather all the people—the elders, the children, and even the babies.* . . . *Let them pray, "Spare your people, LORD!"*

Paris, France – December, Year 1

"The pistol isn't necessary." Dylan swallowed hard as the black metal captured his gaze. "I'll tell you what you want to know." Then, fearing how the man would react, he related to René LeClerc the entire story—about Caleb's blogging, Caleb's kidnapping, the demon encounter at the hat company, Margot's paintings, and how God led them to the catacombs where, with his sister Chelsea's help, they rescued Caleb and Baruch. He described Baruch's role as leader of 144,000 Jewish men who would bring millions to faith during the Tribulation.

When he'd finished, Dylan sat perfectly still, one hand gripping the other until his knuckles hurt. Would this man now turn the gun on them and kill them all in cold blood? Telling him everything had been a leap of faith, but what else could he do?

René's glance settled on each of them. He pocketed his pistol. Then, with moist eyes, he whispered, "Forgive me, my friends."

He motioned for them to rise, and they did. As he stepped forward, Dylan stepped back. But when René raised a hand and shook his head, Dylan stopped. Then, much to Dylan's surprise, René hugged him.

Next, René went to Baruch and kissed him on both cheeks. René took Margot's hands and kissed them, again and again.

"I am so used to the double-dealing, untrustworthy characters of my profession, I sometimes forget there are good people, Christian people, in this world. Thank you for your tale, Dylan Turner. Now I, too, have a confession to make."

"What?"

"Unlike my friend Sergei, when I heard the reports that UFOs caused the disappearances, I did not believe them. Then I heard the theory of the Christian Rapture, and I sought out a fallen priest, a man who came to faith too late. With tears in his eyes, he pointed me to the Christian Bible and the book of Revelation." Then René's voice broke.

"My friends, I–I am now a believer in Jesus as the Son of the living God." He closed his eyes and hung his head. "But I confess, in my zeal to help my fellow Christians, I haven't yet given up some of the unsavory activities of my trade. I have much to be forgiven for."

Dylan and Margot exchanged glances of relief. Baruch clapped his hands, and Caleb smiled.

René paced to the window and returned. "But there is more. Much, much more. Ever since my conversion, I have been convinced we must work against this Antichrist whose evil threatens all believers of the truth. With my extensive contacts, I became involved with a secret organization called the Friends of the Nazarene. I have pledged to them my skills and my life. We are few, but we are establishing a foothold in southern France. One day, we hope to create a European network devoted to helping believers escape persecution. We also strive to thwart the goals of the Antichrist's government wherever we can."

"That is wonderful." Dylan rose and again shook René's hands.

"It is clear your arrival here was divinely inspired." René smiled at each of them. Then he gave them their passports, tickets, and credit cards. He also returned three hundred and fifty euros, what Dylan had paid him for half his fee. "I cannot charge you a fee. Not after hearing your story. But I will need the rest of the money to fund your accounts."

Dylan tried to press the euros back into René's hand. "No, you deserve your fee."

"No. For you, Dylan, and for you, Margot, I have a proposition—

but later. First, we must say goodbye to Baruch and Caleb." He faced those two. "Your flights to Jerusalem and Chicago leave in three and four hours, respectively, so you must begin making your way now to the airport. When you leave the hotel, be sure no one follows you. Take the metro and get off at the Les Halles stop. From there, take a taxi to the Gare du Nord where you will buy tickets for the RER train to the airport. That route may help throw off any pursuers."

The two retrieved their bags from next door. Then Baruch Abramovich stopped before Margot. "I am privileged to have met one upon whom God has bestowed such a gift. And you, Dylan Turner, thank you for arranging our escape. May God go with you both."

After Baruch kissed them on the cheeks and stepped back, Caleb embraced his brother and said goodbye. But as they parted, a sudden shiver crossed Dylan's shoulders. "Don't go, Caleb. Stay here with us."

"What?" Caleb raised an eyebrow. "Why?"

"I have a bad feeling, a sudden feeling, about your returning to Chicago."

"A feeling?"

"Yeah. Just now." Dylan shivered again. "Stay here and help us."

"My apartment is in Chicago. And Tanya is there."

"Send for her. Don't go back. It's not safe there. I feel it. I know it."

The others sent questioning glances his way.

Caleb waved off his brother's concern. "I'll be fine. Too much has happened, and you're getting paranoid. I can't stay here simply because you had a *feeling*." He embraced Margot, and the two left.

When they were alone again, Dylan rubbed his temples. "I fear for him. Something's going to happen in Chicago."

"What?" asked Margot.

"I don't know." He tried to steady his quickening heartbeat. "Maybe it's nothing. Maybe Caleb's right, and I'm getting paranoid."

Margot laid a hand on his shoulder. "So many people have been chasing us lately. It's understandable. I've been feeling the same way."

"You're probably right." He turned to René. "What is this proposition you mentioned?"

René smiled. "For that, my friends, we must meet over dinner. I know a quiet restaurant nearby that serves the best food in the fourteenth arrondissement."

* * *

Dylan and Margot followed René on a circuitous route through the neighborhood. Occasionally, he would glance behind. Twice, he circled back only to resume their original route. The restaurant held only a dozen patrons, and René led them to an isolated table against a back wall. When they were seated and the waiter arrived, their host ordered a bottle of Syrah while Dylan examined the menu.

"I recommend the cassoulet," said René, "white beans stewed with sausages and duck."

After they'd ordered and the waiter departed, Dylan sipped his wine then faced their host. "What is so secretive that—"

René raised a finger to his lips. "Quietly, my friend."

Dylan lowered his voice. "What is your proposition?"

"As I've said, the Nazarene Friends is composed of Christians who came to faith after the Rapture. Our goal is to help other Christians escape persecution." He lit a cigarette and drew in. "We also want to thwart the activities of the Antichrist whenever possible. You may not be aware of this, but new Christians are being taken off the streets every day. Until recently, I attended a small Protestant church here in Paris, but in the last three weeks, five of our number simply disappeared."

"What happened to them?"

"We think Davato's men rounded them up and sent them to an internment camp."

Margot's hand grasped Dylan's, and a shiver raced down his spine. "How do you know this?"

"We bribed a man to spy for us inside Davato's headquarters in Rome. He was seeking the location of the camp when all communication with him stopped. We haven't heard from him since. Most likely, he is either dead or in that camp."

René lit a new cigarette and stubbed out the old one. "That just proves the urgency of our mission. We can't just sit around, waiting for them to track us down and lock up our brothers and sisters. We have a safe house, a villa big enough to hide a number of refugees—fortunately, our spy never knew its location. We also have people out in the communities, seeking new Christians, offering them sanctuary."

"What do you want us to do?" asked Dylan.

"We need people willing to help at the villa. And people willing to go out and pick up refugees."

Margot frowned and cupped her hands around the glass of wine she'd barely touched. "Wouldn't that be . . . risky?"

Folding his arms, René nodded. "Davato's grip on his empire is tightening. Rumor has it he'll soon send groups of men to identify Christians in every arrondissement in France—Truth Squads, they're called, from the Central Security Agency. They will be stationed in every village, town, and city. Right now, they are identifying Christians. Later, CSA agents will come and take them away. That's probably what happened to our church members. So, yes, anyone at the safe house will be at risk. But our villa is isolated, somewhat hidden. You shouldn't think of the risk. Instead, think of it as a chance to serve your God in this time of the end." He took another drag on his cigarette.

"You two are lucky I was still in Paris when you called, mopping up old business. I wasn't even going to take your call, but something whispered to me that I should. In a month or so, I will return to the villa for good. At that time, if you wish, I will take you there. So, now"—he stubbed out his cigarette and straightened—"will you join me and the Nazarene Friends in doing God's work?"

Wanting to say yes, Dylan sat back and faced Margot. But her head shook, ever so slightly, back and forth, and she bit her lip.

The waiter brought their food, interrupting the moment.

When they had finished their meal, René opened his hands in a question. "So, my friends, what is your answer? Our brothers and sisters are being rounded up daily—especially here, in Paris. I admit that what I ask will put you in some danger. But staying here is also risky, and it's clear to me that God has laid his hand on you both. Has he not already set you apart for mission?"

Dylan's glance searched Margot's. "I'm willing."

Again, she lowered her gaze to the table. "I'm sorry, but I–I'm not sure." She folded her hands on her lap. "We've been through so much lately. We just escaped men who were chasing us. Right now, I can't do this. Not yet. I need time."

"I can't do this without you." Dylan's voice was pleading.

"We could really use you both," said their French companion. "Especially after what you've revealed about Margot's extraordinary gift."

Still looking down, she shook her head. "Not . . . right . . . now."

Dylan turned to René. "Give us time to think about it. We'll let you know."

"Fair enough. You have my number. I will pray for your decision." Before he was out the door, he had lit another cigarette.

CHAPTER 4
MRS. PRESIDENT

Daniel 8:23–25a (NLT): *At the end of their rule, when their sin is at its height, a fierce king, a master of intrigue, will rise to power. He will become very strong, but not by his own power. . . . He will destroy powerful leaders and devastate the holy people. He will be a master of deception and will become arrogant; he will destroy many without warning.*

Washington, DC – December, Year 1

A smiling Davato stepped into the Oval Office and received Kamryn Harper's trademark grin, her sweaty, uncertain palm, and her insincere greeting. From the woman's furtive glances, he sensed fear, pliability, weakness. Good. Perhaps he could stop the plans he'd set in motion.

Maybe she would live to see the dawn.

He followed her into the room. "I'm so glad you could receive me on such short notice, President Harper."

She motioned to a cushioned chair then circled to her side of the Resolute Desk and sat. "President Davato, you have accomplished so much in so . . . short an amount of time." Her lips quavered. "All of us here are in . . . awe."

"Thank you. But I have now taken the title of Imperator. I would prefer if you called me by that."

"Yes. Of course, Mister—Imperator. You said our meeting was of the utmost importance?" She picked up a pencil and rolled it between her fingers, but it slipped through and dropped to the desk.

"Yes." Davato sat back. Harper was in over her head and had been since the day she took office. When her President had died of a sudden heart attack on V-Day, the job had been thrust upon her. He'd read the report they prepared for him, and he'd shaken his head in wonder that such incompetence had reached such heights of power. Her only experience with leadership had been as an activist community organizer, then as a half-term senator from the most liberal state in the country. She had no familiarity with business or the military. What she did have was a deep conviction to an ideology that, if implemented to its fullest, would destroy the very nation she found herself leading. He suppressed the mirth threatening to explode in raucous laughter.

As his delight grew, she swallowed.

His mission here today should be an easy one.

"The Unitum Imperium is, indeed, a great accomplishment, but that is only the beginning." His voice now rose with the power of command. "We plan to do much, much more. To complete my grand design, we need more nation partners to align their interests with ours."

Her eyes averted beneath his steady gaze, and she shifted on her seat. "I see." A nervous laugh escaped her mouth, and one hand scratched something behind her right ear. "But how does that affect me—I mean us?"

"It can't have escaped your attention, President Harper, that in population, power, and influence, the Unitum Imperium has replaced your country as the greatest power on the planet. I have consolidated my reign over the nations of the old Roman Empire. Around that core, I am creating a treaty alliance that includes the remaining countries of Europe and the world. Africa and Latin America will soon be treaty partners. And within the next few years, most of the world—excluding China, Russia, and the Islamic countries—will also join. That leaves me with the question of your nation."

She swallowed and reached for a pitcher of water. Her hand trembling ever so slightly, she poured a glass for herself then raised a glance to him. "W–what do you have in mind?" But again, one hand went to her right ear, seeming to poke something back in place.

Did Harper have an earpiece? Was she listening to advice from someone outside the room, someone unaffected by the power of his voice? Frowning, he leaned forward and placed both hands on the desk. "I'm here today to ask for two things. First, would you sign a Treaty of Intent with the Unitum Imperium? Second—and this is just between you and me—I also propose that, when the time comes, you commit the United States to joining the Unitum Imperium family of nations in our forward march of history. My second request might come as a bit of a shock. Between us, it will remain unofficial and private. But I assure you that, within the next three years, every nation on earth will beg to join us. So, what do you say, Mrs. President? Can I count on you?"

"I . . . I . . ." The hand dropped from her ear. Then she tilted her head so he couldn't see the right side of her face. "I don't think that's possible. Your proposal is interesting. But the Senate must approve all treaties, and they would never agree to such a request." Her cheeks were turning red. "I'm afraid we c–can't."

"They don't have to know the final goal, Mrs. President. You can take the first step and sign the first treaty today. You and your predecessors have used executive privilege many times before. You could use it in this instance to override your Senate's objections. If you agree to both of my conditions today, I guarantee you a position of power and influence in the new government. Believe me when I say it would be most unwise for you to refuse."

"I–I—"

A door opened, and an aide walked in. As Davato frowned, the man whispered in her ear. Did she have handlers like her bumbling, incompetent, senile predecessor? Was she even in charge?

The aide stepped around the desk and opened the far door for her.

"I'm so sorry, Mr. Imperator, but . . ." She wiped sweat from her forehead. "But within the hour, I am speaking to Black Lives Matter in the park. My aides tell me it's time to leave for the event." She stood. "Thank you for stopping by today. Rest assured, I will give your proposal the utmost consideration."

"Of course." Davato stood and again shook her hand, and they parted.

He stalked from the building to a waiting limousine then joined his personal aide and bodyguard, Carlo Scutari, in the back seat. Davato waved to the driver, and the car entered DC traffic.

"How did it go?" asked Carlo.

"She didn't agree. Tell our friend at the park to continue with the plan."

His eyes widening, Carlo faced his boss. "Are you sure about that, sir?"

Suppressing a wave of anger at the question, Davato nodded. "As sure as I am about anything."

* * *

When the President of the United States arrived in Lincoln Park before the statue of Mary McLeod Bethune, the crowd of well-wishers, numbering in the tens of thousands, spilled over the grounds into the trees. The Secret Service had advised against the speech, but the President had been undeterred. As usual, agents were scattered throughout, on guard for suspicious persons of hostile intent.

For mid-December, the afternoon was warm and snowless. Still, most in attendance wore winter jackets and hats. This was of great concern to her security detail as so much heavy clothing could conceal almost any kind of weapon.

President Harper mounted the stage erected before the statue of the Civil Rights leader and stepped to the microphone. Sweeping her glance over the upraised faces, she smiled and waved. "I am so glad to be here with you today, celebrating your victory over racial oppression. Though the world has changed drastically in the last few months, that will not deter us from our goal. Our quest for racial equity goes on. We still have more work to do, and we will not be deterred from our goal, even though we have more work to do. Even in these trying times, our quest for racial equity goes on."

As her speech rambled and repeated itself, a white man in a full-length coat wormed his way to within twenty yards of the roped-off cordon around the stage. He removed his winter gloves and pocketed them. He unbuttoned the bottom half of his jacket.

Three years ago, he'd taken the name of Abu Sufyan, the name of the father-in-law of Muhammad himself. Before V-Day, he'd lost a factory job in Baltimore and another in Philadelphia. After being fired as a FedEx driver in New York, he spent a year in Saudi Arabia studying with imams. Then came the vanishing, and he was asked to join the Revenge of Islam, a secret Washington cell dedicated to the advancement of Islam and the destruction of the ruling class of white elites. According to his cell leader, the woman on the stage before him represented all that was wrong with the world and everything the Revenge of Islam was against.

She was not Muslim. She belonged to the white ruling elite. And she was a woman. It was a repugnant, abhorrent situation. Everyone in his cell had agreed.

His right hand slipped beneath his jacket. His fingers found the Bushmaster ACR assault rifle hanging by its cord around his neck. The metal was cold, but his index finger slid easily around the trigger.

His next actions might bring his own death, but he welcomed it. Beyond this life, waited Paradise. Or at least that's what the imams promised. He grinned.

President Harper was facing away from him, addressing the crowd on her right.

Stupid and meaningless, the words kept spilling from her mouth. Everything about the woman screamed foolishness.

All she had to do was turn to the left, toward him. Just a bit farther. He needed a full frontal view.

There.

She'd turned.

In one quick motion, he lifted the rifle from his jacket, slammed the stock against his shoulder, and aimed.

He squeezed the trigger.

The gun kicked back against his clavicle.

A spray of bullets spattered his target. A Secret Service agent threw himself into the line of fire, but more bullets took him down. As the man fell, the President slumped to the stage behind him.

Something sharp bit Abu on the neck. For one instant, his bullets shot wildly across the stage, hitting a second agent. But he ignored the sting. He corrected his aim and squeezed the trigger again. More on the stand fell.

Around him now came screams as the crowd scattered.

He kept shooting until his heart raced with adrenaline and his clip emptied.

Men were now running toward him from all directions. Secret Service agents. Men trained to repel just such an attack. He raised his rifle toward the threat. But it was empty.

An approaching agent fired his weapon.

Abu Sufyan saw the flash, felt something slam into his chest, then dropped to the ground.

* * *

UNKNOWN TO ABU SUFYAN, A man in a jogging suit, known to everyone simply as Smith, had been standing nearby, watching the assassin's every move. Smith had known what his target was doing because he'd created the fiction that was the Revenge of Islam. It was he who had organized the fake cell on behalf of the League of Abaddon. He'd been doing that kind of thing all his life, waiting for the moment when they would call him to act. His cell members had pumped their target full of the right propaganda.

Abu Sufyan wasn't the only one the League had prepared, but today was the right time. This was the right venue. And Abu Sufyan was the right man.

The moment Abu had fired and hit his target, Smith's right hand had reached up with the pencil syringe and shot the poison into Abu's neck. It would take a few minutes to work, but once injected, there was no surviving it. One couldn't risk the chance that the Secret Service would take Abu alive and interrogate him. Even now, his social media accounts and apartment were being scrubbed of all reference to Smith's fictional cell. His men were also erasing Abu's data in all the servers, wherever they existed. Within hours, there'd be no evidence linking Abu to the Revenge of Islam or the League of Abaddon.

After Smith released his poison, he merged with the fleeing, panicked crowd. He was headed for his hotel room. The job was complete, and within the hour, he would receive the substantial bonus promised him by Carlo Scutari.

CHAPTER 5

CALEB

University Village, Chicago – December, Year 1

Caleb's trip from Paris to Chicago had been a nightmare. In midflight, the airline went bankrupt, and his plane made an unscheduled landing in Reykjavik, Iceland, where he was stranded for a week competing with other passengers for a way out. When he was finally able to secure a seat, his next flight was forced to land in Boston to fix a failing turbine. But the needed parts weren't available, and neither was another plane. The company put up the disgruntled passengers in a hotel, and they waited. For days, the airline repeated apologies and assurances that the flight would resume. Again and again, he tried without success to get one of the increasingly scarce rental cars to continue to his destination.

Had everything in the country broken down?

But as time passed, Dylan's parting warning planted a dark seed in Caleb's soul, and he, too, felt a growing danger for the city he called home. By the time his new flight departed Boston's Logan airport, it was a week before Christmas, and his fear was all-consuming.

After landing at O'Hare Airport, he took a taxi and returned to the apartment building he hadn't seen in months. He'd tried to call Tanya from Reykjavik, but her number was disconnected. He longed to be home, to see her, and to get back to normality. But what greeted him after he paid the driver and stepped onto the sidewalk only fed a growing unease.

His car was still parked out front, and, miraculously, its windows were intact. But mixed with the fallen snow littering the entrance was broken glass and garbage. The front door also hung open, its lock busted. Inside, the lights were out, and the elevator didn't work. His heart beating faster, he entered the stairwell and climbed to the third floor in the dark.

At his apartment, someone had replaced the door, and the lock was broken. When he entered what had once been home, he gasped. Someone had ripped every cushion, broken every picture frame, mirror, and bottle. And they'd defaced every wall with obscenities, some blasphemous. His heart beating hard, he stepped carefully through each room. Whoever had done this had destroyed or defaced everything.

But what about Tanya? Was she all right?

Whirling, he raced through the dimly lit hallway to the Baranov apartment. He knocked. No answer. He knocked again. Still no answer. Placing a hand on the knob, he turned it. The door opened.

Inside, all was dark, and he sucked in breath. If she were here, Nika would be racing toward him.

"Tanya?" he called.

Silence.

Reaching into his pocket, he switched on the flashlight from the new phone René had given him and began a search. Someone had ransacked the place, but not nearly as bad as his apartment. On the refrigerator, dark and no longer humming, magnets held a sheet of paper—his name and an unfamiliar phone number. He walked to the light by the window and dialed the number.

"Hello?" came Tanya Baranov's familiar voice. "Who is this?"

"It's Caleb. I'm so glad to hear your voice."

"Caleb!" She screeched with delight. "I didn't know what happened to you. When I called your number, it didn't go through. After they told me to get a new phone, I was afraid we'd never connect."

"That explains why I couldn't reach you. My first plane stranded me in Reykjavik, and the next flight had me stuck for days in Boston while we waited for parts. It's crazy out there. Everything's breaking down. Where are you? *How* are you?"

"It wasn't safe in the apartment. So I went back to that church we attended, and the pastor let me stay with a friend of his. Nika is with me. And I like it here."

His muscles relaxing, he drew a deep breath. "Tanya, we need to leave the city."

"Why?"

"I can't explain it." He strode toward the window and looked down. "But I've been having premonitions that it isn't safe here."

"Premonitions?"

"Yes." Shadows moved in the alley below—gangs? "I'm going to load what I can in the car, and we need to drive as far from here as we can get."

"What brought this on?"

"Trust me in this. We don't want to be in Chicago when it happens."

"When what happens?"

"I–I don't know. Like I said, things are breaking down everywhere. It could get worse. A lot worse." He wiped his brow. Did he sound like a crazy man? "Just trust me."

"Caleb . . ." Her voice showed hesitation. "I don't want to leave. I like it here. Can't we wait?"

"Why?"

"Please. This place is nice, and there's room for you here. Where do you want to go?"

"I–I don't know. I just want to get as far away from the city as I can. Give me your address, and we'll talk more when I get there."

She did, and they hung up.

He loaded what clothing and unspoiled food he could find into his SUV. But when he started the car, someone had drained the tank of fuel. He stopped at a dozen stations before finding one with gas for sale, and then the price was exorbitant. His next stop was a Walmart where he bought a rooftop carrier, sleeping bags, canned and dried food, dog food, and winter camping gear.

"More folks have the same idea," said the stooped, gray-haired woman at the cash register. "They're leaving the city, heading north to Wisconsin or west to the Mississippi. We're out of nearly everything. You probably got the last of it."

Caleb nodded, fished for his credit card, and handed it over.

"I'd leave if I could." The woman rang up the sale. "But at my age, where would I go?"

Caleb shrugged then pushed his cart overflowing with purchases toward the parking lot.

As his car sped through intersections, past lounging National Guard troops and the occasional youth gang, he passed block after block of snow-covered wreckage.

He turned on the radio and the news.

"A spokesperson from the Unitum Imperium's Ministry of Peace has today responded to Russia after that county began massing troops on its borders with the Baltic states. The official statement included this warning: 'Know that if the sovereignty of any member state is threatened in any way, the Unitum Imperium is prepared to respond with all necessary force. It would be a grave mistake to think that the Empire will not give an overwhelming defense of its territory.'

"No official response has been received from the Russian government.

"This adds to fears from the other side of the world where the Chinese are assembling a fleet off the mainland coast opposite Taiwan. Satellite images confirm it includes high-speed landing craft. The latest official ultimatum from the Chinese Communist Party reads as follows: 'Any attempt to interfere with our historic right to reunite Taiwan with the Chinese mainland will be met with a final and crushing blow. We condemn in the strongest possible terms the provocative and lawless exercises now being conducted in Chinese waters. If President William Cole does not withdraw his weak and pathetic navy from Chinese waters in the Taiwan Strait, he may soon find his ships at the bottom of the ocean.' "

For a moment, Caleb took his focus off the road and stared at the radio. Was this what his and Dylan's premonitions were about? Gazing again at the way ahead, he pressed his foot on the accelerator.

Somehow, he needed to convince Tanya. They needed to leave Chicago as soon as possible.

CHAPTER 6

MARGOT'S DECISION

Paris, France – December, Year 1

On Christmas Eve, Dylan and Margot decided to risk it and make a rare visit to René's favorite café. The walk from the apartment revealed no signs that this was the night before the celebration of the birth of Christ. Inside, the only other occupants were a young couple sitting two tables away and a waiter reading his phone.

During their infrequent nights out, the city's atmosphere had changed for the worse. Groups of young men, always three or four at a time, often roamed the streets. But they weren't the usual gangs. They were the Truth Squads René had warned them about, men wearing black armbands emblazoned with the hexagram and globe that was now the symbol of the Antichrist's government. Everywhere, all at once, as if by magic, the six corners of the emblem now contained the six letters of Davato's name.

The squads would stop people at random. While one demanded IDs, addresses, affiliations, beliefs, and the nature of a person's business, another recorded everything on a tablet. Whenever Dylan saw such men coming, he steered Margot to the opposite side of the street or into a shop, or an alley—anywhere but in the path of the new inquisitors.

Tonight, the two nursed glasses of red wine as they waited for their orders of cassoulet.

Dylan waved toward the street. "They've finally done it. Christmas has been completely purged from the culture."

"It's been a long time coming." Margot lifted an eyebrow. "Not a single Christmas display in a single window, anywhere. It's Christmas Eve, and gloom itself hangs over the city."

"You're right, and I want to get out of here." He leaned forward and narrowed his gaze. During their time in Paris, he'd begged her without success to take up René's offer. "Margot, it's been weeks since René asked us to join him. When are you going to decide?"

She rolled her eyes to the ceiling. "I've told you a hundred times. It's too risky. I can best help René's cause by painting, not by manning a way station for refugees."

"But it's our cause too, isn't it?" Dylan tapped the table with his fingers.

"I . . . suppose so."

"Then why not take the risk? René has an entire villa ready and waiting in the country. He's heading down there next week. And like I said—this city is depressing. And it's becoming dangerous to stay."

"It is, isn't it?" She wrapped her arms about her chest and shivered. "But the idea that the Antichrist's men might be seeking out Christians, that they might find the villa and put us in a camp—it scares me. Last time, we barely escaped. I guess I'm not as strong as I thought I was."

He was about to respond when the young couple nearby captured his glance. The woman had been sending furtive glances toward the street. Then the man lowered his head toward his companion, and they began whispering.

With an effort, Dylan turned back to Margot. "You're wrong. Down in the cavern, you were brave, reliable, strong. You locked the gate to keep out the guards then brought the keys to unlock the prisoners' chains. You were wonderful." He reached across and laid a hand on hers. "And wouldn't it be great to be in the country again? There you could paint to your heart's content."

"Yes, to have a studio again would be nice. And last night, I had the desire to paint, but . . ."

"But what?"

"I don't think I could ever paint here, in the city."

"Then let's go with—"

The front door slammed open, and four young men burst in. Each wore the black armband emblazoned with Davato's six-sided symbol. Cold stares bored into the room's four occupants.

Margot's forehead wrinkled with fear. Widened, darting eyes searched his. He reached across, grabbed her hands, and squeezed.

The young man across the room seemed on the verge of rising, but his woman friend laid a hand on his shoulder.

One of the squad members took three steps toward Dylan and stopped. "What is your business here?"

Had they come for Dylan and Margot? Had Davato's agents finally caught them? The blood pounded in his temples, and he wanted to flee out the back. But he forced his voice to remain calm. "Dinner. That's all."

One of the others called the man back. "These are the ones we want."

The man whirled, and the intruders surrounded the far table.

The tallest of the bunch produced a pistol, its black barrel gleaming. "You will stand," he said. "Now!"

The young woman's whole body now shook, and tears streamed down her face as she complied.

Defiance in his eyes, the young man shot out of his seat. "You may have our bodies." He stood erect with head held high. "But you'll never have our souls. They belong to Christ, to the King of the—"

The pistol lashed out. The barrel struck his forehead, and the young man dropped to his knees.

The woman helped him rise.

Wiping blood from his face, the young man stood. He straightened his back. Again, he spoke. "We belong to Christ, to the—"

Again, the barrel struck, but with a sound of a hammer slamming into a side of beef.

Dylan sucked in air.

Like a bull in the slaughterhouse receiving a shot to the head, the young man slumped, unconscious, to the floor.

His companion knelt over him, tears falling on his closed eyelids and upturned face.

"Enough of this." The squad leader motioned, and the black arm-bands hoisted their lifeless prisoner, grabbed the woman by both arms, and dragged the two out the door.

Dylan's gaze followed them through the window glass until they'd gone. But when he exhaled and faced Margot, he found a different woman sitting across from him.

She was red-faced, shaking, and her hands now gripped his with force.

"Th–those animals." Her jaw muscles tightened. Her eyes narrowed. "They had no right."

Startled by the change that had come over her, he struggled for words, found none.

"I've never seen such callousness." She glared at the street where they'd gone. "They were new Christians, only recently converted. And yet, he showed a passion and a conviction that I only showed when painting and the Holy Spirit gripped me. That man who stood up to those bullies showed incredible bravery. It was . . . admirable."

"Margot . . ." Dylan breathed in. "Let's get out of here. Let's go to René's villa and help refugees from Davato's purges escape what happened to those two. It would be a way to fight back."

"It would, wouldn't it?" She released his hands and brushed aside her bangs.

"And maybe in the country, you'll paint again. We need your visions. They were the clues that led us to where God intended us to go. God still has plans for you, for me."

"He does, doesn't he? That's what Baruch said."

"Yes. And Christians are supposed to serve, to advance God's kingdom, not hide from the world."

"I suppose you're right. And it might be safer in the country." She laid both hands on the table. "Okay, I'll do it."

"That's the best Christmas present you've ever given me."

A half-smile lifted one side of her face. "Dylan, that's the only Christmas present I've ever given you."

"Let's go and tell René."

CHAPTER 7
THE NAZARENE FRIENDS

The French Luberon – January, Year 1

On New Year's Day, after Parisians had celebrated the previous evening with heavy drinking and violent revelry, Dylan and Margot escaped south on the A6 with René behind the wheel of his Peugeot.

"Your timing is perfect." René again opened the window to a blast of frigid air and lit another cigarette. "I wasn't ready to leave Paris earlier, but my business here is finished. It's good we travel now as we'll soon see checkpoints on most major highways, and we don't yet have a way to forge the necessary IDs."

As they drove further, Margot turned on the radio to catch the news:

"Physicians are asked to be on the lookout for a mysterious epidemic of psychiatric disorders that may or may not be related to some new, unknown pathogen. Patients exhibit profound, adverse personality changes that include vile cursing, usually of a religious nature. Victims often speak with a voice distinctly different from before they were infected, and they will insist they are someone other than the patient. Some will converse in a foreign language, such as Latin, that they were previously unfamiliar with. They can also become violent, possessed with unnatural, superhuman strength. A few have shown telekinetic abilities and are able to throw objects, such as knives, across a room using only their thoughts. Many are also able to unnaturally cool the room they occupy. One distraught family member described their daughter's room as, 'As cold as a tomb.'

"There is no known cure. Due to a rapid, uncontrolled heartbeat, the disease is often fatal. Until authorities determine the cause and whether or not it's contagious, physicians encountering such patients should consider them extremely dangerous and refrain from attempting treatment. Physicians should immediately isolate infected individuals using whatever force is necessary. They are also urged to report all cases to the nearest office of the Central Security Agency without delay."

Dylan exchanged glances with Margot and René. "Are you thinking what I'm thinking?"

"Demonic possession?" asked Margot.

"It certainly sounds like it," added René.

Nodding, Dylan shut off the radio. "Can the world get any weirder?"

Late that afternoon and half a pack of cigarettes later, they entered Provence.

Out the window, brown and bare fields lay where, last year, lavender had burst in all its purple glory. Only last summer, God's majesty must have shone in glorious color through these fields. But according to the prophecies of what would happen toward the end of the Tribulation's first three years, all that would soon change. Creation itself would turn against man. Ripping his gaze away, Dylan shuddered.

It had been his choice to ask God to stay behind—or had it been God's? And now he must do all he could to honor the Lord in the trying times ahead.

Moments later, they drove through a series of villages, ancient stone and timber, marred on the outskirts by small factories, gas stations, warehouses.

Near Avignon, they passed an art supply shop, and Margot begged them to sop. "The desire to paint has been building ever since we left Paris."

Dylan shot her a smile. "Another vision?"

She nodded, and René parked. A half hour later, an easel, a stack of canvases, brushes, and paints filled the trunk and the empty seat in back.

They made the turn east for the D900 toward Bonnieux and the Luberon region. To the south rose the blue-green mountains of the Luberon. To the east, Mount Ventoux's snow-covered slopes dominated the sky. With stops, they'd been driving for nine hours since Paris. When they took a side road and began the ascent into the Petit Luberon range, Dylan was ready to quit.

After passing through a small village, René turned the Peugeot up a long forested drive and climbed through switchbacks. They stopped before two garages beneath a villa nestled in the hillside.

"It's a short hike to the house," said René as they left the car. "After the vanishing, we bought the place from the son of the owner who died in a plane crash. The son has a larger house on the coast."

Spreading above them on both sides, the two-storied stone château spoke of old-world charm, nestled among bare fields that stretched to tree-covered hillocks. Far to the right, grapevines blanketed the hills. Above and beyond the house, fences bordering a forest enclosed a pasture holding a dozen or so black-and-white Prim'Holstein dairy cows. From here, the only visible human habitation was a distant village beyond the forest in the valley below.

They grabbed their bags and started up the stone steps.

Huffing from the fifty-meter ascent, Dylan waved at the bare fields. "What do you grow here?"

"In the spring, we'll plant wheat, corn, and barley. There's a barn behind the house with a tractor, a plow, and a planter. It has space for the cows in bad weather. Marcel also keeps two horses. I've tried to convince him they aren't necessary, but he refuses to give them up. This fall, the Blanchets were able to harvest enough wheat to make bread for hundreds."

"Are we to become farmers then?" Fearing the answer, Dylan scrunched his face.

"No." René laughed. "That is Marcel and Gabrielle's job. They are new Christians, they grew up on a nearby farm, and they'll look after the livestock and crops."

Dylan let out a sigh of relief.

The house loomed above them, and Margot turned to René. "How many rooms?"

"Besides the master bedroom and fifteen guest rooms, there's a grand salon, a petit salon, a dining room, a library, a billiard room, and a smoking room that was converted to a television and recreation room."

"It looks ancient," said Dylan.

"Four hundred years old. We bought it because it's out of the way. We're at the end of the road, and to reach our nearest neighbor, one must either trek through heavy forest or drive back the way we came then take another road for two kilometers up the slope—perfect for our use. But look. Here are the Blanchets."

From a cement walkway encircling the house, a young couple approached on Dylan's left. Both wore jeans, muddy leather boots, and long-sleeved shirts. Tall and stocky, Marcel gave a smile as wide as his face. "Bonjour, my friends, and welcome to Montagne Verte."

Dylan took the extended hand.

A head shorter, just as stocky, Marcel's wife beamed, with a ruddy complexion and an ever-present smile. She nodded to the newcomers and shook their hands. "You must be tired and hungry after your trip. I will clean up and get supper ready. We'll eat in about an hour." She glanced at her watch. "Around eight?"

"Great," said René. "Thank you, Gabrielle."

"I may be late." Marcel waved toward the barn. "I've got fifteen cows overdue for milking. The fence repair took longer than I'd hoped."

"Come inside." As Gabrielle removed her boots, René led them through a door into the billiard room then upstairs to a second-floor master bedroom. "This one is yours. Margot's is down the hall. The Blanchets have a room downstairs near the kitchen. Take the stairs down and turn right for the dining room."

"How many of you are there here?" asked Dylan.

"Only five, right now, including you two. But in a few weeks, the head of our organization will join us, and we'll start accepting refugees."

René's eyes seemed to darken. "Pasqual promises to bring news of Davato's plans. But of that, nothing good can ever come, can it?"

CHAPTER 8
CHAIM WEINBERG

The South China Sea – February, Year 1

Gunner's Mate Second Class Camden Weinberg's binoculars scanned the horizon from the windows of the bridge on the destroyer, the USS *Avenger*. Today, he stood watch under his nemesis, Lieutenant Grady Wilson, the officer of the deck. Serving on the bridge was unusual for Cam, as he liked to be called. He was here under the commander's orders that all gunner's mates periodically stand watch with him on the bridge.

This morning, Grady Wilson wasn't even trying to hide his dislike for his subordinate. The man's hatred stemmed from Camden's Jewishness. And every moment Cam spent in Grady's presence, he wished he were somebody else.

Camden, whose real name was Chaim, hated being a Jew. He'd always tried to hide his upbringing, never speaking about his New York father and mother, both passed on now. In port, he never attended synagogue. Before V-Day, there'd been camaraderie with his fellow seapersons—yes, they'd beat that term into him at the Great Lakes' Navy Recruit Training center in Chicago. But after V-Day and recrewing in Guam, everything changed.

Two years ago, he'd changed his first name to Camden. But his service record still listed it as Chaim, and many on the ship—including the lieutenant—knew it. Now his life aboard the *Avenger* had become a living hell.

"Starboard engine ahead one-third," came the lieutenant's order, and the quartermaster repeated the command.

"Course two seven zero," added the lieutenant.

"Course two seven zero, aye, sir," came the response. The ship shuddered as one of its four 2,500-horsepower engines turned the ship to the west and into the wind.

Cam glanced behind him to the bridge crew.

"Keep your eyes on the horizon, Hay-eeeem."

Cam had repeatedly told the lieutenant what he preferred to be called. Yet Grady Wilson insisted on calling him Chaim, mispronouncing it every time.

He returned his binoculars to the windows and the expanse of ocean ahead, roiled today by swells and whitecaps. Ashen-gray clouds and slanting rain cut the horizon to a mile. Threatening weather to match the storm swirling through Cam's life.

They had entered the strait between Taiwan and the Chinese mainland. Just ahead loomed the dark outline of the USS *Ronald Reagan*. The *Avenger* would add its firepower to the carrier and to the cruiser and two other destroyers somewhere nearby. Too few for a strike group, but all that could be assembled after years of budget cuts and the crew losses on V-Day.

Last week, when Cam was alone with Grady on the launch deck, the lieutenant had pulled him aside. "Your kind doesn't belong here," Grady had said. "You need to request a transfer to shore duty."

Cam had stiffened and straightened his back. "I don't want a transfer. I want to serve my country, and I can best do that aboard this ship."

"I think you'll regret that decision. I can make life miserable for you." With a sneer, Grady had stalked away.

Two months after V-Day, Cam's nemesis had received praise and a promotion. That same week, Cam had been disciplined for a dirty gun, an unmade bunk, and unstowed gear, even though he was certain he'd cleaned the .50 caliber weapon, pulled his blanket tight, tucked it under the mattress corners, and left his gear stowed neatly beneath. Right before inspection, someone had intentionally set him up. The Jewish thing again.

The odd thing was, Cam did not look at all Jewish. Indeed, by some quirk of cosmic fate, Grady Wilson and Chaim Weinberg, with their dark good looks, black hair, and strong chins, could have been identical twins. Using some imagination, their voices even sounded alike. Once in the shower, two men even mistakenly called Cam by the lieutenant's name. Smiling inwardly and enjoying himself more than he could remember, Cam played along. That worked until he entered the lockers and donned his gunner's mate uniform, after which his embarrassed teammates, silent and red-faced, just stared at him. Perhaps the similarity between him and the lieutenant, maybe more than anything, drove Grady's hatred.

"All engines ahead one-fourth," ordered the lieutenant.

"Aye, sir. All engines ahead one-fourth," came the quartermaster's replay.

Cam lowered his binoculars to rest his eyes.

When he again scanned the horizon, on the lookout for any small threat escaping the ship's radar, the shadow of two destroyers appeared through the rain. The three destroyers in the strike group were of the Arleigh-Burke class. Like the *Avenger*, all were equipped with an Aegis, 360-degree radar array, a five-inch cannon, and six torpedoes for antisubmarine warfare. They had ninety-six missile bays for antiballistic missile interceptors, air-to-air missiles to take out cruise missiles or airplanes, antiship missiles, antisubmarine rockets, and Tomahawk missiles for land attack. They also carried a variety of missiles for antiship warfare, and two 25mm autocannons. It was the job of a gunner's mate to service and man these weapons.

To serve on such a powerful seagoing war machine had been his dream since high school. Yet, on the decks of the *Avenger*, his zeal went unnoticed, unappreciated. All his shipmates saw was one of the Jews whom people were now blaming for the worldwide financial collapse, the bank failures, and the hoarding. Why this anti-Semitism was sweeping the US and its navy he didn't understand. It was as if, when the UFOs took people away on V-Day, they left behind not only anarchy, chaos, and violence, but also a hatred of the Jewish race. Cam even imagined the attitude of the ship's commander, formerly a fair-minded man, had changed.

After his historic treaty with Israel, Davato himself had spoken out in support of Israel and its people. All across the world, countries were voluntarily falling in line with the proclamations coming from Davato's government in Rome. He'd united Europe. The rest of the world, awed by the man's stunning accomplishments and goals, seemed eager to embrace his every idea and pronouncement. Yet when it came to their attitude toward Jews, everyone was suddenly an anti-Semite. Why?

A boatswain's whistle screeched over the microphone. "The commander will now address the ship." The boatswain's pipe rose to the ensign's lips and shrieked again.

"Listen up, crew. This is your commander speaking." Cam lifted his glance from the horizon to the commander standing only yards away. "We are in the Taiwan Strait, and it's time to give you our latest orders. The situation between China and the US is deteriorating day by day. China is making increasingly belligerent threats against us. It's been massing troops and transport ships on its eastern coast. Satellite images show that half of its cruisers, destroyers, and submarines and one of its three-carrier strike groups are holding position and massing about seventy nautical miles to the west. Do not underestimate China's modernized bluewater fleet. In the last few years, they've doubled their number of ships. And with the technology they've stolen, they're almost at par with us.

"And now I must tell you what naval intelligence and the President have long feared"—he lowered the mike and took a deep breath—"a Chinese attack on Taiwan appears imminent."

The normal bustle of the bridge ceased, replaced only by the hum of the engines, the muffled slap of the hull through the waves. Everyone now stared at the commander gripping the microphone in one hand.

"We have just joined the USS *Ronald Reagan* carrier strike group. Our orders are to merge with and shadow two other carrier strike groups seventy nautical miles to the southwest. The three strike groups, bolstered by recrewed destroyers and cruisers that should soon arrive from Guam and Okinawa, will spread out in a defensive line. We don't know where the Chinese fleet will end up or even if they will turn around and this is a bluff."

The commander lowered the mike, cleared his throat, and glanced around the deck. The eyes of every officer and enlisted man were fixed on him.

"Crew, our mission is to detect, intercept, and destroy all missiles aimed at Taiwan. Since we have the capability to intercept ICBMs in space headed for the US mainland, we are also to be on alert for that possibility. Yes, even defending against a mainland attack, though unlikely, is now part of our orders. We are also to engage any enemy submarines, surface vessels, or aircraft coming within striking distance of the fleet and showing hostile intent. In short, we are taking a war footing, waiting only for a signal from Washington or, failing that, hostile action from the enemy."

Again, the commander paused, glanced around the bridge with furrowed brows, then resumed.

"I know you are prepared. You have all trained hard for this moment. And if war comes, we may soon see the fruits of your training. May the fates have mercy on the United States of America and its navy. That is all."

The silence on the bridge was deafening. War with China? Would it really come to that? But could it be won?

He'd heard the murmurings at mess, the complaints that the new navy cared more about diversity, racial division, and "equity" than they did about fighting a war and that West Point and Annapolis were now teaching more about the new leftist ideology than about war strategy.

Cam himself had attended too few classes on war fighting and too many admonishing him not just to accept, but to celebrate the LGBTQs among them. Classes also claiming that, because he was a white male, he was inherently racist. Classes calling him sexist and an oppressor. Of course, they didn't care that he was Jewish. Somehow, when it came to racking up oppressor points, whiteness overruled everything else. All the classes did was make him look askance at some of his fellow crew members, wondering if they got where they were because of their qualifications. Or were they here only because they had checked some box on a diversity checklist?

Even before the vanishing, half the fleet had been idled in port with ships in need of a major overhaul or waiting for spare parts that never came. The US navy, it appeared, was more concerned with fighting racism and promoting "equity" than with fighting a war.

The end result: They were heading into battle ill prepared.

Cam himself was ready. He'd passed with high marks through Recruit Training, the Training Support Center, and then the Gunner's Mate A-School in Illinois. On his first tour of duty at sea, before V-Day interrupted, he'd impressed everyone with how quickly he'd learned his tasks. As a gunner's mate having put in time and with good reports, he should have been in line for promotion—until, without explanation, they quashed it. Again, because he was Jewish?

"Attention on deck," came a new voice.

Cam stood to attention as Lieutenant Sorenson strode onto the bridge. Cam's group had been on watch for twelve hours, and this lieutenant arrived with his own quartermaster, boatswain's mate, and signalman of the watch. Another gunner's mate followed. As the new seapersons stepped forward to relieve the old, Sorenson conferred with Grady about the navigational track, the latest orders, and the position of the fleet they'd joined.

After the lieutenants exchanged salutes and Grady dismissed his crew, Cam headed after the others for the door. He followed a man and a woman down the stairs, making for the mess, and he couldn't help but overhear their conversation.

As they descended, the stocky, short-haired blonde ensign—Marcia Roberts was her name—turned to Ishaan, her companion. "Did you hear that Grady will soon join an advisory panel to the President on naval and military affairs?"

"Advisor to the President?" Ishaan, a young man of apparent Indian descent, cocked his head, and his glance revealed shock. "How did he get *that* appointment?"

"The scuttlebutt is that the brass created a pool of the recently promoted then picked one at random. But I'm guessing that Grady's upper-class Boston family ties had something to do with it. His family is upper-crust rich with DC Senate connections. They're also big supporters of the President's party."

"Naturally." A smile widened the young man's cheeks as he turned to the woman. "If he's leaving for Washington soon, we could see openings for promotion."

"Possibly. Especially if we see action."

"Yes . . . action." He lowered his voice, and his head dropped. "Have you ever seen combat?"

Ensign Marcia Roberts opened the door to the mess and shook her head. "No. Who's ever had the opportunity?"

Cam followed the two into the mess deck. The clanking of forks and knives on plates, the hum of conversation, and the smell of coffee and frying bacon greeted him.

"Are you scared?" asked the man.

The woman shot Ishaan a glance with widened eyes. "Aren't you?"

The man lowered his head again. "Yes."

Cam stumbled, and one foot rammed the back of the woman's leg.

"Sorry," he said.

She whirled and arched a brow. "You! Were you following us? Did you hear everything we said, Hay–eeem?" Again, with the mispronounced name. Had they learned this from Grady?

"I was just going to the mess."

"I don't need the likes of a Jew boy tailing me, listening to everything I say." The woman scrunched her face. "Come on, Ishaan. Let's go."

"Sorry," Cam repeated. He held back, letting three sailors enter the line so they separated him from Ishaan and Ensign Marcia Roberts.

As he waited for chow, Chaim Weinberg wished, once again, that he were someone else.

CHAPTER 9

A FAUSTIAN BARGAIN

Washington, DC – February, Year 1

A few weeks after he was sworn into office, William Cole received a package from the Imperator of the Unitum Imperium. The new President had been warned ahead of time the parcel was coming, and a Secret Service agent met the courier at the gate. When Cole spread the contents over the Resolute Desk, he stared at the shocking photos, the copies of bank statements and wire transfers he had hoped would forever remain secret. How had the information leaked? His sexual affairs with underage youth and his extralegal financial exploits had caught up with him. The package's very existence left his brow covered with sweat, his hands reaching for a tumbler of whiskey.

Overnight, Davato flew in from Italy on a private jet, and the two met alone in the Oval Office with instructions not to be disturbed. As he received his guest, President Cole shivered inside. That such power existed in one man was terrifying. Now his entire future—a future that could easily lead to disgrace, impeachment, and jail time—lay in the hands of a man who was single-handedly uniting most of the world. In the presence of such a towering figure, he wilted to insignificance.

After some awkward small talk, the Imperator said, "You are not a churchgoing man, are you, Bill?"

"No." The Imperator had eyes everywhere. His staff would have scoured the news to ferret this out. So why was he asking what he already knew?

"And you don't really believe in God, do you, Bill?"

Cole shifted in his chair, uncomfortable at the familiar tone, the knowledge behind the question, but he didn't answer. That Davato insisted on talking about this was, again, chilling.

Then his visitor began his offer, an alliance bringing the United States and the Unitum Imperium together, not militarily, but with something new in the world of political affairs. Though each country would remain separate and sovereign, Davato's treaty proposed to mold—unofficially, of course—the goals and policies of the United States after those of the Unitum Imperium. To the President's delight, most of Davato's goals were those his own party had striven for years to achieve—the fulfillment of nearly every liberal objective dear to the President's heart.

Certainly, the man had amassed an incredible amount of power in the short time he'd come on the scene. What troubled Cole was Davato's second proposal—an unofficial agreement between the two men that, sometime in the future, President Cole would agree to officially merge the United States of America with the Unitum Imperium, giving up his country's national sovereignty. Also troubling was how this startling visitor sometimes spoke of himself—as if he were on a par with God himself.

Davato laid two documents on the Resolute Desk. The first was the Treaty of Intent. The second was a private agreement between the two men. "All you have to do is sign, something your predecessor foolishly refused to do."

Cole drew in a sharp breath. Was that a veiled admission that her death was planned? Had she been assassinated? Another shiver began in his shoulders. "But the Senate must approve all treaties."

The Imperator waved away the objection, and his voice deepened, changed. "You can easily sign another executive order. You've already been ruling by fiat." Davato's words seemed reasonable, logical, even necessary, and, as if carried by some supernatural wind, they stormed unhindered into his consciousness.

Then the Imperator stressed that if he agreed, not only would the secret file remain secret, when the time came, he'd be given a commanding role in the new world order.

"But before you sign, you should be aware of one nonnegotiable condition."

Cole looked up. "What's that?"

"When your nation joins with ours and you come under my rule, I must have unquestioning loyalty." The man's eyes narrowed, and his jaw tightened. "I will accept nothing but total, uncompromising obedience. And if I don't get it . . ."

Then the man's visage morphed and darkened, chilling the President to his core. And he wondered if what stood before him was a man at all, or . . .

Pausing, his pulse quickening, Cole stared at the documents, at the Imperator, then at the papers.

He swallowed and reached for the pen.

CHAPTER 10

A NEW WORLD ORDER

Revelation 13:1–2 (HCSB): *And I saw a beast coming up out of the sea. It had ten horns and seven heads. On its horns were ten crowns, and on its heads were blasphemous names. The beast I saw was like a leopard, its feet were like a bear's, and its mouth was like a lion's mouth. The dragon gave the beast his power, his throne, and great authority.*

Daniel 7:19, 23 (HCSB): *"Then I wanted to know the true meaning of the fourth beast, the one different from all the others, extremely terrifying, with iron teeth and bronze claws, devouring, crushing, and trampling with its feet whatever was left. . . . "This is what he said: 'The fourth beast will be a fourth kingdom on the earth, different from all the other kingdoms. It will devour the whole earth, trample it down, and crush it.' "*

New York City – February, Year 1

Outside the United Nations building stood a statue named *The Guardian of International Peace and Security*. Donated by Mexico, it had first appeared on its pedestal in November 2021 only to be removed a month later after an outcry. With the head of a leopard and the wings of an eagle, it was a passable depiction of the symbolic end-times beast described in the Bible.

Unaware of this demonic connection, Chelsea Turner headed for the UN entrance. As if some supernatural force was at work, she glanced at the stature and stopped. There it sat, mouth open, teeth bared, wings unfurled, haunches bunched and ready to spring. A name popped into her head, unbidden, and it was *Davato*. An involuntary shiver started in her shoulders and rippled down her arms.

She hurried on. Only after passing the security checks and entering the General Assembly Hall did she breathe easier.

Then she berated herself. It was only a statue, wasn't it?—not a harbinger of things to come. Why would she have associated it with Davato? And wasn't it silly to fear a simple statue?

A beaming Adam Turner emerged from the crowd then laid a hand on her shoulder. "A wonderful day for the Unitum Imperium, is it not?"

"Yes," was her only reply to her father. He was showing too much enthusiasm, and she wouldn't encourage it.

"Will you sit with me?" He waved toward the front. "I have seats in the premier section."

She flourished her entrance ticket. "Sorry, my seat is in the front row."

A dark eyebrow rose, and he cocked his head. "My daughter in the front row? For some reason, Chelsea, he has greatly favored you."

"I guess." Then she hurried down the aisle away from him. He was her father, yes, and he'd gotten her the job at the security division of Veritas Systems he once headed. Then, overnight, Veritas Systems became the Ministry of Truth, and he had been promoted to head the new ministry. Under him was now the feared Central Security Agency and its growing legions of Truth Squads. In normal circumstances, he was a man to be feared. But she resented his lifelong attempts to run her life, even deciding where she was going to sit.

She smoothed her dress and lowered herself into a front-row seat on the aisle. Two seats away sat the green-eyed Prophet, now engaged in conversation with a man beside her. Why had Davato invited her to this important mission in New York? Why had he given her such an honored seat? Did it have anything to do with their private dinner last fall?

Her glance swept right, then left, then up. No expense had been spared to create the blue, green, and gold interior. Marble hallways. Giant displays of art at the entrance. And for each delegate, plush seats equipped with earphones and state-of-the-art desks. Above, a massive spoked wheel atop a circle of blue black led to a rim of pinpoint lights in imitation of the heavens themselves. The buzz of two thousand delegates and guests now filled the hall. The UN's last charter held 193 member countries. But now the Unitum Imperium had swallowed most of the European state members into itself.

The news was full of disdain for countries refusing to join today's event: Russia, China, Iran, Turkey, and the Islamic states of North Africa and the Mideast.

From a side door, the silver-haired Imperator himself entered, crossed the platform, and stopped at the podium only fifty feet away. When he nodded in her direction, a shiver raced down her back, and she returned a hesitant smile. As Davato's gaze swept the assembled dignitaries from every corner of the globe, the whispered conversations hushed.

"Ministers, presidents, and delegates." Davato gripped the dais and stood to his full height. "Welcome to this final gathering of the General Assembly of the United Nations. Our meeting today is auspicious and history making. And having said that, you now deserve an explanation."

Chelsea shifted in her seat. What was Davato up to? Had he just said this was the *final* meeting of the General Assembly?

"Though we have a long way to go, the world is struggling back from the Great Catastrophe. But for us to move forward, we must be clear-eyed about its cause. The consensus is that UFOs came like a thief in the night to steal from us our friends, neighbors, relatives, and children. But why did they come? For what reason did they throw our civilization into anarchy, chaos, and terror? That is the burning question, is it not? Well, my friends, I will now reveal the answer.

"They came because we have sinned grievously against our planet. We have so befouled the atmosphere with carbon dioxide and pollutants that, in another decade, we will have made the earth unlivable. Not all of us were taken. No, the aliens carefully selected those whom they took. You may have heard that many of the missing were Christians. Yes, my friends, it's true. Those who were taken walked a different path and vibrated to a different life frequency from the rest of us. They were out of touch with you and me and with the earth, and they worshiped the one I will call the Enemy. And because they marched to a different beat, they were enemies of the earth and all who live upon it."

Whispers and startled glances erupted from a few of the assembled. Chelsea turned to look back. Only then did she notice the security men, probably agents of Father's CSA, lining the walls and taking note of the dissenters.

"But what about the children? Why did the aliens take them? Here now is the answer. They took the children because too many of us live on the planet, and by removing the next generation, they saved the earth for those who remain. But do not trouble yourselves about the children. They now live in a new and happy environment where they are being well cared for."

Davato paused, dropped his gaze, but when he again lifted his eyes, they were on fire.

"I will now speak briefly of the one whose name half the globe once worshiped in reverence and awe. Once, that name filled countless churches—now only empty shells, monuments to his arrogance. Once, he claimed to create everything that is, but that was always a lie. The universe existed before him, and it will go on long after he is gone. Now you know of whom I speak. Some called him God. But I call him Enemy."

Again, while Davato paused for effect, the audience shifted in their seats.

"Why do I call him that? Because he and his followers were not of our kind. Their path is not and has never been our path. Their ways are not and have never been our ways. And because their ways were so different from the planet's and from ours, for the good of us all, the aliens took them away." Davato's fist slammed onto the dais, reverberating through the mike. "And that is why we call their leader the Enemy."

Across the hall, a deathly silence now reigned.

"But that is in the past." He smiled, and the muscles of his face relaxed. "Let us now set grievances aside. Let us look instead to the future. A moment ago, I said this was the final gathering of the General Assembly, and now I should explain.

"Today, we sit on the cusp of a new world order, one defined by the Unitum Imperium. Most of those once part of the European Union have joined our great venture. They have seen the vision. They have turned from selfish nationalism. They have allied with the surging tide of humanity that is the Unitum Imperium. After the chaos wrought when the Enemy's people departed, the Unitum Imperium stands alone as the future of mankind, the only hope for peace, progress, and prosperity. And for those who have joined us, I say welcome and congratulations!"

From every corner of the great hall, applause spread out in waves.

Davato waved a hand for silence, and the clapping died out. "Today marks not only the end of one chapter but the beginning of another. Some of you have heard the rumor that the United Nations is being disbanded, and it's true, for its time has passed. Yet from the ashes of the old, a new entity—stronger and firmer of purpose—rises to replace it. What is its name? It's the Unitum Imperium, of course."

A few whispers popped up around the hall. Delegates turned to one another, some with shocked faces, others with knowing smiles.

"But fear not. Though the names and charters may differ, the UN and the Unitum Imperium share the same aspirations, the same goals. After we implement our program of improvements, what was formerly impossible for the UN, the Unitum Imperium will soon realize.

"Where before, there was discord, division, and strife, there will now be unity and harmony.

"Where before, nation-states settled their differences with war and conflict, there will now be peace and security.

"Where before, invisible shackles bound men's spirits with strict dogmas, religions, and arbitrary commandments, we will free the inner man to do what he or she, deep in their hearts, has always wanted to do.

"We will bring about most of the goals of Klaus Schwab and his World Economic Forum, an organization to which I and most of you belong. We will ensure the reproductive rights of women who, at any stage, do not wish to bear a fetus. We will promote the rights and primacy of the gay, lesbian, bisexual, and transgender community—and all the other sexual orientations—and encourage any child of any age to be whatever sex they desire. We will educate the white oppressors who do not understand how their white privilege has disadvantaged other races. We will fight against racism, sexism, and homophobia. We will implement a cashless society that streamlines all commercial transactions. We will work to save the planet from man-made climate change. We will eliminate all national boundaries. We will finally join, hand in hand, with our neighbors, uniting all the countries on earth as one. In short, my friends, we will bring about the new world order you have long dreamed of."

As the room erupted in wild, thundering applause, a smiling Davato stepped back and waited for the clamor to die down.

"So today, under my rule, we are replacing this body with the wisdom, direction, and authority of the Unitum Imperium. To join our loose alliance of nations many of you have already signed a Treaty of Intent, aligning your nations' goals with ours. As of last week, Japan joined. So did Canada and Australia. The Unitum Imperium now has treaties with countries on every continent.

"But today I want to welcome another great nation to our alliance. It is now my great pleasure to introduce to you the Honorable William Cole, President of the United States of America."

As Davato stepped back and the liberal President stepped forward, Chelsea gasped. This was unexpected. The man had been in office less than a month, and already Davato had convinced him to sign this unusual treaty? Standing behind him, giving tacit support by his very presence, was the chairman of the Joint Chiefs of Staff. The applause that followed boomed and echoed off the ceiling.

The US President kept his speech short, and his words paled after the powerful oratory of Davato. But the gist of it was clear. The US would follow Davato's lead in setting policy. The US was still its own entity, but the influence and power of the Unitum Imperium had unmistakably overshadowed what had once been a great nation.

Chelsea's head swirled with the magnitude of what had just occurred. Weren't others seeing the same thing? Or were they so overawed by Davato's stunning oratory, the supernatural power behind his words, that they no longer questioned what he said?

Turning in her seat, she again glanced behind her into the crowd. Most of the faces showed satisfaction, even joy. Amazing how his silver-tongued words had seduced so many. But a handful who had not yet given in to the Imperator were walking out. And the security men were taking notes.

The President and the chairman of the Joint Chiefs left the stage, and the Imperator resumed his position at the podium.

"Now that I have laid out our vision, I must speak of impediments to our cause. Parts of the existing order stand in the way of progress. I speak, of course, of the UN Security Council and the structure of the UN as we know it. We know the names of the naysayers who constantly derail the will of the many: Russia, China, and the countries of Islam. Though they were once part of the entity we called the UN, they chose not to come today. Some of you here may also be in that camp. I hope not, for the world is moving on, and so must those who believe in world unity. Even now, I invite the dissenters to join us. For those who are not with us are against us. Now is the time to unite for peace, progress, and security. Now is the time to join our quest for a united world, one without war, strife, and division. Now is the time to free man's inner spirit from the chains and shackles that bind it. And that, today, is my message to this august world body."

Bowing in a stance of humility, he stepped back and let the assembly's wild applause wash over him. Chelsea joined in but couldn't help but look behind her again.

A few more outcasts who had rejected the Unitum Imperium's treaty were standing, making their way to the rear.

Davato waved goodbye and left the stage, but the clapping went on and on. When the clamor died down, she rose, intending to join the throngs headed for the door.

But a hand touched her shoulder, and she whirled. Before her stood a smiling young man with blond hair, bright blue eyes, and a dark suit. "Chelsea Turner, the Imperator requests your presence for drinks at the Equinox hotel bar in thirty minutes. Can you attend?"

Startled, her mouth opened, closed, then opened again. "Y–yes."

"If you please, you will follow me."

CHAPTER 11

THE ROOFTOP BAR

Revelation 17:1–2 (NLT): *One of the seven angels . . . came over and spoke to me. "Come with me," he said, "and I will show you the judgment that is going to come on the great prostitute, who rules over many waters. The kings of the world have committed adultery with her, and the people who belong to this world have been made drunk by the wine of her immorality."*

New York City – February, Year 1

Trying to control a wildly beating heart, Chelsea followed the young man to the street. There Davato's entourage entered a fleet of black limousines, and, escorted by two armored cars mounted with machine guns, they departed. After what seemed an eternity, another armored car and a limousine arrived to escort her through the Murray Hill area, across town to Hudson Yards and the Equinox. Along the way, they passed burned-out buildings, hulks of charred cars, a few roving gangs, and streets dirty with melting snow mixed with broken bricks and glass. At the towering hotel structure, surrounded now by coils of razor wire, they showed their IDs then passed a half dozen sour-faced armed guards. The elevator passed her room on the sixth floor and continued up to the bar. Through the 360-degree glass-sided room, city lights glimmered in the panoramic metropolitan vista beyond. But half the lights were out. In the corner, a pianist played soft elevator music.

Near the door sat two gay men on a cushion, their thighs touching. Each grasped a drink in one hand, holding their partner's hand in the other. Next to these were a man dressed as a woman and a woman dressed as a man, chatting with each other in voices too deep and too high, respectively, for their appearances. Beyond these at the room's far end, a circle of muscled bodyguards occupied seats outside a cluster of leather chairs. There sat Davato, the green-eyed Prophet, and a young blond-haired man who might be the most beautiful specimen of masculine humanity on the planet. With eye shadow and a pearl necklace visible under an open shirt, the young man held the Prophet's eyes with apparent lust.

"Ah, there you are." Davato rose as did the Prophet and the young blond. "But of course, Sebastien, you have already met Adam Turner's daughter, Chelsea."

From afar, the Prophet's appearance was pleasant, even inviting. His white, rounded beard, his heavy jowls, and his salt-and-pepper hair gave him the appearance of a kindly, wise grandfather. She hadn't had a good look at him earlier. But as she took Sebastien Rey's extended hand, she suppressed a shiver of revulsion at the paleness of his skin, the emptiness behind his green eyes.

"And this is Sebastien's paramour, Robert Young." Davato waved toward handsome Robert Young.

"Pleased to meet you." Again, she offered her hand.

Paramour Robert took her hand, but instead of a handshake, he lifted it to his lips, kissed it, and smiled.

Retrieving her fingers from his lingering kiss, she flushed, for no one should look that handsome. Against her will, a thrill of excitement shivered up her arm. Where he'd kissed, she brought the spot to her lips. Embarrassed by her reaction, she dropped her hand.

"We've just arrived." Davato smiled at her gesture. "What are you drinking, Chelsea?"

"White wine, if you please."

A partial wave of one hand produced a fawning, bowing waiter who took her order.

"Sebastien was updating me on our plans for building a great city in the desert. Sebastien, why don't you repeat what you were saying for Chelsea?"

Before the Prophet spoke, her drink arrived. Grateful for the distraction, she clutched the cold glass then faced Sebastien.

"First, I must give credit to Worldnet as they started this project ten years ago, buying the land and starting construction. Since Davato's rise to power, we've accelerated our building program a hundredfold, but all on Worldnet's foundation. Rome is a great city with a great history, yes, but the shadow of the Vatican lies heavily upon it. And it contains the Pope. And too many former priests. We needed a city designed according to our specifications, not the Vatican's."

Nodding, Chelsea thought back to Davato's rant against God, whom he called the Enemy. Though she had nothing against the Catholic Church, she could see his point about the Catholic presence in Rome.

"First and foremost," continued Sebastien, "our city will contain the greatest temple the world has ever seen. We'll dedicate it to the earth, of course, and to stopping climate change."

She smiled. Climate change had been the cause to which she'd dedicated most of her life.

Nodding his approval, Sebastien went on. "Thousands of earth priestesses will be on hand to entertain male visitors in private rooms. There will also be earth priests to amuse our female guests. Of course, anyone of any sexual orientation will be able to choose the priest or priestess with whom they wish to worship. To accommodate the multitudes, the temple will have thousands of private rooms available."

She swallowed. Just what kind of worship did he have in mind? "Why in the desert?"

"Because the history of that location goes further back in time even than Rome. We've contracted with companies all over the world, and construction has proceeded in earnest. We're building an airport with dozens of runways. There will also be hotels, music bars, restaurants, and event centers. We'll have casinos, communal baths, nude swimming pools, video gaming rooms, and shooting galleries where tourists can pay to shoot a live heretic."

Sucking in air, she tried not to show her surprise. "They'll shoot a . . . heretic?"

"Naturally. It will reinforce the idea that no one can stand against the Imperator without consequences. It's something everyone's always wanted to do—release their anger against one of these self-righteous deplorables. Such a thing would have been impossible under the previous dictatorship of religious dogma. It will be a great catharsis for the populace." When he smiled, a shiver ran down her back. "Other than the temple, the center of our city will be the Coliseum. Yes, Chelsea, we're bringing back the great games of old, with live animals, gladiators, and live victims—all Christian heretics, of course."

"Of course." She buried her nose and her surprise in her glass and sipped. Did that mean Dylan and Caleb were at risk? Perhaps she'd be able to warn them. "So you've started building? Where?"

Davato reached across the table and laid a hand on her arm. "You haven't guessed? It's about eighty kilometers south of Baghdad. We're constructing on a site already begun by Saddam Hussein. We've got agreements with the Iraqis. They think we're building the city for them in exchange for free oil, and the fools believe us. But Unitum Imperium troops are arriving daily to guard the perimeter and secure the site. Eventually, we'll have amassed a force that no one will be able to argue with. The name of the city is New Babylon."

Babylon!

A name associated with hedonism, immorality, and wanton sexual excess. Almost against her will, a thrill rippled down her back. What would it be like to throw caution to the wind—just for a day or two—and join them? Surprised by this part of herself, she blinked, set her glass down, and dug the fingers of her right hand into the palm of her left. Why did this so excite her?

Davato said to his Prophet, "I'd like a few moments alone with Chelsea."

Sebastien waved to handsome Robert Young, and the two crossed to an empty table on the far side of the room.

Sitting back against his leather chair, Davato regarded her with smiling eyes. "I sense you approve of Sebastien's plan for New Babylon, as we're calling it. Is that true, Chelsea?"

"It is . . . intriguing." The feeling of wild abandon she'd fought a moment ago lingered, and her voice showed an eagerness that surprised her. "Very . . . intriguing."

"Good." He slapped a thigh. "Now you're wondering why I brought you here to New York to hear my speech and be part of my delegation?"

"Yes, Imperator, I—"

"When we are alone, Chelsea"—his voice lowered—"please call me Davato."

"Of course . . . Davato. Yes, I am curious."

"The reason for your presence is this: I wanted to give you a glimpse of the great things in store for you if you were to join my team. You've heard Sebastien's vision for New Babylon, but that's in the future. We're only now at the beginning. I'm still assembling a staff, and I would like you to be part of it. So today, I'm offering you the position of personal secretary to the Imperator."

She gasped and brought a hand to her mouth.

"Of course, this will come as quite a surprise. Your duties would be to take notes at many of my private meetings, be a hostess when required, escort visitors, and accompany me on all my travels. Your salary would be tripled, of course. It's a great honor, perhaps the greatest you'll ever receive in your lifetime. What do you say?"

Closing her open mouth, she brought her other hand to her face. Her heart was beating fast, thumping against her ribs. She hadn't lied when she said it was intriguing—but it was also frightening. If she said yes, she'd enter a world of power, excitement, and extraordinary privilege beyond her wildest dreams. But if she said no . . . what would happen to her? They were already planning to execute anyone not part of their ideology, what they called heretics. Would saying no to his offer mark her as one of those?

"I know the rumors swirling about me." He sat back in his chair, his silver hair aglow under the soft lighting. "That all the young women in my orbit have slept with me, and for many of them, it's true. But I promise you, that doesn't have to happen. Not unless you want it to, of course."

She breathed deeply. Yes, that had also been in the back of her mind. She dropped her hands and stared at her lap.

"I'm not asking you to join my staff merely because you are an extremely attractive woman. And you are, Chelsea. Yes, you are. No, I want you because of your background, your skills, and because you are the daughter of Adam Turner, our new head of the Ministry of Truth. What do you say?"

She raised her glance. Then the words escaped her lips. "Y–yes." Somehow—and her words startled even herself—he'd broken down her defenses, and her mouth had hurried beyond where her brain told her to go. "Yes, I'll be your personal secretary."

"Wonderful!" He reached across the table, grabbed her hands, and planted a kiss on them. Then he waved, and Sebastien and handsome Robert Young rejoined them.

In one gulp, Chelsea downed the remainder of her wine and, her heart beating hard, ordered a double brandy from the waiter who appeared as if by magic.

CHAPTER 12
MARGOT'S VISION

Joel 2:28, 30–31 (HCSB): *After this I will pour out my Spirit on all humanity; then your sons and your daughters will prophesy, your old men will have dreams, and your young men will see visions. . . . before the great and terrible day of the* LORD *comes.*

The French Luberon – February, Year 1

Dylan and Margot had been at the villa less than a week. As usual for the evening meal, Gabrielle served, and Dylan, Margot, Marcel, and René ate.

All during dinner, Margot's glance kept going to the stairs, and she only picked at the beef marinated in red wine, topped with mushrooms. Long before the others had finished, she stood from the table. "Forgive me, but I need to set up my easel."

"But you've barely touched your food." Dylan stared at her plate. "And it's so good."

"I'm not hungry." She started across the room toward the door.

"But if you start working now, you'll be up all night."

"I know. But I have to paint. The desire has been building ever since we arrived. And now . . . it can't wait."

As her footsteps echoed down the hall, René turned a worried glance to him.

Dylan shrugged. "When the visions come upon her, it's always like this. But never so late in the day. Whatever it's telling her, it must be important."

Gabrielle swept aside a lock of reddish-brown hair and set down her fork. "We are blessed to have one such as her among us."

Marcel's eyes widened. "She's really a seer?"

Dylan nodded. "Much of what she's painted has come true."

"Maybe the Pope will make her a saint?" Gabrielle's questioning glance caught her husband's.

Marcel laid a hand as big as a slab of ham on his wife. "Each night before she goes to bed, she prays to Isadore, the patron saint of farmers."

René shook his head. "We are all saints, Gabrielle. We have no need of a pope's declaration of sainthood. I doubt your prayers to Isadore will help."

Her lips tightened. "I know that if we ask him, Saint Isadore will give us good crops and make the cattle fat."

"Then go ahead and pray. But don't forget Jesus, the one to whom we owe eternal life."

"I will not, Monsieur LeClerc. And tonight, I will also pray for Margot Durand, upon whom the Lord has surely laid his hand."

* * *

BRIGHT BEAMS OF SUNLIGHT BURST through the window, and Dylan sat upright in bed. Rubbing the sleep from his eyes, he dressed then ambled down the hall to Margot's room—empty, with an unmade bed. Had she been painting since yesterday evening?

At the staircase, he descended to the first floor. He knocked on the door to the room René had assigned as her studio and entered.

"Done!" With bloodshot eyes and hair askew, she swished a brush in a jar of thinner.

"You've been at this all night?" The backs of two easels stood before him. "And you finished two paintings?"

Nodding, she pulled off her smock. A wrist swept aside a lock of black hair. Random spots of paint daubed her cheeks.

He stepped around the easels to see what she'd been working on all night.

And he froze.

The first canvas showed hundreds of long, rectangular gray buildings, each exactly like the other, laid out on a bare field surrounded by razor wire and guard towers. In a cobblestone lot before a stone arch entrance, several vehicles were parked. At the camp's far end, a brick building bearing a tall chimney spewed heavy streamers of black smoke.

It could have been a painting of Auschwitz.

"I've been working on this all night, and it scares me." Her face slack and pale, she pointed an accusing finger at the canvas.

Nodding, unable to speak, he tore his gaze to the second canvas. This one depicted a massive open hall. The great room was divided into more than two dozen stations leading off into the distance. For each station, guards funneled hundreds of blindfolded people through high wooden gates on the right. The gates led to execution platforms on the left, each bearing a guillotine on a pedestal. Upon each platform, guards forced men, women, and youths to lay their necks on bloody slots where a second block held their heads in place. Above the victims, blades hovered—gleaming, dripping red, only waiting for the throw of a switch. Conveyer belts dropped the headless bodies into carts. Women prisoners, gaunt and skinny, their faces drained of all emotion, threw the severed heads into the carts after the corpses.

A shudder began in Dylan's shoulders, shook his torso, and rippled all the way to his legs. He tore his gaze away. "This is what they're doing to prisoners in the camp? To Christians?"

Tears trickled down her cheeks. She could barely nod. "These were the most difficult works I've ever done."

As he embraced her and held her tight, her whole body trembled. "You need to eat and rest. You should have taken a break."

"No." She pushed away and again wiped bangs from a sweaty, paint-daubed forehead. "I had to finish."

Voices approached from the hall, and Dylan turned. Following their host came a tall man, middle-aged, with thick black hair and a twinkle in his eye.

"This is Pasqual Berger," said a smiling René. "He arrived late last night after we went to bed. Pasqual is our organization's founder. He's come to join us at the farm."

Still stunned and grim-faced, Dylan shook his hands, and they exchanged greetings.

"René has told me all about you two, and we are so pleased you will be part of us." Pasqual stepped closer to the easels. "But what is this?" His eyes widening, he waved at Margot's work. "Is this your latest vision?"

"It is, monsieur."

As the men examined the painting, their faces clouded, and they fell silent. Finally, Pasqual spoke, but in a whisper. "We've heard rumors of something like this. We knew there was a camp somewhere. But what you've drawn . . ." He whipped his face toward Margot. "They tell me that every one of your visions has come true. Is that so?"

"Some are still in the future, but yes, monsieur, on the whole, many have come true."

"Your work is so real, it makes my skin crawl." For a time, he continued examining the painting. "At the camp entrance, I see an Italian Fiat truck, a German Audi, and a French Citroen. Margot, when you painted this, did you have any sense of where it is?"

She shook her head. "Only somewhere in Europe."

"Do you know if this is happening now? Or in the future?"

"It could be either. I've painted both present and future events."

After another long examination, Pasqual said he'd seen enough and headed for the door. "René, I'll take you up on that coffee now."

Their host insisted everyone follow him down the hall to the library and its padded leather seats. René poured coffee for all.

Pasqual sat back, swirled his cup, and settled his gaze on the floor. "If we knew where that camp was located, we might be able to mount a rescue mission." He raised his glance. "Does anyone have any ideas how to find it?"

René frowned and lit a cigarette. "The camp seems enormous. Or at least in the future, it will be. We could send someone on a mission to seek it out."

"But they'd have to scour every village from France to Poland. Not possible and . . . dangerous." Pasqual's brows wrinkled. "There must be a better way."

"Perhaps my sister could help," offered Dylan.

As the two men shot him puzzled glances, he explained how they'd convinced Chelsea to join Worldnet as a spy and continue working for Davato's Ministry of Truth. He also told them how she'd relayed the information that allowed them to free his brother and Baruch Abramovich from a Unitum Imperium prison.

"But this is wonderful." Pasqual clapped and sat upright. "Can you convince her to find out the camp's location?"

"I haven't heard from her since we escaped from Italy in November. Her old number no longer works. That was three months ago. But I believe she's on our side. It's risky, but maybe I can call her at work and ask her. Maybe she'd do it."

"*Très bien.*" Pasqual's eyes lit up as he smiled at each of them in turn. "If the Nazarene Friends can free some of those Christians from the fate the Antichrist has in store for them—then even if we die in the process, our lives will have been worth the living."

CHAPTER 13
A TROUBLING MEETING

Rome, Italy – March, Year 1

Dylan sat outdoors with Margot in a café in the Piazza di Santa Chiara near the Pantheon. The warm March sun convinced him to slip his jacket over the back of his chair. He swirled his glass of red wine and glanced again down the sidewalk.

"So where is she?" Margot again checked her watch. "We've been waiting half an hour."

"Give her time. Maybe she had trouble getting a taxi?"

As he reached for his croissant, a woman looking remarkably like his sister strode across the cobbles between the tables. But he had to look again to verify this was, indeed, Chelsea. She'd lost the punk look, and her hair was now its original reddish blonde. And she wore a smart gray business suit.

"Chelsea!" Dylan rose in greeting. He hugged her and held her at arm's length. "We haven't been able to reach you since we freed Caleb."

She took a seat opposite his. "A few days after the fire, I threw away my phone." She pulled off her leather gloves. Gucci? Was she that rich? She slapped the fine leather into a palm. "I got a new number because I was afraid you'd call me. Then they'd connect me with you."

"I know. I had to go through the reception desk at Worldnet. I knew it was dangerous, so I called from a phone in another city." He frowned. "But why were you afraid I'd call you? I'm your brother."

"And in the eyes of the Unitum Imperium, a criminal. No one must ever know my part in what we did. I don't plan on doing anything like that ever again. You don't know how many nights that kept me awake, wondering if, in the morning, someone would cart me off to jail."

"But they didn't. And Caleb is free. And you did your part to fight against the Antichrist."

"*The Antichrist?*" She smacked her gloves on the table. "I don't know where you got that idea. Davato can't be who you say he is. He's doing great things for the world, fighting climate change and bringing everyone together. You're wrong about him."

Dylan's jaws opened then closed, and he narrowed his eyes. What had happened to her? She was spouting nonsense. "We're not wrong about him, Chelsea. The number of his name is 666, and—"

"I looked into that, and using your methodology, a lot of names end up being 666. That proves nothing."

"But he made a peace treaty with Israel, he's brought the old Roman Empire together again, and—"

"And how is that bad? No, Dylan, everything he's done is all for the good. And there's something else you should know about him." She swallowed. "And about me."

"What?"

"I'm now his personal secretary. He's going to take me wherever he goes. I'm recording most of his meetings. He's tripled my salary, given me a nice apartment, and made me privy to the inner workings of the Unitum Imperium. I've never had such an important, rewarding job—much better than what I was doing for Worldnet."

His heart beating faster, Dylan was speechless. Had Davato swayed her with promises of wealth, position, and influence? Had she abandoned all her principles? Or had she somehow rationalized what she was doing, latching onto a new cause—the cult of Davato? After listening to his speeches on TV, Dylan could understand how the man could persuade her.

Would she help them now?

Trying to recover from his shock, he reached for her hand and squeezed. He mustn't alienate her. "Then congratulations, Chelsea."

A weak smile crossed her lips. "Thank you. You asked to meet for some reason." She checked her watch. "I've got fifteen minutes before I'm due back at the office."

"Yes." He released her hand and glanced at a frowning Margot. "We're hoping you can help us. And now that you're in such a powerful position, maybe you can."

"With what?" Still holding her Gucci gloves, she crossed her arms.

"Margot has painted a vision of the detention camp where they're taking the Christians they've been rounding up. We know some folks who would like to know where that camp is." He took a deep breath. "Could you get us that information?"

For some time, Chelsea sat back in her chair. She stared first at Margot, then at Dylan, as if looking at them for the first time. "Who are these folks who want to know this?"

"I can't tell you that."

"And what are they going to do with the information?"

"I can't tell you that either."

She shook her head. "No, Dylan." She began pulling on her gloves. "You're not getting me involved in another criminal activity. No, I won't do it."

"Chelsea!" Now his heart was beating even faster. "They're going to execute the prisoners in those camps. We've got to free them."

"No, you don't. It's none of your business, and certainly none of mine. Those prisoners are standing in the way of Davato's plans for the world, and they're criminals." She stood from the table and shot a glance up and down the street. "I advise you to have nothing to do with whoever's behind this. And don't ask me—ever again—to work against Davato's government." She pushed the chair in and started walking away, then abruptly turned back. "You're my brother, and I love you, but—"

But she made a hesitant turn away from him then strode off through the tables.

Dylan stared after her as she entered the crowded sidewalk.

"They've gotten to her," said Margot when she was out of sight.

"Apparently so." Dylan downed the last of his wine and dropped his head into his hands.

CHAPTER 14

BARUCH ABRAMOVICH

Rev 7:1–4 (HCSB): *After this I saw four angels standing at the four corners of the earth, restraining the four winds of the earth so that no wind could blow on the earth or on the sea or on any tree. Then I saw another angel, who had the seal of the living God rise up from the east. He cried out in a loud voice to the four angels who were empowered to harm the earth and the sea: "Don't harm the earth or the sea or the trees until we seal the slaves of our God on their foreheads." And I heard the number of those who were sealed: 144,000 sealed from every tribe of the Israelites.*

Jerusalem, Israel – March, Year 1

Baruch Abramovich and David Benjamin wormed their way to the center of the crowd filling Temple Square to overflowing. The March sun was too warm for the parka Baruch had brought, and he unzipped the front. Around him, Jews from all over Israel had gathered—ultra-Orthodox Haredi, religious Dati, traditional Masorti, and even the secular Hiloni. Everyone wanted to hear what the Imperator was going to say about Israel and the recently completed Third Temple.

He glanced aside to his friend, the tall, slim immigrant from Denmark.

"What a great day for Israel!" His face alight, David beamed and laid a hand on Baruch's shoulder. "We're beginning the year with the greatest event in Jewish history since Solomon built the first Temple."

Baruch gave a slight nod then glanced toward the dais upon the Temple steps where the Imperator himself would speak. How was he going to tell his friend that the leader of the Unitum Imperium, this man who'd so impressed everyone, was the spawn of Satan, the personification of evil?

"Why so glum, Baruch? The Temple is complete, and Davato himself—he who arranged the historic treaty allowing us to live in peace with our Arab and Persian neighbors—is about to give us his mark of approval. Who could ask for more?"

"Looks are often deceiving. He is not what he appears to be."

"Bah." David dismissed him with a wave. "I know you spent time in their prison, but did they not admit it was a mistake? Did they not apologize?"

"They did. But you don't know the whole story. After his speech and you sacrifice your bull, you and I are going to sit down and have a serious talk."

"About what?" He cocked his head.

"About the truth of what's going on. Believe me, it will change your whole world."

For some time, David stared at him in silence and seemed about to respond when murmuring broke out all around them and heads turned toward the dais.

Someone tapped a microphone, followed by a shriek of feedback.

Then Davato himself appeared on the stage, and the crowd hushed. Sitting behind him was an attractive woman in a smart business suit, with blonde hair and a pert nose. He'd seen her somewhere before. But where? Baruch searched his memory, and then it hit him.

This must be Dylan and Caleb's sister. At the bishop's villa, Dylan had pointed to a photograph of all three siblings with their father and the bishop. She'd been employed at Worldnet and had created the diversion that helped free him. Was she now working for the Antichrist? He shuddered.

"Today is indeed a great day for the Jewish people." Standing tall behind the podium, Davato swept aside his silver hair and beamed. "I am overwhelmed and honored to be here today, giving these brief dedication remarks on behalf of the Unitum Imperium. Today, the whole world is watching as we mark this historic occasion. Not since 70 CE have the Jewish people had such a monument to their faith on this site. For Israel, it is truly the most holy place on earth, and I congratulate your nation on its reconstruction." He took a deep breath and paused.

"But it is well to remember how this came about. Without the treaty that brought peace between the Arab nations, Iran, and Israel, this site would still be barren. Without the intervention of the future Imperator, the Jewish people would still be worshiping in synagogues, still pining for the day when this magnificent building would rise from the rubble. So let us not forget who made it all possible. But I ask not for praise." He seemed to shrink as he cast his glance toward the steps in a stance of humility. "I ask only for gratitude and remembrance."

After sporadic clapping spread through the crowd, he straightened to his full height. "Yes, today is a time for rejoicing, for reestablishing holy rituals the Jewish nation hasn't performed for millennia, and for thankfulness to the Unitum Imperium and its leader for making it all happen." Pausing again, he swept his gaze over the crowd.

"And now, to honor this day and the Jewish people, I have an announcement to make, one I haven't even shared with my staff."

Behind Davato, the woman Chelsea stiffened and turned a startled gaze on her employer. Baruch crossed his arms. What was he going to say next?

"You have all heard that Israel signed a Treaty of Intent with the Unitum Imperium. But what you have not known until now is that the government of Israel, as of last week, has secretly agreed to *join* the Unitum Imperium. We now have a military alliance. As such, I have arranged to move Unitum Imperium headquarters from Rome to Jerusalem."

For several seconds, a stunned silence followed. Then the crowd burst into wild applause and shouts of approval. Many long minutes later, it died down.

"Thank you, people of Israel, for honoring this move. After today, Jerusalem will be the spiritual center of the planet, so where better to also plant the headquarters of the new world order? But this is a day to honor the rebuilding of the Temple. For the time being, enjoy what your hands have wrought." He bowed low then left the stage.

Waves of applause followed, after which a series of rabbis gave speeches, but Baruch lost interest. What had Davato meant by saying, "for the time being"? Was it just a figure of speech? Or a slip of the tongue? Baruch shook his head as another speaker, an Israeli politician, took the platform. The last speaker, a rabbi, declared the start of communal sacrifices and the end of the ceremony.

His eyes alight, David again laid a hand on Baruch's shoulder. "They've given me permission to be one of the first. You will excuse me as the bull I have chosen is waiting."

"I'll watch from the Sacrifice Gate."

"No. Your contribution to the Torat Kohanim has earned you a place inside the Court of Priests. Follow me. Someone will bring you inside."

"Very well. But after you're done and cleaned up, let us meet at the usual place and talk."

* * *

ONE OF THE LEVITES LED Baruch into the inner courtyard and the Court of Priests. From nearby pens, bulls bellowed, and sheep baaed. Did the animals suspect their fate? The smell of manure, smoke, and burning flesh hung heavy in the air. On the far side of the great room, a fire in the altar bowl consumed the flesh of sacrificed animals. Smoke from their burning rose in a thick, boiling cloud toward the heavens.

Baruch followed David across the floor as his friend led his offering for Yahweh—a great black bull, pure, without spot or blemish. Its eyes were wild, and David had trouble goading it into a pen in the slaughterhouse room. As two priests held the reins and Baruch watched from the corner, David laid one hand on the bull's head. "Yahweh, Lord of all Creation," he said, his voice tight with emotion, "accept my penance as I give my sins to this animal." His other hand held a long knife, and with one quick motion, he thrust into the skin and drew it across the bull's throat.

The animal threw its head from side to side, moaned, staggered, then fell.

With advice and instruction from the priests, David began skinning the animal. Long before he was done, Baruch shouted his departure. "I'll meet you at the coffeehouse at five."

His friend nodded and continued the bloody business of removing the hide.

Baruch left the slaughterhouse, the Court of Priests, the Inner Court, and the Temple and joined the crowds streaming through the Dung Gate into Old Town. Today, the streets were overflowing with visitors.

* * *

THEIR TABLE HUGGED THE CAFÉ entrance by an open window next to the street. Pushing his mug aside, Baruch leaned toward his friend. "Do you trust me in all things spiritual? In how I interpret the Torah? In my zeal for the Jewish people?" With the shop full, the buzz of patrons talking, and the cars passing on the street, he had no fear their conversation would be overheard.

"You know I do." His face puzzled, David sat back and slicked damp hair from his forehead. After the ceremony, he'd gone home and showered.

"What I am about to tell you may be difficult to believe, but it's true. This is the most important conversation you and I will ever have—because what I've found will change Judaism forever."

"Now I am intrigued. And worried."

"Then keep an open mind and listen to my tale."

He proceeded to tell how he'd met Caleb Turner in Davato's prison, how Margot Durand painted prophetic visions, some of which led Dylan and Margot to rescue him from the Roman catacombs. He related Chelsea Turner's part and how he'd seen her on the dais today with Davato. He told how Margot's painted prophecies are coming true and what they portend for the world. He related his new interpretation of Isaiah and all he discovered in the Christian New Testament, especially from the book of Revelation.

When Baruch had finished, David sat back, bereft of words, his hands clamped together. "This is a . . . hard pill to swallow." He shook his head. "Is it really true?"

"All of it."

David closed his eyes and gripped his head. "But the Temple? The sacrifices? The Torat Kohanim? Everything we've worked for all our lives . . . ?"

"I know." Baruch softened his voice. "But you and I have always been dedicated to the truth. And now my mission, and hopefully yours, is to bring the truth of the Messiah—this man who's already come to earth, whom our ancestors crucified—to our people."

"These prophecies, this book of Revelation—you say it predicted the vanishing and the coming of this man Davato and his Unitum Imperium?"

"Yes, prophecies from Revelation and from Matthew, Ezekiel, Daniel, Joel, Isaiah, and others. They're all coming true. Revelation told me why we had gathered the Great Assembly. And it agrees with Davato's announcement today that he's moving his headquarters to Jerusalem. When you understand the book's predictions, it all makes sense."

"I have never known you to be led astray or to follow a false prophet. I respect you and admire you as the holiest man I have ever known."

"You are too kind." Baruch opened both hands in a question. "But . . . ?"

"But you are asking me to give up the beliefs I've built my life around. Not only my beliefs, but my life's work, my worship, my reason for living." David cocked his head, and tears came to his eyes.

"I know, my friend. And that impediment is why our ancestors, the Pharisees and the Sadducees, could not or would not believe when the Son of God himself appeared to them. We must not be like them, David. But this is a big decision, and I won't ask you to make it today." Baruch pulled a book from his backpack and pushed it across the table. "This is a Christian Bible. Start reading in Matthew. Pay close attention to the chapters I've marked. Read it with an open mind and in light of all you've heard today. Then we will talk again."

David took the book and, wiping the tears from his eyes, nodded. "I will read it. Yes, let us talk again."

"And, David?"

"Yes?"

"Best to keep the book secret."

CHAPTER 15
THE SECOND SEAL

The Great Throne Room – March, Year 1

In the Great Throne Room of the Lord of Hosts—an expanse stretching for miles in all directions—the archangel Gabriel bowed low beside his brother Michael. On all sides were gathered a great multitude of saints and lesser angels. A mile above them, the diamond ceiling sparkled and glimmered. As he bowed, Gabriel's wings touched the translucent floor of crystalline gold.

The great host had gathered to witness the next phase of God's plan for the end times, and an electric excitement rippled over the heads of the assembly, glowing from the bodies of the angels and saints.

Not far from Gabriel in the center of the vast hall, on a throne towering fifty feet above the assembled throng, sat the Creator of all that was, is, and will ever be. Before the throne, seven fiery torches burned with a wavering, blinding light. From beneath the throne, thunder rumbled, shook the floor, and rolled off into the distance. Smoke rose from behind, even to the ceiling a mile or more above, spreading out to the far corners of the vast hall. Thousands of sparkling, crystalline gems—diamonds, amethyst, rubies, and jasper—rimmed the chair itself. High above all sat the Lord of Creation, shining with a light brighter than a thousand suns, gleaming with a million shades of jasper that sparkled like diamonds, shimmering with a million ever-changing hues of ruby-red carnelian.

Beside and beneath the great throne were twenty-four smaller thrones, upon which sat twenty-four elders.

Across the great hall and above the great throne, a rainbow spread its arc, shining with a million ever-changing colors.

Before the Lord of Hosts hovered the four cherubim, tall and fearsome. Lightning and fire flashed between them. Each had four faces—of a man, a lion, an ox, and an eagle. Each had three pairs of wings—one to cover their faces, another to hover, and the third to point at their feet, which were the hooves of calves, shining like burnished gold. Human hands extended below the wings.

Holy, holy, holy is the Lord God Almighty, they sang in unison, a sound both ethereal and full of power, *the Creator of all that was, that is, and that is to come.*

Each creature floated above an enormous wheel containing an inner wheel, and the outer wheel touched the ground. Gleaming like polished aquamarine, the rim contained all-seeing eyes. The creatures hovered above the wheels without turning, and lightning flashed between them.

Then the lightning ceased, and they faced the Son of the living God, standing a few feet away. *Come!* they said.

The Son of the living God stepped forward. He did not come now as the lamb he first appeared to be or as a Being of blinding light with a body of shining burnished gold. Instead, he appeared with the wounds given him on the day the Roman soldiers drove the foot-long spikes through his wrists and ankles and later shoved the spear into his side. He appeared as the one who took upon himself the sins of all mankind, the only one worthy to open the ancient scroll. The only one worthy to break the seals.

A hush swept the assembled as the Son again took up the great scroll, written at the beginning of time, that recorded the events at the end of time. The pages rustled as they turned, and Gabriel took a deep breath. The Son's hands reached down, grasped the second seal, and snapped it open.

The crack echoed to the ends of the great hall and back. A hush followed, and the vast multitudes fell silent.

The rider on the red horse was unleashed.

To swing his sword among the nations.

To end the time of peace.

To begin the time of war.

CHAPTER 16

WAR

The South China Sea – March, Year 1

Cam Weinberg stood at his post on the starboard deck, cold hands gripping a .50 caliber machine gun. A life vest hugged his chest, and the wind blew cool and wet across his forehead. Beside the destroyer, porpoises arced in and out of the water. Cam loved moments like this, alone on his watch, sucking in fresh sea air, especially when porpoises shadowed the vessel. Ever since the heightened state of war, the commander had ordered that someone man the deck guns at all times—just in case. For days, the entire crew had been on endless watches, and the mood was tense. Another of Cam's crew manned a gun on the port deck.

A quarter mile to his right, the USS *Ronald Reagan* plied the ocean. Weeks ago, their carrier strike group had joined the other two carrier strike groups to form a defensive line stretching across fifteen nautical miles of open ocean. He released his grip on the gun and tucked chilled hands beneath his armpits.

For the last month, they'd been on high alert. The last reported location of the Chinese fleet was forty nautical miles to the west. For weeks, they'd held their position. Now it was sailing toward Taiwan, and everyone expected an engagement.

The repeated warnings from the Chinese Communist Party mouthpieces had grown ever more strident and filled with bluster. "Your continued presence in Chinese waters is a violation of international law and an affront to the Chinese people," said one such statement, even though international law declared the Taiwan Strait to be international waters. Then they repeated a warning given in 2021 by President Xi Jinping, "The Chinese people will never allow any foreign forces to bully us. Anyone who dares to try will have their heads bashed bloody against a great wall of steel." The repeated, increasingly belligerent tone from the Chinese only heightened the crew's tension.

"Why are you not holding your weapon, Hay-eeem?"

Cam stiffened and faced the familiar visage of his nemesis, Lieutenant Grady Wilson. It was like looking in the mirror, and Cam hoped he didn't start to hate the look of his own face.

"Sorry, sir. I was just warming my hands." He grabbed the gun.

Also wearing a life vest, Grady glanced up and down the deck then lowered his voice. "You don't belong here, Weinberg, and I'm going to see you don't stay. You can decide to request shore duty . . . or you can wait until I find something that will send you to the US Disciplinary Barracks at Leavenworth. One way or another, I'll see you off this ship."

Cam stood his ground and narrowed his eyes. "Why do you hate me so, Lieutenant? What have I ever done for you to treat me like this?"

Grady glowered. "Your kind brought on the shortages, the collapse of the markets, and nearly ruined my family. I can't stand the sight of you. Having you on board makes me siii—"

A warning clang ended Grady's speech. It was so loud it throbbed in Cam's chest. On the launch deck, the covers for ten missile silos began cranking open.

"It's begun!" The lieutenant whirled and ran for the stairs to the bridge.

"General quarters! General quarters!" came the shout over the loudspeakers. "*All hands to battle stations!* This is not a drill."

A siren began wailing.

Cam gripped his weapon and scanned the waves for threats.

In the distance, twin-engine FA-18 super hornets began roaring off the USS *Ronald Reagan*'s flight deck. Each would carry some combination of Taurus Cruise missiles and Maverick HARMs (High-speed Anti-radiation Missiles) or JASSMs (Joint Air-to-Surface Standoff Missiles).

Ahead on the launch deck, the roar of rockets leaving their silos rocked the air, and he smashed his hands over his ears. A blinding haze of acrid smoke washed the deck, and he choked, enveloped in a fog of exhaust. After the wind carried it away, seven metal birds arced west toward the Chinese fleet lurking over the horizon. Some might even have been targeted at the Chinese mainland. The other three climbed straight up—interceptors for ICBMs?

More missile doors began opening. From the carrier, dozens more jets rose into the sky. But from the other destroyers, no more missiles climbed toward the heavens. Surely, there were submarines with the fleet. He scanned the nearby waters. Only a few missiles rose from the ocean. Why not more?

When the rockets they'd already fired had disappeared over the horizon, he shuddered. Finally, after all the bluster, the threats, and the posturing, they were at war. But what kind of war? Was it in some way limited?

If those three *Avenger* missiles were intercepting ICBMs, did that mean there would be an exchange of nukes?

What did that mean for the homeland? For New York, the city he called home? He had only a few friends there now, some uncles, aunts, and cousins he rarely saw. And a synagogue he'd vowed never again to attend.

How many would die?

Before the missile doors on the launch deck had fully opened, they stopped.

A bright light burst overhead while, simultaneously, the throbbing of engines, the whir of machinery, the general quarters siren also ceased. In its place—an eerie, unnatural silence.

Ever since he'd come aboard, he'd never experienced such silence.

Four jets still in view became brilliant mirrors of light. They stopped their ascent and began slow, spiraling descents.

A curse from behind, and Grady Wilson emerged from the bridge he'd only recently entered. His face drained of blood, he pointed up, winced, then looked away. "EMP blast! We're screwed."

Cam tried to look where Grady had pointed but quickly averted his gaze. A ball of blinding bright light—a nuclear blast?—had detonated far above them, sending out a deadly electromagnetic pulse. He'd read in class how many of the ship's systems had been hardened against a limited EMP attack. But anything exceeding 50 kilovolts per meter—and a small nuke could deliver four or five times that—would fry the ship's electronics, including the power systems.

The last two liberal administrations had cut the military budget then cut it again, preferring to spend borrowed money on green energy, checks for every child in the country, free college tuition, free food, free housing, and free medical care. They also paid people to sit home and not work. Year after year, they kept reducing the number of missiles, bombers, and warheads on each missile until they had stripped the nuclear force of the deterrent power it once possessed. Included in the cuts—the extra hardening needed for a serious EMP attack.

Now, the USS *Avenger*, the USS *Ronald Reagan*, and every other ship in the fleet was apparently dead in the water.

"Oh no!" Still on the stairs, Grady pointed westward, and Cam's glance followed.

A half dozen missiles were dropping from above—from space?—at lightning speed.

A quarter mile away, the USS *Ronald Reagan* exploded in a fireball as multiple rockets slammed into her deck. Another missile hit one of the destroyers on the horizon, sending up a mushroom cloud of smoke, seawater, and debris.

High above them, many thousands of white streamers striped the sky, racing eastward toward the Taiwanese mainland. But Cam's gaze settled on a single white contrail, growing larger each second, heading straight for him.

It was coming on fast. It was targeted at the *Avenger*.

His heart leaped against his ribs. But what could he do? Where could he go?

It was all a dream, so impossibly unreal. He couldn't move, had no time to react.

Frozen in place, his heart racing wildly, his eyes followed it down.

Before it slammed into the launch deck, he ripped his gaze away.

The day exploded with thunder, smoke, and fire. Angry shrieks of twisted, snapping metal flew by him, spinning in all directions. The shock wave threw him off the deck into the air.

At the last second, before plunging under the cold sea, he gulped air into struggling lungs.

He hit the water so hard, even the life vest couldn't stop him from sinking.

Kicking, he fought his way to the surface, and there he gasped for breath. He treaded water, marveling that he was still conscious, still alive. Nearby, the flames of an oil spill licked the surface.

Rent asunder, the ship had split in half. The bow section stuck out of the water at a sharp angle.

He had to put distance between himself and the downdraft whirlpool that would follow. Using every ounce of strength he possessed, he began swimming.

After an eternity of struggling with wet clothes and shoes impeding his progress, he gained about fifty meters. On the next stroke, his hands hit something ahead, and he stopped. Someone was floating face down on the surface. He treaded water.

"Are you okay?"

No answer.

He reached out, turned the body over, and gasped.

It was Grady Wilson.

But one-half of his skull was missing.

Cam pushed away, shivering, holding his position, staring, not believing what he saw. He jerked to look behind him as another explosion threw fire and smoke into the air. The bow half of the USS *Avenger* slipped under the surface. But he'd gained enough distance to be safe from the whirlpool that would follow.

He scanned the ocean around him, but he was alone. He didn't see his counterpart who'd manned the port gun. Anyone below decks when the missile hit would never have made it out. Was he the only survivor?

Again, he stared at the corpse, his nemesis, this officer, this man who'd been born with all the advantages in life Chaim Weinberg had never had.

Grady Wilson had risen quickly to the rank of lieutenant.

Grady Wilson came from a prestigious, wealthy family in Boston.

Grady Wilson's father knew the President when he was still a senator from Massachusetts.

Grady Wilson was soon to join a presidential naval advisory panel.

Now Grady Wilson was dead.

Cam often wished he were someone else, and now he pondered the possibilities. If rescue came—and that was uncertain—could he start life over from scratch? Could he pull off the grand deception now swirling through his brain?

He swam back to the corpse and struggled to remove Grady's life jacket, his dog tags, and his bloodied shirt with its lieutenant's insignia.

He took Grady's tags for his own. He donned Grady's shirt. He hung his own dog tags around Grady's neck, but Cam had barely struggled one of the corpse's arms into his shirt when the body began to sink. He reached for it, but too late—it sank below the cold, black waters. The outline of the corpse dimmed, grew darker, was gone.

Trying to control his breathing, he raised his gaze to the rocket-striped sky.

Grady Wilson was dead.

But no, he wasn't.

It was Chaim Weinberg who'd died—a Jew formerly known as Cam, a Jew starting life anew as one of the goyim, a child of promise, wealth, and privilege. A Jew now taking the name and identity of Grady Wilson.

CHAPTER 17

DEPARTURE

Duluth, Minnesota – March, Year 1

For the last ten hours, Caleb had driven his Toyota RAV4 north from Chicago through Wisconsin. The trip had taken longer than expected. He'd hurried through ghost towns, stopping only long enough to top off his tank at unmanned gas stations where the pumps still worked and the tanks weren't empty. They'd bypassed countless roadside wrecks. Moments ago, they'd entered Duluth where the late-March snow was still piled deep beside the road.

Tanya occupied the front seat, and Nika slept in back. The other back seat and trunk were crammed full of food, sleeping bags, and camping gear. Each day leading up to their departure, he'd withdrawn the maximum amount from an ATM until he'd gathered over five thousand dollars and the machines stopped working.

"Too bad Brody won't be joining us." Tanya yawned.

"He said he couldn't leave his church."

"The First Church of the Apocalypse." She laughed. "What a name."

"Yeah. But so appropriate." He slowed as traffic entered an underpass. On the other side to their right, idled coal cars clogged the rail yard. The clock on the dash told him it was seven o'clock, and the light was already dimming. They wouldn't make their destination before dark. "It was nice of Brody to let us stay in his uncle's cabin."

"I think he likes you. You two hit it off."

Now it was Caleb's turn to laugh. "We both think alike."

Minutes later, where the road narrowed to two lanes, they encountered a bottleneck. Mounds of melting dirty snow, three feet high, lined both sides of the road. At least up north, someone had manned the plows.

Ahead, a line of late-model cars slowed to a crawl in the most traffic he'd seen since leaving Chicago. Behind, a beat-up pickup bore a layer of unbrushed snow on its hood. Beside them, a semi hauling a bed full of logs crept south. Up at the light, a Kwik Trip flashed the latest price increase. Gas was becoming as precious as gold, and too many stations had nothing left to pump.

Tanya gathered her strawberry-blonde hair into a ponytail, tied it off, then fingered through a knotted clump. "This is crazy, Caleb—leaving Chicago like this. And they've still got winter up here. Northern Minnesota is the coldest place in the nation."

"We'll be warm. There'll be firewood. And it's as far from civilization as we can get. Brody's uncle Vernon will be there." Pastor Brody had been happy to find someone to take care of his ill uncle. "Besides, Brody said the place was stocked with food, and Vernon is expecting us. We'll be safe there."

"Safe from what?"

"Safe when it happens."

She scrunched her face. "What exactly do you think is going to happen?"

"I–I don't know." He gripped the wheel tighter. "But I'm glad you finally agreed to leave with me. And I'm glad Brody's uncle has a cabin."

"Do you realize we're doing this only because of some feeling you had? Do you know how crazy that sounds?"

"I can't explain it. It was more than a feeling. It was as if God was speaking to me, and—"

Light exploded, illuminating the highway and everything around them. The engine died, and the car slowed to a stop. He turned the key in the ignition.

Nothing happened.

"What was that?" asked Tanya. "Why did you stop?"

"I didn't stop. The car just died."

He exited the vehicle and tried to glance at the sky above. But immediately, he averted his eyes. Far to the southeast, a huge fireball filled the heavens.

He searched the road ahead. The vehicles there were also stalled, and drivers were leaving their cars, looking briefly skyward.

Beside him, the lumber truck had also stalled. But from the pickup behind them, a plume of exhaust still rose. Up ahead, the light at the intersection was dark. So was the Kwik Trip sign. The light above them dimmed as the fireball lost intensity. All around the fireball, clouds were fast rolling away in a circle.

The driver of the pickup approached. "Hey, man." He wore a scraggly beard down to his chest and a ragged baseball cap atop his head. "What the hell is going on?"

"I don't know, but"—Dylan pointed southeast—"that looks like a nuclear explosion."

Shielding his eyes, the man tried to look but failed. "Is that why everyone's stopped?"

"Apparently."

The man glanced up and down the road. "Just what we need—more craziness." He pulled out his cell phone. "Dang thing is dead. No lights. No nuttin'."

Caleb tried his phone, and it, too, was dead.

Tanya appeared beside him and pulled out her phone. "It's warm. And it's . . . burning." Smoke rose from the device. Her eyes wide, she dropped it to the ground and jumped back. "What is happening?"

"EMP blast," whispered Caleb.

"Huh?" the others said in unison.

"We must be at war. The Chinese must have exploded one or more electromagnetic pulse bombs, small nukes, above us. That would knock out all our electronics. And our cars. That's got to be what happened."

The bearded man and Tanya stared at him with disbelieving expressions.

"I reckon they'll get everything back up soon," said the truck driver.

"No. I've read that such an attack could melt every generator in every power grid in the country. It might take months, if not years, to fix them all. The problem is—we get the really big generators that run the grid from China. And with no factories running, no trucks or cars or trains moving, no one will be able to get replacement parts for anything. The economy will be completely shut down."

"You're kidding." The man scratched his beard.

"I wish I were."

"What about solar?" asked Tanya. "And windmills?"

"Same thing. Every piece of electronics that wasn't heavily shielded is now fried. And green energy is even more dependent on electronics. And the precious metals needed for wind and solar—we get those from China too. All communications will also be dead—every cell tower and every landline." He gripped his head with both hands. "We're in deep, deep trouble."

"How come my truck is still running?" asked the bearded man.

"How old is it?"

"Maybe forty years. A junk bucket I've been meaning to replace. But I don't have the cash."

"It's still running because it's not loaded down with electronics like all the newer vehicles. You're lucky. Where you headed?"

"My place, west of Grand Marais."

"Could you take two passengers about fifteen miles west of Tofte?"

Again, he scratched his beard, looked at his truck, then cocked his head. "How much you give me?"

"A hundred dollars." Cash would rise in value. Without functioning banks or digital accounts and with no working ATMs, whatever cash Caleb had was all he was ever going to get.

A smile lit up the man's face. "A hundred twenty, and it's a deal."

"Done."

"My name's Ralph. Let's shake on it." After they sealed the deal, Caleb helped Ralph shovel snow from the truck bed to make room for their gear. Then the three of them huddled together in the front seat while Nika warmed Tanya's lap.

But the line of stalled cars blocked their way. They pushed Caleb's car to the side. The driver ahead wasn't happy about it, but he finally agreed to let them push his car out of the way enough so they could get by.

The pickup drove north in the opposite lane. Weaving in and out, they managed to bypass all the disabled vehicles hung up before the light.

The trip north was eerie, unreal. They passed dead cars and trucks, dead stoplights, dark stores, unlit houses. They took the bypass and rejoined Highway 61 where the road paralleled Lake Superior. Out on the lake, sheets of tumbled, broken ice piled up on the near shore while, farther out, whitecaps broke.

The sun had set a half hour ago. Then, without lights, all the dead vehicles blocking the road made the route treacherous.

After nine, with the temperature five degrees above zero, Ralph finally dropped them at the end of a dark drive covered with snow. He helped deposit their belongings in a dirty drift beside a mailbox. Caleb paid him, and Ralph drove off.

"I hope you've got the right address because I'm freezing." Wrapped in a down jacket, with heavy mittens on both hands, and topped with a stocking cap, Tanya gripped Nika's leash but didn't bother to clip it to her collar.

Similarly garbed, Caleb gazed up a snow-covered road that disappeared around a corner. Deep woods bordered the drive. Someone had plowed it, but more snow had recently fallen. "Let's grab what we can and start out."

They pulled on backpacks and hefted boxes of food. They'd probably need four or five trips to get it all.

They trudged through foot-deep snow for a quarter mile until the drive ended at a log cabin surrounded by pines. The dirty windows of a detached single-car garage revealed an ancient truck. Beside the garage stretched a twenty-foot-long pile of firewood under a snow-covered metal canopy. No smoke issued from the cabin's chimney. No lights shone from its windows.

Caleb set down his box and knocked on the door.

No answer.

He pounded on the windows, but the only response was silence.

When he tried the knob, the door opened, and they stepped into a wood-paneled living/dining room/kitchen. Nika padded in after them and shook snow from her fur.

On a corner wall, a bear's head stared down above a hearth holding cold, dead embers. Another wall held a shotgun, a rifle, and a bow with a full quiver of arrows. Hundreds of boxes of cartridges were stacked on the floor beneath. Two easy chairs, both covered with faded, worn quilts, were pulled before a cold fireplace. Beside one chair, a wooden end table bore an empty wine glass, a novel by Dostoevsky, and a Bible. Had the man turned to God after the Rapture? The room held no television, only a shelf overflowing with books, many of them classics. A small kitchen with a dead refrigerator occupied the far end of the room.

It was already so cold, Caleb could see his breath. The firedog beside the hearth carried no logs. Nika looked up at Caleb with questioning eyes then sat beside Tanya.

Stamping his feet to free the snow, he called out. "Vernon? We're here. Are you home?"

No answer. He knelt and untied his boots.

"Maybe he went to town when the power shut off, and he's stuck there?" Tanya knelt to pet the dog then removed her boots.

"But his truck is still here." He tiptoed in stockinged feet past the kitchen into the hall. The bathroom on the right was empty, its toilet stained, in need of cleaning. On the floor, a squat machine, now stood silent, still plugged into the wall socket. A long length of thin transparent hose led down the hall to the cabin's third and final room—a bedroom.

Caleb stepped through the open doorway. On one wall hung a deer-skin. On the other, a picture labeled The High Falls, Tettegouche State Park. A faint smell, as of burned electronics, hovered in the air. On the floor beside a double bed, the tube ended with a discarded cannula. Beside the bed on the floor lay a man with a second cannula around his nose. The machine in the bathroom must have been an oxygen concentrator, and the small box in the man's hands was a portable unit—now silent, without lights, also fried.

The man was still, his face pale, and no warm vapor issued from an open mouth.

"Vernon?"

Again, silence.

Caleb reached out a hand and touched the man's forehead. But the skin was cold. Jumping back, he covered his mouth with both hands.

"Is he . . . ?" came Tanya's whisper from behind.

"Dead." Caleb led her back to the living room. "When the power died, without the oxygen he needed, he must have suffocated. Or he didn't have enough strength to get more wood, and he died of the cold."

Tanya rubbed her mittened hands up and down her arms, her eyes reflecting fear and uncertainty. "Now what do we do?"

"It's freezing in here. Let's bring in some wood and start a fire."

"Then what?"

"The ground won't thaw for another month or two, so we'll have to carry Vernon's body outside and bury it in the snow. After that, we'll bring all our stuff up from the road. Then we'll change the sheets and the bedding, make supper, and start living in the Minnesota Northwoods."

"Your premonition was right, wasn't it?" She wrapped her arms around her chest. "Who knows what would have happened if we'd stayed in Chicago?"

"Yeah." He shuddered. "Unbelievable chaos. Much worse than anything we've seen so far. Mass starvation. The breakdown of whatever order remained. Millions of people are going to die. We're living in the time of the end, Tanya. God allowed this to happen, and Uri was right. We are living through God's judgment on our nation and the world, a world that turned its back on God, spat on his name, and embraced everything he abhorred."

She ran to his side and fell into his arms. "I'm scared, Caleb."

He held her tight. "We'll be all right." But as she shivered in his arms, he wondered.

What lay ahead when civilization itself was collapsing, when people became desperate and might do anything to survive?

Thinking back to his study of the book of Revelation, he shuddered again.

It was bad now. But the worst was yet to come.

CHAPTER 18

CHANGES

The South China Sea – April, Year 1

Lieutenant Grady Wilson—Cam was fast getting used to his new name—floated alone for a day after the remains of the *Avenger* then the USS *Ronald Reagan* sank beneath the waves. Night fell, he was alone with the stars, and he drifted, huddled in a ball to preserve warmth. Morning came, the sun burned hot over the water, and he heard a woman's cry for help. He responded, they swam toward each other, and he met Ensign Marcia Roberts, the short-haired blonde who'd been disgusted that a Jew had overheard her and Ishaan's conversation on the way to the mess.

"Lieutenant?" Her voice was weak and strained, but he smiled inwardly. His lieutenant's uniform was working.

"Aye. It's Ensign Roberts, is it not?" Cam—now Grady—tried to imitate Grady's speech.

"It is, and I'm so glad to find someone else alive, sir."

"Me too."

They floated for another day, too weak for conversation, until a helicopter from a late-arriving destroyer that had escaped the EMP blast plucked them from the sea. When the destroyer's commander found Grady Wilson's name on a VIP list, he sent his high-priority personage east on the ship's helicopter to rendezvous with the only surviving carrier in the Pacific. The carrier was still functioning because, after leaving Hawaii where it was docked for repairs, it was in the middle of the ocean when the war started. Grady then caught a flight on the carrier's twin-engine C-2 Greyhound, with a mission to pick up supplies in Guam. In Guam, he received a new photo ID and orders to report to Camp David. Then he was given a seat on the island's only remaining C-5 Galaxy transport jet charged with ferrying VIPs to the homeland.

Upper brass from the army and navy occupied the seats around him as well as the CEOs of two large companies, recognizable from their TV interviews. After the military transport lifted off from Anderson Air Force Base, a lieutenant approached the row ahead of Grady. There sat a congressman from Maine, another from Illinois, a senator from Nebraska, an army general, and a navy admiral.

"I–I've been asked to brief you five on the state of the war," said the lieutenant, his voice quiet, but not low enough to keep Grady from overhearing. His face was pale, and his eyes were red and puffy, as if he'd been crying.

"Good," said the white-haired senator. "We heard nothing in Japan. Communications in the entire country are down."

"Yes." The lieutenant's hands shook as he held a piece of paper. "Satellite communications are down everywhere across North America, Hawaii, Japan, and Australia—all except for Elon Musk's SpaceX network. But the military isn't on that network, is it? Without the satellites, Emergency Action Messages couldn't reach their recipients. Without an EAM, many of our ICBMs and short-range nukes—especially from our sub-based missiles—couldn't launch. The long antennae on the subs also make them vulnerable to the EMP blasts that disabled the fleet."

The admiral slammed a fist into a palm. "I told them," he whispered. "Again and again, I told them."

"The news gets worse. Much, much worse." The lieutenant cleared his throat and paused so long, Grady wondered if he would continue. "The US homeland was hit with a massive cyberattack followed by multiple EMP blasts that destroyed the internet and the power grid. No one really knows what's happening in the center of the country—no information is getting out. Before the EMPs hit us, our antimissile defenses successfully stopped many of their incoming ICBMs."

"What about our Tranche One satellites?" asked the army general. "Our new distributed, more resilient space communications system?"

"Only a handful were ever launched, and Chinese antisatellites even destroyed some of them. There weren't enough to inform us of any hypersonic missiles in orbit. But someone had the foresight to keep an old SR-71 Blackbird in a hardened hangar. From its overflights, we know that seven of their missiles hit our cities. We're guessing those came from the hypersonic glide vehicles against which we have no defense."

Grady and the man next to him in the second row, a lieutenant colonel from Idaho, exchanged horrified glances.

"Which cities?" whispered the Illinois congressman.

"Los Angeles. San Francisco. Denver." The lieutenant paused again, his voice wavering. "Ch–Chicago." He wiped his forehead. "Boston . . . DC." He sucked in air. "And New York."

The hum of the jet engines filled the following silence, but not enough to mask the gasps around Grady. Or the man two seats over who dropped his head into his hands and sobbed.

For Grady, the news took time to register.

They'd hit New York.

New York, where Chaim Weinberg's uncles, aunts, and cousins lived. And the rabbi at the synagogue he rarely attended. And a few friends from high school, friends he now wished he'd kept in touch with. Were they all gone? Had any survived?

He tried to mourn, but he was so exhausted, so bereft of tears, the news only stunned.

"Chicago?" The Illinois congressman stood, gripped his temples, and faced the others. "We've finally done it, haven't we? One hydrogen bomb landing on one of our cities would kill millions. You've all seen the estimates. If they hit that many cities and if we're without power—we're finished. We'll enter the worst depression we've ever seen. There'll be mass starvation, looting, chaos. . . ."

He dropped his gaze to the floor. "My wife and kids were . . . in Chicago. We are . . . finished." The man couldn't go on, and a woman from the second row, possibly his aide, rose, wrapped an arm around his shoulders, and helped him back to his seat.

Still standing in front, the lieutenant took several deep breaths. "I'll try to answer any questions you have."

"What about our missiles?" asked the army general. "Did they hit their targets?"

"North Korea tried to launch five missiles, and we shot down all but two which then crashed in the ocean. Our response was swift, overwhelming, and . . . North Korea is no more."

"But our counterattack on the Chinese? What happened?"

"We're not sure. We know their EMPs, their antisatellite and space-based weapons killed most of our outgoing missiles in midflight. We assume a few of ours got through."

"But we don't know."

"No." The lieutenant hung his head. "Before their missiles hit the US, we unleashed a massive cyberattack on China that, in theory, should have severely crippled the country. We also know that our destroyers launched maybe a dozen of our own EMP missiles targeted for high-altitude detonation over the country. They were programmed to detonate without GPS guidance. Those two attacks may have stopped a lot of their rockets from launching. It's possible China is now in the same state we are."

"But we really . . . don't . . . know." The general's voice was deep and rumbling.

"No." The lieutenant closed his eyes, shook his head, and reopened them. "We don't."

After a long silence, he took a microphone from a cradle behind him. "This announcement is for all passengers on board: We are scheduled to land at Camp David Airfield in approximately seventeen hours and thirty minutes. That airfield, at least, is functional. On the way, we'll serve sandwiches, coffee, and tea. As you may have heard, nothing around the DC area"—he took a deep breath—"rather, very little survived. If anyone needs accommodations near the camp, raise your hand, and I'll register your name for a room at the hotel we've secured."

Per his orders, Grady took one of the VIP rooms. With a simple name change, he had joined the elite, had been given special treatment apart from the grunts and common folk now struggling to survive. While the rest of the country faced chaos, disaster, and starvation, he had entered a world of privilege, wealth, and power.

But so exhausted was he from the rescue and the travel, he slept most of the way home.

* * *

SURROUNDED BY SOLDIERS, THE LIBERTY Mountain Resort in Carroll Valley, Pennsylvania, had no hot water, and candles substituted for electric lights. But Grady woke feeling better than he had in weeks. After a cold breakfast of cereal—but there was hot coffee—a man from the Secret Service knocked on his door.

"Sorry for the surprise notice," said a middle-aged man in a dark suit, "but we're still trying to establish communications. Your orders are to pack your gear and come with me."

Carrying his flight bag, Grady slipped into the back seat of an ancient, rusting Cadillac for a thirty-minute drive from the hotel in Pennsylvania, past snow-covered fields and forests, up a winding road, to Catoctin Mountain and Camp David. At the gate, two Secret Service men went through the traveling kit he'd put together in Guam and checked his new photo ID.

"Our database of fingerprints and retina scans was fried," said the guard, "but you look like our picture on file." When he waved the car on, Grady breathed out. He hadn't remembered the fingerprints or the eye scans that would have unmasked his deception.

The Cadillac dropped him at the entrance to Aspen Lodge, sometimes called the second White House, and two marines again checked his ID. They took him to an antechamber and left him there, alone. He waited for over an hour until a woman aide led him into a room with an elliptical oak table where sat the remaining leaders of the country.

With the President were two men in ties without jackets and a woman in a gray business suit, probably the secretary of labor. The black man with a beard was certainly the secretary of defense, and the short man in a plaid shirt was the secretary of commerce. Older than the picture Grady remembered from his TV inauguration, William Cole wore no tie. With disheveled hair, dark circles under his eyes, and a pale face, he appeared worn, exhausted. Grady stood to attention in the corner and waited.

"Bill, how are we to communicate without cell phones, landlines, or internet?" With her short hair cut in imitation of a man's, the woman slumped in her chair. "It will take a year, if ever, before we can manufacture generators to get power to anyone. Assuming we can even get the parts. And the rare minerals we need."

President Cole's face slumped as much as the woman's posture. "We're dependent on Davato now. He promised to launch new satellites and

98

bring us new cell phones. And we can seize the SpaceX network. That, at least, is functional."

"But, sir"—the black man sitting beside him held up a hand—"what good will that do? Even if we have a functioning satellite network, how are people down here to get the power to charge their phones? And now nobody even has a working phone."

"Until we get Davato's phones, we're screwed." President Cole drew a hand through his hair. "He's promised us solar-powered phones. They're working on the design now, but it will be some time before they're manufactured and delivered. There won't be many at first, and we'll have to prioritize who gets them. In a year or two, he's promised us industrial-sized generators to get the grid going again."

"A year or two . . ." The defense secretary shook his head. "What will be left of us in a year or two? Might as well be a century."

"What about the fuel to power these new generators?" asked the woman labor secretary.

"All the refineries are down," answered the secretary of commerce. "And people will have to scrounge what's out there. Even before this, we hadn't many functioning oil wells left. Remember our climate change agenda. We got what we wanted. Not much remains of the fossil fuel industry. And the windmills and solar panels? Every one of them is fried! And China manufactured most of them."

Only then did President Cole notice the new arrival standing at attention in the corner. "Oh, I'm sorry, Lieutenant." He shuffled through papers on the table, brought one to the top, and read. "Grady Wilson, isn't it? Come in."

Grady stepped forward.

"I knew your father well." The President's voice was tired. "He was in Boston when it started, wasn't he?"

"I fear he was, sir." Grady didn't know, but he went along with the supposition.

"Sorry to hear it. He was a good supporter. We lost so many." The President sat back, and his chair creaked. "Originally, my predecessor had scheduled you to be on an advisory panel for naval affairs. But all that's changed. We have new plans for you."

"Yes, sir." He stood to attention. "Whatever you have in mind, sir."

"Only a handful left Washington before it was . . . hit." He removed his glasses and rubbed his eyes. "We lost most of the House and Senate, or at least what was left of them after V-Day. What really hurt was losing so much of the executive branch and nearly all my staff. So we are in sympathy with your loss, Lieutenant." He stared at his glasses, shook his head, then put them back on. "I am now in great need of talented people I can trust."

"Yes, sir."

"One need I have right now is for an ambassador, a liaison, to send to the Imperator of the Unitum Imperium. Davato himself has requested this. I know I can trust any son of your father's. And because I am without other options, I am choosing you, Grady Wilson. This is your chance to serve your country—or what's left of it, which isn't much. But I'll give you the choice. Will you accept the assignment?"

Grady gasped and tried not to stare at the President of the country. He was getting in deep over his head. Ambassador to Davato? His heart began racing. He opened his mouth but couldn't formulate an answer.

"It must be quite a shock, but the position will not be a normal ambassadorship. You will not have to negotiate or make major decisions. You will not have a staff. You will need to be diplomatic, yes, and having read your record, I know that might be a struggle for you. But I am confident you can manage it. Your duties will be mainly to relay information between Davato and me. I desperately need a sense of where this man stands on issues. We have a Treaty of Intent with him, but how we are going to follow it now and what it will do for us—I don't know. I'm also asking you to be a kind of spy for your country. But much of that will occur only after we reestablish electronic communications. So, Lieutenant, will you accept?"

Lieutenant Grady Wilson, formerly Gunner's Mate Second Class Chaim Weinberg, stood at attention and swallowed. Then he uttered four words that would change his life forever. "Yes, sir, I accept."

"Good." President Cole smiled. "As soon as transport can be arranged, you will leave for Jerusalem."

CHAPTER 19
THE AMBASSADOR

Jerusalem, Israel – April, Year 1

Chelsea Turner left the elevator in Jerusalem's Clal Center and exited the building. Shortly after V-Day, Davato had purchased the fifteen-story office tower, kicked out the shopping center and other tenants, and moved in Worldnet personnel. After his last stunning announcement, the center's Jerusalem location now served as the seat of power for the Unitum Imperium.

As she stood beside Jaffa Road, waiting for the US representative to arrive from Tel Aviv, she looked up and back. Rescue nets from the previous owner protruded above the building's first floor—nets to catch would-be suicides from smashing their skulls on the sidewalks below and disturbing the shoppers. Even before V-Day, some people lived lives of such despair they felt that was the only way out. She shuddered.

When a car door opened behind her, she whirled to greet a sun-browned, dark-haired man in his midtwenties holding a flight bag and wearing a rumpled suit and tie. "Are you Ambassador Wilson?"

"I am." Dark hair fell over his high forehead before he shook it back. That and the dimple indenting his chin gave him a boyish appeal. He was too young, too cute, to be an ambassador, and his first instinct seemed to be to salute. But when his hand rose halfway to his forehead, he stopped, smiled, and extended a palm instead.

Smiling in response, she took it then introduced herself as Davato's aide charged with taking care of all the ambassadors. To put him at ease, she asked about his trip.

"Exhausting. In the last week since they plucked me from the ocean, I've had only one good night's rest."

"That's right. You're the officer who survived the sinking of your boat." Recalling the summary of his exploits, she looked with renewed respect on him.

"We call them ships. And yes, that was me. But, miss"—he grinned—
"you seem like a nice person, so if you're taking care of me, you should
know this is all new to me. I never expected to be assigned to this post. I
hope you'll forgive me for being such a newbie."

She cocked her head, surprised by his honesty, his naivete, his boyish
manner. He wasn't your typical diplomat, was he? "You're forgiven. But
come. Hopefully, you'll like the apartment we've picked out for you. It's
on the seventh floor, and I promise, it's quiet. Then you must meet the
man himself. He's expecting you."

A shadow crossed his forehead.

"Where are you from, Grady?" His vulnerability was endearing. She
must do what she could to assuage his fears.

"Boston."

"Oh. I'm sorry. I'm from Minneapolis, but for a time, I lived in New
York." As she thought of all the people she'd known there, another shudder rippled across her shoulders. Was Archer among the dead? And her
former coworkers at Green Planet? Had she not left Chicago for Rome
when she did, her fate could have been theirs.

"Yeah." His glance swept the building then settled on her. "Truly
awful. Words can't do it justice. But it's good to meet another American.
I thought I'd be dealing only with foreigners."

"Likewise."

She led him through the galleria food court, used now only for
employees and guests, then on to the elevators and to Grady's seventh-
floor, three-room apartment. He appeared well pleased with it, and after
he dropped his bag, they rode to the fourteenth floor and passed through
security.

"Now, we'll meet the Imperator himself." As another look of uncertainty crossed his face, she smiled. "It will be all right, Lieutenant. I
mean—Ambassador."

* * *

GRADY WILSON FOLLOWED THE WOMAN to the fourteenth floor and a
meeting room serving as a temporary war room where the silver-haired

Davato was conferring with some general. That Grady was here, now, in the presence of this great leader who'd united the world, made his heart race. Was he really living this, or was it some kind of dream?

The woman Chelsea pulled him back and put a finger to her lips, indicating they should wait until summoned. Then she whispered, "That's General Eric Hofmann, supreme commander of all UI forces."

Three technical staff sat at the table's end before laptops. Two aides waited by the far wall.

"Sir, after the bombardment, the Russian tanks are racing westward." Wearing a sky-blue uniform with the Unitum Imperium's six-sided patch and the letters *D, A, V, A, T, O* on each corner, the middle-aged general pointed to a map on the table. "Here, here, and here."

"And what resistance are the Baltic states putting up?" Davato's voice carried all the authority of command Grady had heard on TV. Close and in person, Grady wanted to obey it.

"Very little. They've been in chaos ever since the vanishing." The general gripped his hands together. "I expect Latvia to fall within days, Lithuania by the end of next week, and Estonia a few days after that. By the first week of May, the Baltics will be part of Russia."

Davato pointed to another place on the map. "And Western Ukraine?"

"Right now, the Russians are pounding their defenses with heavy artillery and rockets. Their tanks will probably cross the Donbas frontier tomorrow, at the latest. I estimate the rest of the country will be theirs sometime in June. After the Russians' previous brutal invasion and the Great Catastrophe, Western Ukraine hasn't many left for the fight." The general raised a worried glance. "What should we do?"

"Unless they threaten the Unitum Imperium—nothing." Davato straightened his back. "Do we have an update on China?"

"The news is good, sir. As expected, the Chinese took Taiwan—for what good it will do them. Now they're embroiled in street battles and hill fighting with the locals. It will take months to achieve complete control of the island."

"And the American response to their nuclear attack?"

"The American President followed your advice, sir, and the US response against the Chinese was devastating. The Chinese EMPs checked a full-blown strike, but the North American missiles that got through took out eight cities, including Beijing, Nanking, and Shanghai. The US launched a massive cyberattack, and combined with their EMP missiles, the Chinese internet and electronic infrastructure is fried. Almost simultaneously, seven of China's nukes got through and hit seven American cities."

"And your conclusion?" Davato straightened his back.

General Hofmann grinned. "Before this happened, the Great Catastrophe had already devastated the United States. But after this, well . . . the US may never recover."

"And China?"

"In both countries, we'll see mass starvation, food riots, and a further breakdown of law and order. Both China and the United States have essentially been eliminated from the world stage."

Davato slapped his general on the back. "Perfect. Absolutely perfect. What about nuclear winter?"

"The climate will cool a bit, and crop yields will be down, but we don't expect nuclear winter."

"Excellent. Truly excellent." Turning from the table, he strolled to the window, clapped his hands together, then whirled. Only then did he notice Grady and the woman Chelsea in the corner. Smiling broadly, he waved them forward. "Come in. Come in."

Chelsea introduced Grady to the Imperator, and when Davato smiled and reached out a hand, Grady extended a sweaty palm.

"I read about your rescue, Lieutenant." Davato shook his hand with more force. "That was quite an ordeal."

"Yes, sir." Grady snapped to attention and began raising his hand in a salute. Embarrassed, he dropped the arm. "And now I'm here, representing the United States."

Davato grinned at the mistake. "Yes. It will take time to get used to all the changes. But now you're an ambassador, not a lieutenant, and let's sit. I will tell you why I requested that your President send me an ambassador."

The Imperator beckoned to an aide. As they headed for cushioned chairs in the corner, the young man asked them what they would like to drink. Davato ordered a whiskey, Chelsea a white wine, and Grady a beer. They'd barely sat when the waiter hurried over with their drinks.

"As you may have been told," said the Imperator, "yours will be a different kind of ambassadorship." Both hands pulled his glass to his chest. Then his face grew taut, and his demeanor, so ingratiating and friendly, morphed. In its place was a mask of cold iron.

The change came on so fast, with such force, a shiver ran down Grady's torso.

"Whatever your President told you about your duties here, you can forget." Eyes as black as night bored into Grady with almost supernatural force. "The world is changing, and your country is not what it used to be. Your President sent you here thinking you will be his ambassador and possibly his spy, but I suggest you will perform a different role. First, you should understand that I do not tolerate spies. The penalty for spying on the Unitum Imperium, even by an ally, is death."

Grady shifted uncomfortably on his seat.

"Instead, I want you to spy for me, reporting back to me everything the American President and his incompetent Camp David staff tells him. And when you communicate with Camp David, you will tell them only what I want them to hear and nothing more. If you do not agree with my terms, you will return, tomorrow. But you will go, not seated in the main cabin of a passenger airline, but in a casket in the cargo section, the unfortunate and untimely victim of a car crash. Is that clear?"

So stunned was he by the Imperator's statement and the force with which he said it that Grady could only stare, his mouth open.

Beside him, Chelsea, too, now stared wide-eyed at her boss.

"*Is that clear, Ambassador?*"

"Y–yes, sir." But his voice rose barely a whisper. "It is perfectly . . . clear."

"Good." Davato sipped his drink and sat back, and the kindly, genteel demeanor returned. The change was so swift and unsettling, Grady gasped again.

"You'll find that all who work for me with undying loyalty are amply rewarded and lack for nothing. Isn't that right, Chelsea?"

She lowered her gaze to her glass and nodded.

"My, aren't we quiet all of a sudden?"

"You've given me everything a girl could ask for." She raised her eyes to his. "I lack for nothing, sir."

But behind her quiet acquiescence, Grady sensed in her tone caution, maybe even fear.

"Of course, you don't. I reward everyone who is loyal to me. And woe to those who aren't. They would wish they had never been born." Though his tone had softened, his words had not, and when Davato grinned at his own words—as though at some private joke—Grady shuddered.

Davato faced his new ambassador. "Welcome to Jerusalem, Ambassador Grady, and to the new headquarters of the Unitum Imperium."

Grady swallowed. His only reply was to close his gaping mouth and nod.

YEAR TWO

THE THIRD
AND
FOURTH SEALS

Revelation 6:5–8 (HCSB): *When He opened the third seal, I heard the third living creature say, "Come!" And I looked, and there was a black horse. The horseman on it had a set of scales in his hand. Then I heard something like a voice among the four living creatures say, "A quart of wheat for a denarius, and three quarts of barley for a denarius—but do not harm the olive oil and the wine."*

When He opened the fourth seal, I heard the voice of the fourth living creature say, "Come!" And I looked, and there was a pale green horse. The horseman on it was named Death, and Hades was following after him. Authority was given to them over a fourth of the earth, to kill by the sword, by famine, by plague, and by the wild animals of the earth.

CHAPTER 20

SETTLING IN

The French Luberon – August, Year 2

August brought the first month of the second year of the Tribulation. Long after supper, Dylan took a glass of wine to his favorite spot on the patio. He sat under the trellis and listened to the crickets chirping. He peered at the stars peeking through cracks in the overhanging vines. And as he often did in quiet moments alone, he looked back on all that had happened since last spring. . . .

The warm rains of April had brought red, pink, blue, and yellow hyacinths bursting from the ground. The radiation had been in the rain and the ground but wasn't as bad as predicted. When the storms came, Dylan took the iodine tablets Pasqual gave everyone and helped herd the animals into the barn. But what could anyone do? Some radiation was now a fact of life.

Despite a cooler than normal May, the irises, lilacs, and peonies still bloomed. To everyone's relief, nuclear winter did not come to pass.

Refugees from Davato's purges began appearing at the farm, and the beds reserved for them slowly filled. While Margot served meals, made beds, cleaned bathrooms, and helped the new Christians feel welcome, Dylan found—despite earlier misgivings—that assisting Marcel with the farm chores was somewhat rewarding and better than doing nothing. He also kept company with Pasqual.

With the new arrivals in June came Victor Marceau, a short man with thinning blond hair, wire-rim glasses, and a nervous smile. René gave Victor his own locked room in the basement where he disappeared after breakfast and from which he rarely emerged until evening. When Dylan asked what Victor was up to, René only smiled and said, "Victor is unusually talented with electronics. Someday we will reveal what he's been working on. But not yet."

In the evenings after supper—and after René had his cigarette outside—he and Pasqual would gather everyone in the large dining room next to a crackling wood fire. On some evenings, René would pray that God would hide the new Christians in the cities, lead them to the farm, and thwart the efforts of the Central Security Agency and the growing number of Truth Squads. Pasqual would then thank Jesus for giving them the farm and a place of safety. Others would join in with prayers for each other. On other evenings, someone would give a short message from the Bible after which came a time of lively discussion.

Shortly after arriving, to everyone's surprise, Victor came to the after-supper meeting bearing a guitar someone had found in an upstairs closet. "I can play," he said. And play he did. His fingers plucked at the strings as if he'd been born with the instrument. He played popular songs, Christian songs he learned only the day before, and songs he made up. The group sang along to the ones they knew or just sat back and listened. After Victor's impromptu performance, the group begged him to bring the guitar several times a week.

At the end of such gatherings, Pasqual would remind everyone that, no matter what happened and how bad things got, even if they found themselves facing the Antichrist's guillotines, they were all now members of God's eternal family, blessed and treasured by him, destined to live forever in the light of Christ's all-encompassing love. Dylan thought of him as their pastor, though Pasqual vehemently denied it.

In June, lavender had spread like a violet ocean over the fields in the valley. But it was Pasqual's opinion the flowers' growth was stunted. Still, Dylan was impressed.

The bright colors in the fields below contrasted with the chilling news from Eastern Europe, China, and the United States. Grim-faced TV newsmen reported how Russian forces had secured the Ukraine, Finland, the Baltic states, and Poland. Across the frontier, Unitum Imperium troops were massed on the borders of Germany, Hungary, and Romania, effectively blocking the Slavic advance.

The snippets of news filtering from China depicted a country in a state of collapse. With the head decapitated, the communist grip on the populace was severed. Lawlessness now ruled the cities and countryside. The farm economy collapsed, leading to mass starvation. Without pay, without food, the army rebelled. Riots broke out everywhere, and rival warlords sprang up in the provinces from the former Communist party apparatchiks. These then fought each other for territory.

Before the war, the US was already facing depopulation and a collapsing farm economy. The war brought mass starvation, a complete loss of communication, and a total breakdown of order from coast to coast. Lawless gangs roamed unchecked across much of the interior. Only in a few enclaves on the coasts and Deep South did National Guard and federal troops maintain some semblance of order. It was much the same in Canada.

Dylan's premonition about Chicago had been correct. After no signals were detected from the Windy City, overflights revealed that several nukes had devastated the entire metropolitan region. Since his parting from Caleb last December, Dylan hadn't heard from his brother, and now he feared the worst.

"He could be all right," Margot had tried to reassure him. "He might have taken your warning to heart. Maybe he left the city?"

She meant well, but the lack of news from all points west of Camp David and east of San Diego and Sacramento—California's last major, functioning cities—only fed a conviction that Caleb and Tanya, if not in grave danger, were both probably dead.

In July, Dylan and Margot joined René on his frequent trips to nearby cities to buy supplies or to meet people Pasqual called his "seekers".

"We've sent seekers to various cities, towns, and villages," Pasqual had explained, "a handful of men and women trained to look for those who don't quite fit in, who appear to be struggling outcasts, adrift in this hedonistic age of the damned. This world is not our home, Dylan, even more so in these difficult times, and if we can recognize our own—well, we must save as many as we can."

But every venture outside the compound involved increasing danger. The Truth Squads were becoming more aggressive, stopping people at random, staking out businesses, restaurants, or apartments suspected of being Christian meeting points. Sometimes, agents of the CSA appeared on the streets. They wore green-and-black uniforms with a patch showing a lightning bolt crossing a skull. Rumors returned from the field that the CSA agents were more professional and more brutal than the lesser-trained Truth Squads.

But none of this would stop the Nazarene Friends from pursuing their mission to thwart the will of the Antichrist and his persecution of Christians.

* * *

THESE THEN WERE DYLAN'S MUSINGS as he sat in the gathering dark under the vine-laden trellis in the first month of the Tribulation's second year. With his wine glass empty, he stood, strolled out onto the grass, and lifted his eyes to the heavens. Pinprick stars glistened in a blue-black sky, broken only by a yellow half-moon peeking over the horizon. Competing with the crickets, a scops owl chirped from a nest on the roof, and Dylan breathed deeply of the cool night air.

"Beautiful evening, isn't it?"

Startled by Pasqual's voice, Dylan whirled. "Yes, beautiful. But it's hard to believe all that's happened since last April and that we're living in the time of the end."

"I've often had the same thoughts. Back in Lyon, I attended a church where the pastor often preached about the end of days." Pasqual stopped beside Dylan, his neck craned skyward. "But someone would always complain that such preaching distracted us from living in the present."

"Why weren't you a Christian then?"

"I was a fallen sinner who didn't really know Jesus." Pasqual's voice was quiet. "Like everyone else at the farm, I came too late to real faith. Now I'm reading the books of Matthew, Revelation, Ezekiel, Joel, and Daniel nearly every day. Did you know that twenty-seven percent of the Bible is prophecy?"

Dylan cocked his head. "Is that true?"

"Preachers should have spent more time on those books. Back then, if I had heard what the Bible predicted, if I had known how many biblical prophecies had already come to pass, maybe I would have listened. Who knows?"

"You've got a point. All of us here at the farm have a different story about coming to faith. Now everyone's finally on the right track." Deciding not to revisit his own past, Dylan changed the subject. "René's faith story is something, isn't it?—a former spy who's turned to Christ."

"Oui, but did you know he was also an assassin? I worry about him going back to his old ways. With the situations we find ourselves in, sometimes I fear he'll go too far and forget who he is now."

"An assassin?"

"Oui. And with what we have to face in the days ahead, I also worry about the rest of us."

* * *

A FEW DAYS LATER, UNDER a sunny sky, Dylan ambled from the house toward the hillside where Pasqual was overseeing the excavation of a second storage chamber. After they'd bought the villa, the Nazarene Friends had purchased a skid loader with scoop to accomplish the digging.

"You're almost done." Dylan ogled the thirty-foot-deep hole with a ramp leading down from the surface. Twenty feet wide, it would hold more than a year's harvest.

"Oui," answered Pasqual. "Friday we'll start pouring concrete. By the end of next week, it will be cured."

They'd studied Revelation and the second seal. They knew what was coming. To prepare for the famine to come, they'd already stockpiled much of last fall's harvest in the first chamber. "If only we have as good a yield this year," Pasqual said. "But it's too cool. The wheat and corn are not where they should be. Neither are the grapes. I fear for the fall harvest."

"You've done an amazing job so far." Dylan strolled with his host around the hole's perimeter. "How many refugees have we taken in these last few months?"

"About forty."

Dylan frowned. The villa could hold about a hundred souls. "But there must be thousands of new Christians out there? What will happen to them if we don't have room?"

"We're looking at the island of Madeira. Though they were part of

Portugal, they have escaped Davato's attention by pretending to follow his edicts."

"But so many Christians are being taken to the camp. We can make barely a dent."

Pasqual dropped his gaze to the ground and nodded. "There is only so much one can do. So we do what we can." Then he laid a hand on Dylan's shoulder. "But come to the house. It's time to reveal what Victor has been working on."

Intrigued, Dylan followed as Pasqual gathered Margot and a few others to the basement. Pasqual punched the combination for the lock then pulled open the door. Inside wires, soldering irons, oscilloscope-like machines, and computers covered a table. Victor looked up from a chair and gave them his nervous smile.

Pasqual pointed to an open box filled with cell phones. "Shortly after the vanishing, we bought a number of these throwaway phones."

Dylan cocked his head. "But I thought we couldn't use cell phones as the Antichrist's people would use GPS to trace the call."

"All true for an ordinary phone." Victor rose from his seat. "But I have developed a method to confuse their ability to track us. We can turn off GPS, of course, but there are other ways to track a phone. The hardware in these devices frustrates a network-based approach by varying the power levels and antenna patterns. They have ten times the power of a normal phone, so they can negotiate a signal with cell towers that are one, two, or three hops away. They also vary the SIM data reported to the networks, and they always connect via cell towers, never via Wi-Fi. Wi-Fi would allow someone to further narrow a phone's location. The result— the area from which we're calling is too wide to track us. And they can't identify one particular phone."

"Impressive. Is there a downside?"

"Yes. With my method, it can take longer to switch towers if we're moving, and sometimes we lose the signal. And the phones are a bit larger."

Dylan picked one up then set it down. "But they can still record everything we say. And with voice recognition software, they can also identify who we are."

Victor smiled. "If we're communicating with one of our own, we should only speak over these in an emergency. Instead, we'll send encrypted texts. Anyone watching what we send will only see gibberish from a phone they can't locate."

"What if I want to talk with someone who isn't in our network? Like my sister?"

"It will work like a normal phone. But whoever is listening in will know the location of whomever you're calling. To convey important information without using encryption, you'll have to use code words, just like in the old days."

"Can I still use the internet?"

"Yes, but you'll have to be careful. They'll see everything you search on."

Pasqual stepped behind the table and laid a hand on Victor's back. "He was working on this even before he arrived. Now he's given us a nearly foolproof method to communicate without being tracked. Not only that, he's created a long-range drone we can use to monitor any threats coming up the drive."

Dylan congratulated Victor on his success then raised a quizzical glance to Pasqual. "Since I threw my old phone away, I've been unable to call my sister. I'd like to find out how she's doing and ask her again if she'll help us find the camp."

Pasqual rubbed his beard. "Oui, my friend. But even with all of Victor's safeguards, it's best to make the call close to a big city. The denser the population, the more difficult it is to track us. As it happens, I was about to ask you and Margot to accompany René to Marseilles tomorrow to help him collect a group of refugees. It's one of our more dangerous assignments, and since René possesses all the skills of a trained espionage agent, he's the best one to lead it."

"Then tomorrow it is."

CHAPTER 21

REFUGEES

Marseilles, France – August, Year 2

As René stubbed out a final cigarette and pulled the van off the D5 into an empty drive, Dylan raised his window against the downpour. When driving with the former spy, fresh air inside the vehicle was always welcome. He peered through the car windows at the warehouse where the refugees were hiding. Rain pattered against the glass, exploded on the cement, and splashed in puddles outside.

"Our vehicle is not ideal." René shut off the engine and wiped a hand over the windows on his side to clear the mist. "With the famine getting worse, a food company truck attracts too much attention."

"Then why are we driving it?" asked Margot, sitting between Dylan and René.

"It was the only thing we could get, the only vehicle for which we could forge papers. We didn't have time to change the signage. The refugees have been stuck in this building for two weeks. Now they're running out of food and water, and one needs medical attention. This warehouse has been abandoned for some time. It's the best place we've found to hide people temporarily. But we'll put the next group somewhere else. Too much activity in one location for too long invites trouble."

Rusted forklifts and machinery lay abandoned in a fenced-in yard bordering the highway. At the entrance to the highway behind them, occasional cars and trucks whizzed by. On the way, they'd passed through five checkpoints, and each time, Dylan's heart raced while the guards pored over their forged credentials. But the forgers at the farm, including René, were good at what they did. No one had questioned their work.

Before leaving home, René had handed him a 9mm Glock 17 pistol, a box of ammunition, and an extra clip. When Dylan lifted a questioning glance, René explained. "If we encounter a squaddie bent on putting us or our brethren into a camp, what should we do? Let them take us? Or should we fight?"

"A squaddie?"

"It's what we're now calling members of the Truth Squads."

The term seemed to fit, and Dylan smiled. He balanced the weapon in his grip, the polymer fitting well to his hand, even as part of him recoiled against holding it. "Christians aren't supposed to commit murder."

"In an ideal world, oui." Then René had laid a hand on Dylan's shoulder and squeezed. "Keep it anyway. When the time comes, if it comes, you'll know what to do."

Nodding, Dylan had slipped the black metal into one pocket, the ammunition and extra clip into the other.

In a break in the rain, René exited the vehicle. Dylan shielded his eyes from the drizzle and followed. With Margot close behind, they approached a side door.

Again, he sent a furtive glance to the highway. A black Citroen slowed as it passed the entrance but then sped up and kept going. Probably nothing.

René pushed through into a dark interior littered with broken crates and discarded packing material. A family of rats scampered away. Crossing a floor under water dripping down from a leaky ceiling, they stopped in shadows at a far-side door. René knocked three times, paused, then knocked twice more. They waited for an answer.

A lock clicked from inside, and a long-haired, skinny man wearing jeans and a black sweatshirt opened the door. Beyond was a room outfitted with bunk beds, easy chairs, and a long counter with a sink, hot plates, microwave, and a refrigerator. A woman lay in bed, her face pale and sweaty. Three men lounged on chairs under a string of bare bulbs.

A woman with wavy red hair rose from a chair. "My name is Danielle, and we are so glad to see you!" As though in apology, a sparkling smile briefly crossed her lips. "We haven't eaten in days, and Monique is doing poorly."

"What's wrong with her?" Margot stepped to the bed and knelt beside the woman.

"She's got a fever. And her abdomen is tender."

"I hope it's not serious," said René. "We don't have the medical facilities or the doctor that we should."

"Do what you can," came a whisper from the bed. "I understand."

"Come. All of you." René motioned toward the door. "We must get back to the farm before curfew."

The fugitives filled their packs with what little they'd brought. Then the group left the building in a driving rain. As planned, Margot joined the five in the back of the van. Dylan sat up front with René.

They pulled out of the drive onto the D5 and turned left. As the rain came down, the wipers slapped side to side, and René lit another cigarette. For ten minutes, they wended their way through the outskirts of Marseilles.

Then René pulled off the main road onto a side street and faced Dylan. "You may make your call from here. But be brief."

He still didn't have a private number for Chelsea. Taking out his phone, he took a deep breath. Once again, he was forced to go through official channels by calling Worldnet headquarters, now the Ministry of Truth. He asked the receptionist to speak to Chelsea Turner.

"And who may I say is calling?" she asked.

"Tell her it's her brother."

There followed a long pause, and Dylan's heart sped up. Would they have put some kind of alert on calls coming from him? Would they try to trace him? But Victor's technology should foil that attempt. In any event, he'd thought long and hard about how to arrange a meeting with his sister with a dozen ears listening in.

"All right, sir," the receptionist finally said. "But she's in our Jerusalem headquarters now. Hold on while I transfer your call."

After another long wait, he heard his sister's voice. "Dylan?"

"Yeah, sis, it's me. But we must be brief, and I have an important request."

"You shouldn't be calling me here at this number. They're looking for you. In fact, you should turn yourself in to the nearest CSA office at the first opportunity."

He took another deep breath. She probably had to say that. "Maybe later. Right now, I'd like to meet you somewhere so we can talk."

"Meet with you?" Her voice rose. "Are you crazy? I'm in Jerusalem now."

"That's what the receptionist said. Why Jerusalem?"

"Davato's new headquarters are in Jerusalem, and I go where he goes."

"Right. Of course. But you still travel a lot, don't you?"

"I . . . do."

"Do you remember when we were kids, when Father took the five of us to a certain restaurant in a certain city where Mother spilled red wine all over an expensive white dress she'd bought that day?"

"I remember."

"Let's meet there. Whenever you're in that city next."

"This is ridiculous. Even if I get there, how will I communicate with you? Will you give me your phone number?"

"You know I can't do that. But you can call the man with the white hair who likes his steak rare and his wine red. He can get the info to me. Tell him the date and time, and we'll meet."

"A man with white hair? Who are you talking about?"

"You know him well. He once found you crying and out of breath after you fell from a tree." He was speaking, of course, of Bettino, the caretaker at Father's villa in Tuscany.

"Oh. Yes, I remember."

"Good. I've got to go. It's important we keep our meeting secret. I know you'll arrange this when you can."

"I'm not going along with this, Dylan. I won't do this."

"Sure, you will. I'll be waiting for your call."

When he hung up, René narrowed his eyes and shook his head. "You are crazy, *mon ami*. What if Davato's people figure out where this meeting place is? What if they find out who your white-haired man is? Or what if your sister tells them all the details? If you go ahead with this meeting, you could be walking into a trap."

"I trust her. And unless they ask Father, I doubt they'll discover our secret."

Still shaking his head, René pulled the van back onto the street. As they picked up speed and headed north, Dylan again glanced in the rearview mirror.

Fifty meters back, a black Citroen pulled out of a side street. He couldn't be certain, but—wasn't that the same car that had passed them on the street when they were parked at the warehouse?

CHAPTER 22
TROUBLE IN THE STREET

Marseilles, France – August, Year 2

At first, Dylan wondered if he was being overly concerned. The car behind them was like any other, and this was a busy street. A Peugeot pulled in front of the Citroen, separating the two vehicles. But when René followed a sign for Aix-en-Provence, the black car followed.

"I think someone is following us." Dylan's gaze remained fixed on the back mirror.

"Oui, I've noticed." René sent a glance behind. "But a lot of traffic is heading north. Let's see what happens at the next turn."

At the sign for the A51, barely visible through the drizzle, René turned left as did the Peugeot. But so did the Citroen.

"He might just be going north. I'll make a detour through the neighborhoods and see what happens."

At the next side street, René turned left. The Peugeot went straight.

But the black Citroen followed, and it was the wrong turn to make. The lane they'd entered was narrow, and ahead, a crowd blocked the way. Wearing raincoats and holding clubs, crowbars, and sledgehammers, they were beating on a plywood-encased building.

"Oh no." René slowed the vehicle. "That's a neighborhood market. The mob must be after food."

"And we're driving what looks like a food company delivery van." Dylan shot another glance back. "Look behind you." The Citroen had pulled sideways, blocking the street. Now there wasn't enough room on the sidewalk to get around.

Ahead, the mob had spied their vehicle and was marching toward them. "What do we do?"

"I don't know."

They sat frozen in their seats as the crowd approached. Illuminated by the headlights, gaunt men and women bore pickaxes, hammers, and crowbars. Leading them was a middle-aged man with a wet mop of yellow hair pasted to his forehead. Anger twisted his face. As he neared, he shouted something, and Dylan lowered the window a crack to hear.

"Give us your food, and we'll let you go."

Dylan rolled down the window and stuck his head out. "We're empty. Haven't picked up our delivery yet."

"I don't believe you," came the reply.

From behind echoed the crack of a gunshot. Startled, the mob stopped its advance then began backing away.

Dylan searched the rearview mirror but couldn't find who fired. Then something hard and metallic rapped against the window on René's side. His heart hammering fast against his ribs, he whipped toward the sound.

A pistol in the hands of a man with a squaddie armband rapped again. "Open the window."

René complied with the muffled command.

"Now get out. Both of you. And bring your papers." The man stepped back a few meters.

As René reached for the glove box, he whispered to the side. "Use your gun if you have to. We can't let them take us."

"W—what?"

"Your gun." With the papers in one hand, René reached for the door with the other. "Be ready!"

Beside Dylan's window now stood another man, a young, freckle-faced squaddie who couldn't be more than eighteen. Dressed in jeans and a black shirt, he waved his gun for Dylan to get out. Like his leader, he wore a black armband.

His heart beating fast, Dylan grasped the cold metal handle. How were they going to get out of this? And what about Margot? She and the refugees in back had no idea what was happening.

Outside, the blond-haired youth directed Dylan to join René where the squad leader was examining their forged documents. The squaddie flipped through the sheaf of papers, frowned, then waved down the street. "You are not authorized to be at that market. Why are you here?"

"We must have made a wrong turn somewhere. Hard to see signs in the rain. Isn't this Rue Marcel?"

"It is not. What's in the van?"

"It's empty." René wiped moisture from his forehead. "We haven't picked up our load yet."

The squaddie leader narrowed his eyes and handed back the papers. "We'll see about that. Open the back."

René threw the documents through the open window. With slow steps, he led them to the rear. These men must be new at this as they hadn't checked René or Dylan for weapons. As they walked, the heavy metal inside Dylan's pocket bounced against his thigh. Would he have to use it? Could he pull the trigger?

Twenty meters away, two other squaddies left the Citroen and stood waiting. Both were young and armed with pistols, and they, too, wore no uniforms, only armbands.

"Open it!" The leader waved his weapon at the van and backed away. He directed his youthful partner to the opposite side of the vehicle.

René grabbed the handle but paused. "When I open it," he whispered, "step away from the door, pull out your gun, and shoot the one beside you."

"Shoot him?" Blood rushed to Dylan's head. He wasn't ready to take a life. Was this really happening?

"We can't be taken. Do it!" René placed a hand on the knob and yanked. The door hadn't even opened before he spun to the side, weapon in hand, and fired. The shot thundered off the two-story buildings. The squad leader crumpled to the pavement.

At the same time, Dylan jerked the pistol from his pocket, whirled in the opposite direction, and aimed.

But the freckle-faced squaddie stood frozen, his weapon shaking and pointed at Dylan. "Don't," came the youth's quiet complaint. "Please, don't."

"Let us go." Dylan sucked in breath and held his pistol steady. "And no one will get hurt."

His eyes wild with fear, the young man glanced toward the Citroen. Then he began backing away.

Momentarily stunned after their leader was shot, the other two squaddies now headed toward the van, guns in hand.

To add to the confusion, the four men among their refugees now burst out of the van, crossed behind Dylan, and fled to opposite sides of the street.

"Come back," shouted Margot, poking her head out the back.

"Don't leave us," added Danielle beside her.

But the men kept running—two to the left, the other two to the right.

The young squaddie beside Dylan had already disappeared into an alley, but his two companions at the van were still coming on, undeterred. They aimed their weapons at the fleeing refugees. "Stop, or we'll shoot," said the stockier of the two.

But the men kept running.

Two shots rang out, reverberated off the buildings, and Dylan jumped. Both hit their targets, and the two refugees on the left fell to the pavement.

Even as this was happening, René dropped to a knee and fired back. The stockier squaddie clutched his chest and collapsed. René's second shot missed as the second man fled to the cover of the Citroen.

"Everyone!" shouted René, "into the van!"

Margot, Danielle, and Monique shut the door, and Dylan whirled. The remaining two refugees and the youthful squaddie had disappeared into the alleys. The mob had also gone.

His hands sweating, his temples pounding, Dylan plopped into the front seat and slammed the door shut.

"We can't go after them." René started the engine. "They shouldn't have fled."

He backed the van up then raced for the Citroen blocking their exit from the alley.

René picked up speed and aimed for the trunk. Partially shielded by the car, the last squaddie spread his feet, aimed at the van's windshield, and fired.

Dylan ducked to the side as a circle of glass exploded onto the seat beside him. The bullet missed both René and Dylan. But it punched a hole in the back of the van.

He sucked in air. Had it hit anyone back there?

The van closed the gap to the Citroën's trunk, and Dylan braced for impact.

Metal crashed against metal, and he lurched forward. An airbag exploded in his face. The collision crushed the Citroën's back end and shoved it aside. With a back tire bent inward, the vehicle wouldn't be following anyone any time soon.

The van raced down the street. At the intersection, René headed north and slowed down.

Two kilometers later, they pulled into a side street. Like other city thoroughfares, graffiti covered the walls of some buildings and garbage lay in abandoned piles. René kept going and parked in front of a Renault sedan. For one moment, Dylan closed his eyes and breathed deeply. He exchanged a worried glance with René. They left the front and circled to the back in a pouring rain.

When they opened the door, Danielle was holding Monique's limp body in her arms. Tears streamed down her cheeks, and blood covered her coat.

"She's gone." Danielle rocked her friend back and forth. "It hit her."

Eyes brimming with tears, Margot laid a hand on Danielle's shoulder.

"I'm sorry," said René. "But we have to change vehicles and get out of here." He lifted the lid of a floor compartment, removed some tools, and walked to the Renault. He broke into the car, wired the ignition, and they all moved to the sedan.

"What about Monique?" asked Danielle. "We can't just leave her here."

"I'm sorry, but we'll have to put her in the trunk and bury her when we get to the farm. It's the best we can do for now."

Danielle nodded, and minutes later, with Monique's body hidden in the trunk, they headed north on the A51 in the Renault.

Once on the road, Margot tried to comfort a shaken Danielle in the back seat. While René lit another cigarette, Dylan sat beside him in silence.

The rain beat down out of an ashen sky, and the wipers slapped.

"If the men hadn't run," whispered René, "we could have saved them."

Shaken and exhausted, Dylan could only nod. A storm hovered over the world, and only God knew when and how it would end.

CHAPTER 23

THE SITUATION ROOM

Jerusalem, Israel – August, Year 2

As Chelsea escorted Grady from his room on the seventh floor to the restricted area on the fourteenth, he pondered what he'd seen on his morning walks. Yesterday and today, UI troop trucks and tanks had rolled down several main arteries. The sky was also full of jets, and people were in the streets, talking and gesturing among themselves. No one knew what was happening, but Israelis were clearly upset.

He followed Chelsea into what she called the situation room. Newly remodeled and wired, the room occupied half the floor of the building. The Imperator met them and took them to the far back where a wide dais held a master electronics control center and a handful of plush seats. Maybe here, he'd learn what was going on.

Below the dais, facing the wall screens in a wide arc and filling the room's expanse, were seats with computer consoles for maybe fifty technicians, aides, and military personnel. On the opposite wall hung a bank of twenty large monitors with twice that number of smaller monitors beneath.

Chelsea motioned Grady to look behind him to six, glass-enclosed observation rooms. "The ambassadors from Africa, Australia, Canada, India, Japan, and South America."

He nodded. He'd already met several.

Davato laid a hand on his shoulder. "Today we are fulfilling two important functions, and I want you, Grady, to see what goes on up here on the floor. While I attend to business, I'll let Marcia guide you through what's happening." He waved them to seats beside a smiling, black-haired, attractive Marcia. A few meters away, Davato conversed with General Eric Hofmann as the two leaders focused on the rightmost screens.

"Hi, Chelsea." Marcia shook hands with her, and the woman turned to Grady. "You must be the US ambassador?" After a handshake with him, she pointed to the screens on the left. "Those two monitors are tracking the launch of new Worldnet satellites to replace the ones the Americans and Chinese destroyed."

"Where are they located?" asked Grady.

"It's no secret. The first is the Kourou site in French Guiana. The second is our newly constructed launchpad on Tenerife in the Canary Islands. You're familiar with that, aren't you, Chelsea?"

"I am. I've been in meetings overseeing its construction."

"Have a seat." Marcia nodded to consoles before each. "With the headphones, you'll be able to hear me and the launch technicians."

Marcia's voice now came through the headphones. "The second thing we're monitoring today is the possession of Israel. This is the second day of the takeover."

Grady shot a startled look to Chelsea.

"It's been in the works for some time." Chelsea spoke through a microphone attached to the headphones. Apparently, the three of them were connected.

"The large screens on your right," added Marcia, "show the final offloading of our tanks, troops, and mechanized vehicles at airports at Ben Gurion in Tel Aviv, at Haifa, Bar Yehuda Airfield, and at Kiryat Shmona Airport in the north. The occupation started yesterday morning, and what you're seeing now is the mopping-up operation."

"You're taking over the country?"

"That's right. Israel is now part of the Unitum Imperium, and Davato needs to defend it from hostile forces on the border."

"And that screen on the far right?"

On the far-right screen labeled Knesset, Givat Ram, UI troops were marching down the aisles of a large meeting room. He couldn't hear the sound, but members were leaving their seats and shouting at the soldiers. When one elderly white-haired man walked to the center aisle and extended his arms to block their progress, two of the intruders knocked him aside with their rifle butts. He sprawled over a chair as other delegates rushed to his side.

"We're taking over the Knesset, the Israeli governing body." Marcia waved at the screens. "It's all for the best."

"What's going to happen to them?"

"If they don't resist—nothing."

"And if they resist?"

She shrugged.

The soldiers, with pistols and rifles drawn, cleared the meeting room, and the screen went blank.

Most of the pictures of the invasion showed a completed takeover of military and civilian centers of power—except for a number of screens in the middle. Early yesterday, near the Syrian border, fighting had apparently broken out between UI troops and three rogue companies belonging to Israeli Ground Forces of the Northern Command's Ninety-first Division. The IDF troops refused to give ground, and the conflict continued into today. Marcia explained that more screens had been devoted to the battle until half the wall showed the difficulty the UI troops were having against the highly trained IDF. But the Israeli Air Force had been disabled, and with no air support, the IDF troops were losing.

"I'm told we'll win that battle by the end of the day." Marcia waved at the fighting.

For the next hours, the room was abuzz with chatter, lights, and commands from stocky white-haired General Hofmann and from Davato as the two managed the last of the Israeli takeover. All the high wall monitors were active, and all the consoles in the room below were manned.

Then came a voice from the headphones, "Five minutes to launch," and Grady focused on the leftmost screens.

"There's a lot happening today," came Marcia's voice through the headphones.

Three rockets sat on the pads at Kourou with two more at Tenerife. Plumes of vapor poured from the bottom of each glistening cylinder and trailed away in the breeze. Marcia reached down, punched a button, and Grady could hear the sound of the countdowns from each location. The countdowns were so synchronized, they echoed.

"Five . . . four . . . three . . . two . . . one." Thunder filled his ears. Exhaust clouded the screens. All five rockets lifted off.

Soon all he could see were the white contrails and small black dots rising to the heavens. Grady grinned at Chelsea and removed his head-phones.

She returned his smile, and Marcia turned off the sound.

A smiling Davato left General Hofmann, who was speaking to a tank commander in one of the screens. "They don't need me here anymore. The launch was perfect. And the occupation is in the final mopping-up stages. Grady, do you have any questions?"

"You've taken over Israel?"

Davato's smile faded. "That's right. If the headquarters of the Unitum Imperium is to be in Jerusalem, I must be able to defend it properly. I hope you'll report everything you've seen here today to your President."

"Yes, sir. I will."

"Then you're dismissed." He started to turn away then whirled. "I invite you both to accompany me the day after tomorrow to Temple Mount to hear an important message from the Prophet. Will you attend?"

Both Grady and Chelsea nodded. It was unwise to say no to the most powerful man in the world.

CHAPTER 24

DECISION IN TEHRAN

Ezekiel 38:3–6, 8–9 (NASB): *"Behold, I am against you, O Gog, prince of Rosh, Meshech and Tubal. "I will turn you about and put hooks into your jaws, and I will bring you out, and all your army, horses and horsemen, all of them splendidly attired, a great company with buckler and shield, all of them wielding swords; Persia, Ethiopia and Put with them, all of them with shield and helmet; Gomer with all its troops; Beth-togarmah from the remote parts of the north with all its troops—many peoples with you. . . . in the latter years you will come into the land that is restored from the sword, whose inhabitants have been gathered from many nations to the mountains of Israel which had been a continual waste; but its people were brought out from the nations, and they are living securely, all of them. You will go up, you will come like a storm; you will be like a cloud covering the land, you and all your troops, and many peoples with you."* (Note: Please refer to the Scripture References section for translations of the above ancient place names to modern locations.)

Tehran, Iran – August, Year 2

Jaleel Hasani stepped out of his air-conditioned Mercedes and glanced at the distant snow-capped mountains shimmering in the Tehran heat. After only five steps toward the Office of the Supreme Leader—also Muhammad Najafi's home—he was already tasting the dust of the air and wiping his brow. For a man of his bulk, living in Tehran in August was unbearable. He much preferred the milder climate of his mansion on a forested hill overlooking the Caspian Sea. But his moderate views made him popular with the people, and when half the parliament urged him to run for president two years ago, he'd won. Now he could only get away a few times a year.

He wasn't looking forward to today's meeting with Supreme Leader

Muhammad Najafi, the Grand Ayatollah. Najafi had insisted they must listen together to the worldwide broadcast from Jerusalem. But Najafi clearly disapproved of his president, and whenever Jaleel was in Najafi's presence, he wanted to be elsewhere.

Perhaps the Supreme Leader's dislike stemmed from the parliamentary proposals Jaleel often brought to him—nearly all of which Najafi ordered his parliament to shoot down. Or maybe it was the Western clothing he often sported? Or his fondness for Western food? Or perhaps Najafi had heard the rumors that, behind the walls of Jaleel's expansive villa, he drank French wine? Or was it because of Jaleel's firm view that Iran should spend more of its wealth on schools and hospitals and less on the nuclear program sucking the life from the economy?

The servant Perviz met him at the door, leading him into a cool interior, down a hall, under an arch, and into a library.

"Welcome, Muhammad Hasani." Najafi rose from his chair and leaned on his cane. Years ago, an assassination attempt by the previous regime had injured his right leg. "Hasani, would you take a glass of khakshir?"

"Delighted to, Supreme Leader." Jaleel hated the taste of flixweed seeds mixed with honey—Najafi's favorite drink—but he'd do whatever it took to please his host.

The Supreme Leader waved to his servant, who poured a second glass. "Please, when we are alone, call me simply Muhammad Najafi."

"Of course, Muhammad Najafi. Forgive me. I forgot."

"The broadcast should begin soon. Perviz, would you turn on the set?"

The dark-haired servant, dressed all in white, brought the red drink to Jaleel then turned on the television. The flat-screen Samsung occupied most of the far wall. As Perviz found the new worldwide Worldnet channel, Jaleel sipped the sugary sweet drink and tried to keep from grimacing.

"This new man controlling the West, this Davato, has me greatly concerned." Najafi pounded his cane twice on the complex Persian rug that mixed a hundred shades of blue.

"I agree." There weren't many areas on which the two of them agreed, but this was one. "He is a danger to all Islam."

Najafi nodded in solemn agreement. "This so-called Prophet concerns me even more."

"Again, Muhammad Najafi, your words are pearls of wisdom." Maybe he was laying it on too thick. But how difficult it was to walk a narrow path when one false step could mean disaster. One must avoid at all costs the unintentional insult, the remark in poor taste, the slightest hint of heresy, anything that could lead to a parting and possible fall from grace. How many of Jaleel's friends had disappeared overnight after the Supreme Leader spoke a quiet word to the Revolutionary Guard?

He shivered. To hide his discomfort, he took another sip of khakshir.

"Our friends in Turkey are also displeased with what they are hearing from the Zionist capital."

"As you have said many times."

"It is one reason why I invited you here today. After the broadcast, there will be a conference call to which I have invited the leaders of four nations."

Jaleel's eyes widened. This was unexpected. "To what purpose?"

"To determine if a united course of action is necessary to cut the roots out from under this upstart Davato and his Zionist friends. But it's starting. Let's listen."

As Jaleel tried to wrap his head around the Supreme Leader's startling announcement, Perviz turned up the volume.

On the screen, Jerusalem's Temple Mount overflowed with bare-headed women and skull-capped Jewish men. Up on the stage, the silver-haired Davato and the Prophet sat together with a blonde-haired, bare-headed woman. Jaleel had to admit that the sight of a beautiful Western woman without a hijab brought heat to his loins.

Davato stepped to the podium, made some introductory remarks—in the universal language of English—then introduced the man known as Sebastien the Prophet. Wearing a long white robe as if he were some kind of religious figure, he took the stage. But everything Najafi's spies had learned of him elicited nothing but disgust. Besides being a homosexual, he promoted every sin against which Muhammad warned.

"Peoples of the Unitum Imperium, and all those listening in from countries allied with us, I greet you." Yet, from a distance, Sebastien presented an attractive, almost mesmerizing appearance. And who could argue that the man's words didn't drip like honey into the ears? Jaleel shook his head. No wonder they called him the Prophet. He could be reading a recipe for kuku sabzi and convince the world it was the wisdom of Allah.

"We are gathered here today," continued Sebastien, "to speak of what is true and what is not, to cast off old, false dogmas and beliefs and embrace what is new and right and true. I speak, of course, of religion."

Jaleel shifted in his seat. Beside him, Najafi gripped the sides of his chair and stared at the screen. Would they be able to get through this without one of Najafi's legendary tirades? Unlikely.

"When the UFOs took from us the Christians and all our young children, where was the one they call God? If he truly was the benevolent Being some suggest, why didn't he send one of his supposed prophets to warn us that we were so damaging the planet that the aliens were about to act? Was he then our protector, the one to whom we owe worship? We do not mourn the loss of the Christians, the ones living apart from us, always vibrating to a different rhythm. But we do grieve the loss of our children and the disaster the aliens thrust upon us since the Great Catastrophe. If he were truly all-powerful, why would God allow such a disaster?

"My friends, the UFOs took our children, and God allowed it!" He stepped back and paused for breath.

"Since the Great Catastrophe, we have had nothing but disorder, lawbreaking, and violence. My friends, what the one called God did was nothing but an act of war against the whole of the human race. Once, they called this fiend God, but they also called him Allah and Krishna and many other things. Whatever he was called, he's a fraud, a deceiver, and a murderer. A better name might be Enemy."

Now the Temple Square crowd appeared restless, unsure of what they were hearing. Najafi, too, slammed a fist on the arm of his chair and turned a fierce gaze on his guest. "This is an outrage."

"I agree." His forehead warming with anger, Jaleel again focused on the television and the Prophet.

"Lately, it has come to our attention that the group we thought had been removed from our presence has reemerged. And now, they are working to return us to the ways of old, to the worship of this fiend, our Enemy. In so doing, they strive to undermine all the Imperator is doing, working against all his plans to bring peace, security, and stability to the world. Like a metastasizing cancer, their presence spreads through every country, city, and village. Their work is secretive, insidious, and destructive, and they oppose everything we do."

From the nodding heads and approving shouts on the screen, the crowd portrayed its agreement.

"So today, we are accelerating our plan to root out and gather up these criminal miscreants trying to undo all that the Imperator wants to accomplish on your behalf. We do this to protect you, the people, and return the world to prosperity. So we humbly ask your help by reporting any suspected Christian to the nearest office of the Central Security Agency. Help us find and root out the traitors among us. Only then will we be free of the poison they promote."

Najafi nodded. "That, at least, I can agree with."

Sebastien paused to sip from a bottle before looking up again. "But that is only one of the reasons for this broadcast. Now, I will tell you the second.

"We have mentioned the false religions, dogmas, and creeds that formerly straitjacketed us. We have stated our wish to free mankind from the chains that bound us to all the perverted, rigid, inflexible rules and creeds of the past. Well, today, we offer an alternative, a new religion to unite the world, one that will free mankind's inner self for the greatness that lies within, one that will require from you, not sacrifice, but participation in endless worlds of pleasure.

"Yes, my friends, today we announce a new and worthy object of worship. You know her intimately, for it is upon her we all live. We owe her the very breath that fills our lungs, the food that satisfies our stomachs, and the water that cleanses our bodies. Unlike past deities, she will not make impossible demands or throw a chain of legalistic bondage upon your soul. I speak, of course, of the Earth. Yes, it is to her—the pleasure-loving, benevolent spirit of the planet—that we owe our true worship, not to the false demigods and deities of the past, those who want to strip from us all joy.

"Too long have we ignored her, taken her for granted, and abused her climate. And when everyone finally turns to her, she will revel in our free and unbounded worship, give us abundant crops to eat, clean water to drink, and endless bounty to embrace. And this I promise you: When you become a follower of Gaia—for that is one of her names—you will free your spirit and experience true happiness."

Across the room, Najafi's face was turning red. Was he about to explode? Jaleel held his breath and faced the screen.

"Gaia is a deity, not of rules and regulations, but a spirit of the senses. Under Gaia, you will throw off all restraints, immerse yourself in endless pleasures, and find true inner peace. And when everyone removes the shackles from their inner being, who knows what wondrous things the human race can accomplish?"

As the crowd roared its approval, Sebastien grinned and grabbed the podium.

"But some of you might require more than a spiritual reward. So to assist in the start of this venture, we are offering everyone a one-time cash credit for signing up. On your screens, you will find local websites and phone numbers for the Church of Gaia, advising how and where you can join this new faith. We are building earth temples in a city near you where earth priests and priestesses will fulfill your every desire. I hope you will participate. Imagine how it will be when all peoples everywhere are united in sensual worship. What a great day that will be." He raised one hand high. "Praise and glory to Gaia, the mother of us all, for only when the entire world gives her the worship she deserves, will we be one people." As the crowd thundered its applause, he retreated, the dignitaries left the stage, and the broadcast ended.

Beside Jaleel, the Supreme Leader was shaking. Red-faced and breathing fast, Najafi hobbled across the room, stopped, and rapped his cane hard on the floor. Whirling, he returned to his seat and glared at his guest.

Shaking his head, Jaleel scowled at the screen. This Prophet was a true heretic, an enemy of Allah if ever there was. And yet . . . he had become the religious mouthpiece of the Unitum Imperium, now the most powerful country in the world. Something had to be done. But what?

Najafi breathed deeply. His next words were sharp, directed at Perviz. "Set up the call. Now!"

"Yes, Supreme Leader." Perviz manned a laptop in the corner.

Jaleel tensed, waiting for a conference call that could decide the fate of nations.

* * *

ONE BY ONE, THE SCREEN divided into four squares, and four prominent leaders joined the call. Jaleel recognized . . .

Dour-faced President Suleyman Aydin of Turkey, wearing a black business suit and a tie bearing the crescent moon of Islam.

Kaftan-headed Omid Noor, leader of the Sayf Alsharaf, the Afghani terrorist group in the process of uniting the disparate hill fighters of Afghanistan, Uzbekistan, Turkmenistan, Kyrgyzstan, and Kazakhstan.

Uniformed General Hassan Al-Kalifa. After his successful coup, he became the self-declared high caliph of Sudan.

And Ahmed Umar, chairman of the presidential council of Libya.

"Now that we are all present"—Najafi switched to Arabic, the language of Islam—"has everyone heard the words of the infidel prophet?"

As each man nodded, their faces set into lines of anger and resolve.

"We have discussed the problem of this upstart Davato before. And a possible solution." Najafi's words were quiet, but his tone was sharp as a dagger. Beneath that restrained visage was there a volcano ready to erupt? "But now we hear—straight from his Prophet, his official mouthpiece—plans of a great heresy they intend to inflict upon the world. If anyone doubted our course of action before today, this broadcast should sweep aside all reservations." As though trying to calm his inner spirit, Najafi drew in a long breath.

"But before I ask your opinion, I have some news to relate. Some of you have questioned the strength of Davato's new army. Only yesterday, our spies reported that, when the Unitum Imperium forces invaded Israel, the UI army was weak and ill prepared. It appears that their army is a paper tiger."

Joyous shouts erupted. Hands clapped. Dour faces now smiled.

"Given that news," continued Najafi, "how should we respond to today's broadcast? General, you may start."

Sun-wrinkled and stony-faced, General Al-Kalifa of Sudan spoke. "We must act decisively and soon. Through back channels, we have heard that the UI intends to impose heavy tariffs on any nation outside their orbit that hasn't signed their Treaty of Intent and that doesn't promote this new 'earth religion', as they call it. Our trade across UI borders has already plummeted. If we don't stop them soon, they'll ruin us. I'm concerned about the UI nuclear force, yes, but with Allah's help, we will prevail. Sudan will commit as many troops and tanks as are needed."

Nodding his approval, the Supreme Leader turned to the chairman of the Libyan presidential council, wearing khaki fatigues. "Ahmed, what do you say?"

"I agree," said Ahmed Umar. "This man Davato is aligned with the Zionists, and he will use Israel to destroy the rest of us. If we strike quickly from all directions, we will be so close to him, of what use will their nukes be? No matter the cost, we must stop him now. We are with you."

"What about you, Amid Noor?" Najafi rapped his cane on the floor. "Will the Sayf Alsharaf lend its fighters to the final demise of Israel and this offense against all Islam?"

In Amid Noor's cold eyes and weatherworn skin, Jaleel could almost see the desert and a hand raising an American-made M16, with thousands of hardened warriors behind him. "Nothing on this earth would give the Sayf Alsharaf greater pleasure than to see the scum of Zion and this man Davato driven into the sea. When the Americans abandoned our country with their tails between their legs, they left us with eighty-five billion dollars' worth of high-tech weaponry. Now that the Great Satan, America, has been castrated, we will use their very weapons against the Zionists and its new leader. To die in battle is to gain paradise. We are with you."

"That leaves Turkey." Najafi fidgeted with his cane and shot a sideways glance to Jaleel. "What are your thoughts, Suleyman?"

Looking stiff in his black business suit and tie, Suleyman Aydin nodded. In previous meetings, he'd been cautious, expressing deep reservations about fighting a nuclear-armed Israel. But Turkey had the only real navy, the largest army, the most tanks, and a modern air force. It was also closest to the enemy. After leaving NATO, the country had flirted with sharia law, driven out Western preachers, professors, and advisors, and moved ever closer to its Islamic roots.

Without Turkey, there would be no invasion of Israel.

Aydin sat back in his chair and straightened his back. "Turkey will not—*cannot*—abide what the Unitum Imperium is doing. Since we refused to sign their treaty of infidels, our trade with the rest of the world has plummeted, and our economy has suffered. On top of that affront, the Imperator and his Prophet, as the pretender calls himself, today piled on the worst insult of all—spitting in the face of Allah." He leaned forward and slammed a fist on the table before him. "But I am concerned about the formidable nuclear arsenal Davato can use against us."

"But, Suleyman," continued the Supreme Leader, "what better time to strike the infidels than now? To Ahmed's point, if we attack from all directions at once, what can they do? If they use their nukes, they will surround themselves with a nuclear cloud and poison their own country and their own soldiers."

Suleyman's hands rubbed his temples. "I don't know."

"Without you, my friend," again, Najafi spoke with quiet strength, "the opportunity passes, and the Zionists win again. This is our chance to fulfill our greatest desire—the total annihilation of Israel. In this matter, should we not put our trust in Allah?"

Suleyman pushed away from his table, stood, and walked to the end of the room with his hands behind his back. The screen showed his head dipping as though he were praying. Jaleel held his breath. Everything now depended on this man. Then, as slowly as he'd left, Suleyman returned to the monitor and his seat before the camera. "You are right, Supreme Leader. We must cast our fears on Allah and put our trust in him. Yes, I will commit Turkey to the invasion and final destruction of Israel and this upstart Davato."

Najafi smiled and sat back. "This is good, my friends, swimmingly good."

Jaleel cringed at the Supreme Leader's use of language.

The Supreme Leader cast his gaze on each of the monitors. "I knew all of you would make the right decision. And now I have one more piece of good news I have been saving for last. I have spoken with President Alexander Petrov of Russia. For reasons having nothing to do with our faith, Russia is willing to join us. Indeed, it was President Petrov who approached me and suggested just such an alliance. He wants to lead the venture, and I am willing to let him think that. They have designs on Eastern Europe, and again, I, for one, am willing to give the Unitum Imperium a formidable adversary on its eastern border. Knowing Russian nukes could respond in kind to any nuclear defense of Israel might give Davato pause before entering into any nuclear exchange."

All the screens were silent. Then they all broke out in unanimous, cacophonous agreement. This was the best news yet. With a great power like Russia on their side, how could they lose?

Jaleel should have joined them and shouted for joy. But they were going to war against a nuclear-armed Unitum Imperium and the most powerful world leader since Hitler. Yes, they now had Russia on their side. Yes, Russia had a formidable arsenal of nuclear weapons. Yet an unreasoning fear gripped him, and a vision of death by fire flashed before his eyes. A shudder began in his shoulders, crawled up his back, and rippled down his arms and into his legs.

The men said their goodbyes, the screens darkened, and the Supreme Leader led Jaleel to the front door. Then he laid a hand on his guest's shoulder. "You have been unusually quiet, my friend. After all you have heard today, what is your opinion of our venture?"

Jaleel took a deep breath, faced his superior, and swallowed. "Do not take offense, Muhammad Najafi, but after everyone spoke, I had a terrifying premonition."

As if Jaleel were talking in jest, one corner of Najafi's mouth lifted. "Jaleel, have you now become a seer?"

"Perhaps it was nothing. But for one brief instant, I saw this house in flames. I also saw fire raining down from the sky, killing a vast number of our soldiers and leaving them dead on the battlefield."

The Supreme Leader froze, his hand dropped, and his eyes bored into Jaleel so long, the president shuddered. "My advice to you, Hasani"—his voice was hard and cold—"is to forget you ever said that. Now I suggest you go home and ponder your shortcomings."

As Jaleel Hasani entered the dust and blistering heat of a Tehran afternoon, the door slammed behind him.

CHAPTER 25
THE PARIS RESTAURANT

Paris, France – August, Year 2

As Dylan crossed the street, the 9mm Glock 17 pistol René had given him bounced against his thigh. Two stories up, above and behind him, René waited in an observation room overlooking the square.

Static crackled in Dylan's earpiece, and he stopped to adjust it. As instructed, he held up his cell phone then spoke for the benefit of the microphone pinned beneath his shirt collar. "Are you sure she won't see it?"

"It's behind your ear," answered René. "Your hair covers it. You'll be okay. Now tell me again the phrase to use if you get in trouble."

"It was raining when I called you."

"Right. I think you're ready."

Speaking into a dead phone felt odd, but René didn't want anyone to see him talking to himself.

"It's almost time. You should go."

Dylan slipped the phone into his pocket and entered the square. Last week, Bettino had called to relay the message that Chelsea would meet him at La Dernière Bouchée at eighteen hundred hours the following Friday evening in Paris. René and Pasqual were worried it was a trap, but Dylan must meet his sister.

René now sat before a hotel room's open window with binoculars and a Ruger 10/22 Takedown rifle with scope and tripod. When disassembled, the rifle fit inside a backpack, all the better for discreet travel and for carrying through the lobby of a third-rate hotel.

Before he and Pasqual had left for the street, René had opened the window and began setting up. "Are you going to shoot somebody?" Dylan had asked.

"This is only a precaution. We can't let them take you. Under duress, you could give them the location of the farm. That would endanger everyone."

Standing beside Dylan, his thick black hair falling into his eyes, Pasqual was frowning at a second 9mm Glock René had given him.

Dylan continued the argument. "Really, René, is this necessary? Chelsea won't lead me into a trap."

"Even if you trust her, she may not know what the people around her are doing."

Pasqual was still pondering his weapon, and Dylan challenged him. "How about you, Pasqual? Are you prepared to shoot someone?"

"I . . ." He'd swallowed hard and shook his hair away from his eyes— or was he shaking away the possibility? "I guess so."

René's scowl speared them both. "We've been through this before. Understand, you two—this is not a game. These people want to capture you, maybe torture you until you spill whatever you know, and then they will most certainly kill you. Your pistols are there to protect Dylan in case he gets in trouble. Those weapons could save his life and everyone else's at the farm." He slapped the gunstock in place with a click. "I'm working with two novices. I just hope you don't get one of us killed."

Pasqual pocketed the gun and wiped his brow. "We'll do our best." Then he left the room.

Ten minutes later, Dylan followed him out the door.

August heat now shimmered over the square. A few businessmen and women passed in a hurry. Dry weeds struggled to grow in the central fountain's empty pool. A statue of some long-forgotten officer, his stone sword extended, sat a rearing horse. One couple, holding hands, huddled together on the rim, a bottle of wine and glasses between them. As he crossed the square and approached the canopied outdoor tables, pigeons waddled away. Out of nowhere, two rats scurried across the cobbles, and he waited until they passed.

Odd. That was the second time today he'd seen rats out in broad daylight.

At the far ends of the only two restaurants still open, guards with machine guns lounged. The other six restaurants lining the square had long since closed their doors.

Only four tables were occupied. Men in business suits—probably with high connections to the Unitum Imperium—sat at two of them. A woman dripping with expensive jewelry and a richly dressed man occupied another. The last table held four young men wearing the black armbands of a Truth Squad.

Shuddering, Dylan found a seat far from the squaddies on the edge of the square where René could see him from the window. He checked his watch—17:55.

About seventy meters away, Pasqual pretended to read his phone as he sat with a cup of coffee at the only other open café.

"Monsieur?" A frowning black-haired waiter appeared at his side. "To sit here, one must order something."

"Oui. Bring me a glass of your house red. My sister is coming. We'll order dinner later."

The waiter's frown morphed into a wide smile. He bowed and left.

Still high in the west, the sun beat down on Dylan's back. He glanced up and down the nearly empty square. What if she couldn't get away? But if someone were watching—like the squaddies—he mustn't appear nervous.

From across the square, a man shuffled toward him. As he approached Dylan's table, the waiter brought Dylan's wine then hurried to intercept the man. "What do you want, Gascon?"

"A hunk of bread, if you please." The man lifted pleading eyes, and now the thinness of his face, the flesh clinging to his skull, the stringbean arms, were visible. "Any scrap of leftovers. Anything to feed my children and my wife."

"No, monsieur." The waiter blocked his way with arms crossed. "We want no trouble from you today. You've been here before, Gascon. This establishment is only for those who can pay."

"Just a few scraps?" He held out his hand. "The leavings, the garbage you're going to throw out? Please?"

"You know we must sell the leftovers. And now you must leave. Look! The security men are coming to evict you. Again."

Dylan glanced aside as the restaurant guards approached.

The man identified as Gascon stood his ground and glared. "You sell the garbage, the leftovers, and you cannot even give them to a starving man and his family. Y–you'll be sorry for this." He shook his fist, whirled, and left.

After the man departed, the waiter shrugged at Dylan. "We get them all the time. What can one do?"

The waiter departed, and Dylan shuddered. Was this how it was now in the cities? Starving people begging for scraps of food and being turned away because the restaurants even sold their garbage? He shook his head, sipped his wine, and pulled out his phone. Hard as it was, he must appear like he belonged here.

He found a news site and began reading.

A City Rises in the Desert.

For years, bulldozers, construction workers, and cranes have been airlifted to a site south of Baghdad where they have been working day and night to raise a city from the sand. "Not only will it be a center of worldwide commerce," said a Worldnet spokeswoman, "it will be the world's premier playground. New Babylon will have more casinos, spas, shows, pools, video gaming venues, bars, and restaurants than Paris, London, Monte Carlo, Las Vegas, and New York combined. Our massive Earth Temple will dominate the city center. There visitors will be able to worship Gaia with a willing priest or priestess of their choice. Each worship room will be equipped with a luxurious bed, couch, bar, and hot tub. No worshiper will leave the temple unsatisfied."

When this reporter asked when New Babylon would be open for business, she was told . . .

"Dylan?"

He raised his glance at the familiar voice. Chelsea stood before him, wearing jeans, a sweatshirt, and tennis shoes—the way she used to dress before she left home for New York.

"You're looking good, sis. You've dropped the uppity business attire."

"Just like the old days, huh? I told my attendants I wanted to stroll through the city on my own terms, like I did before I became involved in"—she waved a hand—"all of this."

"What is *this*?" He waved his hands in imitation of hers.

She shot a glance to the squaddies in the far corner and lowered her voice. "Everything having to do with Davato and the Unitum Imperium."

Had she changed? Gone was the haughty air she'd brought to their last meeting. In its place, he sensed weariness, resignation, and maybe . . . fear?

"Were you followed?"

"I don't think so." She pulled out a chair and sat. "I didn't want to get you in trouble."

The waiter appeared with two sheets of glossy paper—menus?—plus a wine list. "I regret, monsieur, that our food selection is diminished. And everything so dear." He waved his hands in apology. "The famine, you understand?"

Dylan scanned the menu and swallowed. A hundred fifty euros for a bread and cheese plate? Four hundred and fifty euros for boeuf bourguignon? Three hundred ninety for coq au vin? The menu contained just five choices. Only the wine was reasonably priced. He couldn't afford this. But when would he ever be able to sit down with Chelsea like this again? He lifted his gaze. "I can only pay for two bread and cheese plates. I'm sorry."

"Get whatever you want. I'm buying."

"Are you sure?"

She nodded, blonde hair slipping over her shoulders, and said to the waiter. "I'll have the boeuf bourguignon. And bring a carafe of your best red wine for both of us."

Dylan swallowed and ordered the same. At the farm, they relied on whatever they grew, and in the car on the way up from the Luberon, they'd eaten sandwiches. He knew the famine was severe, but this . . . ?

Beaming and bowing, the waiter left.

Alone again, Dylan faced his sister. "How are you, Chelsea? I've missed you."

She reached across the table and grasped his hands. "It is so good to . . . to see you, Dylan."

"You don't know how much I've worried about you. I saw you on TV a few times. You're in the big leagues now. But how are you?"

She pulled her hands back and flattened them against the tabletop. "I wish things were different. This job I have—I'm in over my head. I'm hearing, seeing things that scare me."

"What kind of things?"

The waiter brought them the carafe of wine, and she fell silent. After he'd poured a glass for each, Dylan repeated the question.

"I–I can't say. The world is changing. He's changing it. Everything has become so strange and surreal that I . . ."

"That you what?" His heart raced. His carefree, headstrong sister was gripped with fear.

She grabbed her wine glass and sipped. "Have you heard from Caleb?"

He twisted his glass between his hands. "I don't hold out much hope for Caleb and Tanya. They say a couple of nukes devastated Chicago. If he was still there . . ."

"I heard." She closed her eyes then opened them again.

Were those tears forming at the edges of those blue orbs? She seemed so vulnerable today, so unlike the last time they met, and this realization nearly brought tears to his eyes. Had he just said the wrong thing? Had he just killed whatever hope she had that Caleb might be still alive? He wanted to kick himself in the leg.

"Right"—with too much force, she waved her hands again—"just another casualty of . . . all *this*!"

Neither said anything, and he waited for her to calm down. But she'd said something important, and he needed to get to the bottom of it. "You were talking about things getting surreal?"

As if to brush off the question, she shook her head. "I'm working with another American—Grady Wilson. He's nice, and he's the US ambassador. And a most unlikely ambassador he is. He was a navy lieutenant on a destroyer the Chinese sank, and after they rescued him, the President appointed him to the post. Few of the cabinet, the Congress, or the executive branch survived, and the President was desperate to find anyone he could trust. So Grady got the post. And we seem to be hitting it off."

She was talking too fast. She sipped her wine and set it back down again.

"You're changing the subject. But that's great. You've met someone. I'm glad."

"Thanks." Again, she pressed her palms to the tabletop. "Dylan, I'm worried for you."

"In what way? You're the one who seems to be walking a tightrope."

She brushed aside a lock of blonde hair and sent a furtive glance toward the squaddie table. "They're serious about finding Christians and putting them away. If you're still involved with some underground organization, you're in great danger. You have to stop whatever it is you're doing."

"I can't do that, sis. In fact, there are two reasons I wanted us to meet. The first is that I was worried about you and I needed to see you in person, to hear from your lips how you're doing."

"Thanks, I appreciate that." She smiled. "And the second?"

"I'm going to ask you for that favor again. And it's a big one."

"What favor?" Her eyes narrowed.

"We need the location of the camp where they've been sending all the Christian prisoners. All we need is the name of the nearest town."

She sat back, her gaze boring into him, but she said nothing.

"We know what they're doing there, Chelsea, and you don't want any part of it. They're executing them. Just like the Nazis did at Auschwitz and Treblinka and all the other concentration camps."

Again, she closed her eyes. She dropped her head into her hands and spoke to the table. "You don't know what you're asking. I have no way of finding out something like that. I no longer work at the Ministry of Truth near Father. We hardly ever see each other. If I start poking around where I shouldn't, it would be obvious. They'd find me out. Then they'd send *me* to that camp. You don't know what it's been like." Her fingers clawed through her hair, and her voice hushed to a whisper. "Sometimes, at odd moments, I get a sense of such powerful evil, it overwhelms me. Then I have to go to the restroom, and I just shake all over until it passes. Davato is . . . a . . . a monster. There, I've said it. He's a monster. One false step. One wrong word. And people disappear. I'm scared, Dylan, and I don't know how to get out. I can't get out. No one ever gets out."

Startled by her admission, by the fear in her voice and her obvious distress, he reached across and laid a hand on her arm.

"Now you know. Now you see how it is with me. Now you understand why I can't help you." She waved her hands. "Good grief! I can't even help myself."

"It's okay, sis. I understand. If you can't help, you can't help." He looked aside as the waiter brought them their plates of beef bourguignon.

"It's a pleasure serving you, Madame et Monsieur." He bowed low then left.

For some time, Dylan stared at the food. Nine hundred euros for this? He ate in silence, trying to savor every bite. After they'd finished, she presented her credit card, and it was time to part.

He stood and hugged her.

"This has been good," she said. "To see you again, a familiar face from back before things got out of control—it's done me good."

"Take care, sis. I'll be praying for you."

She wiped a tear from one eye, nodded, then strolled across the square.

For a time, he sat and sipped the last of his wine.

Then René's voice exploded in his ear. "Two men with guns are approaching from the north. Get out of there as fast as you can. Now!"

CHAPTER 26

FIREFIGHT

Paris, France – August, Year 2

Dylan shot out of his seat and glanced north. Two men in green-and-black uniforms and lugging pistols marched toward him. These weren't the usual squaddies, not with those hardened faces and that air of professionalism.

He swiveled to the south, but two armed squaddies in jeans and tee shirts with black armbands were closing in from that direction. "What should I do?" he spoke for the microphone. "Tell me!"

"Keep calm and don't run. Head for the fountain. When I tell you, take cover behind it. When I have a clear shot, I'll take them out."

His heart was racing too fast, but his feet—slow down, don't run!—were already hurrying him over the bricks. "The ones in uniform aren't squaddies. Are they CSA?"

"Yes."

He nearly stumbled. He'd never been confronted, face-to-face, by the CSA. His heart pounded harder inside his chest. Sweat burst onto his forehead.

Again, René's voice burst into his mike. "Pasqual, fall in behind the CSA men who just passed you. On my signal, shoot the one on your right. I'll get the other one. Then take cover. After those two are down, I'll get the squaddies."

"I don't know if I can—"

"Pasqual, do it! We're counting on you. And, Dylan, when you hear shooting, duck behind that fountain, draw your weapon, and prepare to defend yourself."

Dylan sent a glance toward the fountain. The young couple had left.

His shoes clopped over the bricks, echoing like thunder.

The sun burned on his neck, drenching it with sweat.

The pigeons ahead burst upward in a cloud, heading for the peaks of the buildings.

The crack of a rifle shot echoed across the square. Like a racehorse out of the gate, he sprinted for the fountain.

A second shot followed.

At the fountain, he dropped to the bricks and rolled behind the cement rim.

A third explosion reverberated between the buildings. Then a fourth. Then a fifth and a sixth. But who was shooting at whom?

With shaking hands, he jerked the pistol from his pocket and peeked over the rim.

Three men, including the CSA agents, lay motionless on the ground across the square. Pasqual was not in sight.

But one blue-jeaned squaddie, his pistol out, was zigzagging toward Dylan, heading for the fountain.

Another shot split the air—this one from behind. Chips of stone exploded above his head. The tip of the cavalryman's sword dropped inside the empty fount.

His attacker stopped, steadied his pistol, and fired twice. Once at the hotel window. A second time at Dylan.

Angry air whizzed past his head as he ducked. He scrambled around the circle of concrete, using the rim for protection, trying to put distance between himself and his attacker.

"I don't have a shot!" shouted René in his ear. "The statue's in the way."

"Should I make a break for it?"

"No! You'll just give him a target. You'll have to take him out. It's all up to you now."

He took a deep breath. What had René said? "All . . . up . . . to . . . you?"

From the other side of the fountain came the scraping of shoes over concrete.

"He's down behind the rim now," came René's voice.

Dylan poked his head up, saw no one, and heard his opponent sliding over the bricks below the rim. The sound came from his right. He stood, gun in hand, and slid into the empty bowl.

One slow foot forward. Dried leaves on the right. He stepped around them and circled to the left, putting the monument between him and the threat.

A few more meters and he'd be behind the man.

Rustling sounds from the right.

Dylan froze, held his gun with both hands, and aimed at the sound. If only the man would peek his head above the—

The man stood, glanced in the direction where Dylan had been.

Dylan's finger was on the trigger, and he aimed. But he froze. His target was young, with muscled arms, red hair falling over his forehead, red stubble on his chin. Except for the red hair, he could almost have been a distant cousin.

"Shoot!" came the voice in his ear mike.

He pulled the trigger. The shot cracked the air. His hand jerked up and back.

Red bloomed on the man's shoulder. He rocked back, rocked forward. Frightened eyes stared at his chest. Then he raised his pistol toward Dylan—

Dylan fell to the right behind the statue.

Another crack shattered the air, and pieces at the statue's base exploded past his face, stinging his cheek.

The monument's base was barely wide enough to hide behind, so he scooted down further. He'd hit the man in the shoulder—or was it the chest?—and there'd been blood. Why was he still standing?

Then came the unmistakable sound of a body slumping onto the pavement, lungs gasping for air, and a gun clattering over the bricks.

"He's down," came René's voice over the mike. "Let's go!"

But Dylan left his hiding place, walked to the edge of the bowl, and looked out onto the square. There lay the man he'd shot, blood drenching the right side of his shirt. He was about the same age as Dylan. Frightened eyes looked up into his. "Help me!"

Dylan glanced toward the observation room. "He isn't dead. He wants our help."

"We've got to go. Let his people deal with him. The square will soon be filled with police."

All the tables were empty now. When the shooting started, even the four squaddies sitting nearby, probably the usual amateurs, had fled. Again, he gazed at the man. "Maybe we should take him with us, find out what we can from him?"

"No! I'm packing up and coming down. Get ready to go to the car."

Dylan pocketed his weapon, stepped over the rim, and knelt beside the man he'd shot. Blood seeped from the wound.

"I won't . . . turn you in," came a pained whisper. "Take me with you. My name is Angelo Pisano. And I was forced to do this."

To be safe, Dylan kicked the gun away then helped Angelo to a sitting position. An involuntary grunt, a grimace of pain, escaped him.

The bullet had passed through the shoulder, but the bleeding wouldn't stop. With Angelo's help, Dylan removed the man's tee shirt. Then he ripped it apart and balled it into two plugs. "This might hurt."

He stuffed one plug into the hole in the man's back, and his patient emitted a cry of pain. He did the same for the front, and again Angelo shook with agony. But the bleeding slowed. Dylan wiped his bloody hands on the remains of the tee shirt.

From the far end of the square came angry voices. A mob was headed toward the restaurant. In the lead was Gascon, the scarecrow beggar whom the waiter had turned away.

Far ahead of the mob, Pasqual was racing across the square toward Dylan.

Behind Pasqual, the waiter emerged from the restaurant and hastily began shutting metal grates that closed off the building's front. The four security guards, who'd disappeared when the shooting started, reappeared with guns in hand, forming a line before the approaching threat. But by the way they kept glancing behind them, Dylan wondered about their commitment.

"Let's get out of here!" shouted Pasqual from across the square.

"Come on." Dylan helped Angelo to his feet. "I'm taking you with us."

By the time Dylan's charge was walking, Pasqual was beside them. Pasqual shifted his gun to his other hand. "What are you doing?"

"He wants to come with us. He might have valuable information."

"You're crazy." Pasqual shot a look across the square and shrugged. "All right, but we've got to go—now!"

Angelo was able to walk, but unsteadily. All three left the square, rounded the hotel, and crossed an intersection to the stares of passersby. As fast as Angelo would let them, they hurried to an alley two blocks away.

René was already in the car with the engine running. "Are you out of your mind?" He pulled out his pistol, jerked back on the action, and pointed it at the newcomer.

Dylan held up a hand. "His name is Angelo, and he wants to come with us."

"I won't turn you in." Angelo's eyes shone bright with fear. "They forced me to do this. My fiancée is in their camp somewhere. If I didn't cooperate, they said they'd kill her." He dropped his gaze to the ground. "If she isn't dead already."

"Do you know where the camp is?" asked Dylan.

"Yes."

Police sirens echoed in the distance.

"All right." René gave Dylan an angry stare then waved to the back seat. "Get in. All of you! We've got to go!"

As the car squealed away, distant police sirens merged with angry voices from the square.

CHAPTER 27

ANGELO

The French Luberon – August, Year 2

After graduating from gymnasium in Brussels, Margot had briefly trained as a nurse before the money ran out and she had to quit. At the farm, when it appeared she was as qualified as anyone, she was elected to treat minor injuries and tend the sick. It fulfilled a lifelong goal, and it made her feel good to help others in need. The new girl, Danielle, also had some nurse training, and they both pitched in whenever there was a need. But when Dylan, René, and Pasqual arrived with this new man, Angelo, on the edge of consciousness and turning feverish, the two faced their most difficult nursing trial yet. Not until yesterday, when Margot discovered a more powerful antibiotic in the farm's inventory, did his condition improve.

Now it was the third morning, and when she entered his room, followed by the red-haired Danielle, Angelo lay in bed with his eyes open.

"How is my patient today?" Margot asked with a smile.

"Better, thank you." When he tried a return smile, he reminded her of Dylan.

"I'm glad." Danielle set down her tray with a glass of milk, a sandwich, and some grapes. "If you weren't better, we were going to turn you in for a quicker healing patient."

Grinning, he sat up. With widened brown eyes, he pulled the tray to his lap. "You have food! I was worried you'd have nothing—like everybody else."

"They have cattle, milk cows, pigs, and chickens." Danielle's eyes brightened and crinkled up at the edges. "And they've stored wheat from last fall's harvest, so there's bread. They have grapevines and wine! They are wonderful!"

"But lately," added Margot with a frown, "the rats have gotten into the granary. They're becoming a problem."

"Yes." He eyed the plate. "The rats are everywhere lately." Then he attacked the food until there was nothing left.

Moments later, René entered, followed by Pasqual and Dylan. "Better, I see." Each day, René had badgered Margot and Danielle about Angelo's condition, wondering when he'd be able to talk. She hoped he wouldn't begin his interrogation until her patient was stronger.

"I am, sir, and thank you for allowing me to come here and stay with you."

"We'll see about that." He turned to Danielle. "Is he able to answer questions today?"

"I am," said Angelo. "I will tell you anything you want to know."

As Margot frowned, Dylan sat in the only chair while Pasqual and René stood on either side of the bed.

Danielle excused herself to sew up a finger that "some clumsy oaf"—her exact words—had cut with his own knife.

"You said you knew the location of the camp where they're taking all the Christian prisoners." He loomed beside the bed, his eyes darkening as he focused on the newcomer. "Where is it?"

"I don't know its exact location."

"You told us you knew where it was." René crossed his arms.

"Only the general area."

René scowled. "Then tell us what you do know."

"It's somewhere in southern Germany."

"Is that it?" René's voice rose. "You need to do better than that."

"I only heard bits and pieces of a conversation. Some of us were asked to accompany a convoy of trucks carrying prisoners, but not me. They planned to stop in Stuttgart then head southeast from there. Someone also mentioned Munich."

"And this group was traveling from Paris?" René leaned forward, his fists digging into the bed.

"Yes."

"How do you know they were stopping in southern Germany? What if they were going on to Austria? Or even to Hungary?"

"I . . . I don't know. I assumed it was Germany."

Pasqual stepped closer to the bed. "Can tell us anything else about this camp?"

"I know that most of the people they send there . . . will be executed."
Angelo's forehead wrinkled, and the hand on the blankets shook. "They
took my fiancée. She's there."

"Why do you say 'most of the people'? Why not all of them?"

"Some they're keeping for interrogation. Others they use to work
at the camp itself—but only a few. I don't know what kind of work."
Intense eyes found René's. "They said they'd allow her to work if I did
what they told me, so I did. Otherwise, they'd kill her. I never wanted to
be part of them. I had no choice."

"And yet you were chasing Dylan with a gun, firing shots at him and
at me, ready to kill us both." René glared. Obviously, he didn't believe a
word.

Angelo hung his head. "Yes."

"What can you tell us about the Truth Squads?"

"Probably not much you don't already know." Angelo's fist closed
around a wad of blankets. "I'm sorry for what I did. You've been kind
to me, and you must realize—if I didn't cooperate, they were going to
execute her."

"Oui, you've said that. And now you feel you have no choice but to
play along with us because you fear *we* might kill *you*?" A sneer lifted one
side of René's mouth before he squelched it. "So how can we trust you
won't just go wherever the wind takes you—like you did before? How do
we know that the moment you're out of sight, you won't turn us in to
protect your sister—like you did before?"

Margot's head jerked up. Dylan had said it was Angelo's fiancée. Was
René trying to catch Angelo in a lie, or had René forgotten?

"No, no, it's not like that!" Angelo gripped the bedcovers with both
hands. "You've treated me well, not like members of my squad—squaddies, you call them. They are only out for themselves, devoted to Davato
and to, to—hate! Yes, that's what it is—they hate you folks with an
unreasoning, mind-numbing hate. But I don't. Honest! I won't turn you
in. I promise."

For some time, a silent, frowning René stared at the newcomer, his
eyes so narrow, his sockets so deep, one could not guess his thoughts.

"Maybe I believe you, and maybe I don't. But you're going to have to give us something more than a vague location. And you'll have to prove your truthfulness—somehow. But you avoided my question. What more can you tell us about the Truth Squads or the CSA?"

Angelo scratched the red stubble on his chin then lifted his gaze with a smile. "How about the login and password they use for one of their main websites?"

René and Pasqual exchanged glances. "What's on this site?" asked René. Then he fumbled in a pocket for his cigarettes and waved one at Margot's raised brow.

"Daily marching orders and warnings about local resistance, area by area."

"Can this site tell us what they're doing here in the Luberon, day by day?" Pasqual's eyes were bright.

"It's for all of France. And they've just changed the password. It might be good yet for several months."

"Well, that's something, isn't it?" offered Margot.

Seeming barely able to contain his excitement, René nodded. When he wrote down the relevant information Angelo gave him, he departed. Then Dylan and Pasqual remained with her.

"Everyone here is a Christian, Angelo." Pasqual laid a hand on the bedcovers. "And you were charged with killing Christians. What is your faith background?"

"I think that's enough questioning for today," said Margot. "He needs rest, not more interrogation."

Angelo waved a hand. "That's all right, mademoiselle. I'll answer. My mother was Catholic, and I went to church as a teenager. But it didn't mean much to me."

"What about your fiancée?" continued Pasqual. "Why did they take her?"

"After my mother disappeared, my fiancée became a Christian. She was always trying to get me to this new church she'd found, but I refused." He shifted on the bed and sat up higher. "But don't get me wrong. I have nothing against Christians. I'm just not sure there is a God. Or a Jesus. Or a Heaven. For how can anyone know if there's anything beyond this world? What if it's all just a myth?"

"You're what we call an agnostic." Eyes twinkling, Pasqual patted Angelo's knee. "What if I were to bring you evidence that the Bible is true, that the events described there did happen? What if I were to show you that many of the predictions the biblical prophets made have already come true? And what if I can prove to you that it was impossible, without divine intervention, for those prophecies to have occurred? Of course, some prophecies haven't yet come to pass, and some we are living through right now—here in the end times."

Angelo tilted his head. "You can prove these things? I mean with facts and evidence?"

"I can. When would you like to hear them?"

"Any time. But maybe later this afternoon. I—"

"He needs rest." Margot stepped forward and laid a hand on Pasqual's shoulder. "He's barely recovered."

"Of course." Pasqual motioned to Dylan that they should leave. As they headed toward the door, Pasqual turned back to Angelo. "Thank you, my friend. If you are being honest with us, there's a place for you here."

Angelo's shoulders relaxed, and his expression softened. "Thanks. I appreciate that."

Margot left her patient and followed the two down the hall.

But they'd only taken a few steps when René caught up with them again. "I was just on the CSA website with Victor"—he stopped, nearly out of breath—"and Angelo is right. It has warnings about resistance activity."

"Does it say anything about us?" Pasqual frowned.

"Only that there is a suspected resistance cell somewhere in the Luberon. But I did find something of great concern, something happening today."

"What?" asked Margot.

"A group of starving people is roaming the area. They number almost a hundred, and they're pillaging and sacking every house and villa in their path. The last report said they were in the village below. I asked Victor to send up his drone to monitor the situation."

"What's the government doing about it?" asked Dylan.

"Nothing. Their orders are to let them be. They are to focus only on finding the Christians—folks like us."

The crash of pounding feet echoed up the stairwell. The door slammed open, and Victor burst into the hall. "Guys." Red-faced, he grabbed his knees and sucked in air. "I was monitoring images from my drone, and—"

"And what?" asked René.

"We're in big trouble. There's a mob from the village, maybe a hundred strong, heading for our road. They're carrying clubs, knives, axes, and guns. Nothing short of an army battalion is going to turn them around."

CHAPTER 28

THE MOB

The French Luberon – August, Year 2

For long seconds, as René, Pasqual, and Dylan stood transfixed, Margot tried to digest what Victor had just said. How could they hold off a mob of a hundred desperate people bent on pillaging everything in their path?

René broke the silence by slamming a fist into a palm. "We'll need every man and woman able to carry a gun down on the road before they see the wheat fields and the livestock. There's a narrow spot between the trees where we can hold them off."

"How many guns do we have?" asked Dylan.

"Last I checked"—Pasqual scrunched his face in concentration—"twelve handguns and six rifles, all semiautomatic."

Something tightened in her chest. "If they're that determined, how can we stop them?"

"Once a few are lying dead on the road"—René's lips flattened into a grim line—"they'll change their minds."

She shuddered at the answer.

"We have to get everyone moving." Then René gave them each a task and a section of the villa to canvas before leaving for the armory room where he would collect the guns.

Then they ran from room to room, asking who had ever fired a gun and was willing to defend the farm against the invaders.

But as Margot gathered her group of five men and led them toward the ground floor, her pulse quickened. This was a battle for survival, wasn't it? Would the men have to shoot to kill to stop this gang bent on their destruction? But what would be the consequences of that?

When her group met René outside, he and three others were burdened with pistols and rifles. Dylan and Pasqual soon joined them. She counted eighteen men, total, for their makeshift army.

René began passing out weapons. Since they had more than enough men, Margot stood aside, watching and saying a short prayer.

Cigarette in hand, the ex-spy examined his cobbled-up band then leaned on the butt of his rifle. Like a general before a battle, he settled his stern gaze on each. "Understand this is a fight for our survival. If we let them get too far up the mountain, they'll see our wheat fields and the animals, and nothing will stop them. They cannot get that far. At the gap, we'll position half of you in the woods on the perimeter, with the other half on the road behind the vehicles." He dropped his cigarette and stamped it out with his boot. "Let's go!"

Over a kilometer and a half long, the access road descended a steep slope between pines and oaks. If the mob had just started the climb, it would take some time to reach the place René had mentioned. Margot drove the Renault packed with men as others drove the Peugeot. René drove the new van they'd acquired. At the narrow gap where deep forest hugged both sides of the road, everyone exited the vehicles.

She peered down the drive, but the mob was not yet in view.

René ordered the van and the Peugeot to barricade the road, giving the men cover behind which they could shoot.

"Don't fire until I give the word," he said. "And when you shoot, shoot to kill. I'll try to talk them out of it, but . . ."

"But they probably won't listen, will they?" offered Dylan.

She cringed at the implication.

"Probably not."

Half the men found positions on either side of the road, hidden in the shadows of tall pines. The other half spread out behind the van and the Peugeot.

With a walkie-talkie, René called Victor, who was monitoring the gang's progress up the drive. After the conversation, René turned to those around him. "They'll turn the corner in about five minutes."

Down at the bend in the road, trees obscured her view. Nearby, men with grim faces and guns ready huddled behind the vehicles. In the deep forest, a few shadows moved, and men waited to do battle. The pungent scent of pine needles mixed with the smell of motor exhaust. Above, a solitary hawk cried and circled.

Would this be a bloodbath? How many would they kill before the mob decided to turn around? Would a group of desperate, starving people ever turn around? And would the resulting melee bring the authorities down on the farm? She gripped her head with both hands. Was there no way out of this?

She moved to René's side and laid a hand on his shoulder. "Wouldn't the squaddies have more food than the rest of us?"

He turned to her, his eye sockets seeming deeper as his brows drew together. "Huh?"

"Don't they always seem to be well-fed?"

"They do." He faced away from her toward the road. "So what?"

"Maybe Angelo can tell us why that is. I'm going to ask him." Without waiting for an answer, she whirled and ran to the Renault parked behind the barricade. The keys were still inside. She started the engine, turned the car around, and squealed up the hill.

In the rearview mirror, a black mass of bodies appeared at the bend in the road, heading for the barricade.

She floored the accelerator. When she reached the garage, she continued up the service drive to the back entrance and slammed on the brakes. Climbing the stairs two at a time, she found Angelo's room, pushed through the door, and shook him.

"Wake up. Wake up, Angelo!"

"Huh?" He opened bleary eyes and focused on her. "What do you want?"

"Does every CSA region have a secret store of food somewhere?"

He pushed himself to a sitting position on the bed. "They do. Why do you ask?"

"Because a mob is heading up the drive intent on ransacking the farm. Tell me. Quickly! How would we find such a storehouse?"

His eyes opening wider, he nodded. "On the website, there's a section called CSA Regional Stores. For each region, they have a storehouse of confiscated food they keep for all the CSA headquarters. One storehouse for one or two dozen offices." Then he proceeded to explain how to find which CSA office held the storehouse.

Whirling, she shouted her thanks over her shoulder and burst out of the room. Pounding down the steps, she found Victor's room in the basement, pushed through, and stopped. "Bring up their website." She grabbed the edge of a counter and tried to catch her breath. "Look for a section called CSA Regional Stores. Quick! We can stop this." Then she explained what Angelo had told her.

Understanding instantly, Victor spun from the drone screen in front of him to a laptop. His fingers flew over the keys. While he searched, the drone screen captured her eyes—the mob was marching up the slope toward the barricade.

"Got it!" Victor rolled his chair from the laptop. "Now what?"

"Call René on the walkie-talkie and tell him!"

"Of course." He grabbed the device, clicked the button to talk, and tried to get René's attention. But there was no answer. He kept trying. "It's probably back in the van. He's probably focused on the mob."

"Right." She whirled away and raced back toward the service entrance. She started the car, spun the wheel, faced the car downhill, and punched the accelerator.

The Renault raced down the road at high speed, barely making the first switchback turn.

When the barricade was in view, the mob was within ten meters of it. Was she in time? Had shots been fired? She kept up her speed, slamming on the brakes and skidding to a halt.

She left the car, passed the men's questioning glances, and hurried to where René was stepping through the gap between vehicles. He took two steps toward the mob and stopped. The horde paused, their faces thin from hunger, twisted in anger. For the first time, Margot saw that some carried firearms.

"Turn around and go back." René held his rifle with one hand, butt resting on his hip, barrel pointing skyward. "We have no food here. We're in bad shape just like everyone else."

"You look pretty healthy to me," said skinny Mallory, the village mayor, the transperson dressed as a woman with breasts, but looking in every other respect like a man. Muscled arms waved a pistol. "Get out of the way and let us see for ourselves."

"Can't do that." René dropped the rifle so both hands held it. He pulled back on the action. "If you keep coming, a lot of you are going to die."

"We need food, monsieur, and nothing's going to stop us from getting it. Get out of the way."

René waved to the forest on both sides. "Men, show him what he's up against."

"It's *she*, not he!" said Mallory.

Brandishing their weapons, the men poked their heads out from behind the trees before the shadows again swallowed them.

The mayor whirled to the mob behind. "Show him what *he* is up against."

A half dozen arms lifted hunting rifles in the air, accompanied by an earsplitting scream.

René began backing up. "If that's the way you want it . . ."

As he turned for the safety of the barricade, Margot pushed through the gap.

"What are you doing?" His tone was harsh. "Get back!"

"No!"

A growing murmur—an angry wind before the storm—rose from the mob.

As they advanced, she whispered to René what she'd found.

He gripped her shoulder with one hand and nodded.

She took a step toward the approaching threat. "We know," she shouted, "where there's a great store of food that each CSA region keeps for all the CSA bases it serves."

"That's right." René came to stand beside her. "And we're willing to tell you about it if you leave us alone."

"Right." The mayor shook her head. "Why should we believe you?"

"You've seen, haven't you, how the Truth Squads and the CSA always seem to be so well-fed?" René put the rifle butt back on his hip. "Well, we know where they keep the supplies for the entire Luberon. For our region, it's in the CSA headquarters in the village below."

"If that's true, then why haven't you taken it?"

"We don't have enough men for the job, but you do. What do you say? You're going to lose a lot of people on this road if you try to pass us."

The skinny woman/man lowered her pistol, scratched her head, and turned to converse with the others behind. Then she faced René again. "All right. We accept your offer. But if you've deceived us, we'll be back. Then nothing will keep you safe."

The mob reversed direction and headed back down the hill.

When they were out of sight, men left the shadows and joined the others at the barricade.

René wiped his brow and laid a hand on Margot's shoulder. "That was quick thinking. How did you find out about the squaddie food stores?"

"Angelo told me, and Victor discovered which CSA base had the storehouse. But I couldn't raise you on the walkie-talkie, so I had to tell you in person."

René smiled. "I guess Angelo has proved his trustworthiness. We avoided a lot of bloodshed today."

"Just think what would have happened if there was a battle." Shivering now that it was over, she hugged her arms around her chest. "The CSA would then surely know about us."

"Good point."

The men had gathered around the two, and René's glance swept the circle. "Starting right now, we'll post a guard here—two men at a time with guns and a walkie-talkie. Who will take the first shift?"

Dylan and another man raised their hands.

As the rest piled into the van, the Renault, and the Peugeot, Margot tried to slow her beating heart. Then she wondered: Were the same out-of-control mobs rampaging all over Europe? Davato had promised peace, prosperity, and security. But the population was starving and desperate.

In the last months, she and Dylan had studied the Bible.

This, then, was the harvest of the third seal. And their troubles were only beginning.

CHAPTER 29
INVASION PLANS

On the Black Sea Coast – September, Year 2

The helicopter blades were still churning, forcing Jaleel Hasani to crouch as he left the helipad. Behind him stooped the Supreme Leader Muhammad Najafi, his robes flying, one hand on his turban, the other clutching his cane.

"Welcome to President Petrov's dacha." A smiling, buxom blonde, speaking in English, waved them up the path between sculpted gardens onto marble walkways.

Before Jaleel, the palace and grounds of the Russian president spread to the horizon. Rumor had it that this massive complex on the Black Sea near Gelendzhik, Krasnodar Krai, had cost Arkady Rotenberg over one hundred billion rubles to build. Arkady, holding insider contracts for electrical transmission and gas pipelines, was a Russian billionaire claiming he'd created it as a resort. But everyone knew he'd built it exclusively for Vladimir Putin, a former Russian leader.

Jaleel had heard of the palace's opulence, but nothing prepared him for the blonde-haired maiden's tour through its amphitheater, arboretum, casino, discotheque, food shops, greenhouse, hookah bar, ice palace, music lounge, reading room, sauna rooms, spa, swimming pool, theater and cinema, Turkish baths, warehouse, wine cellar, and its dozen sumptuous guest bedrooms.

Despite the shameless affluence, three times the group surprised families of rats, sending them scurrying off into dark corners. No matter where Jaleel went lately—Tehran, his Caspian Sea home, and now here at this Black Sea dacha—there were rats. He shuddered.

When the tour concluded, he couldn't help but smile at the irony. Wasn't the last owner, Putin, a former member of the Communist party, an ideology committed to ending the excesses of the upper classes? What happened to the people's paradise? Even the czars had never lived in such luxury.

Petrov had obviously meant the tour to overwhelm and possibly cower his guests. But one glance beside him at the Supreme Leader's scowl convinced Jaleel that Najafi did not approve. When the woman finally led them to the meeting room, under crystal chandeliers and a high frescoed ceiling, Jaleel was ready to ease his considerable bulk into the plush conference chair. After all that walking, he was puffing and drenched with sweat.

Even before lifting off from Tehran, he'd had a bad feeling about this meeting. He couldn't keep his mind off his vision of fire raining down on the invading troops. Was it because of Davato's nukes?

"Welcome, Supreme Leader and President Hasani, to my humble abode." Petrov, speaking in English—the one language with which they were all familiar—wore a dark-blue business suit with a checkered tie. But as he reached to shake hands with Najafi, the Supreme Leader simply folded his arms and bowed. And as Petrov waved them to seats on the opposite side of the ebony table's polished, gleaming surface, Jaleel caught a whiff of strong drink. Against the wall, two black-suited men—FSB agents?—lurked with unsmiling faces.

"We are most honored to join you in your, ah, home." Najafi's face was impassive.

"If there is anything you lack, just ask, and it will be provided." Petrov smiled, and strands of ink-black hair fell across his forehead. As a hand brushes away a fly, he knocked it aside. "But now to business."

"Yes, to business." The Supreme Leader bunched his robe around one arm and laid a clothed hand on the table. "It is past time we rein in this Davato and his Zionist friends. Every utterance from his so-called Prophet is a blasphemy and an insult to Islam. And his demands on those not part of his so-called Imperium are increasingly unacceptable. Now that he has made his home in the Israeli stronghold, the place of our mortal enemy, we must act."

"I am glad you have seen the light, Supreme Leader." But did Petrov's smile betray some private joke, some hint of sarcasm?

Undeterred, Najafi plunged ahead. "We have firm commitments from Ahmed Umar of Libya, General Hassan Al-Kalifa of Sudan, Omid

Noor of the Sayf Alsharaf and his tribal hill fighters, and from Suleyman Aydin of Turkey. All of them will join the fight. At the appropriate time, they will commit men, tanks, artillery, rocket batteries, and ships. So far, all has gone . . . swimmingly well."

As Jaleel cringed at Najafi's awkward turn of phrase, Petrov nodded. Then the Russian leader placed his hands on the table, and his black, intense eyes speared his guests. "This man has been a cancer on the world since the Unitum Imperium sprang out of Europe. And his trade policies are worsening the famine that is wreaking havoc on the Russian people."

"The same for us," added Jaleel. "He has also strangled trade with Iran and all the Islamic nations. He is destroying our economies." Jaleel shifted in his seat, still unhappy about the looming danger of the Israeli, French, and UK nukes, now in Davato's hands. When would someone address that delicate subject?

"Da, he must be stopped." Petrov waved to one of the FSB agents, and from the corner, the man brought a tray holding a bottle of vodka and three small glasses. "In Russia, I always start my meetings with a shot of vodka. Will you join me?"

As Najafi's eyes bulged, Petrov's lackey brought two glasses and set them before the Supreme Leader and Jaleel Hasani.

Jaleel stared at the glass of clear liquid. The odor rose even now to his nostrils. Was this a joke? Did Petrov not know the strictures of Muhammad prohibiting the consumption of alcohol? Maybe it was a test. Or was it simply a blatant insult? Jaleel had heard of Petrov's disdain for all religions, especially Islam. That this atheist was now conspiring with the most powerful leader of the Muslim world was itself shocking.

The Supreme Leader narrowed his eyes and slowly, oh so slowly, shook his head and pushed the glass away.

Jaleel looked longingly at the shot glass, but he, too, pushed it aside.

"Very well. You have your customs. We have ours. To the defeat of the interloper." Petrov raised his glass, threw the shot down his throat, and slammed the glass on the tabletop. "Let us continue."

"Yes . . . President . . . Petrov." Najafi spoke as though each word were strangled. Was he on the verge of an outburst? "Let us continue."

His eyes bright with—humor? inebriation?—Petrov again slapped his palms atop the ebony. "You have done well by gathering so many committed allies to join me. With your forces beside the Russian Federation and its great power, we will destroy this pretender to the world's throne. And when he is rousted from his Jerusalem nest—" Much to Jaleel's annoyance, Petrov again slapped the table. "When he's gone, I will reunite all the former lands of the great Russian Empire. The Baltics, Belarus, Poland, and, at long last, Ukraine, are again ours. But we must add Slovakia and the Czech Republic. And we mustn't forget Romania, Hungary, and Germany."

"We will not stand in your way." Najafi's gaze found his folded hands.

Jaleel had recently reviewed film footage of Hiroshima's destruction and the US atomic tests in the Pacific, and they kept flashing through his mind. He couldn't shake his vision of being burned alive and the fear that, after poking the Zionist stronghold, they all might be fried to a crisp in a bunker somewhere. Why wasn't anyone concerned with Davato's nukes?

"But the first step is to deploy our armies, and that will take time." Petrov pushed his chair back and stood. He paced to the wall, spun, and returned. "This man is wily and smart, and we must take nothing for granted. Therefore, I will send everything I have for the venture. Bombers, tanks, armored personnel carriers, trucks, fighters, helicopter gunships, and as many missile batteries as the land can hold. When the head of the snake is cut off, the tail—whatever is left of the Unitum Imperium forces in Europe—will not long survive."

Najafi grabbed the cane at his side and rapped it three times on the floor. "I am pleased to hear that. Though our cultures, our ways, differ, we stand united against this common enemy."

"Da, Najafi, but your allies control Israel's borders. Can you suggest an invasion strategy?"

"I can. Here is my suggestion for the attack." His hands emerged from the folds of his robe and clasped together. "We will strike from all sides simultaneously. The first front will be from the north, from the Lebanese and Syrian border. Turkey will send its forces there. Secondly, the Turkish fleet will anchor off the waters of Tel Aviv and Haifa to the west, ready to land there. Third, the Libyans and Sudanese will move in from the Sinai in the south. I'm afraid this will anger Egyptian President Kareem, but there's no hope for it. That is the first part of the plan."

"But, Najafi, Russia's forces will dwarf all of yours, and I must lead this venture. Where can we send them?"

Jaleel cringed at this second use of the Supreme Leader's name, and the turbaned leader flinched.

"You can land them at the Damascus airport. Half your troops will join those in Syria and Lebanon, attacking from the north. I suggest we send the other half to open the fourth front from the east through Jordan. If your tanks and armies cross over into Jordan on your way to the Zionist stronghold—well, who's to stop them?"

Petrov raised an eyebrow and nodded. "I like this plan, Najafi. By attacking from all sides, simultaneously, with such an overwhelming force, we will surely crush them."

Najafi frowned and sat up straighter. "A moment ago, you said you must lead the invasion, but Iran must begin it. But it is I, the Supreme Leader, who assembled our brothers in Islam, and it is I who must communicate and coordinate with them on the battlefield. Otherwise, there will be chaos."

Petrov's face reddened. "The leader of this invasion, Najafi, must be the leader of the great Russian people! But . . ." He took a deep breath and exhaled. "I admit—it was you who assembled your Islamic allies. So I will let you *begin* the battle."

The Supreme Leader gripped his cane. Was he going to strike the floor in anger? Instead, his eyes narrowed, and he gave the Russian a slow nod. "That will be . . . acceptable."

"Excellent." Petrov leaned back and smiled.

Jaleel could wait no longer. He shifted in his seat. "But what about the nukes? What will stop them from wiping out our entire invasion force? Or from destroying Tehran, Istanbul, Moscow, and every other city standing against them?"

Both men faced him with somber expressions. Najafi started to speak, but Petrov held up a hand. A smile spread his lips until he was grinning. "I like surprises, my friends, especially pleasant ones. And now I have some news you are going to like."

"What?" asked Jaleel and Najafi.

"One of our intelligence agents was embedded in Davato's headquarters after his invasion of Israel. The Imperator, as he calls himself, had sent some goons to torture the nuclear codes out of the Israeli leadership. Before our man was found out and executed, he was present when they made their report."

The Supreme Leader leaned forward in his chair. "Did they get them?"

"Nyet. Davato did not obtain the codes. The leaders they tortured died with the information." Petrov sat back with a satisfied grin. "The Israeli weapons will be inoperable for some months until they find a way around the problem."

"What about the French and UK nukes?" asked Jaleel.

Petrov waved his hands in dismissal. "They have the codes, but of what use are those weapons? They cannot fire on armies right at their doorstep or the radiation will poison the country and kill their own men. No, those weapons will be useless in this fight."

Jaleel shook his head. "But what if they attack Tehran? Or Moscow? Or Damascus?"

"That is a risk we must take, is it not? But if they dared launch such an attack on our cities, Russia's nuclear forces would respond in kind. Then there would be no Israel left to invade, no countries left of the Unitum Imperium, and Davato himself would be charred to a crisp in a million-degree furnace. He knows this. No, he won't fire his nukes at the Russian or Iranian homelands."

Jaleel took a deep breath. Petrov's argument was sound. Mutual assured destruction it was called, and as long as everyone was rational, an exchange of nukes was not going to happen. All the same, it was good to hear Petrov say it. A smile began forming on Jaleel's lips. Yes, the invasion would succeed. The Zionists and Davato would be pushed into the sea, wiped from the earth. He clapped his hands together. "Yes, I agree. It will work, won't it?"

"Yes, it will work." The Supreme Leader frowned in Jaleel's direction. Expressions of doubt were never welcome in his presence. Then he faced the Russian president. "When should we strike?"

"To position the greatest army ever assembled on the face of the earth will take at least six weeks."

"Then in six weeks, we will destroy the Zionists and this blasphemous upstart." Najafi pushed back from his chair, ending the meeting.

As Jaleel followed the buxom blonde to the rooms reserved for them, he wondered if their host would provide some of that intoxicating vodka for his guests.

CHAPTER 30
A SECRET MEETING

Jerusalem, Israel – September, Year 2

Baruch Abramovich was the last to enter the abandoned restaurant on Jerusalem's outskirts. Despite the September heat, at least five hundred people now filled the space, cleared of tables and chairs for yet another clandestine gathering. He strolled down the aisle and stood in front atop a packing box. He nodded to his longtime friend, David Benjamin, standing beside him. Having recently converted, David now insisted, despite Baruch's objections, that he take responsibility for Baruch's security.

Some of the faces before him were too thin. Even his own stomach growled, for in the last two days, he'd eaten only two meals, probably more than many others here. Volunteers with white armbands were passing out hunks of bread, one for each attendee. The recipients eagerly devoured what might be their only food for the day. Finding the flour to bake that much bread was one of the more difficult logistical obstacles for these gatherings.

As he scanned the crowd, Baruch knew some here might already be, or might soon become, informants. Not everyone would accept the message of Christ's eternal salvation. For those, he grieved.

After he'd returned from the catacomb prison in Rome, he'd gathered the leaders of the Great Assembly and told them everything he'd learned about Christ and the Christian New Testament. They had readily understood how the book of Revelation had prophesied the task ahead and had supernaturally gathered them together, even before the vanishing. That God had so chosen them had awed and inspired each man. To a man, they accepted Baruch's teaching.

All were immediately baptized. Then he sent those leaders to bring the Good News to the men they led. To Baruch's great relief, the entire 144,000 became baptized Christians. Then he sent them to the far corners of the earth to preach the Gospel to a world in desperate spiritual need. He, himself, stayed in Jerusalem. After the Antichrist had moved his headquarters here, it was now the most dangerous place on earth for a preacher of Christ, a danger he reserved for himself.

But he was not afraid. Every day the Spirit of the living God filled him, buoyed him. He felt the Lord's protection even when he passed the dreaded Truth Squads on the streets. He feared not for himself or for the Great Assembly, but for the new Christians and for those about to turn to Christ in meetings like today's. They did not have the same divine protection.

His one prayer at events such as this was that he could convert a few, sealing their eternal destinies before the beast's minions descended and hauled them away.

He smiled and leaned toward the battery-powered microphone that led to a speaker on its pedestal. "Welcome, friends, to this assembly of petitioners before the Lord. You have known me as a true follower of Yahweh, a man who has always been faithful, as much as any flawed human could ever hope to be, to the one who gave us all breath and life and hope. Blessed is he who created the universe. You are here, I hope, because you have heard how I discovered that the Christian Jesus—this man whom our ancestors crucified—was and is the true Son of God. And because you want to learn more about my discovery."

He paused while a few in the audience shifted in their seats or sent troubled looks to their companions. In every event, it was always thus. It was difficult to turn one's back on the habits and beliefs of a lifetime, and some might not have understood the real purpose of this event. His hope for his audiences was that truth would always win out over tradition, ritual, and lifelong habits of thought. Not everyone would convert, and he had accepted that.

Some would now rise in anger and depart. And there—ten men in different locations rose from their seats and headed for the exits. A dozen more followed. But out of five hundred, what were twenty-two lost souls if the rest were saved?

From this point on, he had to be brief and to the point. Some of those leaving might become turncoats and report the gathering to the nearest CSA office. Others might ponder his brief introduction and return to a different assembly at a different time to hear more.

He plunged ahead. He spoke about his time in prison and about the woman Margot and her visions, and then he summarized what he'd discovered by studying the books of Isaiah, Ezekiel, Joel, Daniel, and the books of the Christian New Testament. He laid out his case as quickly and efficiently as possible.

Halfway through, another dozen rose from their seats and left.

But by the time he reached the end, the remainder were rapt with attention, fixed on his every word, ready to believe.

"Yes, my friends, Christ is truly the Son of God, and when you believe in and follow him, your eternal futures will be secure. But you all know the danger we face here today, and we must now end this meeting with all haste. To facilitate the next step for so many, volunteers with white armbands are standing by to give each of you a paper with a location and a time where you can join a house church. There, you will learn more about what it means to be a Christian. And there, if you are ready, they will baptize you. Memorize the paper, destroy it, then guard the location with your life."

He concluded with a quick prayer, dismissed the gathering with an admonition to depart swiftly, and then he checked his watch. Twenty-five minutes. He was shooting for twenty, but it would have to do.

As people mobbed the two dozen house-church members with white armbands, David Benjamin approached.

"Great speech, Baruch, as usual. But now I want you out of here." He lifted the phone to his ear, talked with someone, and ended the call. "I hate to say this, but a squad of CSA agents is out front, looking for you. Another squad—four members—is out back. They want you, Baruch, and they won't give up until they've got you in their prison."

"I've eluded them before." Baruch smiled.

"Yes, but someday, I fear you will not."

"Faith, my friend. Faith."

David frowned, whirled, and motioned he should follow.

The two men left, not by the front or the back, but by a side door leading to an alley. Garbage cans lay on their sides, their contents spilled across the cement—the result of desperate men searching for food. David shot a worried glance in both directions then broke into a jog to the left. Baruch followed, planting his feet around the scattered refuse.

The alley opened into a side street where David stopped his charge and poked his head to the left. "They're here. Quickly! Let's go!"

As David broke to the right, Baruch was close behind. A glance to the left revealed six men with guns sprinting in their direction.

"Stop, or we'll shoot!" cried one of them. "You'll not get away this time."

"The alley . . . on the right," came David's labored directions. He veered into the next side street.

Behind Baruch came the crack of a gunshot. A bullet chipped and sparked against the sidewalk ahead of him, and his heart leaped. *Please, oh Lord*, he prayed to himself, *give us the protection you promised. Do not let these men prevail. My mission is not complete.*

He sprinted after David. But another shot ricocheted off the wall beside him, and something stung his cheek. He turned the corner into the side street. But ahead of him was not a street, but a dead-end alley, only fifty meters deep. He slowed to a halt.

David stood in the center, looking around frantically. His hands gripped the only visible door. He rattled it, over and over, but it wouldn't budge. Then he caught Baruch's gaze, and his voice choked. "Baruch, there's no way out. That door is locked. I have failed you."

Baruch's gaze whipped from one side to another. No exits. No other doors. Not even a fire escape ladder reaching down from the roof. It was a true dead end.

In the middle of the alley, two garbage cans lay on their sides. They'd come from an empty niche in the wall. He headed for the niche and waved David to follow.

"But it's only a meter deep. And it's in full view. The instant they turn the corner, they'll—"

"Ssshh." Baruch put a finger to his lips and whispered. "Stand perfectly still and have faith."

When David caught his gaze, Baruch saw fear. "You're bleeding," said his friend.

"Quiet now. It will be all right." He raised fingers to his cheek where the piece of concrete had stung. His hand came back red with blood. Though he'd said the calming, soothing words, now his own heart began racing, and sweat formed on his brow. He'd been injured, hadn't he? How much faith would it take to save them now?

As they waited, four rats emerged from a corner and made their way toward them. David's eyes widened as he pointed to the approaching rodents. But Baruch shushed him. Everywhere, the rats were getting bolder, more numerous, and no one understood why.

The six men, dressed in the green-and-black uniforms of the CSA with the skull and lightning patches, turned the corner and ran into the alley bearing pistols and stubby machine guns. They slowed then stopped. The lead man—burly, muscled, and frowning—left the others and stalked down the far side of the alley, close to the wall. His glance searched every corner before he yanked on the locked door. He paced along the end, turned the corner, and walked back, only meters from the niche. At the same time, the rats fled from him, toward Baruch and David.

When the leader was three meters from his quarry, his eyes stared straight at the two men. Baruch's heart skipped, and his hands formed into fists at his side. Was this it? Was this the end of his ministry?

But the man's gaze dropped to the ground. "Rats!" he whispered. "I hate rats." He pulled back on his pistol's slide, took a step closer, and aimed.

David gasped, and Baruch slapped a hand over his mouth. The man raised his glance, looked around, his face puzzled.

The rats, perhaps sensing danger, scampered out of the niche along the wall.

The black muzzle followed. The man fired, and bullets ricocheted off the concrete. Two rats lay dead, their bodies destroyed, but the others slunk into a hole in the bricks.

Lowering his weapon, their pursuer returned to his men. "He's done it again. I don't know how he does it, but he's done it again. Come on. Let's go."

The CSA left the alley. Silence descended, and Baruch whispered a prayer of thanks.

Long minutes later, David stepped away and faced him, his eyes wide with wonder. "It was a miracle, wasn't it?"

"The Lord is protecting our mission just as Revelation promised. Now, come. Let us return to the hotel and plan our next meeting."

David grinned. "Perhaps you should fire me from being your 'head of security'. I think I've been replaced." He gave a nod toward the heavens.

Baruch returned the grin, and they left the alley.

CHAPTER 31
BAD KIRCHENSTADT

Southern Germany – September, Year 2

Dylan's trip from the French Luberon to Germany had been fraught with danger. He'd driven alone, taking the Renault. Outside every city, he had to pass through checkpoints, and he sensed that one wrong turn could land him in front of another mob of starving, desperate people.

His destination was Bad Kirchenstadt, a village in southern Germany, and a group whose goals were said to be the same as the Friends of the Nazarene. They called themselves The Worthy. But why they were worthy and worthy of what—no one knew.

Dylan had left at sunrise, and because someone had parked the car outside, he'd had to wipe dew from the windshield. Standing nearby, René and Pasqual had not filled him with confidence.

"The group sounds legitimate," Pasqual had said. "If they are, we cannot let this opportunity pass. But this is our first contact with them, and we cannot take too many precautions."

"All we have are an address and a name," added René. "If what Angelo said is true, the town may be in the same region as the camp. So they'll know the area, and if we can enlist their help, we have a good chance of finding the camp. We've given the Renault bogus plates and scraped off all identifying numbers. When you leave the car, don't leave anything behind that could identify you or the farm. And before you make contact, make sure you do due diligence and have an exit plan."

"What kind of 'due diligence'?" Dylan asked.

"Check the nearby streets and become familiar with the area. Before you go in, watch the address for a time. Find the nearest tram stops, if any, for use in an emergency. Park your car a few blocks away and know how to get out of there, fast. Keep your firearm loaded and ready."

But after hearing René, Pasqual had whirled away from the car, taken a few steps, and returned. "I don't know, René. I don't like this. We're sending him there alone, to an unknown group, in a strange town. What if it's a trap? What if this band isn't who we think they are?"

"You're right to be concerned. But right now, who else can we send? Tomorrow, you are picking up refugees in Marseilles. Ever since the mob attacked the squaddie nest, the CSA presence in the village has tripled, and their forays into the hills have increased. We could easily see another security incident. In case that happens, I'm needed here."

Nodding, Pasqual had faced Dylan. "He's right. So just . . . be careful."

The drive had taken him through Geneva, Lausanne, past Lac Léman, and then through Bern and Zurich with the mountains on his right and to the south. He'd traveled fast through Germany on 96. Traffic was light, but because of the backups at the checkpoints, travel time was longer than expected. The forgeries from the farm had served him well. His papers and the data encoded on his travel card seemed always to be in order. Once again, they'd been blessed by Victor's and René's expertise.

Twice, he'd pulled off onto roadside parks to eat the sandwiches and drink the coffee Margot had packed for him. The farm was stocked with food. Even so, their supplies were diminishing.

When he sat at a bench on the first pull-off, he kept watch for bandits and roving bands of starving, desperate people. But then, perhaps attracted by the smell of food, a dozen rats scurried toward him. He stamped his feet and drove them away. Odd, how so many rats were coming out in the open, even at the farm where they'd been getting into the granary, spoiling some of the wheat. No matter how many they trapped, more appeared out of nowhere.

The next time he pulled over and headed for a bench, a vehicle was parked nearby. But as he glanced inside, he froze. A woman sat behind the wheel, but her face was black and bloated, and her body leaned at an odd angle. No one had yet removed her corpse. How long she'd been like that, who could tell? And what did she die of? When more rats had emerged from the woods, he returned to his car and drove to the next pull-off to eat.

He exited the last roundabout and followed a sign for Bad Kirchenstadt. They'd booked his hotel only a block from the place where he was to meet Kurt, his contact. But he would save meeting with his contact until tomorrow.

On Ludwigstrasse, the main street, he drove slowly past the address. His destination turned out to be a restaurant. This he hadn't expected. The burg was small, perhaps three thousand people, with a main Strasse replete with ground-floor restaurants, small pensions, and two-story hotels. The town's claims to fame were its hot springs and its thousand-year-old church. But the vanishing, the famine, and the ever-present law-lessness had taken their toll. The streets were empty, with few cars and passersby on the cobbled stone walks.

He pulled through the entrance and parked in the hotel courtyard. At first, the clerk eyed him with suspicion, but when he paid with cash, in advance, the man's face brightened. Dylan's room overlooked the street, and from his upstairs window, he could see the object of his mission. The meal provided by the pension that evening was a small portion of sauer-kraut—no wurst—and a tall glass of the local beer. He left hungry, glad Margot had provided him with extra sandwiches.

After supper, he strolled past Das Alte Gasthaus where he was to meet Kurt tomorrow. Strolling up Ludwigstrasse, he took the sidewalk on the opposite side of the street. Like most of the street's buildings, the inn was a two-story affair, with a downstairs restaurant big enough only for a dozen customers and with guest rooms upstairs.

No light lit up the windows, and nobody moved inside. A sign on the door told him they opened at nine thirty tomorrow. He continued to a small park, an open green area with four large oaks and a bench. At the entrance, he passed a beggar in shabby clothes—odd for such a clean, well-manicured village such as Bad Kirchenstadt.

"*Guten morgen*," said the man in heavily accented German.

"*Guten abend*," Dylan responded. Didn't the man realize what time of day it was?

"Can zee spare some euros für a starving man?" The beggar extended a hand and stepped closer.

A strong whiff of body odor sent Dylan backing up. Shaking his head, he hurried to a central bench and sat. When the beggar held his station at the entrance, Dylan breathed his relief.

After he'd arrived, checked in, and if all was on track for tomorrow, he was supposed to send back a message. Pulling out his phone, he typed the code phrase. *Weather is good here. Food is so-so.* He pushed send then started back with the phone still in his hand.

The beggar still stood by the entrance, barring his way. "Five euros, mein Herr? Bitte?"

Dylan reached inside his pocket, pulled out a bill, and started to hand it over when the man snatched it from his fingers. Startled, Dylan jerked back.

He lost his grip on the phone. It clattered to the pavement and bounced.

Dropping to all fours, he lurched for it. But it slipped between the bars of the sewer grate.

He peered into the darkness below.

"Bad luck, bad luck." The beggar shuffled away. "All the time, bad luck."

A gushing of dark water from below convinced Dylan it was gone. He stood, brushed himself off, and started back.

He'd just lost his only lifeline back to the farm.

His trip had not begun well.

* * *

As everyone was about to sit down for supper, Margot held back and faced Pasqual. "I feel the need to paint."

"But it's late." He checked his watch. "If you start now, you'll be up all night."

"When the urge is this strong, I can't resist it."

As Pasqual exchanged puzzled glances with René, she hurried away.

In her studio, she found a fresh canvas, set it on the easel, and brought out her palette, paints, and brushes. It had been months since the desire to paint had come over her, and she wondered why it came now. And why so strong?

As usual, she didn't know where her brush would lead her, only that she must follow the Spirit who guided it. Absorbed in furious strokes, she lost track of time. Two hours later, the outline of a building, a street, and a restaurant appeared.

Only then did she realize what she was painting.

Faded letters appeared over the door—Das Alte Gasthaus. Then came a number—128, the address where Dylan was headed.

She was drawing a vision of the future. Something to do with Dylan's trip. And the next thing to appear were figures at the entrance—men in CSA uniforms, carrying guns, escorting someone in handcuffs.

Her heart beat faster as the face of their prisoner, the blond of his hair, took form.

It was Dylan. Dylan was the prisoner.

For one long moment, she backed away. The painting wasn't finished, but enough was visible.

It was a warning. Dylan was heading into a trap.

A glance at her watch revealed it was midnight. Whirling away from the easel, she raced upstairs and pounded on René's door. When no one answered, she knocked again, rattling the frame.

The former spy opened it, his hair askew, sleep in his eyes. "What is it?"

When she spilled what she had found, René nodded, said to wait while he dressed, then closed the door.

Moments later, after he examined what she'd done, he pulled his phone from his pocket and sent a coded message to Dylan.

They waited but received no answer.

"He's probably asleep." Margot couldn't stop her racing heart.

"I'll risk it and call him." René dialed.

They waited for him to pick up. But again, there was no answer.

He paced across the room. Several more times he dialed, each time without success. Whirling, he slammed a fist into a palm. "Something's wrong. He was supposed to keep the phone on at night, ready at all times to receive a call. He should have answered."

"What if it's just bad reception where he is?"

"Whatever the problem, we need to warn him. And before he meets those people tomorrow." He glanced at his watch. "If I leave now, I might get to him before he enters that building."

"What about traveling papers and a data card?"

"Victor can duplicate what he did for Dylan with a new name. But we have to move fast." Before Margot could respond, he was out the door and down the hall.

Alone again with her painting, she stared at what she'd done. It needed a few finishing touches, so she picked up her brush and began again.

By the time she'd completed the work, no more details were revealed. The original warning remained. She sat back and breathed deeply.

Dylan was in grave danger, and they had no way to reach him.

CHAPTER 32
THE GASTHAUS

Southern Germany – September, Year 2

René had been driving all night and smoking too much. Whenever he was on the road, his desire for a cigarette always increased. A month ago, when they'd raided an abandoned gas station, he'd taken every carton they had. Only he and two others at the farm were still smokers, and the others were smoking less, trying to quit. When his supply ran out . . . Well, he tried not to think about that.

Several times on the trip, he tried to reach Dylan, but to no avail. Reception in the village might be poor. Or maybe something had happened to the phone. Or to Dylan. Whatever the reason, he had to warn Dylan before he entered that gasthaus.

The route had been free of traffic, and he had driven at top speed on the autobahn, passing every vehicle. But the checkpoints were troublesome. No matter how few cars, there was always a line. Now the sun had risen, and traffic was increasing. And just ahead—another checkpoint. He slowed and entered a line of five vehicles. The driver of the lorry now being checked was chatting lazily with the guard. Both were laughing and smiling.

Fortunately, Victor's handiwork was getting him past all Davato's security.

He glanced again at his watch. The inn would open in twenty minutes, and he still had seventy kilometers to go.

Sticking his head out the window, he glared at the guards—as if that did any good. This was no time for small talk and pleasantries. He drummed his fingers on the steering wheel.

He was running out of time.

* * *

Dylan didn't wake until nine fifteen. After traveling all day yesterday, he could use a few more minutes of shut-eye. His breakfast at the pension consisted of a single hard roll, no butter, and no jam. There was also no coffee, only a mug with some kind of weak yellow tea—he'd heard people were now making tea from dandelions. He couldn't abide the taste.

The innkeeper gave his sincere apologies. "Mein Herr, if you are staying, we have nothing for you for lunch." He shrugged. "Is the famine, ja?"

He didn't need lunch, and he checked out. After he took his bag to the car, as René had instructed, he parked the vehicle away from the gasthaus, near the park. By the time he headed for Das Alte Gasthaus, it was nine forty-five.

A morning mist had dampened the street, and his shoes clicked on the wet pavement. As before, no one was about. But when his feet turned onto Ludwigstrasse and approached his destination, a black van was parked opposite the inn, and he slowed.

How odd that here in this sleepy village, he would see a new van, black, with tinted windows, parked near his destination. It hadn't been there yesterday. Then again, maybe he was just being paranoid. A lot of businesses used vans. So what if it was black and new?

To be safe, he continued walking, and as he passed the vehicle, he sent it a sidelong glance. He could see nothing through the black tinted windows. In front, a man in the driver's seat was reading his phone, a man wearing a white uniform. A repair technician?

What had René said to do? Watch the location before entering?

Continuing on to a café three doors down, he found an empty seat by the window. Indeed, all the seats were empty for he was the only patron. He entered, sat, and perused the menu. As elsewhere, most of the food selections had been crossed out. To his surprise, they had coffee, but for the dear price of thirty euros a cup. With cream, it was thirty-five. He gulped.

The waiter approached. "Mein Herr, this seat is only for paying customers. Do you wish to order something?"

He'd been given a wallet full of cash, yet paying such prices hurt. Still, to be safe he had to watch the building and van. Swallowing, he nodded.

"A cup of coffee, bitte. With cream. Is cash acceptable?"

The expression on the waiter's face changed from stern disapproval to a wide smile. "Ja, mein Herr. Of course. I take cash. Not everyone still does, but I do. It will take time to brew the coffee. I make the best—maybe the only—cup of coffee in Bad Kirchenstadt." Then muttering under his breath—something about what had the world come to?—he left.

From Dylan's vantage point, he could see both the gasthaus entrance and the van. This morning, a light was on inside the restaurant, and after a few minutes, a middle-aged, well-dressed man in a suit left with a younger woman, both heading away from the park. From all appearances, it looked like a legitimate establishment. And the longer he watched the van, the more he wondered if he was being overly concerned. Perhaps the driver was just waiting for a partner before going to work?

Was the gasthaus a center for the Christian underground?

Or was it a trap?

When the coffee came, he savored every sip. Months ago, they'd run out of coffee at the farm, and this was a rare treat. A glance at his watch showed ten fifteen, and he had only one sip left. So far, he'd seen nothing unusual.

He downed the last of it and called to the owner for his bill. Time to meet his contact.

* * *

René pulled off the autobahn, weaving too fast through the last roundabout into the quiet burg of Bad Kirchenstadt. He glanced at his watch—ten fifteen. Was he too late? Would Dylan already have gone through the door into the trap? Was he already handcuffed, heading toward an execution in the very camp they were trying to find?

René parked one block south of Ludwigstrasse. Pulling back on his pistol's slide, he put a cartridge in the chamber. He dropped the weapon into his pocket.

Breaking into a run, he crossed a connecting lane and slowed as he entered the main street. Which way were the house numbers going?

Turning right, he passed 45, then 41.

No, wrong way. He whirled and headed the opposite direction. The address lay just ahead.

A man was crossing the street ahead of him. He had his back to René. But his hair was blond, and there was something familiar about the way he walked.

"Dylan!" shouted René.

Too late, his friend opened the door and entered the gasthaus.

René slowed to a walk. What looked like a utility van was parked directly opposite the gasthaus entrance. The driver was talking to someone on his phone while watching the front door. René stiffened. Were there squaddies inside?

When he reached a Volkswagen Beetle, he ducked down behind it. Pulling out his gun, he peered through the sedan's windows. The van driver's eyes were focused on the inn. He had neither seen nor heard René. But there would be others inside the vehicle waiting for the signal to move against their quarry.

He slumped onto the wet sidewalk. Should he enter the inn now and try to get Dylan out the back? But what if there was no back way out and the squaddies moved in? Then they'd both be exposed on the street. Maybe he should wait here and open fire on whoever emerged from the van? That, at least, would distract them. Then they'd have to return fire on René, taking the heat off Dylan.

Neither choice was good.

Deciding on the second course, he gripped the gun tighter and waited.

* * *

AFTER DYLAN ENTERED THE GASTHAUS, he approached a counter, behind which sat a thin-faced woman. The room held no customers. Empty mugs and dirty plates remained on two of the four tables. Cigarette butts littered the floor. The place carried the odor of spilt beer, cigarette smoke, and musty drapes. Against the wall, a buffet table bore empty trays upon which were hunched two rats eating crumbs. But the innkeeper woman either didn't notice the rats or didn't care. Hadn't she heard his footsteps?

"Guten morgen," he said.

She glanced up, once, from her phone then ignored him. From a room in back came the sounds of men playing cards.

Dylan shivered. This did not look like a place where Christians would gather in secret.

He slipped his hand into his pocket and felt the Glock 17's cold metal. Should he back out now? Or carry this to its conclusion?

Frowning, the woman looked up. "Our rooms are full, and we served the last of our food this morning. What do you want?" Finally noticing the rats, she clapped her hands. But they didn't move.

He doubted her statements were true, and he hesitated, sent a glance to the door.

"Mein Herr?" The woman's frown deepened. "What can I do for you?"

Nothing about this place seemed right. But he'd come all this way. How could he back out now? His hand remained on the gun. "I'm here to see Kurt."

"Who did you say?" She cocked her head and leaned forward, laying both hands on the counter.

"Kurt. I was told to ask for Kurt."

For long seconds, she examined him in silence. "Then wait here." She left the counter and entered a door in back. After she closed it, the sounds of the card game ceased.

Glancing around, he saw no exits other than the door the woman had entered. He strolled to the front window. Out on the street, the van was still there. But—wait! The driver was opening the rear door, and men were getting out. His heart raced.

He whirled to the sound of footsteps behind him. Two men had emerged from the back room. One of them, a bearded man wore a black armband and held a pistol.

"Don't move!" The man waved his gun. "You are under arrest."

The front door was only five steps away. Dylan ducked and bolted for it.

A shot exploded from behind. It shattered the glass front. He slammed the door open and pushed through onto the sidewalk.

Across the street, four men wearing black armbands—more squaddies!—were racing toward him.

Then from the right—a pistol shot.

He winced and ducked again. But one of the squaddies on the street clutched his gut and fell.

Then he heard a familiar voice. "Dylan! Over here!"

It was René. Dylan ran east toward his friend.

René fired twice more. Behind Dylan came cursing and men scurrying for cover. His friend was hiding by a Volkswagen Beetle. Before Dylan reached him, a shot echoed from behind. Stone chipped and sparked off the sidewalk. Then came another shot, and something stung his calf. He slid behind the car's protective cover as René fired back.

Dylan slumped down, breathing fast, trying to catch his breath. "Am I glad to see you!" His hand reached for the spot on his leg where blood now soaked his pants. His fingers came back red. He gritted his teeth at a sudden jolt of pain.

"You were hit." René frowned.

Dylan opened the tear in his pants made by the bullet, ripped it wider, and examined the wound. "It only grazed me."

"Good." René poked his head up and fired again. "We need to get out of here. Can you run?"

"I think . . . so."

"Where is your car?" He popped out a magazine and clicked in another.

Dylan pointed beyond the squaddies toward the park.

"Drat! We'll have to leave it and take mine. On my signal, stand and fire. If we both keep shooting, they'll have to take cover." René threw a nod to the east. "If we can make that intersection, my vehicle is only a block away. Are you ready?"

His heart beating wildly, Dylan took another deep breath and said he was.

"One. Two." On three, René stood and fired.

Dylan rose and shot at the men hiding behind the van. His bullet punched a hole in the metal, and heads ducked out of sight.

Only one body lay in the street.

He fired at a head sticking out from the inn, and glass exploded nearby.

"Run!" came René's order, and Dylan ran.

Each step brought a stab of pain, and he limped. But adrenaline pumped through his veins, propelling him past the pain into a sprint.

Behind him, René fired twice more. Their ploy must have worked, as he heard only one return shot, and that went wild, ricocheting off the storefront bricks over his head.

At the intersection, Dylan veered right and slowed until René caught up. Then they ran to the next block where a left turn brought them to the Peugeot. René got behind the wheel, and they peeled away with a screeching of tires. Before the next turn, Dylan shot a glance back.

Two men emerged from the side street, aimed, and fired. But both shots again went wild. René spun the vehicle through the next intersection back onto Ludwigstrasse, and they headed for the autobahn.

"Did they see our plates?" asked Dylan.

"Doesn't matter. We'll pull off somewhere, and I'll change them. There's a first aid kit in the glove box."

He pulled up his pant leg. The wound wasn't deep but still bled. His pants below the knee were soaked red. Wincing, he dabbed the wound with iodine, put on gauze, then bandaged it. "How did you know to come for me? I dropped my phone into a storm drain."

"So that's why we couldn't reach you! What a klutz!"

Dylan returned René's smile.

"Margot painted a picture of you being arrested in front of the gasthaus, but when I couldn't reach you, I had no choice but to come here in person. I've been driving all night."

"Thanks." Once again, Margot's paintings—led by the hand of God—were leading them. He faced the way ahead. "The whole setup back there was a trap. And we almost took the bait."

"Oui. And that was our only lead. Now, we have no idea how to find that camp."

Another bout of pain shivered up his leg, and he flinched. "What if, after my wound heals, I returned to this area? I could scour every small village and inquire about a nearby camp."

René shook his head. "You'd have to visit every burg in the entire region. And we don't even know if it's in Germany. It might take weeks, maybe months. Someone would surely notice. Far too risky."

The Peugeot entered the autobahn, and René sped up. The scenery whizzed by.

"What other choice do we have?"

René shot him a worried glance. "I don't know."

CHAPTER 33

PLAGUE AND PESTILENCE

Revelation 6:7–8 (NLT): When the Lamb broke the fourth seal, I heard the fourth living being say, "Come!" I looked up and saw a horse whose color was pale green. Its rider was named Death, and his companion was the Grave. These two were given authority over one-fourth of the earth, to kill with the sword and famine and disease and wild animals.

Jerusalem, Israel – October, Year 2

Baruch Abramovich left Temple Mount where he'd convinced a few worshipers to come to the next meeting tomorrow. Attendance at the Temple was sparse. For the last month, since mid-September, people were staying in their homes, hiding from the epidemic. Now he was headed for the Beit Shalom Garden for a bit of peace and meditation. But he'd barely left the square when he passed the bodies of an old man and a young woman lying unclaimed beside the walkway. Like others he'd seen, their faces were black and bloated, their necks bulging with open sores. He shuddered. The death trucks couldn't keep up.

It was happening all over the city—a mysterious illness spreading through the populace, killing even the rats whose populations had recently exploded. And a moment ago, two men wearing yarmulkes had hurried past him from the Temple, their faces newly wet with fever, twisted with worry.

Surely, this was the harvest of the fourth seal, this disease following the famine. All that was missing was more war. And with the news reports of enemy troops and tanks gathering on Israel's borders, this, too, couldn't be far off.

A horde of rats—hundreds, with naked tails and ears—swarmed across the walk ahead. Rising from the pack came a fingernails-on-chalkboard chorus of high-pitched squealing. Grimacing, he backed up ten meters and waited. The rodents no longer feared people. They seemed to be everywhere. He'd even heard reports from the poorer quarters of babies lying in their cribs and of drunks lying in alleys being eaten alive by the foul creatures. When the path was again clear, he walked on.

The garden was in sight when a man ran up behind him. "Baruch Abramovich?"

Baruch turned and found one of the men who'd promised to come to the meeting tomorrow. "Shalom, Doron Goldman."

"Shalom, Rabbi." Despite the famine, Doron seemed well-fed. His tailored suit also announced he was well off. Nowadays, only the wealthy, or those who had prepared, were eating well.

"What can I do for you, Doron?"

"I am eager to hear what you have to say about the vanishing." He stopped to catch his breath. "I've heard the official explanation about UFOs, and it's rubbish. We've also heard that those who were taken were all Christians. Is that so, Rabbi?"

"Yes, but in my talk tomorrow, I will touch only briefly on that event."

Doron swept a hand through a thinning mane of white hair. "So perhaps you could tell me your thoughts on the subject now?"

Baruch's glance went up and down the walk, but they were alone. David Benjamin had impressed on him, again and again, that everywhere he went he must ensure he wasn't being followed—not necessarily for his sake, but for the safety of those he was with. "Come with me. I know of a quiet bench nearby."

Doron nodded, and Baruch led him at a leisurely pace to a favorite overlook from which to view the city below.

When they were seated, Baruch faced his new admirer. "I come here often to rest my soul, to pray, and to bring my petitions to God. What do you want to know about the vanishing?"

"Specifically, Rabbi, was it prophesied? I have heard this, and if so, this would greatly strengthen my faith."

"It was, my friend. There are several passages, but one in particular from First Thessalonians 4:16 goes like this: 'For the Lord Himself will descend from heaven with a shout, with the archangel's voice, and with the trumpet of God, and the dead in Christ will rise first. Then we who are still alive will be caught up together with them in the clouds to meet the Lord in the air and so we will always be with the Lord.' "

Baruch paused while Doron took a pen and pad and wrote down the reference. "That, my friend, is precisely what happened on the day the world turned upside down. And those of us who did not yet believe that God had sent his Son to earth, who were not yet followers of Jesus, were left behind. Except, of course, for those of us who were meant to stay and help others find their way."

Baruch gave him more references, after which Doron put away his notebook. "Rabbi, I have recently bought a copy of the Christian Bible on the black market. Only days ago, I started reading."

"That is good. Here is something to ponder as you read: Though this Davato claims to be a friend of the Jews, that will soon change. He is a liar, a deceiver, and a tool of Satan himself."

Startled, Doron's eyes widened. "This is true? This man is not who he claims to be?"

"When you get to the last book of the Bible—to Revelation—you will find a description of him. Davato is the Antichrist, also called the beast and the man of lawlessness."

The man's gaze found the horizon. "It makes sense. So many things about him have puzzled me—his mesmerizing personality, his thirst for power, and more recently, his apparent hatred of Christians."

"Then you are a discerning man, my friend. Only a few recognize the danger he poses."

Closing his eyes, Doron let out a deep breath then faced him. "Baruch, I am a wealthy man. I have read the account of the rich Zaccheus in the book of Luke, and my heart is troubled. I confess I have many sins to atone for. As such, I wish to give your organization a large contribution. Will you accept my offering?"

Surprised, Baruch laid a hand on the man's shoulder and smiled. "It's not your gifts or your deeds that will save you, Doron. It's your heart. Do you believe that Jesus died on the cross for you and that he is the Son of God sent to earth? Are you willing to hold fast to him through the great trials ahead?"

Doron swallowed. "I . . . do."

"Then that is what is most important. That is what makes you a child of God. In that case—yes!—I will accept your contribution." He then told Doron that someone would be at the meeting tomorrow to work out the details of the transaction.

Smiling ear to ear, Doron thanked him, bowed, thanked him again, and then left.

Finally alone, Baruch prepared himself for his original purpose in coming here—to rest his soul with prayer.

He breathed deeply of the chrysanthemums growing in a pot near the bench. The sweet scent offered a welcome change from the foul smoke of burning bodies always thickening the air, rising even now from the streets below. There were now so many dead that the government could no longer deal with the problem. Neighborhoods had begun their own collection centers, creating great pyres of burning corpses in the streets.

A few news outlets had initially reported that the disease was the bubonic plague and that antibiotics were the cure. But nearly all the rest, including all the social media companies, slavishly followed the government's dictates. All were now squelching the antibiotic "theory", as they derisively called it, canceling the accounts of anyone daring to tell the truth. The government even ran ads warning people about the dangers of unauthorized antibiotic use.

Last week, Baruch did an internet search and found it scrubbed of the fact that certain antibiotics did, indeed, cure the disease. According to the internet, there was not now, nor had there ever been, a cure for the bubonic plague. Only after he went in person to the National Library and sat down with a set of printed encyclopedias did he confirm what he'd remembered. But this week, when he returned with a skeptical David Benjamin, all the encyclopedias were gone.

The truth was that the shadow darkening Europe and the world was indeed the Black Death. And the government was hiding the fact that the antibiotics no one could obtain were the cure.

The reason for the scarcity was obvious: Supply chains everywhere had collapsed. Stores were running out of everything, not just antibiotics. For the last year, pharmacies had complained that their drug orders were not being filled. Manufacturers protested that they couldn't get the raw materials needed to produce most drugs. And after the Great Catastrophe, when lawlessness had erupted everywhere, many stores had been broken into, looted, and then closed.

Two-thirds of the people believed the news media. They were the ones now dying in droves. The other third had long ago learned to be skeptical of the authorities' lies and half-truths. For them, the rumors of a cure had created a vast underground market for the remaining lifesaving drugs that were now more precious than gold.

Today, Baruch's heart was troubled by the famine, by the plague, and by those who had died. Most of them would face a bleak eternity.

He closed his eyes and prayed. He thanked the Lord for protecting his followers in the Great Assembly. He asked that tomorrow people might hear his words and believe. He praised the Father for the hope of a blessed future with Christ in Heaven.

How he longed for an end of suffering, pain, and death! How he yearned for the New Jerusalem, the New Earth, and the eternal Holy City! Yes. Each day, it became clearer and clearer.

This world was not his home.

The clatter of mechanized vehicles disturbed his prayers. Down in the valley, tanks were rolling through the city. Hundreds of diesel engines rumbled and roared. Thousands of wheels squeaked. Thousands of chains clanked over pavement. The noise became deafening—even up here on his overlook. Following the tanks was an endless caravan of armored trucks carrying troops. Then came missile batteries, supply trucks, and machine-gun-mounted jeeps. A cloud of diesel exhaust rolled over the city, rising along the line of their passing. Even here, he caught a whiff of diesel fumes. Even up here, the planter with the chrysanthemums rattled, and the ground beneath his feet shook.

As far as he could see, from south to north, troop carriers, camouflaged tanks, armored vehicles, and mounted missile batteries thundered north.

These last few days, the news had been filled with warnings about the massing of Islamic and Russian forces on Israel's borders. Everyone feared there was going to be a war. Some people had even fled to the hills. But until Baruch had seen this, that news had been distant, unreal.

Finally, the convoy passed, and all was again quiet.

Then he lowered his head for a final prayer. "Lord, let your will be done."

CHAPTER 34
UNDER A CLOUD

Jerusalem, Israel – October, Year 2

Chelsea hurried with Grady through the city's empty streets. Their destination was only blocks from the Clal Center, but even here, they passed corpses lying in the gutters, on the sidewalks, in the alleys. The bloated, blackened faces of the dead testified to the utter failure—or was it intentional?—of the Unitum Imperium to provide the antibiotics needed to quell the plague. As if it could stop her shivering, she clutched her arms around her chest and hurried on.

Despite extraordinary measures, the rats had somehow infested every floor of the Unitum Imperium's Jerusalem headquarters. But Davato had stockpiled the antibiotics he needed, and when several staff, including Chelsea, experienced the first symptoms of the plague—headache, fever, swollen glands—those in his employ received the cure and recovered.

A hundred meters beyond the smoke, they reached their goal, an upscale café that was still open. Only one other couple—well-fed and wealthy by the look of their clothes and jewelry—occupied a table at the room's far end. Chelsea and Grady sat near the front by an open window.

With his UI credit card, Grady ordered falafel and coffee for both. Only the rich or those in the UI's employ could now afford to eat in restaurants, and the proprietor had raised his prices accordingly. Even so, Chelsea shook her head whenever she perused a menu.

"This is a terrible time to leave the command center, but maybe not." Grady breathed deeply. "Everyone's attention is on the borders."

"I wonder when the attack will come. It must be soon."

"We should eat then hurry back before we're missed. But I haven't been out in a while." He threw a frown at the street. "What I just saw out there—it's troubling."

"Nowadays, everything is." She opened her arms as if to encompass the whole city. "Especially Davato."

Grady raised a finger to his lips. "Not so loud. If anyone found out what you were saying . . ."

She shuddered. "I had to talk with someone, and I think your views are the same as mine. Did Clemente approach you recently?" Clemente was one of the Italian technical wizards Davato had recently brought from Rome.

Grady narrowed his eyes. "No. What did he say?"

She lowered her voice even further. "He took me aside. Through a roundabout and rather weird conversation, I got the impression he was deeply disturbed by what Davato is doing."

"What else did he say?" Grady frowned.

"He asked me if I was ready to do something about it. I then asked what he meant by that, and he said something like, 'He must be stopped. We cannot allow him to go on. He must be removed.' I responded, 'What do you have in mind?' "

"What did he say to that?"

"He looked at me and drew a finger across his throat. Then he asked me if, when the time came, could I help get him to the right place at the right time?"

"Oh." Grady's face paled. "That kind of talk is extremely dangerous."

"That's what I told him. At that point, we were in the hall, someone was approaching, and I wanted nothing to do with his plans. I said we couldn't talk of such matters at work, and I hurried back to my desk. But afterward, I got to thinking: Why did he approach me, of all people? Have I been *that* transparent in my doubts about Davato?"

For a moment, Grady was silent. "That tells me we must be even more careful. Especially you."

"Even so, I need to talk with someone about what's going on, or I'll go crazy." She shivered, then reached across the table, and touched his hands, bringing a smile to Grady's lips.

"Chelsea, we are two Americans swept up in something far bigger than us. And it's getting scarier every day. But I want to change the subject." He swept a hand through his hair. "I've been waiting to get you alone. And now I'd like to say something to you, something personal."

"What?" She cocked her head.

"From the moment we met, I liked you." His hand covered hers and squeezed. "No, it's more than that. I've never met a woman like you, and I feel a deep and growing attraction for you."

Heat radiated from his touch, up her arms to her neck. "Why, Grady, that's nice. Really nice. And I like you too."

He lifted her fingers to his lips and kissed them. Her heart began racing.

The waiter brought them their coffee, and he released her. Was he falling in love with her? Though she liked him, she didn't think she was ready for a deep relationship. She cleared her throat. "Perhaps we should wait and see how we feel in a month or so?"

He winced and furrowed his forehead. "I suppose this is a surprise to you—my feelings for you?"

"No, I just think we should go slow, see how it goes. There's so much going on right now. The famine. The plague. The coming war. . . ."

"I understand."

Now *she* needed to change the subject. "What did you think about the Prophet's last declaration?"

Grady shook his head. "His claims about Davato, especially to the staff, make him appear almost as if he's some kind of god. He's very convincing, and many people seem to believe what he's saying. I'm not a religious person, but . . ." He frowned and seemed to turn inward.

"But what?"

"Why do so many believe him?"

"They're afraid, Grady." Chelsea sipped from her mug. The waiter had made the coffee *Americano* style, just for them. "The Truth Squads and the CSA agents are everywhere, terrorizing the people. When you see your neighbor taken in the middle of the night, when a wrong word spoken in truth brings the black vans to take you away, along with your father, sister, or fiancé—word gets around. Then people start to accept what they know is not true. And after a time of accepting what is false, repeating it out loud, and looking the other way, it changes you. It's like a poison—always agreeing to these untruths—and it embitters the soul. I know because, before all this began, it was happening to me with the woke thing."

"I think you're right." He narrowed his eyes and focused on something out on the street. "Maybe that's what I'm experiencing. I'm glad you said it. Because sometimes, I believe Davato and the Prophet. And I think it's changing me."

"Don't let it, Grady. Fight it." She gripped her mug, and her glance speared him. "We need to get out. We're trapped. We're living in fear that, by accident, we'll say what we believe, and then we'll disappear and end up in that camp. Clemente must have sensed that. And if he did, maybe Davato does too."

"There is no way out." His gaze wandered again to the street. "Not for us. We're on the inside now, and they know everything about us. And we know too much about them. The moment we tried to escape, they'd come after us with everything they've got. Admit it. We have to go along with whatever they say."

"No, no, don't say that." She brought both hands to her mouth. "We're trapped now, yes, but if we can find a way out, we'll be all right."

"I wonder if any of it will soon matter. This war that's coming may be the end of all of us."

"You've got a point. The forces building against Israel right now are overwhelming." On the street, an older couple passed by, hand in hand. Would they be among the dead? Would she and Grady? They *had* to find a way out. "I don't see how we're going to prevail."

"You said 'we'."

"As long as we're working in Davato's headquarters, our fate is tied with his. Maybe when the bombs start to fall, in the confusion of war—that will give us an opportunity to escape?"

"I doubt it. But quiet now." He faced the café's interior. "Here's our food."

The smiling waiter crossing the floor bore two plates of falafel with rice.

* * *

AFTER EATING, THEY RETURNED TO the command center by a different route.

Only a block from their destination, they entered an intersection where two masked and gloved men were pulling corpses from a flatbed truck. The lifeless limbs flopped as they left the heap before the men tossed them onto a great funeral pyre. The fire sent up clouds of thick, black smoke. A sickening haze, reeking of burnt flesh and bones, hovered about the street.

Chelsea gagged. Barely able to breathe, she groped in her purse for a handkerchief to cover her nose and mouth. Though her heart raced out of control, she paused, mesmerized by the rising flames, the crackling bones, the hissing flesh.

What was it about the pyre that so transfixed her?—this gruesome vision of blackened faces, open sores, and bloated corpses. The bodies of old men. A child of perhaps fourteen. The middle-aged housewives. A businessman still in his suit. So many dead from all walks of life. So many corpses, some now sliding off the side of the truck bed onto the street. The enormity of it struck her with sudden, unexpected force, and she gasped.

Beside her, Grady grabbed her hand and yanked. His touch snapped her out of it.

When they were a hundred meters down the street and breathing cleaner air in front of the Clal building, she stopped.

She spun toward him and brought her hands to her face. "What is happening . . . to the world?" Her voice cracked, mirroring the rip the pyre seemed to have rent in her soul. She waved a hand down the street. "Everything is falling apart. Davato. Famine. Plague. Rats. Death every-where. And now—the threat of war. The world is ending, Grady, and I don't know what is happening anymore." A shivering, like nothing she'd ever felt before, gripped her. It started in her shoulders, moved to her torso, and rippled down her legs. She lifted pained eyes to him. "I've never felt so scared."

His eyes bored into hers. When he spoke, his voice trembled, and he looked away, afraid to catch her gaze. "I have an idea about this, Chelsea, and it t–terrifies me."

"What?"

"Do you believe in God?"

"I—I don't know. But I'm beginning to come around to the idea."

"Well, I don't believe in God. What I do believe in is evil people, and I know that we humans have royally screwed things up down here. What if some power greater than ourselves—maybe it's not God, but the earth, like Davato suggests—what if such a power has looked down on the sorry state of humanity and given up on us? I'm not Jewish, and I don't believe in the Tanakh, but a prophet in that book—Isaiah, I think—says that when a people turn away from God, he will turn away from them. But the principle is the same. What if we have so messed things up that whatever power is above us has become so disgusted with us that it's decided to wipe us off the face of the planet? So *that* is what I think. And you know what else?"

"No, what?"

"I think this is only the beginning."

She'd never heard him talk like that before. Rarely had he spoken of God or what he called some vaguely defined higher power. It didn't surprise her that he didn't believe in God.

Another shiver started in her shoulders and ran down her spine, and then she knew, deep in her heart, Grady was wrong in one respect—there was a God.

And yes, maybe this *was* God's judgment on the world.

CHAPTER 35

ON THE BRINK

Ezekiel 38:14–16 (HCSB): *"Therefore prophesy, son of man, and say to Gog: This is what the Lord GOD says: On that day when My people Israel are dwelling securely, will you not know this and come from your place in the remotest parts of the north—you and many peoples with you, who are all riding horses—a mighty horde, a huge army? You will advance against My people Israel like a cloud covering the land. It will happen in the last days, Gog, that I will bring you against My land so that the nations may know Me, when I show Myself holy through you in their sight."h*

Khan Alsheh, Syria – October, Year 2

Jaleel Hasani wiped at the sweat dripping from his brow. It was eleven o'clock in the morning, and the long-awaited hour for Israel's destruction had arrived. Despite the heat—excessively warm for October—the mood of everyone inside the field tent outside of Khan Alsheh, Syria, not forty kilometers from Israel's Golan Heights, was jubilant. From this tent, Najafi—the Grand Ayatollah, the Supreme Leader, the commander-in-chief over all of Iran's forces—had decided to direct the battle.

Jaleel regarded with longing the two air-conditioning units set into the tent wall behind the computers and monitors. But by the time the breeze passed the equipment and got to him, the hot breath of the desert had already reclaimed it. He had begged to stay in Tehran, but Najafi had insisted the country's president must be present at command headquarters with the rest. "As a show of Muslim solidarity against the heathen Davato and the Zionists," he'd said. "Besides, our forces are so overwhelming, no one will be in any danger."

Their arrival at Damascus International Airport had been troublesome. Their landing over the uneven tarmac was rough. The plane bounced, jerked from side to side, took off, and then landed again. He was still in his seat when he'd lost the copious lunch he'd eaten before takeoff. Then, to his chagrin, he discovered they wouldn't be staying in the four-star hotel he'd picked out.

The Supreme Leader insisted that his entourage move to rat-infested army field tents two dozen kilometers southwest of Damascus. Jaleel hadn't had a shower for three days. And now, instead of eating in four-star restaurants, he'd been given barely edible army field rations.

Each night, he'd been awakened to the sound of sporadic gunfire—soldiers shooting rats in violation of orders. But who could blame them? The vermin were everywhere. This morning, only the prospect of Israel's imminent annihilation softened his mood.

With him now under the canvas were iron-faced General Mir Ansari, commanding the Islamic Republic of Iran Army. Impatient to get underway, Ansari beat his trademark switch against his thigh. At his side was Bayat Mahdi, chief of the Islamic Revolutionary Guard Corps. A long scar on his cheek marred the man's thin visage, reminding Jaleel of a nightmarish scarecrow he'd seen in one of those banned Western horror movies he'd smuggled into his palace.

As usual, when the Grand Ayatollah entered last, he wore a black ankle-length robe with white turban. While the others stood, he sat. The rest, including Jaleel, wore desert camouflage and berets. But the uniform chafed, the heat was oppressive, and he wished he were in his country house above the Caspian Sea where the midday breezes didn't burn the skin.

The fifth man of importance inside the tent was the Russian liaison, Colonel Vladislav. Decked in mottled green-and-brown desert camouflage, the stocky, stone-faced Russian looked on the proceedings with apparent disdain.

With the leaders were Najafi's servant, Perviz, and some twenty technicians and aides hovering about the monitors and computers, ready to squash any technical glitches and keep the information flowing, the computers humming, and the leaders served with tea, water, and food.

General Ansari was about to explain what was happening on the monitors to everyone when an army lieutenant—too young for his position, possibly the son of some important general—burst into the tent.

"Yes, Lieutenant?" The general's normally crusty expression soured further. "What is it?"

"General, sir, excuse me, sir, but I was told to bring you an urgent report from the hospital field tents."

"The fighting hasn't started yet." He whopped his leather switch against his leg. "What could possibly be the problem?"

"Sir, there is much illness among the men. Fevers, chills, headaches, weakness. Excuse me, sir, but I was told to report to you that the hospital tents are nearly full."

Ansari shook his head and closed his eyes. "The plague?"

"Possibly." The young man lowered his eyes and took a step back.

"Either it is, or it isn't." Ansari's opened eyes so speared the uncertain lieutenant that he cowered.

"Yes, sir. I believe it is."

"There's nothing we can do about it now. We have a war to win. Whoever is fit enough to fight, must fight. Tell the hospital people that, when the wounded arrive, they should move the plague victims outside to make room for real casualties."

The lieutenant, finally showing some backbone, started to object, but Ansari brushed him off and turned to Najafi.

"Sorry for the interruption, Supreme Leader." He straightened his posture and waved his switch at the nearest screens. "The monitors in front of you show our forces in Syria."

Jaleel's gaze followed the general's stick. He marveled at the five armored tank divisions, the row upon row of trucks bearing seven army divisions, and beside them, the two divisions of Republican Guard troops. Behind the troops, missile batteries were lined up as far as the eye could see. One monitor showed an air base far in the rear and a runway filled with Grumman F-14 American Tomcat fighters and Mikoyan MIG-29s from the Russians. Plus, dozens of American helicopter gunships left behind in Afghanistan.

"Impressive, indeed." Najafi raised his cane, a signal for the general to proceed.

"The displays on the left are from drones we've sent aloft. They'll give us an overall view of the Russian armies in Lebanon, the forces beside us here in Syria, and the Russian army that has already taken up positions in Jordan. We can also see into the Golan Heights. The two on the far left are flying above the Sinai."

"Have we heard from the king of Jordan about these incursions?" Najafi faced Jaleel. "Or from Egyptian President Kareem?"

"Yes, Supreme Leader." His uniform now soggy and clinging to his chest, Jaleel again wiped at his brow. "I had conference calls with both this morning. I assured the Jordanian king that the Russian forces are only passing through. The king's response was a weak objection followed by silence. Likewise, after I assured President Kareem that the invasion forces would soon leave the Sinai, he merely nodded. Then he said it was in the will of Allah to finally drive both the Jewish obscenity and the blasphemous upstart from the land. He then gave us his blessing."

"Excellent." Najafi returned his gaze to Ansari.

The army general pointed to his right. "Those screens will display images from cameras embedded with the Turkish fleet, the Libyan army, the Sudanese, the Ethiopians, and the tribal fighters of the Sayf Alsharaf." Ansari raised himself to his full height. "In all, I am happy to report that Iran has committed two hundred fifty thousand men to the fight. The Russians—another three hundred fifty thousand. I estimate that, counting all the forces arrayed against the Zionist and Imperium stronghold, we have well over a million men."

"Very good, General." Najafi thumped his cane three times in approval. "Swimmingly good, indeed. It has all gone swimmingly well."

Jaleel cringed at the Supreme Leader's use of words but nodded his agreement.

Then Ansari crossed his arms, his iron-faced visage seeming to harden. "But now I must relate that in all cases we experienced a good deal of resistance from our so-called allies to placing cameras with their units. There seems to be"—he cleared his throat—"mistrust about our motives. I had to insist in the strongest possible terms that, if we are to coordinate, we need to see the entirety of the battle from these headquarters."

Najafi turned to Vladislav, a man who spoke both Farsi and Arabic. "Did that objection also come from the Russians, Colonel?"

"Da." Vladislav crossed his arms. "We understand you Iranians planned the strategy and you will start the operation. But that is where your command will end. It is President Petrov who will lead. So these cameras inside our units"—he waved a hand at the screens—"is like mother-in-law standing over shoulder, questioning everything. It betrays a lack of trust."

"I am sorry the Russians feel that way. But my generals thought it necessary."

Najafi's servant Perviz looked up. "The Russian president is calling you, Supreme Leader."

"Answer it."

Dressed all in black, Perviz struck some keys on a laptop then set it on a pedestal before the Supreme Leader. The laptop was already plugged into one of the larger screens on the wall. After Perviz punched more keys, the face of President Petrov appeared on the wall monitor, his dark hair slicked back, his eyes on fire. Walls of another field tent filled the space behind him, along with half a dozen, stony-faced Russian generals.

Petrov's face was red and flushed as if he had been drinking. "Najafi, why are you spying on me and my troops?" He'd spoken in English, the one language they all knew.

The Supreme Leader wrapped his black robe about one arm and straightened his back. "No one is spying on you, President Petrov. If you are referring to the cameras"—he gripped his cane tighter—"we placed them in all units to properly coordinate the fight."

"So you say. I am suspicious of these cameras. You have also overruled my orders as to the placement of troops and the order of battle. I reluctantly agreed—reluctantly, I say—that you would start this war. But after that—" He stood, stalked from the table where he'd been sitting, returned, and leaned down to the camera. Jaleel imagined he could smell vodka through the glass. "After you have given the signal, I—the leader of the great Russian people—will lead this fight. *I*, not you, will command."

Najafi stiffened. "President Petrov, everything is in place. This is no time for second-guessing. We must proceed as originally agreed."

Petrov stared at the screen, lowered a hand, and brought it back with a shot glass of clear liquid. He downed it in one gulp. "We agreed you would start the operation, and that is all we agreed to. Is my liaison present?"

Jaleel cringed at the Russian's disregard for the proper respect due the Grand Ayatollah.

"He is here." Najafi's tone was cold.

Perviz turned the laptop so its camera faced the Russian liaison.

"Colonel Vladislav," said Petrov in Russian, "please inform me at once of any further irregularities you observe at Iranian headquarters." Jaleel understood enough Russian to catch the meaning.

Vladislav bolted upright, saluted, and answered that he would.

His face reddening, Najafi leaned down. Then he himself pushed the key to end the call. After taking a few deep breaths, he turned to Generals Ansari and Mahdi. "Is everything in readiness?"

General Mahdi, who'd already called units on his satellite phone, straightened. "The Revolutionary Guard is ready to deliver a crushing blow to the Zionists and the interloper."

For his part, Ansari slapped his switch against his thigh. Then he picked up his satellite phone and began checking in with units. There were some twenty points of control, twenty calls to make, excluding the Russians. Vladislav had his own sat phone, and he walked away from the others to make his call. When Ansari and Vladislav had finished checking with their units, both said they were good to go.

The Supreme Leader scanned each man in the room. "This day will long be remembered in the history of Islam as the day the Zionists were driven into the sea. Never has such a force been assembled against Israel, now occupied by this blasphemous upstart." He swept a fierce gaze from General Ansari to Colonel Vladislav. "Begin the attack!"

Ansari picked up his satellite phone and gave the word. Colonel Vladislav and General Mahdi did the same.

As his eyes focused on the displays of Iranian and Russian missile launchers, Jaleel's heart raced. This was the moment they had long awaited. After the missile and air attacks, would there be anything left for the ground and tank troops to do? They expected Israel's Iron Dome defense to stop some of the incoming rockets. But the projectiles heading toward the enemy were so numerous, coming all at once, that the defenders had no hope of stopping all of them.

All across the vast field where the missile trucks had been parked, mobile launchers raised their canisters to the sky. From behind thousands of launcher vehicles, exhaust fumes washed the ground. Thousands upon thousands of missiles left their launch platforms and rose, streaking the sky with so many white contrails, they merged into one great white cloud.

Other screens showed hundreds of missiles rising from the Turkish fleet in the west.

Then, even before the missiles had finished leaving their canisters, the jets behind them began taking off. One after another, they followed the missiles, heading toward strategic military targets in Israel.

Jaleel took a deep breath and smiled. The imminent destruction of the Zionists and the upstart Davato was only moments away.

CHAPTER 36

IMPOSSIBLE EVENTS

Jerusalem, Israel – October, Year 2

Davato watched Chelsea and Grady Wilson return from lunch together—again. He didn't like how close they had become. Both were Americans, and perhaps it was understandable they were drawn to each other. Grady might have potential, but Davato still harbored suspicions about Chelsea after that Paris meeting with her brother. Unfortunately, his agents had been unable to hear their conversation. Sure, he understood why she would want to meet with her brother, especially since they'd been close. But she'd been secretive, and she'd never reported the meeting. Fortunately, she'd been unaware of the events in the square after she and her brother parted.

Still, her brother was a rebel, and her duty had been to turn him in. They would find and deal with him. And, whenever she was in a foreign city, he'd have her followed. If she didn't prove loyal to him and his goals, there was room in the camp for one more.

But today his focus was on the invasion. Never since he'd come to power had such doubts and fear gripped him. He faced his commanding general. "Hofmann, tell me we are prepared to deal with what's coming."

General Hofmann shook his white mane and wiped sweat from his brow. The man hadn't slept in the last twenty-four hours, and the circles under his eyes sagged. "We've done all we could. Our forces have dug in opposite wherever the enemy has positioned themselves. But, my lord"—while Davato smiled at the new appellation he'd asked everyone to address him with in private, Hofmann opened his hands in apology—"the forces are so overwhelming. I have done everything I could, but . . ."

Davato narrowed his eyes. "You will prevail. You *must* prevail." He whirled away from his general and slammed a fist into a palm. Could everything fall apart here, now, on this day? He'd read the Enemy's book, but he didn't believe anything was preordained. No one, not even the

Enemy, could predict the future. Only in the present situation did he hope the book was correct.

"My lord." Hofmann hurried to one of the consoles. "Look!"

Davato whipped his gaze to the monitors. All along the front line of the Syrian, Jordanian, Lebanese, and Sinai borders, missile contrails were rising into the sky. His heart pounded. "Shoot them down!"

"Of course, my lord. Our men have standing orders. It should happen any moment now."

But as he watched the screens displaying the Israeli Iron Dome launchers, nothing happened. He spun toward the general. "Why aren't they firing? They should be firing."

Hofmann had already picked up a sat phone and was talking with someone. The conversation became heated. Then he hung up and called another unit, but with the same result. Again wiping the sweat from his eyes, he called yet a third unit. That conversation, too, was impassioned.

When the general hung up, the life seemed to have gone out of him, and his shoulders slumped. "Something has happened. None of our missiles are firing."

But another monitor where even more missiles had risen from the Turkish fleet drew Davato's gaze. The screens also showed hundreds of fighter jets streaking after the missiles.

"How . . . long?" His heart hammered against his ribs. His tongue was thickening. Could the Enemy have abandoned his own book? Would it all end now?

"For the missiles—only a minute or two."

Silence descended on the control center as the monitors showing their impending doom drew everyone's complete attention. The Clal Center would surely be first among the targets.

Filled with sudden doubt, Davato staggered toward the exit and left the room. He entered the hall where a bank of windows faced north. He could see them now with the naked eye—thousands upon thousands of rocket contrails, each carrying a load of high explosives, many of which would be aimed right at him. Some surely carried the deadly vacuum bombs that filled the air with poisonous fumes before they imploded the lungs. But wait!

The contrails were disappearing in midflight. Where they should have completed their arcs downward, they . . . simply . . . stopped. He rushed back inside to the monitors.

"They're vanishing!" Hofmann's hands gripped both sides of his head. "They're dissolving in midair."

Hofmann ordered the cameras to zero in on one section of sky. Yes, it was as if every contrail's arc had been erased. The moment the missiles began their descents, they simply vanished.

Davato found the screens showing the launch of the fighters. The same thing was happening there. Every jet simply disappeared in midair.

Ten minutes later, it was over. Every missile, every fighter jet, every airborne weapon had ceased to exist.

Hofmann turned to Davato with open mouth and disbelieving eyes. "It's a miracle. It's not possible."

"And yet, it happened." So the Enemy's book, in this case, was correct. Taking a deep breath and smiling, Davato called to Chelsea. "Bring me a sandwich. And a beer."

Her head jerked up, her eyes narrowing at his response to events. Then she nodded and hurried from the room.

* * *

As the missiles and jets vanished in midflight, a silence filled only by the malfunctioning air-conditioning units gripped the command tent southeast of Khan Alsheh. Jaleel wiped sweat from his eyes and tried to focus on the screens. This couldn't be happening. None of this was possible. Every one of the thousands upon thousands of rockets and jets seemed to have been destroyed—vanished? erased?—in midair.

"What is this?" As if to see the monitors better, Najafi rose from his seat and leaned forward on his cane. "Why aren't they reaching their targets?"

"I—I don't know, Supreme Leader." General Ansari picked up a sat phone and called someone. After six more such conversations, he staggered to a chair and slumped into it. "There is no explanation. The missiles, the jets—they are no longer showing up on radar. They are simply . . . no . . . more.”

Najafi dropped back into his seat, a bewildered gaze seeking each man in the room.

Vladislav stared at the screens then at the others. “What kind of trickery . . . ?”

Bayat Mahdi dropped his head in his hands.

Light-headed, Jaleel turned his gaze away. Such things were not possible. He asked an aide for water, and the man brought him a warm plastic bottle. He opened the cap and guzzled half in one swig. But when his eyes again fixed on the screens, nothing had changed.

The missiles, the jets, had not reappeared.

The Supreme Leader stood and rapped his cane hard against the chair, breaking the silence. “It doesn’t matter. We still have overwhelming forces. Order the mortar and artillery bombardment!”

“Yes, Supreme Leader.” General Ansari leaped from the chair, found his sat phone, and dialed.

Mahdi also made his calls.

From Vladislav’s heated exchange and the shouts leaking from his sat phone speaker, President Petrov must have been swearing. Vladislav faced the Supreme Leader. “President Petrov orders you to begin your mortar bombardment.”

“Tell him we have already sent the order,” said Najafi.

Jaleel took a deep breath. Was there hope yet for victory?

The Russian artillery opened fire first with a thunderous volley felt even in the Iranian command tent. The Iranian long-range mortars followed. Their shells climbed into the sky, reached their apogee, and should have begun falling. All eyes in the room turned to the drone videos showing the targets. Any moment now, the monitors should show a blossoming of mushroom clouds, explosions by the hundreds of thousands spreading across the Israeli front lines. Jaleel gripped his hands together, tensing. Any moment now.

“What’s wrong?” The Supreme Leader faced Ansari. “Something’s wrong.”

Again, all parties began calling their artillery units. And again, the response came back that, though they’d fired and continued to fire, none of their shells were reaching their targets.

Indeed, every shell, after reaching its apogee, seemed to have vanished.

When Ansari turned with pale face and shaking hands to report this, the Supreme Leader was close to apoplectic.

But whatever had happened to the missiles, the jets, and the artillery bombardment, the massive ground assault was yet to come. Jaleel said a prayer to Allah that the same fate would not await the main attack.

CHAPTER 37

THE BATTLE OF GOG AND MAGOG

Ezekiel 38:19–22 (HCSB): *"I swear in My zeal and fiery rage: On that day there will be a great earthquake in the land of Israel. The fish of the sea, the birds of the sky, the animals of the field, every creature that crawls on the ground, and every human being on the face of the earth will tremble before Me. The mountains will be thrown down, the cliffs will collapse, and every wall will fall to the ground. I will call for a sword against him on all My mountains"—the declaration of the Lord GOD—"and every man's sword will be against his brother. I will execute judgment on him with plague and bloodshed. I swear in My zeal and fiery rage: I will pour out torrential rain, hailstones, fire, and brimstone on him, as well as his troops and the many peoples who are with him."*

Jerusalem, Israel – October, Year 2

When Chelsea returned from the kitchen with a club sandwich and a can of German pilsner for Davato, everyone was now staring at a new event—an artillery and mortar bombardment that, like the missile attack before it, was stillborn. None of the shells from the thousands of Russian cannons and Iranian long-range mortars made it to their targets. At the peak of their arcs, they simply vanished.

Following this, the artillery and mortars themselves disappeared. The Russian 9A52-4 "Tornado" MLRS. The BM-30 "Smerch" MLRS. The 2S7 "Pion" 203mm heavy artillery. Also the long-range Iranian mortars—the 120mm Razm and the 160mm Vafa.

All of them. Gone.

A cheer erupted from the normally somber UI leaders and support staff. The Prophet, who usually sat in the corner during military events, beamed and moved beside Davato to congratulate him. General Hofmann, after looking haggard and worn, rose from his chair with a bewildered smile.

For the moment, the monitors showed no movement. Closing her eyes, she breathed deeply, glad for a break in the action to slow her racing heart.

"Thank you, Chelsea." Davato took bites from the sandwich and swigs from the beer. Then his eyes sought hers. "I have noticed, lately, that you and the American ambassador seem to have grown rather close."

Her heart sped up again. If he'd noticed this, she'd better not deny it but downplay it. She held his gaze. She was becoming adept at hiding her emotions before the Imperator. "Yes, my lord, we have much in common."

He finished the beer and crushed the empty can. "Do not get too close to him. Personal entanglements can affect one's usefulness to the Unitum Imperium. And if one's usefulness ends . . ." He dropped the can into her open hands.

Swallowing, she nodded and bore away the remains of his lunch. More often lately, Davato's intentions toward those who could no longer serve him frightened her. They became like the crushed aluminum can—useless refuse to be discarded without hesitation.

Moments later, she returned to her seat behind the Imperator.

Then the enemies' tanks began moving.

The Russian tanks and their troop carriers started first. All along the Lebanese and Jordanian border, armored hunks of metal began rolling over the arid flats—thousands of the medium armored Russian T-80s, T-74s, and T-72s. Behind them rolled the heavily armored Russian T-10s, T-10Ms, and IS-4s. Pictures on the wall above identified each of the enemy's weaponry. Then came the Russian self-propelled antiaircraft guns, the ZSU-57-2s and the 2K22 Tunguskas.

On the Syrian, Egyptian, and the remaining Lebanese front lines, hundreds of the new Iranian Karrar battle tanks with their electro-optical fire control systems began moving. Following these came the Iranian T-72Z Safir-74 battle tanks. Drones from the Sinai showed a similar picture.

As the others in the room turned worried faces to the Imperator, Davato faced General Hofmann. "When will they be in range of our Spike antitank missiles?"

"My lord, our commanders in the field know what to do. They have orders to fire when the enemy is within range." Hofmann swallowed. "But there are so many, we do not have enough missiles or time to take them all out."

"Do what you can."

Chelsea shivered. An eerie calm seemed to have settled on the Imperator, as if he knew something the others didn't.

As the fleets of armored tanks raced across the desert, dust rose in a great cloud. Behind them came the transport trucks and troops marching on foot. From the air, they appeared like an army of minuscule locusts swarming over the land. In the south, African troop trucks raced across the Sinai desert.

Then the floor began to shake.

As Chelsea rose to her feet, her chair tipped over behind her. The building swayed, and one of the monitors slipped from its table and crashed to the floor. Behind her, a woman aide screamed. Chelsea fought to maintain her footing.

The building heaved, and after being thrown in the air, she found herself on all fours.

Hardly a man was still standing. Pieces of ceiling crashed to the floor in front of her. The lights dimmed, went out, came on again. Then all the monitors went blank.

On and on it went.

It seemed as if the entire world was shaking apart.

* * *

IN THE COMMAND TENT SOUTHEAST of Khan Alsheh, the gazes locked on the massive land attack changed from admiration to shock. Far worse than in Jerusalem or the Golan Heights or Paris or Mogadishu or Tokyo or Camp David, the quake that struck the Islamic-Russian front line was unlike any that land had ever seen.

When it started, Jaleel, like everyone else in the room, had wondered how any power could hope to stop the thousands of tanks and troop carriers rolling across the desert.

Then the earth trembled.

It hit with such force, his head slammed into the canvas above him. The monitors were thrown off the table, and he followed them down as they crashed and spread over the ground with a shattering of glass and plastic.

He landed hard on cables and splintered plastic and blacked out.

When he came to, he glanced up. The tables were overturned. The monitors lay in broken heaps. And the smell of burning wire, blood, and fear swelled his nostrils. He was shaking like a rat caught in a trap, breathing so fast, his chest hurt. Once more, the ground rolled beneath him. He grasped for the carpet, but it wouldn't hold. Yet again, he was flung into the air, this time landing hard on all fours.

Deep beneath the tent, the earth moaned and rumbled. It was as if the planet itself had awakened in anger and was wreaking its terrible wrath upon all who dared live on its surface.

Still on hands and knees, Jaleel began scrambling madly toward the exit.

Again and again, the heaving earth threw him. Each time he landed, he crept like a wild, drunken spider toward the exit. Others were doing the same, some staggering crazily on their feet, others crawling fast beside him.

Wave after wave of earth rippled and rolled beneath him.

Above, one of the massive poles holding up the canvas cracked, a sound like a gunshot. Then came the whoosh of canvas, the thud of poles hitting the ground, the crunch of wood smashing piles of broken glass and plastic.

He glanced back.

The Supreme Leader lay motionless at the edge of the canvas, his skull crushed by a broken pole.

Fighting to keep his gorge down, Jaleel whipped his head from the sight and crawled faster.

Relentlessly and without mercy, the planet's surface tossed and heaved, tossed and heaved.

The tent plunged into darkness. Three meters ahead, light from the opening showed the way out. Between waves of surging earth, he stood and staggered through the exit then sprawled onto the sand, under a yellow sky now shrouded with dust.

The ground heaved again, throwing him into the air. Behind him, the rest of the tent collapsed with snapping poles, ripping canvas, and muffled screams.

He raised his head from his prone position on the sand.

Others, including General Ansari, Bayat Mahdi, and Colonel Vladislav had also made it out. Ansari, covered with grit, lay on his side, his eyes dazed and unfocused. Only Vladislav still held a sat phone.

Yet another wave hit. And another. And another.

Trembling, Jaleel coiled in a ball as the earth threw him hither and yon. Again and again, he prayed to Allah. But the angry earth continued to shake and rumble beneath him.

Finally, it stopped.

Then he, like the others who'd made it out, lay on the ground—stunned, shaken, and unnerved, waiting for the next wave.

But it was over.

Jaleel uncoiled and, shaking uncontrollably, stood. He felt something warm below his waist. Looking down, he realized to his shame he had wet himself.

A glance toward the desert showed that, fifty meters away, a gap had opened in the sand wide enough to swallow a jeep. A thick haze of dust now hovered over the land, and he couldn't see further than seventy meters. The other tents of the vast encampment—those within view—had also collapsed.

Only Colonel Vladislav still held onto a phone, and as he talked with the Russian units, his forehead scrunched into a frown, and he moved away from the others.

General Mahdi's gaze searched the survivors. "Where is the Supreme Leader?"

"Dead," said Jaleel.

Mahdi closed his eyes and gripped the top of his head.

General Ansari stood and brushed himself off. After glancing at the Russian, he straightened to his full height and faced some of his surviving support staff. "May Allah welcome him to Paradise. But we have a battle to win. Get me a sat phone out here—now!"

The underlings looked at each other, but no one moved.

Ansari's voice rose. "I say get in there and get me a phone—now!"

Four men finally crawled back under the canvas. Moments later, they'd produced two.

As Ansari took his phone, the Russian stalked up, his face red, his fists clenched. "What is going on, General? Your Iranians are firing on us."

"No, no, you must be mistaken. Those are probably Israeli units you are fighting." Ansari began making calls.

After some heated exchanges, he returned to the Russian. "It is unclear who is firing upon whom. My men say it's Davato's forces. Whoever it is, they opened fire on us first. I'm told our men are simply defending themselves."

"I think not. I am told your troops attacked ours." Vladislav scanned the nearby desert, spied a jeep, took two steps toward it, then whirled back. "Ansari, I am finished with this command. I will take that vehicle and rejoin our forces."

"Don't, Vladislav. Remain with us so we can coordinate."

The Russian planted both hands on hips. "Your coordination, as you call it, has led to disaster. From here on, as originally agreed, we will proceed under the leadership of President Petrov." He turned, strode to the jeep, started it, and drove north—probably to find a way around the newly opened crevasse.

For a time, Ansari stared while the dust swallowed the Russian and the jeep. Then he waved his hands. "Let him go. They have always been unreliable, arrogant allies." Then he and Bayat Mahdi began calling unit leaders on their sat phones. But the longer they talked and the more units they contacted, the more agitated both became.

When the last call had been made, Ansari faced Mahdi. "They're fighting all along the line. We are engaged in tank battles with an unknown opponent."

"Yes, that's what my commanders also report. They suspect the UI forces counterattacked under cover of the dust cloud."

"And the Russians think it is us. We're taking heavy casualties, both with the armored units and with our troops on the ground." Ansari had somehow managed to keep his switch, and he now slapped it hard against his thigh.

"It's all falling apart, isn't it?" General Mahdi pounded a fist into a palm and whirled away.

As Jaleel watched the two generals, he gripped both sides of his throbbing head. Events had spun out of control, and there was nothing he could do about any of it. He should be back in Tehran, not stuck out here in some Allah-forsaken desert. He was here only as window dressing, to please Najafi as a show of support for what was supposed to be a massive victory for Persian hegemony.

He wiped blood from his eyes and searched the dust-shrouded horizon.

With the Supreme Leader dead, the power of the presidency would naturally increase, if only temporarily. Yet that thought didn't bring comfort. Right now, he wished he could give up the weight of that responsibility. More than anything, he wanted to be sitting on his porch at his Caspian Sea resort with a glass of French wine in his hand.

Off to his right, something fell from the sky.

Raising a hand, he peered through the dust. Flames were consuming one of the tents. Then something landed on the command tent behind him—a ball of fire as large as a car. The tent burst into flames.

His heart raced uncontrollably. His hands flew to the top of his head. What was happening?

Behind him, someone screamed. He whirled. The ground around General Ansari was a pyre of burning pitch. The general himself was a tower of flaming tar.

Jaleel spun. As fast as his portly frame could move, he waddled toward the desert.

Everywhere around him, hailstones began dropping out of the sky, hitting his head, covering the sand. But some of them were burning.

Burning hail? In the middle of the desert? Was he hallucinating?

He stopped, panting for breath, spots bursting before his eyes.

Something slammed into him from above.

The last thing on earth that Jaleel Hasani experienced was a searing, crackling heat, a burning fire that drilled through his clothes, deep into his flesh, all the way to the bone.

CHAPTER 38
JALEEL'S JOURNEY

Hades – October, Year 2

When Jaleel woke, he was in a new body, deep underground, in a place of deep darkness. Some kind of goo pressed in on him from all sides.

The terrible agony of the flame was gone. In its place came a crushing weight of black ooze. He tried to move an arm, but the slime held him fast. His nostrils filled with the smell of decay, offal, and feces, and he gagged.

He tried to scream. But the sound died in a cocoon of goo.

From nearby came an unearthly sound, as of some giant, unseen creature slithering through the muck. It sent a wave of fear rippling through his naked body. And yes, he now realized he was naked.

Following this came a sense of loneliness so deep and profound, it shook him to his core, and tears came to his eyes.

What was this place?

Then, in a flash, he knew, as with some sixth sense, that the Allah he worshiped had never been the god who ruled the world. He was, instead, a warped, incomplete portrayal of the one true God. He also knew that Muhammad was a false prophet, a mere man deceived by Satan.

No, the true deity, the true Creator of the world, was now, and had always been, the God of the Jews and the Christians, whom Jaleel's people had hated and oppressed. Then he also realized that, in the world he'd left behind, it was that very God whose love and care had sustained him. And the absence of that loving presence now left him with such a terrible sense of unbearable loss and unquenchable loneliness. For here, in this place, the God who had sent Christ to earth had forever rejected those who had rejected him.

Jaleel also knew that from this place there was no escape.

Something wriggled in from the slime and sank into his flesh. Pain, even worse than the searing fire that had killed him, drilled into his leg. Something else wormed into an eye, and though he struggled, he couldn't raise a hand through the muck to stop it.

He tried to scream. But his mouth filled with goo, and no sound came out.

Even worse than the wrenching pain came a new thought. This torment would go on and on, forever and ever—

And there would be no end to it.

CHAPTER 39
THE FINAL BLOW

Jerusalem, Israel – October, Year 2

When the Clal Center had stopped shaking, Chelsea helped clear away the debris and untangle the maze of wires. Most of the equipment had ceased functioning. Only a handful of the surviving monitors, those with pictures from overhead drones, now showed the progress of the battle—if one could still call it that.

After the quake, General Hofmann and the Prophet both appeared pale, shaken, and stunned, as did everyone else in the room. Hofmann finally collected himself and began calling units to determine their status.

Only Davato seemed to have taken it in stride, as if he had known all along what was going to happen.

"Have our forces reacted to the enemies' advances?" asked Davato.

Hofmann shook his head. "They've done nothing. None of the enemy tanks or troops have even come within firing range."

"And yet, they've reported gunfire and explosions from the enemy positions?"

"Yes, my lord. We have no explanation. Our troops remain untouched, waiting for the attack."

Nodding, Davato pointed to a far monitor. "What is happening there?"

On a screen to the far right, the dust cloud had lifted. Fires burned in several places. As Chelsea clenched her fists, multiple red, glowing streaks dropped from the sky, landing on a group of Iranian tanks. Flames engulfed the vehicles. There followed a series of explosions as ammunition and fuel ignited. More fire—burning pitch?—hit the ranks of troops behind. The flaming torches of men staggered in crazy circles until they were consumed and dropped.

Soon, thousands of falling streaks of fire dotted the entire field of vision.

General Hofmann found a chair and plopped into it. "It's a miracle. We've done absolutely nothing. Yet our enemies are being obliterated."

"Yes, General, a miracle." The Prophet stepped forward. "And I know the name of the power behind it."

Chelsea turned toward him. What was he up to?

"I know who performed this miracle on our behalf. Think! For whom have we been building a grand temple in New Babylon? To whom have we asked the world to give worship? Do you see now? Our benefactor was the spirit of the earth. She saw how the enemies of her people came against us. And she acted."

Davato appeared to suppress a frown. After some hesitation, he stood. "This will do for the time being. Yes, I concur with Sebastien. Surely, we have been blessed this day by the spirit of the earth. What else could account this stunning victory?"

Chelsea sucked in breath. She'd heard the words, but she couldn't swallow them. With all her heart, she believed in the threat of climate change and in doing all one could to stop it. But crediting this miracle to the spirit of the earth?

"The spirit of the earth?" General Hofmann drew a hand across his furrowed brow, and he looked toward Sebastien Rey.

"Yes, General." The Prophet's green eyes narrowed. "The spirit of the earth."

"Of course." Hofmann lowered a defeated gaze. "We are blessed to have such a deity on our side."

An aide brought another monitor online, and it captured Chelsea's gaze.

With the deluge of burning pitch now came hailstones, some of which were also burning.

Everyone in the room stared, transfixed by the monitors as unimaginable destruction poured down on the invaders.

CHAPTER 40

THE ANGEL OF WRATH

Zechariah 12:3 (HCSB): *"On that day I will make Jerusalem a heavy stone for all the peoples; all who try to lift it will injure themselves severely when all the nations of the earth gather against her."*

Ezekiel 39:6 (HCSB): *"I will send fire against Magog and those who live securely on the coasts and islands. Then they will know that I am Yahweh."*

Somewhere Over Syria – October, Year 2

The Angel of Wrath had traveled far from the heavenly realm. He had hovered high over the Syrian Desert. He was able to see the smallest detail of every event happening on the ground below, even through the haze of dust thrown up by the quake.

His purpose—to ensure the fulfillment of a terrible prophecy.

Though the Antichrist had taken the chosen people's homeland, he and his entourage would be spared. His time had not yet come.

A simple wave of his sickle had obliterated all the missiles and jets in midflight.

Another wave had taken out the rows of Russian artillery and the long-range Iranian mortars.

He had aimed a third wave at the planet itself. The massive quake that followed spread in an ever-widening arc, shaking every country on earth. The worst of it hit beneath the advancing tanks and troops of the unholy alliance of Russia, the Islamic coalition, and the mid-Asian countries of the former Soviet Union, known to the heavenly host as Magog, and their alliance leader, Russian President Petrov, known to the heavenly host as Gog.

Even as the dust cleared, he whispered to himself, "It is time for the final blow."

He left the desert and flew high over the earth. He'd waved his sickle, sweeping it in a longer, more encompassing arc.

Burning pitch dropped from the sky. Clusters of fire landed on the men of the invading army, on their tents, tanks, and weapons. Huge balls of sticky flame consumed their communication centers, their aircraft, their warships. Everywhere on the battlefield, fire consumed Gog, the leader of the Rosh, and the peoples of Magog. Following this came a deluge of fiery hailstones large enough to knock a man unconscious, stones as big as cannon balls, covering every place the invaders had fouled.

He flew even higher. Once more, he waved his sickle, this instrument of judgment. The skies over the nations that sent the invaders opened up.

Burning tar and fiery hail engulfed every mosque, every center of Islamic power, every city that worshiped the false god Allah and his prophet Muhammad.

Flaming pitch fell from the sky, covering the major centers of Russian power, its armies, air force, and navy, its missile silos, its Black Sea dachas, and command centers. Only some did he spare—those east of the Urals. Meteors as large as houses plunged into the seas, seeking out the submarines, killing every undersea war vessel in the Arctic, the Atlantic, the Pacific, the Indian Ocean, the Black Sea, the Caspian Sea, and the Mediterranean.

Moscow, St. Petersburg, Riyadh, Mecca, Tehran, Baghdad, Ankara, and all the cities that had sent the enemy and where the false god Allah was worshiped—gone. And when all had been incinerated—

When every last invader from north, south, east, and west and their supporting infrastructures lay dead or destroyed—

When every center of power and false worship had been obliterated—

Then came a deluge of rain to quench the fires and flood the enemies' cities.

Only then was God's wrath complete. Only then did the Angel of Wrath turn his back on what he had wrought and, his mission complete, return to his heavenly home.

For then, if any have eyes to see, they will know that He is Yahweh.

CHAPTER 41

THE BROADCAST

Colossians 2:8 (HCSB): *Be careful that no one takes you captive through philosophy and empty deceit based on human tradition, based on the elemental forces of the world, and not based on Christ.*

The French Luberon – October, Year 2

Margot was still with Dylan inside the forest, only meters from the farm's pasture, nearing the end of their morning hike. It was late October, and brilliant red leaves already decorated the great oaks covering the mountain's lower elevations. For the last five days, they'd helped assess damage from the quake. But the repairs had been minimal, and this morning, she had insisted they spend time outside in the fresh air.

On the bald rock of the mountaintop, they'd eaten their packed lunch and listened to the birdsongs, the wind through the trees, the squirrels rustling in the grass nearby.

But that was two hours ago, and now the farm peeked through the trees below.

She stopped and grabbed Dylan's hand. "Look, a fox!"

Fifteen meters away, the animal stood motionless, its head up, its wary black eyes alert.

"Do you think it knows what's happening to the earth?" whispered Dylan. "Do the animals have some sixth sense that something is terribly amiss with the world?"

"I bet she does." Margot couldn't help but admire the animal's red coat, her sleek body, her furry tail, held erect. "I bet she's looking at us and thinking to herself: You people and your evil ways have done this to us. We animals had a good thing going until you messed everything up."

Dylan laughed. "How do you know it's a 'she'?"

"I just do."

The fox turned and slipped between the ancient trunks.

Still watching the animal's progress, she said, "I've been thinking about the future, Dylan. What's going to become of us? The rest of the Tribulation lies ahead." She covered her face with her hands. "And I'm scared."

He placed his hands on her shoulders and slowly turned her toward him. "We must have faith that God has a plan for us. Look what he's done so far. Your paintings have predicted the future. They helped us rescue my brother and Baruch, a man whose mission is to save hundreds of thousands—maybe millions—of souls. We both had a part in that. After all that, do you think God will let bad things happen to us?"

"I . . . I don't know." She released his hands and wrapped her arms around her chest. "I was reading Revelation yesterday and what lies ahead—and it frightens me."

"As it should. But we are Christians. We shouldn't fear death. There's a Bible passage—somewhere in Luke, I think—that says we are not to fear men, but God, the one who can throw the soul into Hell for all eternity."

He was right, of course, and she nodded. Still, the prospect of facing the terrors to come made her shiver.

Dylan pulled her close and planted a kiss on her cheek. Then he hugged her. "Does that make it better?"

"Yes." She smiled. "Yes, it does."

"While you've been thinking about the future, I've been thinking about the past." His gaze wandered to the farm and beyond that, to the valley below. "How strange it is to be here in the French mountains, so far from home. Lately, I've been remembering the summers I spent with my aunt on East Gull Lake in northern Minnesota—where you could hear the loons calling at night over the still water, where the quiet of God could seep into your soul, where the world was peaceful and orderly."

"You sound almost poetic." He rarely talked like this, and she looked at him with admiring new eyes. "I wish we could go there."

"It was a time so far removed from this; it seems impossible it even existed. But it's gone now. Gone forever." He shook his head then waved toward the field. "Come on. We'll be late for the broadcast."

* * *

DYLAN, MARGOT, AND MOST OF the others gathered in the farm's main dining room around a wide-screen TV. The new girl, Danielle, sat beside Victor. Ever since her arrival, the two had grown close.

For four days, no one had had any news of what had occurred in the east. Rumors had come back from the village that a great battle had been waged in Israel. But ever since the quake, electricity, internet, and all television service had been out. Speculation ran wild, and Dylan was eager to hear what really happened.

Yesterday, services had been restored. Then every social and communications media were filled with continuous messages from Jerusalem telling the world that the Prophet would make a major announcement.

"Since the quake, they've taken over every communications medium." René drew a hand through his hair. "They used the disaster as an excuse. I don't trust them."

"Nor should we." Pasqual sat next to Margot and Dylan. The others—perhaps fifty souls—sat in a wide circle. Another thirty were watching from the downstairs library. "But I agree—it's troublesome."

"Look." Victor controlled the remote, and he turned up the volume. "It's starting."

The screen filled with a panoramic view of Temple Mount. Thousands of people swarmed over the square before a platform erected on the Temple steps. As the camera panned away from the crowd and zeroed in on the figures behind the podium, Dylan stiffened. Seated in a row were Davato in the center, flanked by the Prophet, a man in a general's uniform, and a woman with a pert nose and reddish-blonde hair.

He rose from his chair and stepped closer to the screen. "That's Chelsea!"

"It is, isn't it?" Margot also rose from her chair.

"That's your sister?" asked Danielle, her eyes wide and staring at Dylan.

"Quiet. Davato is about to speak," came a voice from the back.

Dylan returned to his seat, troubled by how close his sister had become to the center of evil.

The Imperator stepped to the microphone, and his gaze swept the crowd. "Ladies and gentlemen, Madames et Messieurs"—speaking English, he rose to his full height as his voice thundered across the square—"it has been five days since the planetwide earthquake that disabled most of the world's transmissions media. But now that we have restored most communications in the Unitum Imperium, it is time to inform you of events.

"Five days ago, a vast army of Russians, Iranians, Turks, Libyans, Somalis, and Islamic nationalities, including tribal hill fighters, surrounded our host country, Israel. Never in modern history has there been such an army of tanks, troops, and missiles assembled against one nation. What was their aim? The total destruction of the Unitum Imperium and your Imperator."

His jaw hardening, his eyes aflame, he paused before gripping the podium.

"What was the outcome? They failed, of course. And to give you the reason why and who was behind it, I relinquish the stage to Sebastien Rey, known to many as the Prophet." He waved to the man dressed in a white robe then returned to his seat.

From a distance, the Prophet's round white beard, his salt-and-pepper hair, and his heavy jowls gave the appearance of a wise, kindly grandfather. But Dylan had heard the rumors—of the green eyes, the pale skin, the revulsion people felt when meeting him face-to-face.

Sebastien Rey leaned toward the mike and smiled. "Citizens of the Unitum Imperium and those of you listening from allied countries, a great miracle has occurred. The armies launched against us were so massive, no one could possibly have stood against them. But where are they now, you ask? And where are the nations that sent them?

"I am here today to tell you that they have been utterly, totally obliterated. Did the Unitum Imperium destroy them? Did our armies crush them in one mighty battle?

"No, my friends. We did not fire a single shot." He stepped away from the mike as gasps erupted from the people around Dylan. The camera panned over the crowded Temple square. The faces there also showed puzzlement.

"What really happened?" The Prophet opened his hands in a question. "The missiles they fired, the shells from their cannons, the hundreds of jets streaming toward us—they simply vanished in midair. What about the tanks, the troop carriers, the ships, and the hundreds of thousands of soldiers heading toward us with evil intent? First came an earthquake that rocked the entire world. But beneath the enemy, it was so severe, it stopped the armies in their tracks, throwing them into confusion, opening fissures in the ground, and killing many. Next, burning pitch and hailstones fell from a clear, blue sky, engulfing whoever was left. Not a single enemy soldier, tank, or aircraft survived the terrible onslaught."

He drew himself to his full height.

"Yes, my friends, it was a miracle. But that's not all. Every nation that sent the gods of war against us was also destroyed. More burning fire fell from the sky onto the ruling elites and power centers of Russia, Iran, Libya, Sudan, Turkey, and the other nations who dared strike against us. The cataclysm befalling those countries was so great, they have essentially been eliminated from the world stage.

"But now the question you are all asking is this: Who sent this great miracle on behalf of the Unitum Imperium and its Imperator?"

Dylan shifted in his seat. He'd read Ezekiel and Revelation. He knew who'd sent the earthquake and the burning pitch. But he doubted that the Prophet would credit the God of the Bible.

"Now, my friends, I give you the answer. The great disaster that wiped out the enemies of the Unitum Imperium came from the hand of she who brings the rain that fills our rivers and oceans, from she who allows our crops to grow in her soil and provides the air we breathe. This miracle came from the one who is the source of life itself.

"Of whom do I speak? I speak, of course, of the earth upon which we live, and the living presence and power within and beneath the earth. Yes, my friends, our protector is Gaia, the spirit of the earth."

A stunned silence overtook the room as Dylan's startled gaze met Margot's. "Are you kidding me?" she whispered.

From Temple square came a smattering of applause. But the camera stayed focused only on the speaker.

Sebastien Rey cleared his throat and went on. "Only someone with the powers of a god or goddess could have performed such a miracle. And she did so because we of the Unitum Imperium have been worshiping and honoring her like no one in modern history has ever done. Even now, we have built a great city in the eastern desert whose center is a temple devoted exclusively to her. And that, my friends, is why she performed this great miracle. That is why she defended us from the greatest army ever assembled." He paused to allow his words to sink in. Then his glance swept the crowd.

"So, today, I implore you again to join the Church of Gaia to honor this goddess who saved your government and its leader. To encourage you, those who join this week will receive extra ration points and travel permits. And now, I will introduce you to the basic tenets of this religion—the commandments, if you will, of Gaia."

Pasqual shot out of his chair, paced to the end of the room, and returned. "This is beyond belief. This is the Devil's work if ever there was."

"Please," said Victor, "I'm trying to hear."

Pasqual plopped into his seat.

"Listen and take heed." The Prophet lifted a sheet of paper. "For these are the six Commandments of Gaia:

"One. Revere and honor Gaia, the spirit of the earth, the eternal essence of the planet upon which we live, for it is she who gives us life, health, and prosperity.

"Two. Revere and honor the Imperator. Give to him your allegiance, your obedience, and your tithes, for he is uniting the peoples of the earth and he rules in the name of Gaia.

"Three. Remember to observe the Sixth Day with eating, drinking, and uniting in sexual union with whomever you wish, of whatever age or sex. Humankind was made for pleasure, not useless contemplation.

"Four. Release yourselves from the restraints of biological motherhood, fatherhood, and the outdated concepts of male and female. Your true mother is Gaia who wants to free you from all arbitrary constraints. Your true father is the Imperator. And your true family is the Unitum Imperium.

"Five. Blessed are those who root out and destroy Gaia's enemies and their property, for their feet walk a different path, and they vibrate to a rhythm opposed to ours. That includes all Christians and anyone speaking against the Imperator."

A murmur now swept the room at the farm, and Dylan again caught Margot's gaze. René slammed a fist into a palm and muttered. Pasqual just shook his head.

Sebastien Rey went on. "And finally, six. Covet property, wealth, and pleasures for yourselves in abundance. You were put on this earth to enjoy earthly things, and the greater your wealth and pleasure, the more you will have to share with the world and with Gaia."

The Prophet lifted his gaze to his audience. "I will say more in future broadcasts, but I now return the microphone to the Imperator."

A smiling Davato stepped forward. "As you can see, these are not hard rules to follow. They are things we have all been working toward for a long time. They are designed to free the inner person from the artificial restraints that have oppressed us for so long. Let no one stand in the way of your pleasure, however you wish to take it."

As Dylan shifted in his seat, he noticed Pasqual's deepening frown, René's crossed arms.

"I am confident everyone will enjoy this new kind of worship, especially the Sixth Day celebrations that I decree should start immediately. I encourage every city, town, and village to set up places of worship each Saturday where people can gather to eat, drink, partake of their favorite mood enhancer, and enjoy physical intimacy with whomever they wish, in whatever way they wish. When everyone has joined the Church of Gaia, we will be well on our way toward universal peace, prosperity, and security." Weak applause met his glance as it swept Temple square.

"But this is the day for announcements, and I have a final declaration to make, one of momentous importance. Though Jerusalem remains the spiritual center of the world, the city does not have the resources necessary for true commercial success. You have seen on the news the massive preparations we have made to rebuild a great and ancient city in the Iraqi desert. Well, today, I can tell you that construction is complete.

"The name of the city is New Babylon, and starting next week, we are making it the commercial capital of the Unitum Imperium. For years before the Great Catastrophe, my company, Worldnet, was already working toward this goal. Since then, every corporation of any importance on the planet has joined us. Most of them have already relocated or are in the process of moving their headquarters there.

"For the average person, the city will be a vacation destination extraordinaire. It has more bars, casinos, game rooms, pools, spas, and pleasure dens than anywhere else on the planet. We have also erected there a great temple to Gaia that includes thousands of worship rooms where earth priests and priestesses are waiting to entertain guests. Yes, my friends, whoever visits New Babylon will marvel in awe at the wonders and pleasures awaiting them. They will never want to leave."

When he stepped from the microphone to a thunderous applause, Dylan wondered who now comprised the audience for these announcements in Jerusalem.

Following the broadcast came a commercial announcing the digital euro, the new backbone of a world currency system replacing the old system of physical cash. All commercial transactions would soon be mandated in this new digital currency. When a second message launched into the benefits of the new religion, Pasqual asked Victor to shut off the set.

"Though this was all predicted, it's still difficult to swallow." Pasqual walked to the front. "The Antichrist and his false Prophet are readying the world for the first of two false religions—the Church of Gaia."

"It will make the climate change people ecstatic," said Dylan.

"Exactly." René stood, joined Pasqual, and, ignoring Pasqual's frown, lit a cigarette. "Through the World Economic Forum and dozens of woke billionaires, Satan has been preparing the world for this for a long time. Nearly every aspect of woke ideology fits perfectly with the Antichrist's agenda. They've convinced nearly everyone that global warming is the greatest threat to humanity's existence. How else can one explain a belief so irrational and damaging to human interests? What kind of logic rejects cheap and abundant resources, that has thrown hundreds of thousands out of work and into poverty, and that has made free nations dependent on tyrannical regimes like Russia and China, the main suppliers of the rare minerals and manufacturing needed for their 'green energy' solutions?"

"But we've always been told that humans have been warming the planet, leading to disaster," said a woman in the center.

"That was certainly their rallying cry." René waved his cigarette. "But the planet has been warming since the last ice age, and man had nothing to do with it. If you investigate their claims, every one of them, without exception, turns out to be false or wildly misleading—especially the one about a 'global warming scientific consensus'. As usual, such people find ways to obscure and twist the facts. When the data refused to show a warming planet, they created new terminology, calling it 'climate change'. Now, every tornado, hurricane, heat wave, and cold snap supports their new ideology."

"Oui." Pasqual resumed pacing. "And now we see how it's prepared the people for a new religion with the planet at its center."

"It all makes sense, doesn't it?" added Margot.

"Unfortunately, it does."

"I have an important question." Victor stood and raised his hand.

"Oui?" asked Pasqual.

Victor pointed to the cooks bringing sandwiches and grapes to the serving table at the room's far end. "When is lunch?"

Danielle slapped him playfully on the shoulder, and he leaned far to his left, pretending he'd been hit a mighty blow. "We learn of earthshaking events sweeping the planet," she said, "and Victor is concerned with lunch."

Everyone laughed, and Pasqual ended the gathering with a prayer.

CHAPTER 42
ISRAEL AWAKENS

Ezekiel 39:21–22 (HCSB): *"I will display My glory among the nations, and all the nations will see the judgment I have executed and the hand I have laid on them. From that day forward the house of Israel will know that I am Yahweh their God."*

Jerusatlem, Israel – November, Year 2

After his message had finished, Baruch stepped down from the pallet serving as a makeshift platform. On the hillside below, five hundred Jews from Jerusalem and the surrounding countryside began to disperse. They had gathered to hear about the Christ who offered deliverance from a fiery eternal fate. Besides a half dozen smaller gatherings, this was the tenth big event since the earthquake and the Unitum Imperium broadcast.

The crowd now besieged the dozens of men with white armbands standing at the edges, waiting to get the new converts in touch with one of the underground churches springing up everywhere. Baruch's last warning to the crowd was to take down the address they were given and leave as quickly as possible.

David touched his arm. "Baruch, we must get you out of here. Surely, these crowds will attract the CSA."

Baruch again took in the sight of all the people eager to hear the gospel message. Some had come on foot, others on the bicycles, motorcycles, and cars that lined the road on both sides. "I hope they can all get home safely."

"Yes, and now we'd better leave. The CSA might be here any minute."

Nodding, Baruch followed David to a waiting car. When both were inside, he entered a line of vehicles leaving the site. He leaned toward his friend. "Has my ministry booklet come back from the printers yet?"

"It will be ready this afternoon. The quake delayed the printing."

"The material will help the new church leaders understand the basics of Christianity and keep them from straying into false belief. What about the New Testaments?"

"Same problem. We need so many, our rogue printing operation can't keep up. Your ministry is really taking off, Baruch. I can barely answer the requests to bring you to the next preaching event."

"Amazing, isn't it?" Baruch smiled. "Whatever Davato had intended with his broadcast, it had the opposite effect, at least here in Jerusalem. Jews are reading Ezekiel and realizing we're in the end times. They hear the Prophet's blasphemy and, suddenly, they see the threat Davato poses. They lived through the earthquake. Images of the devastation wrought on the Russian and Islamic armies are popping up everywhere. And when they combine this with Ezekiel's prophecy, Isaiah, and the book of Revelation, they are awakening in droves."

David swerved the car around a group of bicycles. "The grapevine is also working overtime, telling the Israeli people about your messages. And somehow, we're escaping capture and discovery at these events. But I fear one day they'll catch up with us."

"Have faith, David." Baruch laid a hand on his friend's shoulder. "God is protecting us."

"He may be protecting you, but shouldn't we be concerned about all the people back there?" David waved a hand.

Baruch nodded, but the masses leaving on foot beside the car captured his gaze. How often hadn't he prayed that the Lord would raise a shield of protection between these people and the Truth Squads? How many nights hadn't he spent petitioning Jesus, Lord of Lords and King of Kings, to sway the hearts of those attending these meetings, to save them from the eternal fire to come? It was right of David to ask. But concerned? Oh, he was more than concerned. His soul was gripped with longing that all the unsaved men and women and youths would seal their fates with God before it was too late, before the minions of the Adversary and the Antichrist took them away. "Yes, David, you have a right to be concerned. Which is why we must make these meetings as secret and as short as we can."

"Yet somehow, the Truth Squads are always showing up well after these events are finished. Only the stragglers get caught."

"Which tells me God is also giving them some measure of protection." Was that God's answer to his prayers? Baruch smiled. "The same thing is happening in the other cities where the Great Assembly is preaching. Time is running out. Israel and the world are finally awakening to the truth."

David sent him an admiring glance. "I am blessed to have known you, Baruch. And all those who hear you are blessed. May the God of Abraham, Isaac, and Jacob hear my words: Let Christ's will be done."

CHAPTER 43
NEW BABYLON

Revelation 17:3–6 (NLT): *So the angel took me in the Spirit into the wilderness. There I saw a woman sitting on a scarlet beast that had seven heads and ten horns, and blasphemies against God were written all over it. The woman wore purple and scarlet clothing and beautiful jewelry made of gold and precious gems and pearls. In her hand she held a gold goblet full of obscenities and the impurities of her immorality. A mysterious name was written on her forehead: "Babylon the Great, Mother of All Prostitutes and Obscenities in the World." I could see that she was drunk—drunk with the blood of God's holy people who were witnesses for Jesus. I stared at her in complete amazement.*

New Babylon, Iraq – March, Year 2

After the flight from Israel, Chelsea found the room assigned for her exclusive and permanent use inside New Babylon's World Casino. It was one floor below the penthouse suite where Davato resided, and one floor above where all the ambassadors, including Grady Wilson, were quartered in similarly opulent surroundings. The plan now was to spend a few weeks in Jerusalem, and a few more weeks in New Babylon.

But she'd just finished the daylong city tour, and her feet ached. She dragged herself to the refrigerator, opened a bottle of Chardonnay with a gold-plated opener from the counter, poured some into a crystal glass, and sank into an easy chair. A gold-embossed plaque on the wall announced "God Is Dead" in flowery letters. Everything about the city was excessive. The one thing they didn't have in abundance was food. Like everywhere else, meals were expensive and skimpy. They made up for it with copious supplies of beer, wine, and liquor. When a knock came on the door, she called out that she'd left it open, and Grady entered.

"I'm still awed by what we saw." He and several late-arriving ambassadors had taken the tour with her, and he already held a can of beer. "This building alone must occupy ten square miles. But it's not a building, is it? It's a complex, a city all by itself."

"My mind still boggles." She slipped off her shoes and rubbed an aching foot across the plush carpet. "We've seen enough gaming floors to replace every casino in Las Vegas, Reno, Atlantic City, and Monte Carlo. It has more slot machines, roulette wheels, and craps tables. More black-jack, poker, and baccarat tables. More keno tables and bingo halls. There are even six indoor dog tracks and two horse racing tracks."

"Yeah, and the spas, the naked pools, the naked baths with the orgy rooms that you said we shouldn't enter." He plopped into a chair oppo-site. "Then there are the opium and marijuana dens, and the LSD, meth, and heroin chambers. I've never seen so many zonked-out people staring off into space. But they did look happy."

"It's a false happiness. When it wears off, they'll be miserable."

"Still, one wonders what it would be like to join them—just for a day." He grinned.

"Sometimes, Grady, I wonder about you." She waved a hand in dis-missal. "This whole place, this New Babylon—why, it's already as big as New York City. How did they do it?"

"Worldnet was working on it long before Davato's rise to power. Since then, he must have looted every European treasury and bank. And he's placed a hefty tax on the corporations who've moved their headquar-ters here. The pace of construction must have been breathtaking."

She stood and followed his gaze out the window to all the new build-ings, gleaming and wavering in the desert heat, stretching to the horizon.

He went on. "Can you believe that the airport has two dozen run-ways? And between here and the airport, they've raised two thousand skyscrapers to house all the relocated corporate headquarters. And the tens of thousands of apartment buildings, all so opulent, it takes one's breath away."

"Yes, Grady, and the massive Coliseum where on Sunday they are going to release lions, tigers, and rhinoceroses into an arena full of Chris-tians." The muscles of her arms tensed, and she gripped the glass harder. "Are they really going to tie the Christians to stakes, cover them with tar, and burn them?"

"Barbarous. Like ancient Rome. Maybe worse."

"Then there's the Earth Temple." She pointed to its massive dome-like structure. Painted with the European and Asian continents, it blocked half the horizon. "Another five square miles of structure filled with ten thousand 'worship' rooms. I must say, Grady, I've never seen such handsome and enticing men, such beautiful, seductive women, and all so scantily dressed, manning those worship rooms. For anyone so inclined for a quick tryst, they will be hard to resist. And each room looks like they copied it from the most expensive brothel ever conceived, with gold door handles, satin sheets, perfumed whirlpool tubs, and silver-bordered mirrors on the walls and ceilings."

"Yes, and don't forget the temple's central amphitheater with its giant gold statue of the earth goddess. And the dancing men and women on either side, all naked, of course. But I must admit—the women they've got here are quite fetching."

"Grady, you don't mean it!" She shuddered. "But the temple wasn't the worst of it."

"You mean the shooting galleries?" He grimaced, and for a moment, neither spoke.

"Yes, the shooting galleries." Closing her eyes, she couldn't speak aloud what she'd seen there. The tour had ushered them into one of many chambers holding twelve long aisles. At the far end of each aisle, naked men and women were brought out and tied to posts. Around their chests were hung cardboard targets bearing concentric red circles superimposed with phrases like: "Fool for Christ", "Christian Believer", "Saved by Her Belief", and "Enemy of Us All". At the near end of each aisle stood eleven contestants, each holding a weapon of their choice—bow and arrows, pistol, or rifle.

The "game mistress", as she called herself—a short, attractive woman with red hair—announced the rules. Each contestant was allowed ten shots, with points awarded for how close to the target's center each shot came. More points for arrow hits. Fewest for rifle shots.

When the shooters began their work, Chelsea closed her eyes and tried not to be sick. She cringed at every explosion from every firearm.

After the last shot was taken, the game mistress declared an end. With eyes averted, Chelsea hurried into the hall. There she heard machine gun fire, as the woman finished off the few victims unlucky enough to be paired with a bad shot.

"They even paid to do what they did." She guzzled a long draught of wine, shivering still. "And did you see that woman who was with us on the tour and how she kept praising Davato everywhere we went, telling everyone what a great man he was, what great things he'd done? And then when there was an empty aisle and a free spot, she volunteered to take up a rifle. I cannot get over the glee, the eagerness, in her eyes. That woman couldn't wait to shoot those Christians. How can people do such things?"

"Probably because the winner of each round gets free lodging, airfare, and meals for their entire stay in New Babylon. And the advertisements ginning up hatred of Christians are everywhere."

"It scares me that there are such people in the world. And here we are—in the midst of them." After all she'd seen today, she felt none of the illicit thrill that had overtaken her when Davato had first described New Babylon. She was now ashamed of how she felt that day.

She checked her watch and rubbed her eyes. "It's been a long day. I'm scheduled to have dinner with Davato and his staff in an hour, and I need to rest."

"You and me both." Grady stood and headed for the door.

After he'd gone, she turned off the lights and laid on the bed. But all she could think about was how strange life had become, how she was getting deeper and deeper into a world from which she wanted desperately to escape. And she had no idea how to do it.

YEAR THREE

THE FIFTH SEAL

Revelation 6:9–11 (HCSB): *When He opened the fifth seal, I saw under the altar the people slaughtered because of God's word and the testimony they had. They cried out with a loud voice: "Lord, the One who is holy and true, how long until You judge and avenge our blood from those who live on the earth?" So a white robe was given to each of them, and they were told to rest a little while longer until the number would be completed of their fellow slaves and their brothers, who were going to be killed just as they had been.*

CHAPTER 44

THE THIRD YEAR BEGINS

Joel 1:15, 17–18 (HCSB): *Woe because of that day! For the day of the LORD is near and will come as devastation from the Almighty. . . . The seeds lie shriveled in the casings. The storehouses are in ruin, and the granaries are broken down, because the grain has withered away. How the animals groan! The herds of cattle wander in confusion since they have no pasture. Even the flocks of sheep and goats suffer punishment.*

The French Luberon – August through October, Year 3

August began the third year of the Tribulation.

The summer's harvest had been poor, and Marcel waged an unceasing battle to keep the rats out of the granary. He fretted constantly over the crops' progress. At summer's end, the wheat and corn did not stand as high as it should, and the grapes were weeks behind. Less milk was also coming from the cows, and despite Marcel and Gabrielle's ministrations, one-quarter of the herd had died of some unknown malady.

Pasqual theorized that the nuclear explosions and the volcanic eruptions in the Aleutians, Sumatra, Japan, and Chile had thrown so much ash into the atmosphere, it reduced the sunlight enough to affect not only the crops but also, in some way, the cows. But no one knew for sure.

Victor and Danielle had become an inseparable pair, and everyone enjoyed Danielle's wisecracks, her winning smile, and her winsome manner. She even showed some technical expertise and helped Victor with some of his projects. The group agreed she was now part of the Nazarene Friends core.

All summer, periodic earthquakes had rocked the farm. Most were mild, but one cracked the villa's foundation.

In August, Pasqual and René traveled to Marseilles to meet with a freighter pilot. There they arranged for a ship to take refugees to the

Madeira islands off the African coast. Though the islands' ruler paid lip service to Unitum Imperium allegiance, in practice they ignored everything coming from Jerusalem and, increasingly, from New Babylon. To facilitate the delivery of refugees, the farm bought an Opal Vivaro van. Each Monday, Pasqual or René would fill the van with as many Christians as would fit, drive to the Marseilles docks, and drop off passengers for the voyage.

In September, they began rationing food, preparing smaller meals, and everyone lost weight. They weren't as bad off as those in the village or in the cities, but each night, everyone went to bed wanting more. The rats had done their work. Famine had finally come to the farm.

Pasqual pleaded with Marcel to get rid of the farm's two horses, but he refused, insisting they must keep the mottled Percherons to which he was attached.

By October, most of the refugees had been sent on their way. This helped stretch their supplies, and the only extra mouths the farm had to feed were new, temporary arrivals. Though they couldn't return to full rations, they hoped to avoid starvation come winter.

Despite Davato's pledge to bring peace and order, lawlessness and anarchy ran amok. Nearly every day, the television news channels reported one, two, or three mass shootings or stabbings somewhere on the planet. The news seemed to revel in the reporting.

On future missions, to avoid Dylan's problem in Bad Kirchenstadt after he lost his phone, Victor created a number for everyone to memorize on a special phone to be called only in an emergency. The caller could be tracked, of course, but Victor's special phone would scramble its GPS so much that the call would take much longer than normal to connect, making its destination untraceable.

The CSA headquarters changed its password, and the farm lost access to the CSA website. Being blind to the squaddies' plans put them in greater danger as a new threat emerged from the village below. It came in the person of Mallory, the trans-mayor with breasts who dressed like a woman but otherwise looked and spoke like a man. No one at the farm ever attended the "earth services" she officiated in the village square each Saturday—Pasqual called them disgusting orgies of immorality.

And whenever someone drove down for their monthly supply run, it was impossible to hide the farm folks' full faces and limbs when they walked into her store.

"What are you eating up there on Montagne Verte?" Mallory would ask with a frown. "Do you have some to share with the rest of us?"

If it was Dylan's turn to shop, he would shrug and say something like, "The same as you, Mallory. Nothing more."

After the great battle in Israel, the farm was picking up more refugees from Marseilles, Grenoble, Nice, and even Lyon. Something about the miracle of the battle in the desert and the worldwide earthquake had turned a few folks, not to Davato and his new earth religion, but to Christ. The farm rescued as many Christians as they could, shipping them off to Madeira. But the Truth Squads and CSA agents captured even more.

"We need to discover the location of the camp," Pasqual would often say.

"No matter the danger," René would add, "someday we will free them."

But as the months passed, they came no closer to discovering its location.

CHAPTER 45
THE TWO WITNESSES

Revelation 11:3–5 (HCSB): *I will empower my two witnesses, and they will prophesy for 1,260 days, dressed in sackcloth." These are the two olive trees and the two lampstands that stand before the Lord of the earth. If anyone wants to harm them, fire comes from their mouths and consumes their enemies; if anyone wants to harm them, he must be killed in this way.*

Jerusalem, Israel – February, Year 3

Chelsea and Grady were just returning from lunch in the Old Town when people began running south. "Come and watch," said a passing woman. "Two fools are begging to be executed in front of the Temple."

A smiling Grady grabbed her arm and pulled her after the woman, now joined by others. "Come on. I don't want to miss this."

Seeing an execution wouldn't brighten her day. But with Grady so insistent, she agreed to follow.

What awaited her in Temple Square wasn't what she expected. Two men with long beards—one white, the other mottled gray—stood in the square's center. Each held a wooden staff, and their garments were of coarse burlap. They looked like they were dressed for a play about biblical times. Among the smartly dressed but hostile crowd gathering around them, they appeared woefully out of place.

Some of the men standing in a circle about them shouted jeers and curses. But most watched with smirks and knowing smiles, as one might put on when watching two fools.

The gray-bearded man stood with his feet spread wide, his eyes on fire, and his head held high. "Turn from your sins and toward the Lord God above, the one who created earth and sky, Heaven and Hell, and everything in between."

"Believe in the Lord Jesus, the Son of God," said the second man with the white beard. His voice thundered across the square. His face was weathered as if he'd lived in the desert all his life, and he, too, stood erect, his arm stretched out, his staff planted on the cobbles. "Turn from the one sent by the Deceiver, or you will follow him to your destruction in the abyss. Turn instead to the Lord Jesus, he who gives eternal life to those who follow him."

"Repent of your sins," echoed the first ancient with the gray beard. "Believe in the Son of the Most High, and he will cleanse you of your sins."

"Go away, you old fools!" shouted someone behind Chelsea. "Before Davato finds you."

"Salvation waits for all who believe," said the white-bearded man. "But you must abandon the silver-tongued son of the Devil, the wicked one sent by Satan himself who will lead you to a fiery eternal fate."

Beside Chelsea, Grady wore a silly grin. He poked her in the arm. "This should be good. That woman was right. What fools if they think they'll get away with this."

"I don't know." She crossed her arms. "I think they're rather brave. Brave, but as you say, foolish."

"Look!" Grady pointed off to the side. "It's Davato himself."

Indeed, a grim-faced Davato was crossing the square. With him came a platoon of CSA agents in black-and-green uniforms. Some carried truncheons, others machine guns. He stopped a few meters from the ones dressed in sackcloth. "Stop this at once or pay the consequences!"

The white-bearded ancient pointed his staff at the Imperator. "Son of the Devil, son of Satan, begone and take your demands with you! We speak for the Lord God on High, the Lord of Heaven's armies, and for the King of Kings, the Lord of Lords, for Christ the Son!"

When the first man dropped his staff, the gray-bearded man raised his and pointed it at Davato. "You, Davato, calling yourself Imperator, are the man of lawlessness, the beast spoken of in prophecy, the son of destruction. Your doom is certain, as it will be for all who follow you."

His face now red and flushed, Davato said something to the four men beside him, and they started toward the two ancients.

But as soon as their hands reached out to grab the gray-bearded man, an astonishing thing happened. As if their mouths had become flame-throwers, sheets of fire shot from their mouths and engulfed the four agents. Davato's men became pillars of flame, and the sound of their burning was like the roaring of four great bonfires. The men writhed and screamed. They ran this way and that. They rolled on the ground. No matter what they did, the flames only increased in intensity. Soon they lay motionless as the fire burned with supernatural fierceness over the corpses.

Chelsea gaped as the four human pyres burned down to four black heaps of smoldering ash.

The crowd now shrank from the two old men. Stunned silence and frightened eyes replaced their previous mirth, jeers, and curses.

Across from Chelsea, Davato's face had hardened into grim resolve. He whispered something in the ears of two more CSA agents, but the men shook their heads and stepped back, horror in their eyes. Then Davato spoke so all could hear. "You will do as ordered, or you will not leave this square alive."

Slowly, the two stepped forward. Instead of approaching the two prophets—for that was who Chelsea now realized these men were—they raised their submachine guns and aimed.

Before a single shot left their weapons, fire again leaped from the mouths of the two old men. Flames wrapped themselves around Davato's agents.

Chelsea turned her gaze from the supernatural fire that roared with a hissing of flesh, a crackling of bones. She could feel the heat even from where she stood, some fifteen meters away. When she looked back, two more piles of smoking, white-hot ash lay at Davato's feet.

Red-faced and shaking with rage, the Imperator whirled and stalked across the square.

"That's right, you son of a viper, you spawn of Satan," shouted the white-bearded man. "Flee to the Temple you have defiled."

The gray-bearded man faced the crowd. "Follow him and go to your destruction. Turn instead to the Lord Jesus, the Son of God, King of Kings, and Lord of Lords."

"Here and now, we declare a six-month drought," shouted the white-bearded prophet.

"Let no rain or snow or dew fall upon the earth for the next six months." The gray-bearded man raised his staff and slammed it down upon the square. The sound echoed like thunder back from the Temple.

The white-bearded man faced the crowd. "Six months to reject the beast, the man of lawlessness, six months to give up your iniquities and turn to the Lord," added White Beard.

"Six months without water, without rain," added the first prophet. "Six months to embrace the truth and to ponder your eternal destiny."

"Come on." Grady, suddenly pale and without mirth, laid a hand on Chelsea's shoulder. "Let's get back to work."

But as they left the square and began walking back to the Clal Center, the image of the six men who'd burnt alive, the roaring of the flames, and the power of the two prophets left her troubled and questioning.

Without a doubt, these men had been sent by God. What if they were right? What if a drought really was going to spread across the earth?

And what if she was following Davato to her doom?

CHAPTER 46

MARGOT'S LAST PAINTING

The French Luberon – April, Year 3

Toward the end of April, Margot woke in the early morning hours and headed for the room assigned as her studio. A powerful desire drove her, and she had to paint. In the hall, she passed Victor clutching a cup of coffee.

"Up early, aren't we?"

She barely nodded before entering the room and locking the door behind her. Rummaging in the corner, she found a new canvas and set it on the easel. She pulled out her palette and brushes, squeezed the first color—brown—onto the board, and began. As usual, she entered a state of intense, timeless concentration, focused solely on the work, giving herself wholly up to the vision. Twice that day, someone knocked—probably Dylan—but she ignored it.

Though she never knew precisely how it would turn out, she sensed that today's painting was different—deeply personal. For the first time ever, she didn't want to finish, didn't want to know what the future held. But when the visions came upon her, it was impossible to resist.

As the hours passed, a line of prisoners in ragged, dirty clothing appeared. Guards drove them under a massive barbed wire gate and across a barren yard. She painted a sign above the gate, but the letters weren't clear. Two rows of barbed wire, separated by two meters of gravel and broken occasionally by machine-gun towers, ringed the camp. Upon the prisoners' faces were etched fear and resignation. Their destination was somewhere among the low, corrugated metal barracks. Thousands of such buildings filled the canvas's center. In the far distance rose a chimney stack from which spewed a column of thick, heavy smoke.

As she painted, she could almost smell the stench of burning flesh, thick and pungent in her nostrils.

The colors she chose were those of death and despair. Gray. Brown. Black. Dirty white. In her work today, there was no joy.

A new figure appeared—a woman, short in stature, with black hair and bangs, and thick, dark eyebrows. And before Margot drew another stroke, she gasped. For the woman beneath her brush was herself.

She stepped away from the canvas, her heart beating fast. This was the camp where they sent Christians to be executed. Was she destined to be among them?

Another knock rapped on the door, and Dylan's muffled voice came through the wood. "It's evening, Margot. Are you okay?"

She opened the door to let him in.

He approached the easel. "I figured you were deep in concentration, so I didn't want to bother you. But it's getting late, you've missed supper, and—" But when his gaze caught her painting, he stopped.

"It's me." Her voice cracked. "I'm in . . . the . . . camp. And everything I've painted so far has come true."

"Oh no." He held her at arm's length. "This cannot be."

Gently, she freed herself from his grip. "But it's the Holy Spirit, not me, who guides my brush. It's God who's given me this warning. So it must be true."

"Have you ever painted something that hasn't occurred exactly as your paintings have predicted?"

"Well . . . no."

"Wait! Yes, you have. You painted me being taken in handcuffs in front of Bad Kirchenstadt, and it didn't happen, did it?" He paced to the wall, spun, and returned. "We're not going to let this happen. Maybe we *can* change the future."

"I don't know. I felt this painting was really going to happen and that I am meant to be in this camp. It must be for some purpose."

"No, Margot, don't say that."

She closed her eyes, breathed deeply, and opened them again. "It must be God's will."

"No, no, no." Dylan put his hands on top of his head.

In his eyes, she saw pain, and tears came to her eyes. Not because of his pain, but because she realized how much he cared for her. She laid a hand on his shoulder then kissed his cheek.

Victor knocked on the door and stuck his head inside. "Ah, there you are. René has called a meeting in the dining room. We're all waiting for you."

She grabbed Dylan's hands. "Come on. We'll discuss this later."

* * *

IN THE DINING ROOM, THE new core of the Nazarene Friends had gathered—René, Pasqual, the new girl Danielle, and Angelo.

Still troubled by Margot's painting and what it implied, Dylan found a seat.

René sat in an easy chair and inhaled on a cigarette. Somehow, Pasqual's pleas to keep his smoking outside too often went unheeded during these group events. Sitting beside him, Pasqual eyed the cigarette for a time then asked, "Okay, René, what is this about?"

The former spy walked slowly to the front and faced the group. "Folks, with next week's trip to Marseilles, unless we find more refugees, we will have sent the last of our folks to Madeira. But you know that, and that's not why I've asked you here."

"Then why are we here?" asked Victor.

"Just listen, silly," whispered a frowning Danielle beside him.

"I am increasingly concerned with the scrutiny we're arousing from the village."

"It's the mayor, isn't it?" said Angelo.

"Oui. It's the mayor." René sucked on his cigarette and blew out. "We need to be more careful than ever when going into town. And should the need arise, we need to make plans to abandon the farm."

"Abandon the farm?" The surprise on Pasqual's face mirrored everyone else's.

"I'm afraid so. Operation Elba is what I'm calling my plan." Then he described what they needed to do in case of a raid by the CSA. But after he was done, Dylan had grave doubts that such a plan would ever succeed.

CHAPTER 47

RIDING

The French Luberon – May, Year 3

"Come on." Carrying a backpack, Margot pulled Dylan over the stones toward the barn. "We're going riding."

"Riding?" He cocked his head. "Why?"

"Because I'm tired of sitting around doing nothing. I want to do something *fun* for a change. Besides, Victor and Danielle went riding last week, and *they* had fun. That gave me the idea."

A silly smile lifted one corner of his mouth, and he followed.

After they'd saddled and led the farm's two Percherons from the barn, they met Marcel holding a pitchfork. "It's about time you rode those two. Take the trail up the mountain through the woods. Even without the rain, it's still beautiful."

She thanked him and mounted. Back in Brussels before the vanishing, her father had paid for her to spend every Saturday morning at a riding academy. For six months before the desire to paint came so powerfully upon her, she reveled in those morning rides.

Behind her, Dylan mounted his horse with ease. Pleased how naturally he took to the saddle, she wondered if all Americans knew how to ride.

"Circle the field," called Marcel from behind. "Go to the northwest corner, and you'll find the trail."

Nodding, she kicked her mount, and they started off. The Percherons were gentle breeds, friendly and intelligent. And her mottled gray seemed eager to start out on today's trek. Behind her, Dylan kept up, and when she looked back, he gave her a thumbs-up.

The trail started just where Marcel said it would, with the dried-up skeletons of white lilies bordering the entrance. As their mounts climbed the needle-covered path, the smell of pungent pine tickled her nostrils. In the treetops, bright yellow serin birds performed a symphony of high-pitched trilling.

For the next hour, they rode until they arrived at a rocky overlook where she dismounted. "Time for lunch," she said.

"So that's what you've got in your pack. Great. I'm famished."

"Aren't we all. But don't get your hopes up. It's meager." They tied their mounts to branches. Then she laid a blanket on a flat rock, brought out a bottle of red wine—the farm still had plenty of that—and produced a cluster of grapes and a small cheese sandwich, already cut in half and wrapped in paper. She poured them each a glass, said a short prayer, and bit into her half.

Dylan eyed his sandwich and turned it over. "They say we've been eating well compared to folks in the valley. Yet I'm always hungry."

She watched him gobble his in four bites. "At least it's something. Down in the village, they're fighting over food. But I don't want to talk about troubles today."

"What do you want to talk about?"

She brushed crumbs from her jeans and smiled. "These are probably the most terrible times to live through that a person could ever have picked, but . . ."

"But what?"

"But these are also the times when being close to someone should mean more than ever." She raised her glance to him. "Dylan, I've been wanting to say something to you for some time, and I didn't know when or how or if I would ever say it, but . . ."

"But what?"

"But I've grown to . . . to love you."

For long moments, there was only the wind through the trees, the trilling of the birds.

Then his hand reached across, touched her chin, and raised it. His eyes sought hers, and he whispered, "Margot, I already knew. And the feeling is mutual."

Before she knew what was happening, he leaned across, and his lips pressed against hers. Energy and warmth surged through her. When they parted, both were breathing fast.

For some time after lunch, they lay on the blanket with their backs on the ground, holding hands, looking up at the sky, and soaking up the sunshine.

On the ride down the mountain back to the farm, she floated on air, and where his lips had touched hers, she still felt a tingling warmth. And she marveled that, even as the world around her was ending, she was able to find joy and love.

She never wanted this day to end.

CHAPTER 48

A PLOT UNDONE

Jerusalem, Israel – May, Year 3

Chelsea and Grady followed the other Unitum Imperium employees into the street outside the Clal Center. Men with black armbands ushered the group into a growing circle. Smoke from nearby funeral pyres drifted overhead, dimming the afternoon and wafting the stench of burning corpses. Beneath Chelsea's feet, the once level concrete was now uneven and buckled. Weeds were already poking through the cracks from the earthquakes. Not a building had escaped damage, and many had been reduced to rubble.

"What's this about?" asked Grady.

"I have no idea." Her glance swept the puzzled faces of the crowd. No one else knew either. The throng grew until she and Grady were on the innermost ring of perhaps two or three hundred. Was this Davato's entire staff?

Then came murmurs, a commotion, and a way parted through the crowd for two men wearing black-and-green CSA uniforms and dragging a man behind them. At first, Chelsea didn't recognize their victim. His face was beaten, puffy, bloodied, and one eye was swollen shut. Dried blood stained his shirt, and he could barely stand. But then she knew, and her heart hammered against her ribs.

It was Clemente.

Two more CSA agents followed the others into the center. One carried a wooden bench. The other bore a medieval battle-ax with a blade nearly half a meter wide.

When she saw the ax, her heart thumped harder.

Behind this procession came the Imperator. His face grim, his eyes narrow and dark, he stopped beside Clemente. Straightening to his full height, Davato pierced the crowd with a withering gaze. "Today, we have among us a turncoat of the worst kind, a man who plotted to undo everything you and I have worked so hard for. You knew him by the name of Clemente. He once walked among us, and we trusted him. But today his name is Traitor, a plotter of crimes so heinous, we cannot speak them aloud."

"Y–you, not me," came words from Clemente's mouth, "are the . . . evil one. Y–you—" But the butt of the ax poked his jaw and sent his head lurching sideways. The end of the bench slammed into his ribs, and he doubled over, fighting for breath.

Davato shook his head. "There is only one penalty for a man who would speak and plot against their Imperator, and it is death." He nodded to the four CSA agents.

The man with the bench set it on the street. The two holding their victim forced Clemente's neck upon it. He fought them, but one agent grabbed a handful of hair, yanked him into position, and slammed a foot on the back of his head.

The man with the ax gripped his weapon and stepped to the side. Brawny and deep-chested, he drew a deep breath. He raised the blade. Even in the dim light beneath the overhanging clouds, the edge gleamed. His muscles tensed.

The ax swept down onto Clemente's neck with a crunch of bone, a spurt of blood. The restraining foot jerked aside, and the severed head rolled onto the concrete.

Gasps and horrified glances swept the crowd.

Chelsea whipped her gaze away and fought to keep her gorge down.

"Now get back to work!" shouted Davato. "And remember well what you have seen here this day." Then he strolled with head held high through the circle and disappeared into the building.

Most of the crowd instantly obeyed, edging away from the corpse toward the entrance. But Chelsea shot a worried look to Grady, and, as if both had the same idea, they ambled in the opposite direction. Behind her, CSA agents were stuffing Clemente's remains into a body bag.

"It will t–take time for everyone to return up the elevators." Grady's voice shook.

She nodded and strode until they turned the corner, until she could no longer see the corpse. "Do you think he told them who he spoke to?"

"If he had, they would be there beside him today."

"I suppose." She shuddered then stopped. Something on the ground drew her attention, a crumpled flyer with dried mud on one corner. She picked it up and read:

Do not follow the son of destruction, the deceiver, the lawless one. He is the instrument of Satan. There is another way that is true—believe in Jesus as the Son of God, the one who is coming soon! Seek someone who believes in the truth, someone among you. You will know who they are. Save yourself from the trials to come. Your eternity is at stake.

Her hands shaking, she stared at the flyer, marveling that it had appeared here and now. Wasn't this what Dylan had been trying to tell her? Could he have been right all along?

She let the paper flutter to the ground.

"What was that?" Grady asked.

"Nothing." She faced him. "Grady, I'm scared to death, and I don't know what to do about it. How can we get out of this?"

"We can't get out." He grabbed her hand and squeezed. "We just have to keep quiet and do what we're told. I don't want to end up like Clemente."

"Nor me."

He pulled her close and embraced her.

Closing her eyes, she gave herself to his hug, feeling his warmth against her chest.

But when she again opened her eyes, a man wearing a black armband was watching them from the corner.

CHAPTER 49

TROUBLING PLANS

New Babylon, Iraq – June, Year 3

The walk from the World Casino to New Babylon's central park was several kilometers and by the time Chelsea and Grady arrived, waves of heat rose from the asphalt, and she was sweating. For some reason she couldn't remember, she'd agreed to meet Lazzaro, Davato's food taster, and Ernesto, Davato's chauffeur, by the benches at the naked nymph fountain. She and Grady arrived first.

With the drought, park maintenance had stopped running the sprinklers in a city surrounded by desert. When she and Grady had taken a shortcut across the brown grass, it crinkled beneath their feet. The fountain ahead boasted the statue of a naked nymph. But no water spouted from her breasts today. Four similar fountains, dry and empty, circled the wide cobbled center where workers were erecting the foundation for some massive, unknown structure.

They hadn't waited long when the two men arrived—Lazzaro, with his long thin face, and Ernesto, with his white beard. Now, as she saw the couples of all sexes strolling over the dead grass, the workmen sending glances their way, and the four members of a Truth Squad eyeing them as they passed, she regretted this meeting.

The two men approached, and Chelsea and Grady stood.

"Is it safe to talk here?" Grady glanced at the backs of the Truth Squad heading toward the new construction.

"As safe as anywhere in New Babylon." Lazzaro always talked barely above a whisper, and when he spoke, he had difficulty looking a person in the eye. "Before we begin, I have something for you, Chelsea."

"What?"

From his pocket, he pulled out a small leather-bound book, maybe two inches on a side, and passed it to her. "It's a Bible. The Psalms and New Testament. I think you'll find it interesting."

She gasped. "B–but, if they find me with that . . ."

"They'll send you to the camp. Or the shooting gallery. Hide it well."

"Are you a Christian?"

"We both are." Lazzaro dropped his gaze and talked so low she could barely hear him. "But we're struggling."

"I can imagine," added Grady.

Lazzaro's chin rose, and he peered into her eyes. "Do you realize that on this site in ancient times, Babylon was the capital city of Nimrod, the first world ruler? And that city was also steeped in hedonism, debauchery, and evil."

"So?" She scrunched her face.

"So ancient Babylon was also the place where man organized the first mass rebellion against God, building the Tower of Babel to glorify man, not God."

"What's your point?"

"Well, here we are, thousands of years later in New Babylon, and this man Davato has again created a religion and built a massive city— but all in rebellion against God. Don't you see? We've come full circle. It's as if something that began here eons ago is now approaching a conclusion on the same site. There's a kind of cosmic inevitability and sense of completion about the whole thing. It tells me we are at the end of all things."

As she grasped Lazzaro's point, a shiver ran down her spine. To see history repeat itself in such a powerful pattern was eerie, as if God himself had orchestrated it. And if the circle was complete, did that confirm they were living in the end times?

"I see . . . your point." She shook herself and checked her watch. "But you didn't ask me here only to make an observation about history. I have a meeting in one hour."

"You're right." Ernesto's glance swept the area. Then he moved closer and lowered his normally booming voice. "We'll get right to the point. Lazzaro and I are convinced that this man Davato is a grave threat to me, to you, to everyone who works for him, and, most importantly, to the world. We asked you here because we intend to do something about it. And we have observed that you two might be candidates to join us."

To hear Ernesto confess his opinion that she and Grady might be likely coconspirators was troubling. Were they *that* transparent? She swallowed. "What do you have in mind?"

Ernesto glanced to Lazzaro, who raised his gaze from the ground. Lazzaro then said aloud the word that she feared to hear—

"Assassination."

She caught Grady's startled glance, and they both fell silent.

"I don't like this." Grady shuffled his feet and looked away. "I want nothing to do with this."

"Nor I." Chelsea took a step back. "Look at what happened to Clemente."

"But we suspect you believe as we do." Ernesto's pleading eyes caught hers, then Grady's. "Were we wrong?"

"Yes," answered Grady. "I'm no conspirator. My goal right now is to keep out of trouble. We have to go along with whatever Davato says, and I'll never do anything to put myself at risk."

Chelsea shot him a troubled look. Was that really true?

Ernesto shook his head and turned to her. "What about you?"

"I–I don't know. I understand why you want to do something. But look what happened to Clemente."

As she spoke, Grady lifted an eyebrow.

"Of course." Ernesto pressed on, undeterred. "But won't you consider this: Clemente planned poorly and was indiscreet. We will be more careful."

"Yet here we are." Grady waved a hand. "We're meeting in a park in full view of a Truth Squad. And how do you know there aren't cameras and microphones in those trees?"

Chelsea glanced to the trees and shuddered.

Grady laid a hand on her shoulder. "Come on. Let's get out of here."

As Ernesto and Lazzaro stood with disappointed faces, she shrugged and followed Grady down the path.

Ernesto's voice rose. "You're just like all the other sheep. When the wolf comes, you lay on the ground and open your throat."

She accompanied Grady back to the World Casino, but the charge stung. Ernesto was right. Doing nothing in the face of evil was evil itself.

Yet neither she nor Grady had the courage to join the conspirators in what they planned to do.

* * *

Chelsea followed Davato into a conference room on the World Casino's top floor. She glanced out the twentieth-floor window at the Earth Temple and the expanse of New Babylon, shining in the blinding desert sun.

She sat then nodded to the Prophet on her left, to Vice Imperator François Desroches one seat beyond, and to two tech wizards at the end of the table. Opposite her was Aldo Conti, Davato's head of the Department of Prosperity within the Ministry of Charity, a group in charge of taxation, supply chains, transportation infrastructure, and food and fuel distribution. Aldo was a large man with hairy arms, a bald head, and a permanent scowl, and when she smiled in his direction, he looked away as if she didn't exist. Beside him sat stern-faced Dino Castiglione, now head of the Central Security Agency. Next to Dino was his boss—Adam Turner, her father. Father shot her a quick smile.

Still standing, Davato motioned to Chelsea, and she opened her laptop, ready to take notes.

Then the Imperator turned to her father. "What progress are you making with the cleanup?"

Adam took a deep breath. "The task is monumental, my lord. The Jews have been at it for seven months now, but every night some return to their homes in secret, and we have to conscript more to replace them."

"Jews!" Davato's hand slapped the table. "We'll soon deal with the lot of them. But what about the rotting bodies and the wreckage from the battle? When will it be gone?"

"I'm happy to report that my crews have removed nearly all the corpses. But tens of thousands of skeletons are still lying out in the sun. And the workers haven't even started on the weaponry. The amount of twisted, burned up metal is"—he waved his hands—"beyond imagining."

"Keep at it. I want it all gone. Every bone. Every hunk of metal. Every reminder that such a force ever dared come against me. Get rid of it all! I gave this task to you, Turner, and you *will* see it through to the end. Clear?"

His eyes widening, Father swallowed. "Yes, my lord."

Breathing deeply, Davato laid both hands on the table, and his gaze swept the assembled. "Now to the main business at hand."

"Your invitation did not declare a topic, my lord." Aldo's voice was high-pitched for his bulk. "Can you tell us the purpose?"

Davato nodded then stepped to the whiteboard, grabbed a marker, and drew the six-sided hexagram with lines running to a central picture of Europe and northern Africa. Around the edges, he wrote the six letters of his name: *D, A, V, A, T,* and *O.*

"This"—he tapped the board with his fingers—"is why we are meeting today. Sebastien, why don't you explain the plan?"

As Davato sat, the green-eyed Prophet took his place. "You all know this symbol. From the beginning, it has represented the Imperator and the Unitum Imperium. What some of you haven't known until today is what we are now going to do with it. The Imperator is preparing a directive for January of next year, only eight months from now, when we will require everyone to receive this mark. It will be indelibly imprinted on the right hand or, failing that, on the forehead. That is why we invited our tech team here today."

Though the others appeared puzzled, Father's smile revealed he already knew the secret.

"And what is the purpose of this?" Dino Castiglione held Sebastien's gaze with a stony-faced scowl. He had formerly occupied the cubicle next to Chelsea in Rome's Worldnet headquarters.

"The purpose?" Sebastien grinned. "Is to identify who is with us and who is not. Too many rebels and enemies of the state still walk among us, and we don't know who they are. Many of them are Christians and Jews who have given their allegiance to the Enemy. We propose to bring an end to that kind of opposition. Starting next January, anyone wishing to buy or sell must show this mark on their person before engaging in any type of commerce."

Silence, broken only by the sound of jets overhead, filled the room as they pondered the ramifications.

Dino Castiglione cocked his head. "And if a person refuses to take the mark . . . ?"

Davato slammed a fist into a palm. "They will be excluded from the buying and selling of all goods and property. They will starve."

Aldo Conti's face broke from its usual frown into a slow grin.

As the words sank in, Castiglione nodded his approval.

Chelsea's father was also grinning.

Though she continued to type, recording the questions and answers, her heart was racing, and she began to miss letters. A permanent mark identifying the followers of Davato? A mark required before a person could even *eat*? What would that do to Dylan and his friends? Or to Caleb, if he was still alive?

"So today," continued the Prophet, "we will discuss how to implement the Imperator's planned directive."

The rest of the meeting centered on how to commandeer or create the tattoo parlors that would place the mark on the right hand of every person on the planet. They talked about how the Central Security Agency would set up checkpoints where they would require all passersby to take the mark. They came up with plans to educate store owners, with severe penalties for anyone disobeying the directive. And once the global payments and credits system was complete, the accounts of anyone without the mark would be locked.

By the time the meeting ended, Chelsea was nauseous. As she walked alone down the hall toward the elevator, she remembered a phrase that had echoed through the culture before the vanishing, a phrase that had become a sort of joke, but which now struck terror into her soul. Because Davato was about to turn that phrase into policy. It was—

The mark of the beast.

* * *

BACK IN HER ROOM, SHE skipped her usual white wine and poured two shots of brandy over ice. All the way down from the top floor, she'd pondered what Davato was about to do, the decision he was about to force upon everyone.

But what did it mean to take the mark? She didn't know. Dylan had tried to convince her that Davato was the Antichrist, and now she was ready to believe him. She'd hidden Lazzaro's tiny Bible above the cupboard in the kitchen. Now, she pulled up a chair to bring it down.

At the kitchen table, she looked at the index and flipped to Revelation. At least she knew that much about this. She started reading. As she did, much of it was obscure, but she understood enough that sweat came to her brow. When she came to Revelation 14:9–11, her heart nearly stopped. It read:

> Then a third angel followed them, shouting, "Anyone who worships the beast and his statue or who accepts his mark on the forehead or on the hand must drink the wine of God's anger. It has been poured full strength into God's cup of wrath. And they will be tormented with fire and burning sulfur in the presence of the holy angels and the Lamb. The smoke of their torment will rise forever and ever, and they will have no relief day or night, for they have worshiped the beast and his statue and have accepted the mark of his name."

Rising, she went to the window and looked out at the massive earth temple. They were worshiping the earth now, but, apparently, they would soon be worshiping Davato himself. Then what would happen to Christians like Ernesto and Lazzaro if they refused to take the mark? What about Dylan and Caleb? What would Grady do?

To refuse the mark meant starvation and death. She didn't want to die. She pressed her hands against her temples until they ached. What would she do?

She didn't know.

CHAPTER 50
THE MAYOR'S REVENGE

The French Luberon – July, Year 3

On a heavily overcast morning in July, Margot and Dylan drove down to the village. It was their turn to make the farm's monthly run to restock miscellaneous items.

While he left the van in the village lot at the head of the street, she noted the unusual number of vehicles parked there. Some carried plates from the Marseilles region.

This morning, Dylan's mission took him to a garage on the village outskirts to pick up a battery for the Citroen Pasqual had bought last week. As he headed off down a side street, she took her list down the cobbled lane that passed for a main street.

As usual, her trip involved a stop at Mallory's Castorama. She hated going into the mayor's store, but Mallory's was the only hardware store in the village. As she entered, Mallory—formerly Maurice—stiffened and placed both hands on the counter.

Margot ignored her—him?—and headed toward an aisle.

Normally, at this point, a scowling Mallory would follow three steps behind whatever farm folk were visiting the store. But today, she hovered about the register, glancing occasionally toward the street. And when Margot turned the corner into an aisle in back, she heard the mayor talking with someone on her cell phone.

Margot brought her purchases—a toilet repair kit and two boxes of nails—to the front counter where she produced her credit card.

Usually at checkout, Mallory would sneer, and her man's voice would spout some veiled insult. But today, the mayor avoided eye contact. "Where is the other one?" she asked.

"Errands," answered Margot, trying as usual to keep conversation to a minimum.

For some reason, Mallory was taking forever to ring up the sale, and she kept glancing toward the street. After such odd behavior, Margot began to suspect something was wrong.

She put the items in her bag and hurried out the door. But the instant she stepped into the street, she froze.

Down the lane to her right, two men in green and black with the CSA's skull and lightning patch strode toward her. Farther on her left came a second agent.

She knew the village well. There was only one option.

Dropping her bag, she sprinted for an alley two doors to the left of the Castorama.

"Stop!" came a warning from behind, but she kept on.

As she entered the alley, heavy clouds dimmed the light. Panting, breathing fast, she slowed and searched for a hiding place.

Footsteps, a single pair, clicked on the pavement behind her then stopped. "You can't escape," came a man's deep voice. "Turn and give yourself up."

A doorway on her right was open a crack. She sprinted for it, pushed through, and slipped into darkness. Her shin hit some kind of box, but she recovered and circled around it. She plunged deeper into—what? An abandoned store? Rats squealed in the darkness ahead, tiny feet scraping the floor. She stifled a gag at the smell of dust and rat feces.

From behind came a curse as her pursuer entered the dim light.

Hands in front of her, she planted one foot silently ahead of the next, edging hopefully toward some nook that would keep her safe, anything to hide from her pursuer. Her hands hit cold, rough concrete, and her fingers followed the wall in the gloom.

But the man had stopped at the entrance. Why wasn't he following?

Something bumped her head, and she felt an overhead wall. Was this a closet or a niche? Sliding down onto hands and knees, she crawled as quietly as she could into the space. Something scurried away, and she shuddered. Rats again. She was now as hidden as she could make herself.

A light appeared, a weak flashlight from a phone. The light searched the room's opposite side, and she gasped.

"Where are you?" came the voice. "You can't hide. I'll find you."

As if to make her profile smaller, she rolled into a ball.

Another voice called from the alley, and her pursuer told his companion to guard the exit. The only way out was blocked.

Twenty meters away, the light played along the far wall, crept over empty boxes and packing crates. The rat family squealed and skittered through the darkness.

The light hit her cranny, passed over her, and moved on. Would she somehow escape?

Then a thought rose from the recesses of her mind, a terrible conviction she fought against but finally gave in to. The painting said this must happen, didn't it? Was it not in God's plan that they should capture her? Almost against her will, she crawled out from the alcove. On trembling limbs, she stood.

"I'm . . . h–here." The words escaped her lips, and she couldn't believe she'd said them.

The light flashed back and shone into her eyes. She blinked.

"Raise your hands where I can see them."

Her heart hammered against her ribs. Tears ran down her cheeks. But she raised her hands.

* * *

AT THE GARAGE, DYLAN'S TRANSACTION had taken far too long. The owner was meeting a man about some food, and the son hadn't known where the battery might be. In apology, the young man offered Dylan coffee, a rare treat, and he accepted. The owner finally appeared thirty minutes later. As Dylan lugged the battery out of the garage toward the parking lot, he expected Margot to be waiting for him at the van.

She wasn't there. And the parking lot, formerly packed with cars, was empty.

After storing the battery in back, he walked down the lane they called main street, entered Mallory's Castorama, and approached the counter.

"Was there a woman in here earlier?" he asked.

Mallory jumped and raised a startled glance. Her wide, frightened eyes told him something was wrong. Instead of answering, she slowly reached for her phone.

He grabbed her hand to stop her. "Why do you want to call some-one? Answer my question: Was there a woman in here this morning?"

"I–I—" She ripped her hand away and backed up. "No."

"You're lying. She was here, wasn't she?"

Venom narrowed her eyes, and she began edging down the counter away from him. "Yes, she was here. But they took her away some time ago. They'll soon take you too, you and all those wretched Christians in that hideout of yours up on the mountain." She raised her phone and began punching numbers.

Stunned by the mayor's declaration, Dylan froze. They'd taken Margot? And this quisling had reported the farm to the CSA?

Snapping out of it, he whirled and ran into the street. He sprinted up the lane to the lot, started the van, and squealed away. He took the side street to the main highway that led to their mountain road. But as he approached the drive and was ready to turn, he slowed and kept going.

Dozens of vehicles, black CSA vans and sedans, were parked up and down the drive and in the grass-covered gap on either side of the road. Beyond the vehicles, a cluster of men stood around one man, as if waiting for instructions. There was no way to get past them.

His heart pounded in his chest, and his fingers gripped the wheel. The CSA was about to raid the farm, and he had to warn them. Keeping one hand on the wheel, he pulled out his phone with the other. Then he called René.

"Oui?" came René's voice.

"They've taken Margot!" He breathed out. "And there are dozens of vehicles massing at the end of the drive. They're about to raid the farm!"

It took a moment for René to recover from the shock. Then his voice was tense, but calm. "Can you get up here through the Dennel villa?"

"I think so."

"Good. It's time for Operation Elba. If you can't reach us in time, you know where to go."

They hung up, but Dylan had serious doubts whether they could carry out René's risky strategy ahead of the CSA. René named the plan for the way Napoleon survived after his defeat at the battle of Leipzig. But when Dylan had pointed out that Elba was the island of Napoleon's exile, René had replied with a smile, "Oui, but he rose again and wasn't truly defeated until Waterloo."

Dylan followed the highway for another two kilometers. The next drive led to the Dennel villa, and he turned up the narrow lane. He climbed the winding strip at high speed, stopping below the sprawling two-story country retreat. His was the only car here. The rich Marseilles Dennels only used the place occasionally on weekends.

He exited the van and sprinted into the forest. The sole route left to him was a kilometer and a half through dense pines.

He trotted parallel to the slope as fast as his feet would take him without tripping over fallen branches. Pine needles slapped his face, pine boughs grabbed at his shirt and legs, and he sucked in air pungent with the smell of pine. He weaved between trunks, clambered down a gully, crossed a rocky streambed, and raced through brush on the other side. Even the bracing mountain air didn't cool the flush from his face.

He tried not to think about what was happening to Margot and where they were taking her. Was she already on her way to the camp? Or was she locked in a van at the bottom of the drive? Either way, he could do nothing for her now. What he must do was keep the same thing from happening to the others at the farm.

Drenched with sweat and out of breath, he reached the garage below their villa. He slowed to a stop before the group—they hadn't left yet!—and grabbed his knees, breathing heavily. They were gathered at the Peugeot and the Citroen, each holding a pack, and presumably, the emergency IDs Victor had prepared for this moment.

"They're beginning to move." Victor looked up from his tablet's screen. He must have sent up a drone to monitor the CSA's progress. "They're just starting up the drive."

René waved to Dylan. "Glad you made it. Get in. It's time to go."

Victor, Angelo, and René entered the Citroen.

Dylan climbed into the Peugeot's back seat behind Pasqual at the wheel. Danielle already sat up front beside Pasqual. She turned red eyes to Dylan. "They took her?"

He nodded.

Tears running down her cheek, she held his gaze, tried and failed to smile, then faced the front.

But when Marcel and Gabrielle stood unmoving beside the Peugeot, Pasqual opened the window and waved them to get in.

Marcel shook his head. "I cannot leave the farm."

"But they'll take you." Pasqual's voice was pleading. "And they'll take the animals."

He spread his hands as if to encompass the land God had charged him to care for. "We'll ride east into the forest above the Dennel place. There's a cave about four kilometers up the mountain. We'll wait a few days until after they've gone then return."

"We're taking the Percherons and Chloe," added Gabrielle. Chloe was one of the milk cows. "We'll be all right."

"Then may God go with you both." Pasqual started the engine.

"And may the Lord go with you as well," added Marcel.

As the farmers waved goodbye, the two cars headed up the slope toward a tractor path and an access road bypassing the wheat field.

* * *

ON THE FIELD'S FAR SIDE, René's plan diverted them onto an old, overgrown jeep trail. After the vehicles left the tractor path, the group covered their tracks and the trail entrance by moving a pile of prepositioned brush and logs. From there, it was a bumpy, rutted ride, nearly shaking apart the two vehicles unsuited for such rough terrain. Their progress was slow.

When they were half a kilometer up the trail, Victor's drone told them that Marcel and Gabrielle had indeed escaped into the forest ahead of the CSA. The farmers had left with heavy packs and not one, but two cows. And by the time the passable trail ended and the six refugees began climbing on foot—only then did the CSA exit the villa and begin searching the surrounding forest. At that point, Victor recalled his drone.

They covered the vehicles with brush and abandoned them. Following Operation Elba, they hiked up a deer trail for another kilometer to an empty creek bed. They left the path and clambered up a rocky gorge until it reached a deadfall. Turning east from there, they trod through a pine forest on a bed of needles that left no footprints. This brought them to the summit where similar paths led them to the bottom and a cluster of abandoned houses.

It was now dusk. After searching a dozen garages, they found one that held an old, dust-covered van. René wired the ignition, and with half a tank of gas, they drove off.

"Won't we have a problem with the plates?" asked Dylan from the back.

"Not anymore." Victor spoke from the front. "With so many car thefts and abandoned and wrecked vehicles, the government vehicle registration system is useless. At least that's what we gleaned from the CSA website before we lost access."

"I can vouch for that," said Angelo. "When I was with my squad, the system had already become so unreliable, we stopped using it."

By the time Pasqual drove them through the village and onto a main highway heading south, it was dark. For long minutes, the silence of exhaustion overtook the vehicle's interior.

Victor was first to speak. "Operation Elba worked, but now I know how Napoleon must have felt when he was on that ship heading into exile."

"We escaped all right"—Dylan's voice betrayed not just weariness, but defeat—"but not Margot. How are we ever going to free her now?"

Danielle turned around from the front seat and reached out a hand. Dylan took it, and she pressed it lightly against her cheek. "It's a terrible thing to lose a friend." She turned her face to kiss his hand then released him. "She was my good friend too."

"Take heart, people." René glanced back from behind the wheel. "We lost a battle today, but with God's help, we will rise again."

Dylan shook his head in the dark.

Beside him, Pasqual must have seen his gesture as he laid a hand on Dylan's shoulder. "Did she not paint this outcome? Did she not say many times that her capture must be in God's will? Should we not have faith that this was meant to be?"

"I–I have trouble believing that." He remembered her painting of the camp—the room with the long lines of Christians marching toward the guillotines—and he shuddered. "How can being in that camp be in

God's will?"

"I don't know, but perhaps we can take comfort in Romans 8:28: 'We know that all things work together for the good of those who love God: those who are called according to His purpose.' And consider this: Were not you and Margot called 'according to his purpose'?"

"Maybe . . . we were." As the headlights of oncoming cars shone through the window, he held Pasqual's gaze. "But what if that purpose is for her to be executed?"

To that query, Pasqual only shrugged and faced away.

As the van rolled on through the dark over a nearly deserted highway toward Marseilles, Dylan turned his gaze toward the dust-streaked window.

Tears rolled down his cheeks.

Silently, he prayed: *Dear Lord, everything is falling apart. Please keep Margot safe. Please make clear what you want us to do. And please, guide us all to safety. I ask all of this in Jesus's name, amen.*

CHAPTER 51

THE CAMP

Matthew 24:9–10 (NLT): *"Then you will be arrested, persecuted, and killed. You will be hated all over the world because you are my followers. And many will turn away from me and betray and hate each other."*

Weisserwald Uranmine, Germany – July, Year 3

When they captured Margot Durand, they took her to a van in the village parking lot where a man injected her with something and she lost consciousness. And when she woke in darkness, lying on her side, she had no idea how long she'd been out.

Now her hands were bound, and plastic ties cut into her wrists, swelling her fingers. Wherever this was, the place was moving. She felt the vibration, heard the whine of tires outside and the Doppler rush of vehicles approaching then passing.

She struggled to a sitting position and peered left to where a slit of light revealed she was not alone. Huddled along both walls and sprawled over the floor were the slumped shadows of men and women, bound just like her. Was she inside a truck?

"How long have I . . . been here?" She spoke to the shadows, her voice cracking from thirst and disuse.

"Who knows, sister?" came a young man's voice. "After the last pickup, we've been gone at least twenty-four hours. But they keep stopping."

"Where are we going?" she spoke to the dark.

"Don't you know?" answered an old man. "To a death camp."

She'd guessed that, of course, but hearing someone say it aloud shook her.

Another voice, a woman's, broke the silence. " 'The LORD is my shepherd; I shall not want.' "

She was reciting the twenty-third Psalm, and now others joined in.

"'He makes me lie down in green pastures.'" The voices calling out comforted and soothed, and Margot joined them. "'He leads me beside still waters. He restores my soul. He leads me in paths of righteousness for his name's sake. Even though I walk through the valley of the shadow of death, I will fear no evil, for you are with me; your rod and your staff, they comfort me. . . .'"

A half hour later, the truck slowed and turned off a main road, shifting bodies in the dim light. Tires ground over gravel then stopped, but the engine kept running. A whiff of diesel exhaust crept into the cabin.

For long minutes, the truck idled while men stood outside, talking, joking, and a whiff of cigarette smoke mixed with the diesel. Then the truck moved slowly, not far, before backing up and stopping. After a clanking, the back doors creaked open, and dim daylight flooded the interior. Someone yanked on a metal ramp. It rattled out of its cocoon, extended, and crashed to the ground.

The light now revealed over a hundred bodies crammed into the van—men, women, and youths stretching limbs, squinting toward the exit.

"Get out!" The command came from a stout woman with her hair in a tight bun, wearing a black-and-green CSA uniform with the six-sided patch of the lightning bolt and skull. She peered into the cabin then beat her truncheon on the metal ramp. "Schnell! Schnell! Get out!"

Margot followed the others as they headed toward the light. At the top of the ramp, she had her first view of the camp—much like what she had painted. . . .

Endless rows of one-story, corrugated metal barracks stretched to the horizon.

Two rows of razor-wire fence, separated by a two-meter gap, enclosed the perimeter.

In the distance, a tall chimney spewed black smoke above a low building—a crematorium?

But off to the left was something new—a cone-shaped mountain of slag.

Outside the gates to her right stood a decrepit structure needing paint with broken windows and a sign in faded letters: *Weisserwald Uranmine*. So, the camp was located on the site of a former uranium mine? But looking around she saw no evidence of a "white forest" as its name implied.

"No gawking!"

The sting of the truncheon smacked her leg. She stumbled, nearly fell, then limped off the ramp into the crowd. The weather had turned cool, and she shivered.

Surrounding the prisoners at the bottom were at least two dozen CSA guards, some holding submachine guns, others with truncheons. All wore pistols at their belts.

Behind Margot, an old woman tripped and sprawled forward onto the ramp. The woman guard rushed at her, struck her repeatedly with the club, and threw insults and curses. "Get up, you old Christian cow! Get going. Or you'll die right here."

An old man, possibly her husband, helped the victim rise to her knees, then to her feet. More blows from the guard rained down on both.

When the prisoners were off the truck, the guards herded them toward a high gate leading into the interior. A sign stretched above the entrance: Death Is Freedom.

Black ash drifted down, and the acrid taste of burnt flesh and bone soured her tongue, fouled her nostrils.

Inside the gate, a new group of guards separated the men from the women. Teenagers mingled among them, all above the age of fourteen.

The guards marched the women past long rows of barracks, each as bleak and gray as the next, until they came to a building with the number 1,679 painted above the door. In the space leading to the door were placed two tables. The first was empty. The second was piled with striped uniforms.

A kind of black snow now fell upon the women, the tables, the uniforms. Ash from the crematorium?

"Your souls, your minds, and your bodies now belong to me!" shouted the woman guard. "Now strip. Leave your clothes and grab a uniform."

The prisoners looked at the guard with uncomprehending, blinking eyes.

"Strip, I say!" The guard sheathed her truncheon, yanked her pistol from its holster, and pulled back on the slide. She fired a shot in the air, and Margot jumped.

Margot slipped out of her blouse and jeans but kept her bra and underwear as she reached for one of the striped uniforms.

"Everything!" The guard shouted again. "Even your underwear."

Hesitating, Margot removed her underpants and bra. Shivering even more, she stepped to the second table and pulled on a pair of thin cotton pants and a shirt. Moths had eaten holes in the back, and it hung loosely over her chest. An old bloodstain surrounded a tear in one leg.

"You, there." The guard walked to the end and waved her pistol at an old woman—the same one who'd tripped on the ramp. "I told you to strip."

"No." With effort, the old woman straightened her back. "I will not."

"You . . . will . . . not?" The guard's expression morphed to one of gleeful astonishment.

"I will not." The woman straightened to her full height in a gesture of defiance. "You might take my body, but my mind and heart and soul belong to my Lord Jesus."

Appearing to be over eighty, she held her head high, and her jaw tightened. The lined, weathered skin of her face stretched into a thin smile. For one brief moment, standing there, erect with gentle defiance, she could have been a classic statue some famous sculptor had carved. *Ancient Dignity* would have been the title. For Margot in that moment, the woman became the embodiment, the archetype, of timeless grace, gentle dignity, and quiet resistance in the face of mindless evil. Like everyone else here, she was a new Christian. But she wouldn't renounce or turn away from her faith. Rather than surrender her soul to outrage, the woman would take the consequences, whatever they were.

Margot sucked in breath, fearing what would come next.

Grinning, the guard sheathed her pistol and took out her truncheon. Then she began beating the woman. Blow after blow rained down as her victim crumpled to the ground. The woman raised arms above her head, but the truncheon smacked a forearm so hard, Margot heard the snapping of bone followed by a cry of agony.

With the blows, the guard cursed God. She railed and blasphemed against Jesus, spouting an endless stream of vile curses, directed not at the woman, now lying unconscious in the ash-black dirt, but at the Lord of Heaven and Earth. Though the limp body no longer moved, the attack went on. Sickened to her core, Margot forced herself to watch. The skull was now misshapen, crushed, and oozing gray matter. The face was no longer recognizable. Still, the guard continued to rain blow after blow on the motionless corpse with all her might.

Finally, out of breath and covered with blood, the guard straightened, looked at the dead woman, and faced the rest of the group. "Anyone else?"

No one else objected, and Margot buttoned her uniform in silence.

The guard had been filled with such an unreasoning rage Margot sensed it must be demonic. It had always been there, that kind of Satanic, mindless hatred of Christians, of Jesus, and of the morality God desired for mankind. Now, here in this camp, it had exploded in full bloom.

Inside the barracks door, a scarecrow of a woman with fearful, darting eyes asked Margot her name and wrote it down. Then the woman handed her a blanket, a wooden bowl, a wooden spoon, and wrapped a plastic band around her wrist. The woman told her to find the empty bunk with the number matching her wristband.

The only windows were ten-centimeter-high slits cut into the corrugated metal below the ceiling. The translucent paper covering them let in just enough to reveal the dying sunlight. In the dim light, Margot groped to her bunk. It was on top, nothing but bare wooden planks.

When everyone had found a bunk, the woman guard rapped her truncheon on a wooden bedpost by the door. "Line up with your bowls in the yard. Supper is in five minutes."

As women rushed for the door, Margot pressed a hand to the ache in her middle, realizing she was famished. In the fading light, she joined the end of the line.

Guards herded the prisoners around the barracks into a main thoroughfare between buildings. The line crawled toward a huge metal stewpot hanging over a fire where a thin-faced woman dropped a single ladle of soup into each bowl. All up and down the thoroughfare, as far as Margot could see, women from other barracks were lining up before similar stewpots.

She took her supper back to barracks number 1,679, crawled up to her bunk, and sampled the watery stuff in her bowl. It tasted of sawdust, and she gritted her teeth. But needing to keep up her strength, she finished it. She found only two slices of potato in what they called supper.

As darkness filled the room, the door slammed open, and the stout German guard again banged her truncheon. "Achtung! Anyone leaving the building without permission will be shot. Tomorrow or the next day, you will work. Anyone not willing to work will be shot." Then she slammed the door shut, followed by the harsh metallic click of a lock from outside.

Margot laid her head on the bare wood. Shivering, she pulled the blanket over her head. The guard had said they would work. Was there hope they wouldn't be executed as her painting suggested? Or was that statement a ruse to keep the prisoners under control?

Outside, a searchlight played over the window slits before moving on.

Inside, women turned on their beds, elbows bumping against wood. Someone coughed. From others came the sounds of weeping. From a few—whispered prayers.

She huddled beneath her blanket, and tears streamed down her cheeks. She'd never felt so alone, so scared, so vulnerable. But her painting had predicted this, hadn't it? And the Holy Spirit had guided her brush. Somehow, though she couldn't possibly imagine why or how, this was God's will.

What had the sign above the camp's entrance said? Death Is Freedom?

Though her captors didn't know it, for the Christian, this was true. Even if she died here, what waited beyond this life was a blessed eternity with Christ.

Yet that was the future. She was here, now, in this death camp, and though she didn't fear death—or so she tried to tell herself—she feared death would come slowly, painfully, and without dignity. She feared a slow starvation. She feared the ugliness and brutality of this place. And she feared being separated from Dylan, Pasqual, René, Danielle, Victor, and everyone she'd come to love back at the farm. Finally, she feared the horror of the moment they would lead her to the guillotine.

A wave of uncontrolled shivering racked her body, and she bunched her blanket inside a fist.

"Dear L–lord Jesus," she whispered through chattering teeth, "give me the strength to endure this. L–lead me to do what is in your will. Whatever that may be. And if it's to die here . . . then . . . let me die with dignity and grace. Amen."

Her prayer stopped the shivering and brought a measure of warmth and comfort. She laid her head on the wood and tried to sleep.

AUTHOR'S NOTES

Now About the Ending

I apologize to the reader for where we left our characters in this book. I never wanted any of my books to be downers or, worse, to promote the nihilism we find in so much secular literature. Originally, I had a different ending in mind, but as I was writing, I discovered that to leave our folks in a happy place would make this second book too long. Then I decided that if it was going to be bad, it would be *very bad* indeed.

After plotting the entire series, I also discovered that to be true to the biblical storyline, my original three-book series must grow to five. But if you've read the Bible, you know how history ends. So I promise the reader that those characters who persevere and stay true to the faith will see the glorious end that Christ has planned for those who are his, be that in this world or in the next.

The Battle of Gog and Magog

Described in Ezekiel 38 and 39, the Battle of Gog and Magog will be a world-shaking event. One result will surely be to show the hand of God to an unrepentant world, leading many to Christ.

There is speculation among biblical scholars about where, in the Tribulation timeline, this event will come. Some suggest it might come before the Rapture. Others place it at the Tribulation midpoint. But it seems more logical that the battle is a result of the opening of the second seal that brings worldwide war. That would place it somewhere in the beginning of the seven-year period.

The Bible also tells us that the Antichrist will, at some point, take up residence in Jerusalem. And if the Antichrist is residing in Israel before the battle, it seems logical that the nations of Islam would then have two powerful reasons to invade that country: 1. Their historical, rabid hatred of Zionism, and 2. Their desire to strike back at the Antichrist and bring down a regime that stands in opposition to them.

That Russia will be part of and will lead the attacking force is also a matter for debate. The Hebrew word *Rosh,* as used in Ezekiel, can mean head, top, or summit. Or it can be a proper name referring to a specific place. Respected Hebrew scholars such as Wilhelm Gesenius and C. F. Keil hold to the view that *Rosh* should be translated as a place name. Some of the more literal biblical translations also refer to it that way. So does the Septuagint, the Greek Old Testament translation written only three hundred years after Ezekiel.

Ezekiel also says that Gog, the leader of the Rosh, comes from "the remotest parts of the north." The nation furthest north from Israel is Russia. Thus, it makes sense that Russia will be part of the invading coalition and that a Russian will lead it.

We can see the setup for this battle in our world today. For some time, Russia has cozied up to Iran. And Russia's invasion of Ukraine has made it a pariah for just about every nation on the planet.

Turkey is among the end-times invaders, and for some time, Turkey has been at odds with NATO, of which it's currently a part. It, too, is cozying up to Russia and is moving steadily toward a full embrace of Islam. Someday soon, look for Turkey to completely part ways with the West.

The pieces on the board all seem to be moving in the right direction for the Battle of Gog and Magog.

OF WAR, PLAGUE, AND PESTILENCE

Before any of the seven seals are opened, the Rapture will have inflicted on the world economic disaster, lost population, and decreased productivity.

After the Rapture, the second seal will bring war, further disrupting supply chains, preventing farmers from tending their fields, and sending civilization to the brink of collapse.

Then comes the third seal—worldwide famine. Famine often leads to disease, and without factories and supply chains to bring needed antibiotics, it's more than possible that some disease we were once able to cure, such as the bubonic plague, or Black Death, could return with a vengeance.

The fourth seal sums up the results of the previous two, decreeing that one-quarter of the earth's population will die "by the sword, by famine, by plague, and by the wild animals of the earth." This novel presumes that rats fall under the category of "wild animals". It postulates that a supernatural infestation of rats, with their accompanying fleas, might bring a return of the Black Death. In book three, we'll see a battle with wolves.

With COVID-19, for some inexplicable reason, the CDC, NIH, and FDA joined in a conspiracy of leftist media, government, and tech giants to suppress the knowledge of and deny the use of certain drugs that study after study proved were safe and effective against the virus—even more so than the officially sanctioned drugs.

Given that sordid history, when some disease such as the bubonic plague supernaturally sweeps the planet and when the Unitum Imperium is unable to provide the necessary antibiotics, officialdom, with their powers of censorship, will surely deny and suppress the knowledge that antibiotics are the cure. In doing so, they will only be following the path of lies and deception established by the authorities, governments, and media of today.

THE TRIBULATION CASTS ITS SHADOW BEFORE IT—BUT CHRISTIANS HAVE HOPE

It's been said that the Tribulation will cast its shadow before it. And with end-times events occurring almost daily, the statement seems prescient. Who could have imagined in the fall of 2019 how quickly the world would descend into the state it's in now?

Worldwide plague.

Anarchy in our cities.

Mainline churches abandoning the Bible and preaching apostasy and social justice instead of the risen Christ.

A spirit of lawlessness is sweeping the land. It's in the streets with rampant crime. City prosecutors favor criminals over victims. The national government—and some state and local governments—have abandoned their founding principles and refuse to enforce the law.

Across the world, morality has broken down with an embrace of practices, beliefs, and ideologies totally repugnant to God: abortion, LGBTQ, gender confusion, earth worship, and the insidious, twisted ideology of wokeism that encompasses all the above.

The political winds have shifted so far to the left, they are in direct opposition to God, toward a kind of "woke fascism", a term coined by Dr. Michael Rectenwald. It's an ideology derived from socialism, requiring one to conform and pledge allegiance to new norms dictated by the woke collective. Under woke fascism, one's heart, mind, and soul belong—not to God—but to the whims of the mob.

And who would ever have thought that the government would institute a Ministry of Disinformation? It's straight from George Orwell's dystopian vision in *1984*.

In the last days, there is no mention of the United States. One wonders, given all of the above, if the country's recent, swift decline is a result of the divine will.

But the rest of the world is no better off.

Russia ignores world opinion and invades Ukraine.

Iran marches unrestrained toward acquiring nuclear weapons with the goal of annihilating Israel.

A belligerent, increasingly authoritarian China builds up its military and threatens any country daring even to speak of Taiwan as anything but part of the mainland.

Everywhere we see a litany of woes and troubles, a compendium of demonic ideologies, a testimony that this world is not our home, that it's under Satan's sway.

But if you are a Christian, take heart and hold on to hope.

What we are seeing today is only a preview of the Tribulation to come. For the one who believes in Christ, who has put his or her faith in Jesus—they will be spared when today's troublesome preview becomes tomorrow's divine judgment when God decides that enough is enough and it's time to usher in his kingdom.

It is in God's word, not in the deeds of sinful man, that Christians must put their faith.

Take heart from 1 Thessalonians 4:16–18 (HCSB): "For the Lord Himself will descend from heaven with a shout, with the archangel's voice, and with the trumpet of God, and the dead in Christ will rise first. Then we who are still alive will be caught up together with them in the clouds to meet the Lord in the air and so we will always be with the Lord. Therefore encourage one another with these words."

Encouragement, indeed. The Tribulation is a time of God's wrath, a wrath meant for the unredeemed and the unrepentant, for those following the ideologies and doctrines of demons, not for those God calls his own. The coming judgment is not meant for God's people.

So take heart and have hope. Before the great and terrible day of the Lord, we who are in Christ will be spared the Tribulation to come.

SCRIPTURE REFERENCES

- Year One Section Heading: The opening of the first and second seals brings the Antichrist who promises peace but who instead brings war and slaughter. Revelation 6:1–4 (HCSB)
- Chapter 1: With his lies and wiles, the Antichrist will deceive many and lead them to destruction. 2 Thessalonians 2:9–12 (NLT)
- Chapter 3: A plea to gather the people to the Lord and save them before the end times. Joel 2:11–13,16,17 (NLT)
- Chapter 4: The Antichrist will rise to power and destroy powerful leaders with his wiles. Daniel 8:23–25a (NLT)
- Chapter 10:
  - An image of the beast (the Antichrist) coming from the sea (the abyss) with ten heads and seven horns, an image briefly replicated by a statue placed before the UN headquarters building in New York in 2021. The ten heads represent ten leaders he appointed to rule the world. The seven horns represent the seven empires that came before the Antichrist—Egypt, Assyria, Babylon, Medo-Persia, Greece, and Rome. The dragon is Satan. Revelation 13:1–2 (HCSB) (Also repeated in Daniel 7:6–8)
  - The beast who is the Antichrist will devour the whole world, creating one world government. Daniel 7:19, 23 (HCSB)
- Chapter 11: A description of the judgment that will fall on the prostitute (New Babylon) who rules over many waters (the nations). The kings of the world committed adultery with her (first with a false religion, next by worshiping the Antichrist). Revelation 17:1–2 (NLT)
- Chapter 12: At the day of the Lord, God will give women and men visions. Joel 2:28, 30–31 (HCSB)
- Chapter 14: God sent four angels to supernaturally protect the 144,000 Jews who accepted Christianity and went out to preach the Gospel. Revelation 7:1–4 (HCSB)

- Chapter 15: This chapter describes the Lord's throne room in all its glory. Revelation 4:1–8

- Year Two Section Heading: The opening of the third and fourth seals will bring famine and death to one-quarter of the world's population. Revelation 6:5–8 (HCSB)

- Chapter 24: God is against the countries that gather to invade Israel in the Battle of Gog and Magog: Rosh is Russia; Meshech & Tubal are Turkey; Persia is Iran; Ethiopia is Ethiopia; Put is Libya; Gomer is Turkey; Beth-Togarmah is Southern Turkey. Ezekiel 38:3–6, 8–9 (NASB)

  – Note: More description in Ezekiel 39:6 describes Magog belonging to this pact. Magog includes the Islamic republics of the former USSR, including Kazakhstan, Kyrgyzstan, Uzbekistan, Turkmenistan, Tajikistan, and also Afghanistan.

- Chapter 33: The harvest of the fourth seal: death to one-fourth of the population by war, famine, plague, and wild animals. Revelation 6:7–8 (NLT)

- Chapter 35: A description of how, in the last days, Gog, prince of the Rosh, will lead a mighty horde from the remotest parts of the north (Russia) against Israel. Ezekiel 38:14–16 (HCSB)

- Chapter 37: A description of the Battle of Gog and Magog. There will be a great earthquake. The invaders' armies will turn against themselves. Then torrential rain, hail, fire, and brimstone will fall on the invaders. Ezekiel 38:19–22 (HCSB)

- Chapter 40:

  – In the last days, God will make the nations pay a heavy price when they come against Israel. Zechariah 12:3 (HCSB)

  – God will send fire against Magog and the other nations that go against Israel. Ezekiel 39:6 (HCSB)

- Chapter 41: Paul's warning to guard against worldly philosophies and ideologies not based on Christ. Colossians 2:8 (HCSB)

- Chapter 42: After the Battle of Gog and Magog, the nations will see God's glory, and Israel will know that Yahweh is their God. Ezekiel 39:21–22 (HCSB)

- Chapter 43: A description of a prostitute (New Babylon) sitting on a beast (the Antichrist). By her opulent dress, we know she brings prosperity to those who follow her. But she is filled with immorality and is drunk with the blood of martyred Christians. Revelation 17:3–6 (NLT)

- Year Three Section Heading: The opening of the fifth seal describes those who turned to Christ during the Tribulation and were martyred for their faith. Revelation 6.9–11 (HCSB)

- Chapter 44: The Day of the Lord will bring famine. Joel 1:15, 17–18 (HCSB)

- Chapter 45: For 1260 days, two witnesses stand before the Temple and preach the Gospel. Fire comes from their mouths, killing anyone who tries to stop them. Revelation 11:3–5 (HCSB)

- Chapter 48: Anyone who accepts the mark of the beast and worships the Antichrist will be tormented with fire and brimstone forever. Revelation 14:9–11

- Chapter 50: All things work together for the good of those who love God and are called according to his purpose. Romans 8:28 (HCSB)

- Chapter 51: Jesus warns that, in the end times, Christians will be hated and persecuted. Matthew 24:9–10 (NLT)

MARK'S BOOKS

Christian Historical Fiction:

- The Bonfires of Beltane: Following St. Patrick Across Ancient, Celtic Ireland
- The Medallion: An Epic Quest in A.D. 486
- The Slaves of Autumn: A Tale of Stolen Love in Ancient, Celtic Ireland

General Market Historical Fiction:

- Death of the Master Builder: Love, Envy, and the Struggle to Raise the Greatest Cathedral of the Italian Renaissance

Days of the Apocalypse, a Series of Christian End-Times Thrillers:

- Book 1: The Day They Vanished
- Book 2: Days of War and Famine
- Book 3: Days of Trial and Tribulation (coming soon)
- Book 4: Days of Death and Darkness (planned)
- Book 5: Last Days of the End (planned)

The Scepter and Tower Trilogy, a Christian Fantasy Series for Young Adults:

- The Stolen Scroll, A Novella Prequel (eBook only)
- Book 1: Quest for the Scepter
- Book 2: Into the Druid's Lair
- Book 3: Return to the Tower

To learn more about Mark's books please visit:
www.MarkFisherAuthor.com

Made in the USA
Columbia, SC
07 October 2022

68581060R00190